Uncharted

Uncharted

Lewis and Clark in **ARCANE AMERICA**

Arcane America series created by
Kevin J. Anderson, Eric Flint, Walter C. Hunt,
Eytan Kollin, and Peter J. Wacks

KEVIN J. ANDERSON
AND SARAH A. HOYT

A Baen Books Original

Baen Publishing Enterprises
P.O. Box 1403
Riverdale, NY 10471
www.baen.com

ISBN: 978-1-4814-8323-0

Cover art by Dave Seeley

First Baen printing, May 2018

Distributed by Simon & Schuster
1230 Avenue of the Americas
New York, NY 10020

Library of Congress Cataloging-in-Publication Data

Names: Anderson, Kevin J., 1962– author. | Hoyt, Sarah A., author.
Title: Uncharted / Kevin J. Anderson and Sarah A. Hoyt.
Description: Riverdale : Baen, [2018]
Identifiers: LCCN 2018008462 | ISBN 9781481483230 (hardback)
Subjects: | BISAC: FICTION / Fantasy / Historical. | FICTION / Alternative
    History. | GSAFD: Fantasy fiction. | Alternative histories.
Classification: LCC PS3551.N37442 U53 2018 | DDC 813/.54—dc23 LC record
available at https://lccn.loc.gov/2018008462

10 9 8 7 6 5 4 3 2 1

Pages by Joy Freeman (www.pagesbyjoy.com)
Printed in the United States of America

When Halley's Comet was destroyed above our Earth in May 1759, so was our old way of life, along with the natural science I had studied so intently. The Sundering did just as its name suggests: it sundered the Old World from the New.

This dramatic event created an entirely separate American continent where the laws of magic vie for equal, and sometimes superior, place with the laws of nature. The Sundering created an America where sorcery and science sit in unlikely and uncomfortable partnership. As for Europe...no one knows. That continent is lost to us. The great barrier across the Atlantic has proved impenetrable to all our best efforts, even mine, even now that I control the powers of lightning!

But Europe need not be lost to us forever. The passage east across the ocean appears closed permanently. So, my darling Keira—and any else who read these words—we must consider that the way west may be open! Unknown, yes. Perilous, undoubtedly. But open for anyone who dares to explore.

Ah, would that I were seventy again!

—*From The Arcane Autobiography of*
Dr. Benjamin Franklin, Printer, Scientist & Mage

Fire and Parry

My Dear William,

I am writing you to request you join me in a great and exhilarating enterprise. There is no one else I'd rather have at my side than you, and I am thus hastening to tell you before my mind has even ceased reeling.

But first I suppose I should explain how I came to be called to this great mission of discovery. As you might know, I was lately in St. Louis with the charge to discover a medicinal plant said to be a cure-all to the French settlers in that area.

During my visit, the great sorcerer Benjamin Franklin was also due to make an appearance. As you can imagine, I could not resist going to see, if only from a distance, a man of such immense age and such wise learning. Little did I know what I would actually witness. It changed my life forever.

—Letter from Captain Meriwether Lewis to
Captain William Clark, St. Louis, February 10, 1803

IN THE WARM SUNSHINE, MERIWETHER LEWIS REALIZED THAT HE should not have worn his greatcoat with its many capes. It wasn't exactly warm in St. Louis in early February, but it was warm enough to make the icicles drip from the eaves of the great white houses, and the ice that covered the street mud crackle underfoot. As he walked along, swinging his cane, he began to feel too warm.

Of course, the heat he felt might also be due to his excitement.

When he'd come to St. Louis to procure black sage—much mentioned in the correspondence of the French Colonists in this city as being a sovereign remedy against pain when made into tea—he'd never expected this would give him a chance to cross paths with the ancient wizard Ben Franklin himself.

Since the cometary explosion and the magical aftermath that had isolated these American shores from the rest of the world, Ben Franklin had made the sort of name for himself that in other times would have made him a demigod.

Maybe that was true, regardless, with the New World shaking and resonating with all the changed rules of unleashed magic. And Meriwether now had a chance to meet the great man....

He quaked with trepidation and subdued excitement. As a rational man, he knew it was not likely that Franklin would even notice him. Everywhere the great wizard went, he was surrounded by admirers, well-wishers, sycophants, and those who would be his pupils to learn the arcane sciences. If Meriwether managed to see more of the man than (what remained of) his famously coiffed locks bobbing amid the crowd as the man spoke his famous witticisms, he would be greatly satisfied, even thrilled.

And yet, he felt a strange sense of expectancy.

In the more than forty years since the comet's arrival and the shift in the world, Meriwether couldn't say the coming of magic had done much for him. He had been born into it, fifteen years after the change, and so this was the world he had always known since childhood. Perhaps the increased magic had enhanced his ability with herbal healing, which he had learned from his mother in childhood. Or perhaps not. Who could say? He did possess a sense that when he touched a plant he could know what it might do, but how was he to know whether that had always been in this world, even before magic started working? His mother had certainly displayed a similar skill and talked of his grandmother having it, too, which was well before the 1759 return of Mr. Halley's comet.

But Meriwether had also experienced odd, unnatural dreams from early childhood—the feeling of wings and fire, the portent that something was about to burst forth within him. Though he was a man of twenty-nine now, he still had those dreams, still felt that brooding presence. He both feared it and *desired* it in a way he could not explain.

The streets here in St. Louis were more spacious than those in the east. Those original American cities had modeled themselves after the cities of Europe, the cramped and crammed-together sort of life one could expect in the weary continent that had birthed and been swallowed by civilization. But in the west, the proportions of sky and land allowed for expansive building such that in many streets three carriages could have driven abreast without danger of collision.

And yet, as he approached the Government House where Franklin was due to speak in a few minutes, Meriwether could barely move through the throngs in the streets. Well-dressed men and women walked cheek to jowl with people in work clothes, all moving in the same direction. Only with the greatest determination could Meriwether make his way to the outer edges of the plaza outside the Government House. Then his progress halted completely.

And so that's it, he thought, half amused and half exasperated. *I should have known it was foolish to hope for even a glimpse of old Franklin, much less dream of making his acquaintance. At least I shall be able to describe to my friends in Virginia the press of people occasioned by an appearance of the great wizard from Philadelphia.*

Meriwether debated turning back to escape the overwhelming crowd, which would entail moving against the prevailing flow of people, but he decided to stay here, hoping he might hear some hint of his speech passed back through the crowd, sure that Franklin's words would be distorted and exaggerated by unreliable listeners.

What he heard instead was a loud scream close up ahead.

At first he took it to be an expression for excitement of the occasion, an overexcited man or a nervous and flighty woman, but he quickly realized that something was genuinely wrong. The scream held too sharp a note, containing too much shock and fear. And then another scream resounded, and another, coming from the other side of the plaza, right across from Government House.

Perhaps the famed wizard had let loose with his notorious electrical magic. Meriwether strained to see above the turmoil of bodies, hats, coats. Then he heard the sound—not the zap of electricity, but more a sound like when the household staff would beat the rugs in spring. It was a flap, flap, as of a great piece of fabric against the air—except the fabric must be truly immense, and the sound was coming straight toward—

Though the bodies were packed together in the St. Louis square, the crowd managed to move like a living thing as people screamed and ran. Caught by surprise, Meriwether swung his arm and his cane to ward off the panicked crowd about to trample him, but he lost his footing and almost went under onto the dirty street.

Thrashing, trying to save himself, he twirled and swung his cane in all directions, forcing the maddened and blind crowd to deviate around him. When he cleared a small space, he barely managed to pick himself up, prodding with his cane to ward off the human stampede.

As he dragged himself back to his feet, he was aware of other people stumbling and being trampled. He heard the screams and sounds of pain and wished to help, knowing he could not.

Meanwhile from above came that infernal sound again, the flapping of enormous rugs in the air. He nearly gagged with a smell of brimstone.

He risked a glance upward and saw a big, red bulk swoop around in the air and head for Government House again, which launched a fresh stampede, and new screams.

Dragon, the back of Meriwether's head said. *Dragon!*

And just like that, he found himself running, not with the crowd in blind headlong flight, but against it. His movement was so fast, so desperate, that he bowled people out of his way with the force of it. He had the strange, irrational thought that only he could protect the people of St. Louis from the dragon. It was the same reckless feeling that made him go *into* fever-ridden households, to help and save whomever he might. Arrogance, perhaps, but some part of Meriwether Lewis's constitution led him to the certainty that matters sometimes depended on him.

When he broke through the scattering crowd into the clearing in front of the Government House, he came upon sheer confusion. A carriage was now on fire, completely engulfed in flames. The horses, still in their traces, reared and pulled, spreading the fire to tree and bush as they went.

Government House was on fire, too, the tall wood and brick mansion set ablaze in an instant. Yellow flames and black smoke strained skyward.

Meriwether rushed toward the horses, desperate to free the screaming, terrified animals. Embers from the burning carriage sprayed on their hides, driving them into greater frenzy. He could not bear to let even the poor animals be consumed in his sight.

As he reached the horses, using all his knowledge of frightened creatures acquired through years of woodcraft, he avoided the pounding hooves and saw that another man was running to the horses from the opposite side. Without much thought, he registered that the man looked like the representations of old wizard Franklin he had seen, all the way down to the suit of inexpressible pink velvet. But this man looked maybe seventy years old, spry and showing his age, but far too young to be the ancient wizard, who was said to be very nearly a hundred years old. Now he was sidestepping the terrified animals with as much grace and ease as Meriwether himself.

Seeing him, the old man called out, "If we each get hold of the pins where they attach to the carriage, sir, we can release these unfortunate animals." He puffed slightly, out of breath as he spoke. "Even if they drag the traces behind them, they will find it a better alternative than burning alive."

Without wasting breath on an answer, Meriwether dashed to the burning carriage, using both hands to grab the pin that held the long poles to the burning carriage. With the spreading fire, the pin was hot even through his thin gloves. He inhaled smoke and coughed, but he grabbed hard at the pin, yanking it with all his might. The other man was fighting to do the same on the other side. Meriwether's eyes watered, and he was sure he could feel ashes and embers sifting down on his head.

Though he struggled, the pin would not budge. Due to the heat of the fire, the metal had expanded and now fit more tightly than ever. He felt as if his flesh were burning. The horses screamed, dragging the conflagration with them.

The pin gave so suddenly that Meriwether stumbled backward, and the other man must have experienced success at the same time, because the horses galloped free and the burning pile of carriage lunged forward and collapsed. He jumped out of the way.

Now he watched the old man in fine clothes standing in place, waving a wand about, jabbing toward the sky. Up in the sky, the monstrous dragon had flapped away, gaining speed and altitude, and now came back for another pass. Like a cat playing with a mouse.

Any minute, Meriwether was sure, he and the old man would

become cinders. The people had fled the square and the empty circle around them was like a killing zone. The older man stood defying the dragon, as if confident he would not be consumed by the furnace breath. There was nothing Meriwether could do to help.

Behind them, he heard the noise of feet and hooves retreating, or perhaps it was the sound of his blood beating a drumbeat past his ears, making it impossible to think. Meriwether could not make himself run away from what was sure to be certain death, and he couldn't even tell why. *It depends on me.* He simply knew that as long as the stranger in his soot-stained pink velvet suit stood there, he could not leave.

"Sir!" he cried, but his voice came out unaccountably small and squeaky, as though he weren't a full-grown man. "Sir," he said.

Ignoring him, the man swept his hands apart and uttered words that Meriwether thought might be Greek. Maybe the man was a foreigner, trapped here for nearly fifty years since the magic severing of America from the rest of the world?

"Sir!" he cried again.

When the man spread his hands and swept his wand about like an orchestra conductor directing a great piece, cracklings of electricity and lightning united his two hands like a rope.

Meriwether could only gasp, his ears blocked by the panicked spinning of his blood. The back of his neck prickled, and his hairs attempted to stand on end. Seeing this obvious magic, he was more certain than ever that this was truly the wizard Benjamin Franklin. This was the great man he had come to see.

But he hadn't counted on a dragon....

The red monster hove into view directly overhead, its shadow darkening the sky, Meriwether realized that Franklin could not possibly defeat the thing. The creature was as large as the plaza, end to end. Meriwether felt the wind from its wings, smelled its hot pumice stench. Rows of fangs filled the gigantic mouth that yawned open, large enough to swallow whole buildings if it tried. At the back of the reptilian throat something flared like the spark given off by flint and steel.

Meriwether had no weapon to fight a beast like this, but he grabbed for the knife in its sheath at his waist, an affectation of his walks in the woods; he felt naked without it.

Before he could draw the blade, an explosion occurred—and

it did not come from the dragon. A stream of light like a captive lightning bolt escaped Franklin's hands, a roiling ball of electricity like a giant, spinning ball of dazzling blue and white. It hurtled through the air toward the dragon's open mouth and struck the monster with a sound like a deafening, suspended musical note. It seemed to echo from the beginning of time and would sound until the world itself vanished in blackness and chaos.

When it ceased, two more balls of lightning flew from Franklin's hands, slamming the dragon between the eyes, and the giant reptile keened like a creature slain. The second crackling sphere singed the great flapping wings. The old wizard from Philadelphia hurled two more electrical balls, and then two more.

Meriwether stood rooted on the street, his begrimed clothes rough and heavy upon him. His eyes and his throat burned, and his body seemed to vibrate with an echo of magic. And as he watched, aghast, the dragon shimmered and shifted. For a moment, hanging in midair, it wasn't a great primeval beast, but instead became a conjunction of geometric patterns: circles and triangles, squares and shapes, all glowing angles and strange junctions flowing into each other.

He blinked the stinging sweat out of his eyes, and he found himself looking at the dragon again. The huge wings flapped like scaly rugs, and Meriwether felt something touch his mind for just a moment.

More ball lightning flew, fast, fast, from Franklin's hands, too fast for Meriwether to even see which parts of the dragon were hit.

"Be gone!" The magic echoed in Franklin's voice, resonating with the same loud and unbearable cadences he'd heard before.

The dragon spun, a streak of movement, a dancing center of magic, too graceful and quick for a beast so big and unwieldy.

Meriwether no longer had the strength to stand. Awareness and force flowed out of him, like a liquid seeping through his feet. Before darkness swept over him, he heard a sentence, not in Franklin's voice, but in another, stranger accent—*inside his head.* "We will meet again, Meriwether Lewis...son of Wales."

He was absolutely sure it was the dragon speaking.

A Greater Calling

MERIWETHER WOKE UP WET. UNFORTUNATELY, THIS WAS NOT AN unknown experience for him. Having learned from a young age to procure and use magical healing herbs, he had often slept out in the open in the woods of his native Virginia or Georgia. In the hot and humid summers, he often took a midafternoon nap on the verdant grass beneath the pines. More than once, too, as he slept, a thunderstorm would soak him through and he'd awaken in sodden clothes facing a long walk back home.

But this was an entirely different situation. Instead of the blue Virginia skies, he blinked and gazed up at a gray-black sky. Instead of the woods, he was in the middle of a city, a burning city. It reeked of manure, soot and fire. The insistent ringing of a bell made Lewis's head pound. He woke up fully to see a bucket brigade attacking a fire that engulfed the roof of Government House. He turned, rolled over, saw that he lay close to a charred pile of remains. He must have got water tossed on him while—

With a shock, the entire scene came back to him, the unlikely wizard, the dragon.

He sat up, which made his head swim. It wasn't like him to swoon like that, to remain unconscious even when doused with water. Normally when he got soaked through, he woke up. He'd had to fight his mind before, but never his body, which had stood him in perfectly good stead, no matter what he demanded of it.

"Easy, Mister," said a voice just behind him, and he turned to see two men eyeing him warily. He might have been concerned

9

if they looked at all ill-dressed or shady, but they appeared to be prosperous men of St. Louis. "We thought you'd lost consciousness because of the magics." The man's voice had a trace of a French accent. "And we didn't know what succor to give."

"But how do you feel?" the second man asked. "Are you also a wizard?"

Meriwether surprised himself by laughing, a short sound between a bark and a cackle. "No, I'm not a wizard. Definitely not."

"Then you are in the retinue of the great man for other reasons?" asked the first man. "We saw you fight the dragon alongside Franklin."

With a start, Meriwether understood their assumption. If they thought him to be one of old wizard Franklin's traveling companions, maybe they had left him lie unaided in the mud of the street, doused with the water used to extinguish the fires, because they were afraid to approach.

Much had changed since magic had returned to America, and undoubtedly many such changes had been beneficial to society. He knew that some places had devices powered by magic that did the work of men, thus making slaves unnecessary. But despite their familiarity with the arcane changes in the nearly half century since the Sundering from the Old World, people still feared magic—and well they should. A single gifted individual, if trained and of a disposition to do such a thing, could level half a city.

Meriwether grinned ruefully as he caught traces of apprehension in the men's eyes. He picked himself up, looked at his sodden clothes. "No, no," he said, in an easy tone. "You've got me all wrong, my friends. I only just met the great man, by happenstance and desperation. I'm not traveling with him. In fact, I arrived yesterday, and I'm staying at Chez Marie Bayard's." The men exchanged a look at the mention of the comfortable but undistinguished hostelry; surely, the wizard Franklin stayed in far more exotic and expensive lodgings. "I just came here hoping to catch a glimpse of him at work, not fight a dragon beside him!"

The joke must have caught up with the men. The first chuckled, and the second said, "Some glimpse you got, Monsieur."

"Indeed." He drew himself up and swayed against a sudden dizziness. "Meriwether Lewis from Virginia. For years now, I've been the personal assistant and household healer to Thomas Jefferson." Jefferson's name might have been unknown to the men, but he wanted to emphasize the location and the respectability of his position.

They came forward to shake his hand, and then offered to help him to his lodgings. He accepted their help, thankfully. As night fell and the last of the scattered fires were doused, the city assumed a carnival aspect. Townspeople gathered on the street, discussing everything that had happened. Meriwether heard comments as they passed by.

"Three dragons—three!"

"And all the houses around Government House set alight and all burned to the ground, not a bucket of water in sight."

Meriwether felt the water trickling down his back, his coat drenched from the efforts of the bucket brigade, but he decided not to contradict the gossipers. Other comments were as outlandish, ranging from declarations that a whole group of magicians had come to rescue the town from dragons, to those who insisted that several carriages—and horses—had been incinerated in the square.

His head was still dizzy, and he wondered if it was an after-effect of proximity to magic. He couldn't forget what he perceived as the voice of the dragon in his mind, and he wondered if it was correct that he would meet the monster again, and under what circumstances. Though he was a natural scientist at heart, Meriwether did not look forward to the opportunity.

Finally, his new friends delivered him to his hostelry, in a building that had once been a commodious colonial house. The building permitted a large common room in the front, and several small rooms on the second floor. Meriwether parted from the men at the door, with much enthusiastic hand shaking and much apology for having been the cause of such trouble, while the men in return assured him it had been no trouble at all. They apologized in a roundabout way for not having intervened on his behalf earlier, before his clothes got, surely, ruined by the water and the mud.

He entered the warmth of the inn's crowded common room, which at nightfall had the aspect of a dining hall mixed with a tavern. Men sat at tables, arguing, laughing, talking about the day's remarkable events, playing cards. A large haunch roasted in the vast fireplace, filling the air with a smell of burnt fat and meat. For some reason, it hit him wrong, perhaps too near a reminder of how close he and Franklin—not to mention the two terrified horses—had come to being roasted meat themselves. Meriwether felt his gorge rise, choked it back, and hurried toward the narrow stairs that climbed up the left side of the room to the upper rooms.

A voice called out to stop him, "Mr. Lewis, if you will?"

The hosteller's younger son, a twenty-year-old gentleman with an uncertain complexion, pushed his way through the crowds in the common room. He must have been doing his turn as the ale dispenser, as he wore a stained apron and smelled strongly of beer. "Pardon me, sir," he said, out of breath, reaching Meriwether after frantic progress through the closely packed tables. "Pardon me, but the wizard has sent word that he'd like to talk to you."

"The wizard?" He stood near the stairs, dripping, aware that eyes were turning toward him. Waterlogged, muddy, and singed, he was not fit to be seen in society.

"The wizard Franklin, sir. He called for you, sent word right here to the inn."

Meriwether realized he sounded thick-witted. "For me?" Granted they had risked death together to save the horses from the dragon, but how did old wizard Franklin even know who he was, much less where he stayed? And how could he get a messenger here so quickly?

The innkeeper's son nodded. "Yes! His secretary is waiting to lead you to where the wizard stays. It's not too far, but he does want you to come right away."

For a moment, like a madness, he considered refusing. Here he stood in sodden clothes, shivering with cold, ravenously hungry yet queasy, desperate just to stretch out in bed. And yet, Franklin had been so confident that he would accept the invitation he had left his servant here to wait for him.

Meriwether had been eager just to catch a glimpse of the ancient, powerful man, hoping even that would give him something to brag of in his old age. How could he refuse actually meeting the legendary wizard? And at Franklin's own request?

While his thoughts spun, the innkeeper's son waved forward a well-dressed man—much less flamboyant than Franklin—and now Meriwether felt even dingier by comparison. The manservant clutched a hat with a modest crown and a sensible brim; he wore a somber black jacket and knee breeches, both of precise cut.

He bowed slightly to Meriwether, and to his credit, managed to stifle any look of dismay or disdain. Straightening, he offered his hand. "My name is Albert Middleton, sir, and I have the honor to be Mr. Franklin's secretary. The wizard has sent me with the hope I might procure your presence at his dinner table tonight."

Meriwether bowed and then clasped the proffered hand. "It would be an honor." He plucked at his disheveled suit. "But you must grant me the grace of a few minutes to change my attire."

"Of course," Middleton said. "We wouldn't wish to put your health at risk by having you travel about town in soaked clothes. I shall wait."

Meriwether ran up the narrow staircase to his room. He would just have to pretend to be fresh enough to listen to Franklin and memorize his witticisms.

After undressing, he was not surprised to find he was soaked to his smallclothes. Fortunately he had traveled with two other suits of clothes, one a buckskin shirt and pants, with matching rugged boots, fit to go clambering around the wilds near the Mississippi River, as he'd expected to do. The other, a respectable set of evening attire, much like the one Middleton wore.

He changed quickly into the suit, but picked up the overcoat he'd brought for more adventurous work. Though perhaps not as presentable, it would keep him warm in the freezing night outside, and the wizard had seen with his own eyes how Meriwether had ruined his more presentable overcoat.

Returning to the common room, he joined the manservant, who briskly led him through the darkened streets of St. Louis. "I'm afraid we must walk, sir," Middleton said apologetically. "Mr. Franklin's carriage..."

"Indeed, I was present when it...ah...became incapacitated."

"Mr. Franklin has described how you helped rescue his horses, though one of them has not been returned to him yet. He suggests he might put the word out that the beast is infused with a magical spell that will kill anyone who has acquired it illegally."

Meriwether hesitated, deciding how to phrase his question. "And...does it?"

The manservant shook his head. "I'm afraid not, sir, but people believe Mr. Franklin can do practically anything, and so he often makes use of their superstitions rather than his own powers of magic. Magic is not the working of miracles with no cost and no limit, despite what the public believes, and therefore he enjoys making fun of such fancies. His horses are a matched pair, and he would very much like the missing one returned to him."

"I see." The opening presented himself. Lewis asked, "Speaking of the cost of magic, I trust Mr. Franklin was undaunted by the use of force he hurled against the dragon? And that no mishap has come to him?"

"Oh, my master is very well indeed. He collapsed, as often happens when he expends so much magic at once, but it is nothing to worry about. After half an hour of recovery, he's as well as may be. He was in the house and planning his dinner with you in no time. He sent me to you straightaway."

"If it's not an imposition...How did Mr. Franklin find me? Was it some sort of identification spell?"

The servant continued to stroll along at a brisk pace. "Oh, he sent several of us from the house to enquire at the plaza. It wasn't difficult to learn you were the out-of-town gentleman staying at Chez Marie Bayard's, and in turn I ran to your lodging. I'd only just arrived when you came into the common room yourself, sir."

From these points of information, Meriwether decided that he must have been unconscious for more than an hour, unusually long considering he had suffered no direct injury. He also decided that, even though guided by his newfound friends, he must have walked to the inn slowly indeed, or perhaps by a very roundabout way.

They reached a very large house, and Meriwether paused to drink in the details. Other than its size, the house looked as raw and newly built as the others around it, but it was lit with a warm and dazzling glow that suggested every chandelier in the place must be lit. Meriwether realized it must be a wealthy house, or Franklin himself was paying the enormous expense for the candles. Just how rich was the most prominent wizard in the American territories?

As they approached, a liveried servant opened the door. He was as well dressed and as well mannered as any at Monticello. Another servant rushed forward to divest Meriwether of his coat as soon as he stepped through the door. "No hat, sir?"

Meriwether touched his head. "I lost it in the tussle with the dragon." Alas, it was his only hat.

Several more men in livery bowed, and conducted him past

exquisitely appointed drawing rooms to a dining room that he
imagined rivaled anything in the richest houses in lost Europe.
The dining table alone, set with numerous candelabra each blazing with multiple candles, could have seated fifty people without
crowding.

Now, though, the table sat a single man dressed in bright
green velvet. He filled a chair at the far end of the table, but
the numerous candles shed enough light to clearly illuminate
the neat, longish white hair and the wrinkled and smiling face
of Ben Franklin, which Meriwether had seen so many times in
woodcut and painting.

Stepping into the dining room, he bowed. "Mr. Franklin, it
is a pleasure to meet the foremost wizard of our age."

A chuckle answered him. "I'm sure it is. You did meet me
before, Mr. Meriwether, even if we had no time for introductions,
as we tried to keep my horses from becoming roasted—for which
I thank you. Please come in. I've taken the liberty of having a
place set for you up here, next to me." He gestured to his right
side, where there were indeed plates and silverware laid out. "Pardon my presumption, but when you get to be nearly a hundred,
one no longer wishes to gaze across a vast expanse of table, let
alone conduct a conversation by shouting."

Meriwether hastened to the place prepared for him and sat
down. True to legend, Franklin's gaze was indeed filled with
humor, but also acute as he peered through his spectacles.

Unfolding his napkin, and making minute adjustments to
his silverware, more to disguise the fact that he was aware of
being scrutinized than for any actual purpose, Meriwether said,
"It is an honor to be invited to dinner with you, sir. I came to
the Government House and joined the crowds there in hopes of
catching a glimpse of you. I did not expect—"

Franklin interrupted him with a chuckle. "Neither did I
expect to be attacked by a dragon. Life, young man, is a series
of surprises, and those of us who survive have to learn to profit
from and benefit from them."

"Yes, sir," Meriwether said, not sure what else to say.

"You must forgive me. Old men have a habit of lecturing
the young and expecting you to be grateful for the privilege of
our aphorisms. The truth is I sent for you because of what you
did for me in saving the horses. I had some idea of thanking

you for your undaunted courage, by offering you a fine dinner." He narrowed his sparkling eyes, leaned closer to his guest. "But since then my thoughts have taken another turn."

Meriwether looked on expectantly, wondering if he detected an ominous tone in the wizard's words, but Franklin laughed. "Not during dinner, my new friend. I find speaking politics at a meal sours the stomach and causes indigestion. We shall discuss my idea soon enough, but first let's enjoy our repast with some light talk. I trust that will prove soothing after what has been a very difficult day for both of us."

Meriwether enjoyed, and endured, a dinner with a prodigious number of courses, a custom that he was sure Franklin remembered from his younger years when he had traveled across Europe, long before the appearance and destruction of Mr. Halley's comet in 1759. "I confess I am ravenous, Mr. Lewis. Expending my magic as I did today drains the energy in my body, and my only recourse is to refuel. Hence, this glorious feast!" He piled his plate yet again.

To Meriwether the fare of this banquet had a definite feel of the frontier rather than the great houses of England or France. Meriwether especially liked the venison prepared with gooseberries, and a dessert that somehow managed to include turkey eggs.

"A noble bird, the turkey," Franklin said. "Fed the first pioneers to the land, fierce in defense of its young. We should all be very grateful to the turkey."

The dinner conversation led them through Franklin reminiscing about his early adventures in England, after magic had become apparent in the world to himself as well as a few other people, but before the Sundering cut off the colonies from the Old World. Meriwether listened, enchanted.

"I always say," Franklin mused, "that the reason for my success is not the presence of great magic on my person, but more the great power of a mind inclined to natural science when applied to magic. I don't know why no one else has considered magic that way throughout the ages. Magic is, in fact, very much like any other science, and can be learned with a little logical thought. Or a lot of logical thought."

The dizzying variety of food and the endless clatter of dishes being removed went on for more than two hours. Meriwether was more than sated, utterly exhausted from the ordeals of the day, and fascinated by the company.

Finally, the servants cleared the table, and provided the men with glasses of brandy, leaving the decanter along with a deep dish of nuts in their shells. The brandy, a rare indulgence for Meriwether, tasted like golden sunshine on his tongue, finally cleansing the uneasiness that he'd had since the dragon's mind touched his, that he was confined to some land of discomfort and cold from which he could never quite emerge. It was good to banish the feeling, which reminded him overmuch of the melancholy turns his mind sometimes took, rendering him incapable of any work or clear thought for months.

"I am sorry for boring you with my rambling, Mr. Lewis," Franklin said, as he cracked two walnuts in his long, thin fingers that yet showed no sign of being withered with age.

Meriwether stifled an embarrassing yawn. "You didn't bore me, sir. In fact—" He felt heat rise to his face, because he'd always been intrigued by people who had known the world as it used to be. "In fact, I was very much interested in the descriptions of France and England, before... you know—When they were still accessible."

Instead of laughing, Franklin nodded in agreement. "I'm fond of saying that there is no such thing as knowing your own land until you travel abroad. Since the Sundering, we have formed several nations and experimented with various models of government in our world but I doubt there is enough variety to truly cultivate the mind by exposing it to the unknown. All the lands left to us are as recently colonized as our own, the landscape explored all the way to the mighty Mississippi. All our buildings, our food, our entertainment, are shaped by the exigencies of the frontier, and of newly conquered land. And here lies St. Louis, right on the very verge of the known." He gave his guest a keen look. "I understand your interest in longing to see a world that had already been lost when you were born." He considered for a moment, and made a sound with his tongue against his teeth. "But that isn't the only world in need of exploration." His eyes twinkled again. "Which brings us in a roundabout way to what I wished to talk about."

Meriwether sat up, intently interested. "Yes?"

Franklin leaned back in his chair, cradling the glass of brandy between his hands. "I came to St. Louis, the edge of the frontier, ostensibly to give a lecture on magic. It's a habit of mine, wherever I'm bound, because despite decades of usefulness and use, magic still scares the superstitious."

"I saw that with my own eyes," Meriwether said. "After the dragon fires were put out, I lay in the street, unconscious and untended, because the people were afraid I was somehow a sorcerer like yourself."

Franklin chuckled. "Exactly the sort of superstition I meant! But it isn't magic they fear, but the *unknown*. Before the Sundering, magic was the province of charlatans and swindlers, its study quite unbecoming to modern and civilized men of a scientific disposition. Magic, like science, can lead to great harm, and great ill. The same electricity I harness with magic can be harnessed by science and used either as a powering effect for devices—if an unreliable one—or to cause pain, harm, and even death." Franklin set his glass down, picked up another walnut, cracked the shell, and delicately extracted the meat within. "Surely you know the same is true in your avocation, which I'm told is healing? Herbs with potent properties?"

"Yes. We say the poison is in the dose. The same herb that can relieve a condition can also kill a patient if the dose be too large. And sometimes the efficacious dose is so large, so near the lethal dose, we have to work by very small increments to avoid taking a life." Meriwether found it curious to think of magic as botany.

"That is what my lectures were about," Franklin said. "But coming here to address the French frontiersmen was something of a pretext, too."

"A pretext?"

"I didn't expect the dragon," Franklin said, as though talking to himself, "or at least not in such a traditional form, considering the roots and manifestations of magic among our varied cultures. Now, I would not have been surprised if some magical beast, a great bear or some other animal native to these wild lands, had lurched out of the unknown to attack us. But I did not expect a dragon from old European folklore. It seems out of place, and it goes against my formative hypothesis...but I have been told of something very similar."

The old wizard leaned forward. "You see, my...observers, as varied a number of persons as you'd care to know, have been receiving reports that the inhabitants of this unknown land, from wild men, to fur trappers, and everyone in between, have been witnessing disturbances. Tribes that were once friendly to white men have vanished altogether, or else have become hostile. One of my informers sent verified reports of a large beast that kills men and sets fire to forests, and of other incredible creatures that some say are like the primal things that walked the land before the Deluge. One can only guess what miracles and nightmares remain to be found in the unknown territories of the Americas, the unexplored vastness beyond the Mississippi."

He adjusted his spectacles. "We might find a tribe of Welsh Indians, as the intrepid Welsh were said to have sailed this way, long ago. Or lost Viking tribes, who settled here long before the Sundering. I don't believe all the reports of strange beasts and marvelous happenings though." Franklin paused, and picked up his brandy snifter. "Or rather, I didn't believe them, but I am beginning to change my mind. I occurs to me that given what has happened to this world since the comet changed the rules of science and magic, perhaps I should not assume that the same parameters of natural science apply any longer. So many strange things we thought were legends have returned to this world."

Meriwether thought he understood, and he respected the still-inquisitive mind of the century-old wizard and scientist. "So, you wished to come to the border of the unexplored territories to find out what they might harbor? Are you ... are you sure you're up to such an undertaking, sir?"

He knew he would very much like to explore that immense land. What plants, what animals would he find there? What things arcane and strange, legendary creatures made manifest? Meriwether itched to find out for sure, but his resources were lean. His father had died young, and his stepfather preferred to favor his own progeny, so Meriwether had to work for a living. He could never afford to hire the men or purchase the equipment and supplies for such an expedition. As for tramping by himself all over the unknown territory, as he often did back east, he doubted he would long survive either wild beasts or encounters with the natives in the unexplored, arcane territories. The Cherokees were long friends of his, excellent sources of knowledge about herbs, but who knew what strange and bellicose people lived beyond the river?

He realized that Franklin was making a face. The wizard said, "You are exactly right, Mr. Meriwether. While I might try to convince myself that such an undertaking to the wild lands would be exciting, I find I have grown too fond of my own creature comforts." He took a long sip of his brandy. "I am convinced it is a worthwhile endeavor. But not for me."

"Who, then?" Meriwether asked. His heart was suddenly pounding.

Instead of answering the question, Franklin seemed to fall back into the lecture he had intended to give in the square outside the Government House. "As you know, young man, since the Sundering we are confined to these territories by the magically created barrier that cuts us off partway out into the Atlantic. For nearly fifty years, we have not been able to sail to England, or even know if an England still exists." He narrowed his eyes. "But we know from tales of fur trappers and the accounts of Portuguese and Spanish sailors in older times, that our land of America extends, perhaps largely unbroken, all the way to that *other ocean*, known as the Pacific Ocean, which in turn gives route to China and India... from whence, after a long voyage, it would be possible to once more reach old mother England and the civilizations of Europe."

Meriwether found himself caught up in the idea. No ship had been able to sail east to Europe for half a century, since the comet arrived. But sailing west...

"Assuming Europe is merely cut off rather than destroyed, I confess I wish to know what they've discovered about magic, how they have created useful techniques for the benefit of mankind. All of the sorcerers like me in America are like isolated natural scientists, with no comparative information. Like science, magic benefits from more minds on the task, more people to discover what makes it work and how."

He lifted the decanter, removed the stopper, and refilled his brandy glass, then Meriwether's. The younger man didn't even remember finishing his brandy, though he could still taste the warm glow in his mouth.

"I never thought of the need for a worldwide investigation of magic," he said.

"That is because you were born to this smaller, more confined world. When you hear an old man like myself speak of England or France, those other lands are like descriptions of fairyland. You cannot know what it was really like, my dear Mr. Lewis.

Coffee and tea both thrive in Virginia, and if people say it isn't as good as what they remember from India or China, that is just old people talking."

Meriwether nodded. The old wizard continued, "We find ourselves here in a very limited world. People will have children, and those children will need farms to support them. We're already seeing that food is sometimes very dear in the eastern territories, the crowded original colonies. If we don't make a push to find and tame more land, America will become as crowded as Europe, and with such crowding comes a certain calcification of the mind." He made a gesture as of closing a book. "The mind which despairs of new horizons in the world will find no new territory in the realm of thought, either."

Meriwether frowned. "I am somewhat confused, sir. You insist on the importance of exploring the unknown lands to the west, but who would you wish to take on this role?"

Franklin laughed. He'd chuckled or cackled before, but this was the first time Meriwether heard him laugh without reservation. It shook the room and reverberated from the silver and crystal on the sideboard. Even the lights of the candles trembled. "I wish the lands *explored*, Mr. Meriwether, but I have no intention of doing it myself. Now, if I were twenty years younger, I might brave it. Although I age more slowly than most people, I do still age. I'm too old, my reflexes too slow, my body too full of its own crotchets to undertake such a thing. And why would I need to, now that I've made your acquaintance? I was never like you, a man of woods and streams, a man of adventuring in the wilds and learning much from plants and animals. No, I am too much a part of cities, of older civilization."

He raised his brandy snifter to Meriwether in a toast. "If beer is proof that God loves us and wishes us to be happy, then brandy is proof that he loves us very much indeed and wishes us to be overjoyed. Though there have been some experiments with vine growing and even distilling a passable sort of homemade whiskey, this land does not yet have the capacity to make any fine liquor that rivals Europe's centuries of tradition." He laughed again, just as sincere. "Yet another vital reason for us to find a way back to England and France."

He seemed amused by his own comment, then grew serious again. "While we have a great deal of knowledge that was preserved here before the Sundering, not to mention what we have discovered on our own since, what we do not have is..." He rubbed his thumb across the fingers of his right hand, as though feeling some soft and precious fabric. "What we do not have is the sense of time and history from those places, the deep knowledge of human civilization. If America remains isolated, we will be impoverished. In addition to needing room and cropland for our people, in addition to needing to learn what the rest of the world knows about magic, we desperately need that *weight of history* for our people, lest it be forgotten. Because history is the teacher of the future."

Absorbed in his own thoughts, Meriwether found himself daydreaming about all those unexplored lands. "I wish there were a way to do it, sir, with all my heart."

"There is, my dear young man. There is." Meriwether sat up straighter, and the old wizard continued. "I told you that I came here to see how things stood on the frontier, maybe to hear from the fur trappers who venture into that wilderness. What if it is possible to cross the Mississippi and travel the width of the continent all the way to the Pacific? It was truly just a dream, but one that took hold of me. I imagined I would give my cycle of lectures, talk to the natives of St. Louis, for I'm as fluent in French as in English, and learn from them how big the enterprise would be, how enormous the undertaking. For I intended to finance it myself."

Seeing Meriwether's expression, he sniffed. "Do not look at me that way, Mr. Lewis! Thanks to practicing magic for almost fifty years and financing highly successful magical instruments—among other endeavors—I am fabulously wealthy. It will be nothing for me to make sure you have the necessary resources to lead, staff, and supply such an expedition."

Meriwether could barely speak. "I?"

"You, Meriwether Lewis. Once I saw how you endured the attack of that dragon, and once I learned your name, I did some investigating. I got in touch with some friends through—" He frowned slightly. "Well, through magical means that I don't care to disclose. I like your past, Mr. Lewis—your army record, your knowledge of woodcraft and plant life, your easy and amicable relations with the Cherokee, your interest in the unexplored. Find people to go with you, buy boats, supplies, weapons, and organize an expedition. Be optimistic, and be curious. I want you to cross the uncharted territories, hopefully all the way to the Pacific. You, alone, could open a way back to civilization for all of us."

Meriwether tried to demur. "I have...I have sometimes fits of melancholy that render me quite unable to work or—"

Benjamin Franklin nodded. "Well, you'd be free to choose your companions and maybe a co-captain to the adventure, someone perhaps who understands your quirks and is willing to compensate for them?"

Meriwether's mind blurred, and he suddenly heard an echo of the dragon's words, "We will meet again, son of Wales."

But he was too excited about this prospect to pay it much attention. He grabbed hard at the edge of the table, and said, his voice sounding wavery and strange to his own ears, "But—"

Franklin snuffed his concerns. "I will promptly write to Jefferson, whom I know from correspondence. I will convince him to dispense with your services for a few years. I assure you, you will be well compensated for your efforts both before and after the expedition."

"You mean it, then?" Meriwether was half-sure he would wake up once more back in the square, soaked in bucket-brigade water. "You mean to do this thing?"

"I mean for *you* to do it. We must make friends with the natives in this vast unknown territory, and we must discover what lies in it, for our very hearts and souls. If the nearby Missouri River will, as I expect, provide an easy route to the Pacific, and if the Pacific isn't also blocked by the magical barrier, we shall find our way back home."

Franklin set the snifter down. "Let me send for maps, and I'll give you my thoughts on how such an expedition should proceed, and you will begin to contemplate what you'll need in the way of help and provisions, horses, boats, guns. Then, if you agree, we shall start making all the arrangements."

Meriwether nodded, still too dumbfounded, too dazzled by the immense prospect before him to actually speak. The old wizard sent for the maps and rearranged the candles to illuminate them.

They talked long into the night, and Meriwether fell into a sort of dream, a combination of exhaustion and excitement. Deemed too weary to return to his own inn, he fell asleep in a spare bedroom in Franklin's borrowed house, and he dreamed of vast open lands, of never-seen mountain ranges. His vivid dreams were barely disturbed by the dream-memory of wings that flapped like enormous rugs, and the sense of the dragon that was like a cat pursuing a mouse.

Then the dreams got lost in a welter of lists and half-awake ideas of what he would need for the expedition. Meriwether woke up standing by a desk, barely conscious but penning a letter to his good friend, Captain William Clark, under whom Meriwether had served when he was first in the army. He could think of no one else with whom he'd rather share such an adventure.

My Dearest Julia,

I promised I would write to you and tell you of these, my adventures, in hopes that they might amuse you, or at least give you some idea of the momentous enterprise in which I'm involved.

Until recently, I believed I was settled in my ways and had quite abandoned the adventurous life, as I told your esteemed parents when I asked for permission to court you with an eye toward making you my wife. But a month ago, I received a letter from my old friend Meriwether Lewis, whom I'm sure I have mentioned in conversation before. My friend happened to be in St. Louis when the great wizard Benjamin Franklin visited, when the unexpected dragon attacked and set fire to parts of the city. The commotion was reported in many newspapers throughout the land, and the eyewitness reports are quite indisputable.

After my friend Meriwether assisted the old wizard during this battle against the remarkable creature from myth, Franklin was so impressed that he hired Meriwether to lead a bold expedition into the uncharted arcane territories west of St. Louis, perhaps even to find a path all the way to the Pacific Ocean, if it still exists after the Sundering.

Meriwether invited me to accompany him as his partner on the expedition. He wrote me a letter filled with perfectly sensible points and making a strong case to go out there. This, Franklin insisted, was a possible means—via the western sea—to sail back to Europe, and it was also an unparalleled chance for civilized men to study the native fauna and flora, to learn about the rest of our land, in which we now find ourselves stranded.

Those reasons alone should be sufficient, but then, other things transpired, related to the dragon attack and other similarly profound events occurring near St. Louis.

It seems that someone or some arcane force fueled by magic is uniting the native tribes west of the Mississippi and Missouri Rivers, making them hostile to Europeans. Franklin doesn't know if it is an evil person, creature, or force, but that will be part of our duty to investigate.

I apologize for not writing you sooner, but I have been over-whelmed with purchasing and organizing supplies for such an enormous undertaking, funded by Franklin himself. I am due to meet Meriwether in St. Louis in another month.

I know you will chide me for risking myself on this mad enterprise before our wedding, but I promise to do my best to return to you and keep our engagement. Though we encounter perils and adventures, I will be back to claim your hand, my dearest.

I will send letters when I can if we send couriers back east, for I know your curious mind will wish to know of all the new things we find and the dangers we vanquish.

Yours in fond regard,
William Clark

—Letter from William Clark to Julia Hancock,
April 28, 1804

Heroes Assemble

MERIWETHER LEWIS HAD STRIPPED TO HIS SHIRTSLEEVES—AND the shirt a humble homespun one bought recently—as he supervised the assembling of men and supplies, ready to go into the wild. By supervising, mostly it meant waiting around till Clark should arrive.

For weeks, as the men trickled in by one and by two, Meriwether had found them lodging and franked their expenses, both in daily living and in materials for the expedition, from the largesse dispensed to him by Benjamin Franklin.

Each of the men had suggested additions to the expedition and things they should take, from well crafted, watertight wooden boxes to oilcloth, from dried meat to trading goods.

Meriwether now walked between the boats, where these various goods were being stowed and a stand, upon which he kept his ledger, which had become blotted from many a hasty note made with an ill-trimmed quill.

In fact, Meriwether realized his hands too had become blue with ink.

Most of the men were people either he or Captain Clark had known from their army days, though a few had been recommended by Benjamin Franklin himself. And though this was not a military expedition, most of the men had a fine military bearing and military discipline.

There were men that Captain Clark had recommended, having esteemed them much in the war, Sergeants Nathaniel Pryor and his cousin Charles Floyd, who was so excited by the expedition as

to have volunteered to keep "a very precise journal of all occurrences." Having been privileged to see Sergeant Floyd's prose,
Meriwether was somewhat amused by the enthusiasm and the
care with which the young man had brought a bundle of bound
journals, ready to receive his writing. But then, despite his pecu-
liar spelling and sometimes enthusiastic phrasing, the young man
was, after all, another set of eyes, another set of observations to
complement those that Meriwether himself intended to make.
They were going into the unknown, after all, and who was to
say which of them would survive, or which set of diaries would
come through intact?

Another of the men from Kentucky was John Ordway, also a
sergeant, whom Clark had recommended for his close knowledge
of native ways. While growing up, he had consorted much with
native tribes and learned ways of survival that would help should
all their supplies fail.

Clark had also recommended Patrick Gass, a carpenter, who
had served in the war and who Clark thought would be able to
contrive repairs to the boats, should such become needed, but
they'd run into a snag, as the young man's present patron—a
wealthy landowner—didn't wish to dispense with Gass's services.
Meriwether had thought to leave the man where he was, until
he'd received a pleading letter from the man himself, begging
for the opportunity to come on the expedition.

Perhaps it wasn't old Franklin's imagination that they were
in fact sore confined, great though this land was, and in much
need of a place to explore and expand.

In the end it had taken an appeal to Franklin and a letter
from Franklin himself to free Gass to join. He now wore brand
new buckskins, and was stowing his tools with some care, his
face shining with excitement at the upcoming expedition.

William Bratton, one of the best young woodsmen in this
part of the country and a gunsmith besides, was carefully stowing away various guns. Meriwether hadn't yet seen the one he
had, himself, ordered. He waited its delivery in some excitement.

Another young man, John Collins, known as a skillful hunter
even if on recommending him, Franklin had said he might be
overmuch fond of spirits, and perhaps Meriwether should take
care to keep him from temptation, was helping William with
the guns.

John Colter, five foot ten, with piercing blue eyes, stood a little apart. He'd been recruited by Meriwether himself, on account of his hunting prowess. Since he was also an excellent woodsman, Meriwether had been surprised to find him disablingly shy, except of course that he was familiar with his own patron, Benjamin Franklin, who often became mute in company.

Pierre Cruzatte, taller than Colter and very dark, had turned up with his own bedroll and supply of dried meat. Half native, half French, he'd made his living from the fur trade in and around the uncharted territories. Meriwether regarded him with some doubt, as the man seemed to stand apart from the other men in the expedition, whether by choice or because he looked so different. But he spoke the Omaha language and was skilled in sign language. The expedition could not spare him.

Joseph Field and his brother Reubin Field, from Culpeper, Virginia, and known to Meriwether from childhood, had eagerly answered Meriwether's letter of summons, as had Robert Frazer from Virginia, a solid and resourceful man, never daunted or afraid.

George Gibson, also from Kentucky, had won a marksmanship contest Meriwether had set up the week before. Silas Goodrich had made his way into the expedition with certified letters from many notables calling him an outstanding fisherman. Since they'd be following the river for much of the expedition, if not all of it, his skill would come in handy. Hugh Hall, though accounted a fine hunter, was one of the men that Meriwether was none too sure about, as already, in the week he'd been in St. Louis, he had twice got in trouble with the local authorities for drunken and disorderly behavior. Another such was Thomas Proctor Howard of whom the men had started saying "Thomas never drinks... water." If they became a disciplinary problem in the expedition, Meriwether would certainly have to send them back. They'd promised not to let their fondness of liquor impair the expedition.

Hugh McNeal, John Shields, John B. Thompson, Peter M. Weiser, William Werner, John Whitehouse, Alexander Hamilton Willard and Richard Windsor, were all known to Lewis and Clark from the war, and had been picked as men who would both embrace the trek into the wilderness and be of aid in charting the arcane territories. So too had John Potts, a German giant who spoke with a strong accent.

Meriwether had just made a note about the various weapons, when he heard Bill Bratton call, "Captain, Captain!"

Looking up, Meriwether saw the man approaching, running, evading the others in the crowded staging area, carrying a very beautiful polished wood gun case in his hands.

He deposited it on the stand, atop the ledger book, and looked up at Meriwether, "It's here, Captain. It's arrived."

The rifle that had Bratton in such excitement was called a Girandoni rifle, designed by an Italian called Girandoni. His design had somehow made it across the ocean before the Sundering and now the weapon was made by Isaiah Lukens, horologist and gunsmith of Philadelphia.

It had been recommended by Franklin, always an admirer of exquisite instruments. Meriwether had heard much of it, and now removed the detachable stock to examine every part. The rifle was supposed to work by air pressure, and when fully pumped it held air at a pressure of eight hundred pounds per square inch, which meant it fired its .46 caliber round balls with as much force as any powder weapons, but did so silently and could fire twenty-two times before needing to be reloaded and forty times before it lost any muzzle velocity.

Meriwether simply had to try it, and started pumping up the air pressure, which he knew to take quite a few pumps—fifteen hundred strokes in all—before it achieved maximum force. He started upon it, while Bratton hovered nearby, visibly impatient, barely restraining himself from seizing the pump. Meriwether smiled at the man, understanding his impatience and said, "Easy."

He was almost done fully pumping the air rifle when he heard loud, piercing shrieks from a dog, coming from somewhere beyond the staging area of the expedition.

Meriwether liked dogs. He'd always had dogs, who often accompanied him on his expeditions into the wild. He knew that in these frontier towns the men were rough, and often abused animals and women. But he could not resist the appeal of the cry of a dog who sounded little more than a puppy.

Meriwether detached the pump, attached the stock, and ran towards the sound of the cries.

It was worse than he expected. There was a large, shaggy puppy, tied, and a band of young men—boys, really—scruffy and unkempt, setting up to stone him.

Meriwether barely stopped running just short of the dog, who must have cried at being tied, as only one stone had landed nearby and not on the animal.

He brandished the rifle. "Stop!"

A big man came from behind the scruffy boys, "Who are you, sir," he said, "to interrupt our amusement?"

He was a large man, well dressed and wearing a new hat with a rather tall crown. He had a kerchief held up against his right index finger, and there was some red on the fabric.

"Fine entertainment," Meriwether said. He levelled the rifle at the large man, aware but not turning to look at Bratton who had come up behind him. "Why do you abuse this poor animal?"

"That poor animal, sir, is an untrainable beast. A Newfoundland puppy I myself had brought from the east at great expense, who straight out of his crate, made to bite me." He lifted his index finger and pulled away his handkerchief, to reveal a tiny little nip.

"You mean to say that the puppy, confused by travel and strange noises and stranger smells, nipped you when you, doubtless, tried to force him from his crate?" Meriwether asked, irate. One of the things he detested and had always loathed were people who abused animals. Dumb brutes the creatures might be, but they didn't mean to offend. Dogs, in particular, were always eager to please those who treated them with kindness.

Though he brandished the rifle, Meriwether had not indeed had any intention of using it. But then the man said, "Well, I will have no unruly beast under my care. He shall be stoned to death for his impudence, and I shall find another and more obedient dog." He then ordered, "Carry on with stoning, boys!"

Meriwether circled the rifle around and threatened, "The one who throws a stone shall be shot."

"Oh, ignore him and throw the stones already. What can he do when I own the dog?"

That was enough. A demon of rage possessed Meriwether, who—had he not had a rifle to hand—might very well have punched the man. But he had a rifle, and as the man had retreated to a distance, he ventured to aim at the man's hat and shoot it. Not only did he shoot the hat, but he shot it five more times before it fell.

The rapid-fire shots, with no relief, made the boys who'd been poised to throw the rocks stop, hands in the air, as though they'd become frozen statues. As for the well-dressed gentleman, he gaped at Meriwether for a solid count of ten, until Meriwether took it upon himself to shoot balls at the dirt at his feet.

The impacts and fountaining dirt made the man jump backwards, and finally run.

As a cheer went up, Meriwether realized the men from the expedition had gathered around and seen his exhibition.

"Is it not a marvelous rifle?" Bratton said. "It fires so many times without reloading and has no smoke or sound. I'm quite convinced the natives will think it magical."

"Quite likely," Meriwether said, but as the puppy was crying most piteously, he handed the gun over to Bratton and stooped to cut the ties cruelly binding the poor animal so he could not even stand. He cut carefully, as he'd not have been surprised if the animal had nipped at him. Not because he was an ungovernable beast, but because he was scared and had been hurt.

But as soon as he unbound the creature enough—and though a puppy, he was the size of a normal adult dog, being of a very large breed—the puppy leapt into his arms, licking his face.

Meriwether laughed and called to one of the men nearby to bring water for the beast, then noted a tag on the creature's collar, identifying him as Seaman. He smiled. "An odd name, my friend, since I'll take you with me into the wilderness, but maybe you'll justify your name by helping us reach the Pacific."

Which is how Captain Clark came to find Meriwether Lewis, when he arrived a scant half hour later. Meriwether was squatting near Seaman and petting the strong head of the sturdy puppy.

"I thought I'd find you so," the redheaded captain said, smiling, as Meriwether stood to shake his hand. "Petting some stray dog as usual, Lewis?"

"I am so glad you've arrived, my friend," Meriwether said. "There is no one else I'd trust to lead this expedition!"

"Lead? But I thought you'd lead it?"

"Well, you were my captain in the war, sir, and I was at your command. I thought I'd turn over the ledgers and command to you, and you'd make all the hard decisions from here on."

"Not I! It wasn't I that Ben Franklin trusted with his precious expedition. It was your idea to send for me, but he wanted you to organize and lead this expedition."

Meriwether hesitated. On the one hand he had assumed that Clark would be in command, simply because Clark had always been in command when they'd done anything. On the other hand, he had to confess he felt odd relinquishing control over this group of men he'd watched assemble, and over these supplies he'd gathered so carefully. And Franklin had told him he should lead the expedition. "Well," he said. "What say you, then, to our being co-captains, equal in command?"

"That pleases me very well," Captain Clark said, offering him his hand. "And if we should find we do not agree we'll ask your little beasty to decide." He gestured towards Seaman. "From the size of those paws, he'll soon outweigh us both and likely become the real captain of this expedition."

They were both laughing when Pierre Cruzatte approached, "Captain, there are two men here I've known a long time who I think can be useful to your expedition."

As two swarthy men wearing buckskins approached, smiling, Cruzatte introduced them as Francois LaBiche and Jean Baptiste LePage. "They are hunters and fur traders," Cruzatte said, "and have much knowledge of the tribes we'll encounter, and their languages."

They were also, as Meriwether apprised at a glance, of the same undefinable mixture of Indian and French as Cruzatte himself. But that was of little consideration. They would need people to bridge the gap between themselves and the peoples they might meet.

Meriwether was about to give consent, when he realized he'd just given half of his command to Clark. Looking over at his co-captain he said, "Well?"

"I like the idea very well indeed," Clark said, his gaze consulting his friend, who smiled.

"It seems we are in perfect accord," Meriwether said. "Cruzatte, see that they gather all they need before we set off, and to send the reckoning to me."

"I've also brought York," Captain Clark said, gesturing to his freedman, who had accompanied him in the war. "He said he'd never forgive me if I left him behind on such an expedition and I refuse to anger someone who knows where I sleep."

Meriwether always felt awkward around York. He'd grown up around freed slaves, and of course there were plenty of them at Monticello. But York was more like a brother to Captain Clark, the two of them having been raised together. So he was neither just a freedman nor a comrade, and Meriwether didn't know how to treat him. He smiled tentatively at York, who gave him as refined and elegant a bow as if they were I some salon back east, before turning around to see to the stowing of Clark's baggage.

"I believe," Captain Clark said, "That we are about to embark on the adventure of the century, my friend."

Into the Wild

*The beat of wrongness in the land felt like the cawing of Raven...
if Raven had gone mad. It was like the taste of bad meat in the
mouth. Something was wrong and getting worse.*

*I told Toussaint Charbonneau, the man who had claimed me
as wife after winning me in a poker game, that things were getting
worse, that we were in a realm of wrong magic. Charbonneau told
me to keep my mouth shut.*

*We pushed deeper into the wrongness. I didn't want my child
to be born in the realm of bad magic. The feel of the land beneath
my feet thrummed like the beating of a war drum. And I did not
like the dance.*

> —Sacagawea's dictated diaries, Archive of the University
> of Virginia, Department of Arcane Studies

BENEATH THE CANOPY OF TREES AND THE FLIMSY CANVAS OF
his tent, Meriwether Lewis twitched, muttered in half-protest
without wakening.

Seaman barked and whimpered, pawing at Meriwether, but he
failed to wake the captain. As he slept in the wilderness, Meriwether was in a dream where he traveled a land he'd never seen.
It was quite different from the rugged wilds of Virginia or even
the lands of the frontier's edge he had traversed for eleven days
now since the departure of the expedition. Instead, his dream
landscape was wild in its own way, an expanse of low green hills
and modest homes. He recalled the wizard Franklin's words, the

idea of terrain where the past was submerged as deep as water, where the land remembered peoples long vanished and ways of life no longer recalled by anyone living.

In his ethereal state, Meriwether traveled the land from above, somehow flying smoothly over it, his nostrils filled with the acrid smoke of burning peat. Yet he felt right and proper, as though he'd done this many times before.

And he had . . . but only in dreams. He felt his arms extended, his wings like giant rugs against the resistance of the wind, the sky beneath him, the ground far below. He twitched his tail—

His tail?

He let out a cry of surprise, but it came out as a roar. He felt the taste and burn of flames in his mouth.

Meriwether heard a laughter larger than any man's laugh, as though the land itself laughed at him, mocked him. As the words formed in his head, he let out a cry in a voice he'd heard once before, *Ah, dragonling!*

"Lewis! Lewis, wake up, man!"

Meriwether sat up, startled and disoriented. He'd been sleeping in his buckskins and shirt, covered with a light army blanket. As he drew his knees up to his chest, Seaman jumped close, licking at his face.

He simultaneously patted the big dog and pushed him away. "No, Seaman. Down!" Having settled the dog with an arm around his furry neck, Meriwether looked to the entrance of the tent, where a worried-looking Clark knelt, looking in.

"Yes, Captain?" Meriwether asked, addressing him out of habit, though he was no longer under William Clark's command.

"You screamed, and the dog barked. The whole camp heard it. I thought perhaps some creature had got in the tent with you."

Some creature? Some creature perhaps, but in my dreams, not in the tent. Something like a cold finger ran up his spine. What was this curse? What was that strange land of dreams, and what sort of creature did he become in those dreams? He knew of mythical beasts created by magic since the Sundering, and of people who could transform into ensorcelled creatures that then lay waste to the countryside. He remembered stories from the old country, long before the magic had returned, stories of beasts like werewolves and weretigers who killed people and livestock.

Stories to scare children. Had to be.

Meriwether forced a laugh that sounded unconvincing, even to his own ears. "It was but a nightmare. I'm prone to them, just as I'm prone to my melancholies. You should know that by now, my friend. Nothing really. I can't even remember it."

Clark gave him a worried look and a smile as brittle and strained as his own. Clark backed out of the tent. "You might wish to rouse yourself, as the men have coffee and some freshly caught fish. Today we will face the Devil's Race Grounds. A fine way to test the mettle of our boats and our men this early on."

Meriwether knew about the dangerous rapids in the river. "Sounds as exciting as a wild hog race." Now he managed to chuckle normally.

After washing himself in the river, drinking a cup of middling Virginian coffee and eating excellent fried cakes with his pan-fried fish, he felt more up to the day. His disturbing dream was no more than that, a thing contrived of the day's exhaustion and the night's fancy. Even though he'd long dreamed of turning into a flying reptile and even though he'd encountered a real dragon, it neither meant that the two were related, nor that the dragon's voice in his mind was real.

Now that the expedition was under way and as more days passed from the attack in St. Louis, he began to think he had dreamed the dragon's voice all along. As he watched the men pick up the campsite and pack things once more in their designated places in the keelboat, Meriwether thought that the attacking dragon had done him a favor. Surely, the beast was the very catalyst for the entire expedition he now led. He was dousing the campfire when Clark clapped him on the back. "Ready to face the river rapids, my friend? The Devil's Race Course is aptly named, or so I hear."

Meriwether responded with a nervous chuckle. "Despite my dog's name, which was his name when I acquired him, *I* am no seaman—nor even a boatman. I shall follow the banks, while you do your charting on the boat."

Clark seemed up to the task. When he'd first joined the party, the captain had a pale complexion from living mostly indoors, but now he had a reddish tan from spending every day outdoors. The tan made the wrinkles of mirth at the corner of his eyes more obvious. "Not much to chart yet. You taking the dog with you?" Was that concern in his eyes and voice? Concern for Meriwether or the dog? Though the dog strayed a little to harass unfamiliar wildlife or to explore the land around them, Seaman always returned to his side.

Was Clark afraid for Meriwether? Or *of* him?

"Yes, indeed," he said. "Seaman shall protect me from any devil in that race."

Dearest Julia,

We have just survived a very bad stretch of river called the Devil's Race, and I don't mind telling you we had a hard time of it.

The current sets against some projecting rocks for a good half mile on the side of the river, and the water was so swift and so strong that it wheeled the boat around and broke the tow rope, nearly oversetting the boat. It took everyone on the upper side getting out and lifting the boat up so the sand washed out from beneath it.

By the third time the boat wheeled around, we managed to get a strong rope tied to her stern and by means of strong swimmers, we towed her ashore, where we then pulled her over the soft sand, by means of pulleys, thereby giving up—quite—on the Devil's Race!

Before you fret, none of us was in any danger, and may this be quite the worst we face from the mighty river, though in my heart I know it won't be. Captain Lewis met us at the shore, alarmed, but he doesn't trust the waters, being a woodsman.

Since I have a few moments' respite to write, I thought you might wish to learn of this little adventure, which will be quite forgot in the course of our further travels. I want you to know how exciting our days were while you sat in your schoolroom, sewing samplers.

Yours, faithfully,
William Clark

—Letter from William Clark to Julia Hancock,
May 24, 1804

The boat was back in the water, and Meriwether made his way through the leafy shrubs along the bank of the river. For a change, Clark walked beside him. As his companion had said before, there wasn't much to chart as of yet, and perhaps the captain had experienced quite as much of water as he could stand for a day.

The two friends walked side by side in silence, with Seaman now and again bounding back to sniff at them, as though to make sure they were still themselves, before crashing through the forest undergrowth again.

Once or twice, Meriwether heard Seaman bark, and then a scurrying, a pattering, sometimes a squeak. He didn't know if the Newfoundland was actually pursuing prey, but he doubted it. The dog had eaten more than his share of breakfast, in addition to begging some of the dried meat the men had eaten after their travails in the water.

They had not traveled far from the civilized areas around St. Louis, so Meriwether doubted they'd encounter any creature exotic enough to be stuffed and mounted for shipment back to the wizard Franklin. He let Seaman run at will with his puppy energy.

Once, Seaman treed some animal and stretched himself with front paws on the tree trunk, barking loudly, until Meriwether and Clark caught up with him. Meriwether snapped his fingers, and Seaman came back, with a longing glance back at the tree, as though asking for help to corral whatever prey he had treed.

"What do you think he has up there?" Clark asked.

"Likely a squirrel," Meriwether said, peering into the welter of leaves and seeing nothing. "He's very fond of treeing them, as I found before we ever left St. Louis."

They walked onward in silent companionship until Clark suddenly put his hand on Meriwether's arm, squeezing hard. With his free hand, he put a finger to his lips, commanding silence.

Meriwether stopped and listened. Slowly, he felt his hair standing on end.

It wasn't so much what he heard as what he didn't hear. The whole forest around them had gone silent, the emptiness punctured only by the muted sound of the river, which itself seemed distant and muffled. They couldn't hear the voices of the men, though they were certainly still nearby. And they heard no other sounds. Birds, squirrels, and insects had all gone eerily silent.

As if a predator were about.

Meriwether glanced at Seaman to find that the big dog had also gone very quiet, looking expectantly at his master.

Clark lowered his finger, and cautiously the two slowly stepped forward. Meriwether had been in tense wilderness situations before. He had walked through portions of dense woods in Virginia, where everything fell still and the very light seemed dimmed and faint, then a hundred paces on, the normal life and sound of the forest resumed. Here, he didn't expect a bear to come careening out of the undergrowth or a cougar to crash down from a thick branch overhead. This was another type of silence, he thought.

Here, the more he and Clark walked forward, the more the light seemed to dim and darken, even though he could see clearly. It was more as though some quality of cheer or joy had been extracted from the surroundings, until the trees and river, the mossy forest floor seemed cheerless, stark, like a painting of something lifeless and inflexible.

The path along the river had always passed a line of cliffs cut by the river itself, which pressed closer to the water, narrowing the viable area for them to walk. Now they felt increasingly hemmed in by river and rocks. The trees had no purchase, and the underbrush became little more than the occasional shrunken shrub.

Meriwether glanced up and saw a glimpse of wing against the clear blue sky, something very like what he'd seen a year before, when Benjamin Franklin had fought the dragon. The sight captivated him.

He heard Clark shout, "Good God, Lewis, where are you going?" Seaman howled, like a dog lamenting the loss of a friend.

And he suddenly realized he was climbing the bluff, as if in a daze. He caught himself, shouted back something that likely made no sense—but how could it make sense? He was pursuing a giant winged creature, a dragon that seemed to be taunting him and had been doing so ever since the fiery encounter in St. Louis.

He kept climbing up the rough sandstone bluff face, grabbing treacherous handholds that crumbled in his grip. Pine needles, moss, and dried leaves added extra hazards, and his boot slipped from a foothold. Occasionally, he even needed to jab and brace himself with his knife.

He passed a shallow cave alcove and recalled the report of a local fur trapper about a place called Tavern Cave, a deep overhang in a prominent bluff called Tavern Rock, which had served as a resting place for weary travelers, even for storing provisions.

Above, he kept catching glimpses of the angular wings in the sky. That drove Meriwether to greater exertion, but as he climbed higher, the sound of beating wings became elusive, the sight itself nothing more than a blur in the sky. He blinked his burning eyes and was sure he heard the beating-rug sound again, clearly saw an extended hooked claw and a scaled, fang-filled muzzle. All of which seemed mingled with a sound, or a feeling, of laughter in his mind.

The rush of beating wings sounded like a disturbed flock of sparrows or ducks.

Out of the sky rushed a black cloud of birds, a murder of crows that swooped around Meriwether in multitudinous attack. As he found a stable place in the rocky bluff, clutching for his balance, the black birds flung themselves at him, pecking at his hands, smashing into him, until all he heard was a tumult of cawing, all he felt was bird beaks stabbing at him, drawing blood.

The sandstone and moss against his hands and under the heels of his boots slipped and gave way. He caught a glimpse of the gorge below, the rocky shore, the river current. He scrambled desperately, and finally he stabbed the point of his hunting knife into the soft face of the cliff, digging deep into the leaf mulch and loose sand—but it was more than just finding purchase. He held on with something magical, a force that stabilized him... or maybe with the knife he had broken some kind of spell.

Suddenly the attacking birds were gone—flitting off in a raucous, chittering swarm and dispersing back over the forests. The elusive dragon overhead had slipped away from the sky. Finding himself in a precarious position on the bluff, Meriwether suddenly saw clearly again. Holding on, he drew a deep, shuddering breath and grabbed onto the rock with his other hand, keeping his knife in place.

He'd thought he was dead.

"Lewis!" Clark shouted frantically from far below, and he called back words that he hoped were reassuring. The shallow opening to Tavern Rock Cave was in front of him, and seeking refuge he crawled more than climbed into it. Shaking, he sat on the ledge, aware of the cool, somber shadows around him. But the oppressive silence that had smothered him lifted suddenly, leaving him tired, raw, but alive.

He tried to collect his thoughts. There had been a dragon, that terrible presence hunting him. He was sure of it, even though he had seen only deceptive glimpses, not any clear view of the monster. At the same time, he had felt the evil laughter in his mind, and he was doubly sure the dragon had indeed been there.

Which brought him to the ravens attacking in great numbers. Had they even been real? After leaving Virginia, Meriwether had noticed more and more ravens as he moved west, great black flocks as ubiquitous as the doves that supposedly crowded plazas in old Europe, according to the histories (or legends) he had read. But this was different. He looked at his hands and found myriad little wounds, spots of blood from sharp puncturing beaks, as though he'd been poked repeatedly with nails. He found claw scratches, too, as if he'd plunged his hands repeatedly into a spinney.

So the birds had been real after all.

He took another deep breath to calm himself, and heard a succession of scuffling sounds, heavy breathing. Fearing some other monster, he leaned over the lip of the cave overhang to see Captain Clark scrambling up the bluff the same way Meriwether had come. "What's gotten into you, man? Are you all right?" he asked when he pulled himself up to sit on the ledge beside Meriwether.

"Yes, I do believe I am," Meriwether said. "I'm not sure I trust my own senses. When I began to climb, what did you see?"

"A devil of a thing." Clark put his fingers to the ridges above his eyes, to emphasize his recollection. "I swear I saw something flying high above this rock, though it was never clear—a very large, bright bird? And then suddenly there were ravens, a great many ravens covering you."

"Yes," Meriwether said, "attacking me." He extended his hand to show Clark the numerous small but bleeding wounds. "They tried to make me fall."

"How did you get rid of them?"

"I don't know. I struck the rock with my knife and it... somehow it broke the spell. They all flew away."

Clark remained quiet for a long moment. "Walking along the river, as we approached this cliff, it seemed to me that we were entering some strange place. The sunlight dimmed, not darkening like night, but a place where light was... filtered. Like walking into a sack, with the light and sound receding and becoming fainter."

"Yes," Meriwether said, reassured. "Exactly as I felt." So many times in his life, in struggling with his great melancholic fits, he had found that he often perceived the world differently from others. At least he and Clark had seen the same thing along the mysterious river.

Clark scraped his hand down the stubble on his face. Though

they were both military men, since this was a privately funded voyage of exploration, without military discipline, they had decided to forego the effort of shaving every single morning. "The first night when we stopped in Saint Charles, I heard that this cave here was something more than just a sheltered place for travelers. The local natives considered it a magical place. Apparently, if you look on the walls inside, there are some very fine drawings within, from time before anyone can remember. Drawings of magic. And now, after the Sundering, maybe that magic really does hold."

"You suggest that I did indeed encounter a spell?" Meriwether said. "And that my knife dispelled it. The iron in the blade?"

Clark made a face. "I hate to speak of things I don't know, and I know very little about magic, my friend, but I understand some of the native magics are not capable of withstanding the touch of metal. Metal is foreign to them, never smelted or worked by the tribes of this region, which makes it powerful against anything based on this uncharted land. That is why we find such a trade in our knives and guns, for they carry the ability to fight magic."

Meriwether didn't know what to believe. In the Virginia of his upbringing, magic, like science, was a force known to few, controlled by few, established within boundaries. The magics of the eastern native tribes were no great threat to the colonizers, and he knew that the people had little to fear from their rituals and shamanistic fits.

But this was the unexplored west, untamed, and the magical occurrences out here might well be more powerful in unimaginable ways.

And that is why the wizard Franklin found it so important to send us out here.

He and Clark turned to the inspect the interior of the cave. It was a shallow alcove hollowed out of the bluff, showing signs of human occupation, from a pile of ashes and half-burnt branches on the floor near the front and soot smears on the wall and ground. Tiny colorful beads were scattered in the scuffed debris, as well as a thin leather thong, snapped in half, possibly a moccasin tie, cast into a corner.

As their eyes grew accustomed to the gloom, the walls came alive with drawings and symbols. The figures were simple, if colorful, shining with ochre and other pigments. Here and there, the sandstone had been incised and the pigments bit deep, seeming to glow from the rock.

The first scenes depicted hunts: human figures hunted large animals, the likes of which Meriwether had never seen anywhere in the Americas. He remembered an old book of his father's, left to his mother after the man's death, and oft perused by the young Meriwether. He would dream of the world lost to them after the Sundering, places that had disappeared beyond a magical barrier, including the continent of Africa. In that book, he had seen a large creature with a stocky body and a pendulous nose, called an elephant. The creature drawn on the cave wall looked similar, but much hairier, and it dwarfed the natives hunting it, apparently the size of a covered wagon. Another drawing showed an ungainly, long-legged creature with humps.

The hunting scenes extended from the ceiling of the cavern to the floor, but other depictions showed various rituals, one of which made him gasp. It showed a human figure swamped by ravens. Clark called his attention to other creatures: doglike animals that walked on two legs, and an ominous-looking man with antlers on his head.

As the complex mural continued, they saw the appearance of white men, as distinguished by tall hats, as well as horses. Pictures showed battles between the natives and white men. Guns, the flare of fire. And then...

And then on the far right of the cavern, a single figure had been sketched life size, its head lost near the cavern ceiling, its feet on the floor. It was a man, but not quite human. Broad-shouldered and sturdy, with muscular arms, strong legs. From the sketch he could not tell whether its breeches and tunic were of European or native manufacture. The features were hidden behind magic enigmatic symbols, curlicues and wedges. Meriwether could not interpret them.

The extended right hand of the figure unleashed a flock of ravens. His left hand, partly closed, held a tribe of natives. Creatures frolicked at his feet. But seizing Meriwether's attention were the angular wings that sprouted from his shoulders.

"What an odd creature," Clark mused. "Some sort of demon?"

"I think those are dragon wings," Meriwether said, despising himself as his voice cracked. He disguised it by clearing his throat. "Like the dragon that Franklin fought in St. Louis."

Clark bent down to look at the animals massed around the figure's feet "What are these?"

Meriwether bent to study the elephant creatures, camels, buffalo, and...and words failed him. Taller than even the hairy elephant, he saw creatures of fang and claw, one standing on its back legs.

Clark's voice grew quiet. "I certainly hope, my dear friend, that the creatures represented here are but a fanciful outgrowth of some savage's imagination."

Meriwether had a sudden cold feeling in the pit of his stomach. He'd met the ravens, and he'd met the dragon, and he did not doubt that he'd meet the other horrors this demonic winged figure could summon. The mural on the wall felt like a threat rather than a story.

From the foot of the cliff, Seaman was barking, and Meriwether clambered down to calm the dog. But there was a cold presentiment in his soul.

Very Bad Things

"THEY SAY THEY ARE KICKAPOO," SAID NATHANIEL PRYOR, A hardy frontier boy in his early twenties wearing a beaver hat with the tail hanging behind his head. He bent over so that Meriwether and Clark, who were sitting on the ground side by side, could hear him.

Four figures had appeared in the darkness, looming just outside the fire circle. Meriwether thought the strangers looked monstrous, hunched and with horns, like the drawings in the cavern.

"They each bring a deer," Nathaniel continued to explain, "as a peace offering." He seemed more troubled than his words warranted.

"That is normal enough, is it not?" Meriwether asked. "While preparing for the expedition in St. Louis, I witnessed all sorts of trades between fur trappers and natives. Friendship and business flowed back and forth, as one would expect of human beings in a hostile and isolated territory."

"Normal enough," Nathaniel said, still sounding doubtful. "But—but they wish to speak with our chiefs, they said." He shrugged. "They say they bear warnings and information you'll wish to hear. Should we just give them something in trade and run them off, so as to cause no trouble?"

Clark seemed about to agree, but Meriwether broke in, "No, don't do that. What if they do bear vital information, and genuine warnings? Who would venture into the unknown without some intimation of the dangers that lie ahead?" After the narrow escape

47

that afternoon, he needed to pay attention to the dangers in the uncharted lands. As Benjamin Franklin suspected, some great magical work was happening beyond the known territories. "Have them come and speak to us. Let us hear what they have to say."

The four Kickapoo strangers approached the fire and dropped the deer they'd carried across their shoulders. Men from the expedition hastened to the carcasses, ready to clean and dress them. They had been so busy negotiating the river and the rapids, and exploring the shore, that they had settled for dried meat as their dinner, but fresh venison was far preferable.

Leaving the offerings, the Kickapoo walked around the fire, carrying themselves with immense dignity, their bronze faces set in impenetrable calm. The front man wore a cloak with as much style as any European ruler would have worn it. His hair was long, smooth and black, hanging all the way down his back; from the front he wore a sort of feather bonnet. Not in regular arrangement, like what Meriwether had seen the Cherokees wear. This headdress was a riotous affair, as if someone had put feathers willy-nilly, like flowers stuffed at random into a too small vase. The feathers ranged from black to bright red, and were of varying lengths, giving the effect of having grown in a tumult from the man's head.

Meriwether had seen more bizarre fashions worn by women in Richmond; this was an odd and elaborate look, which suggested the man must be a person of some importance. As though to emphasize this, his three companions flanked him, one on either side, and one at the back. The two to the sides also wore deerskin cloaks, but they were shorter and didn't convey the same momentous dignity as their leader's. Their bonnets had fewer feathers, though the man on the right compensated with some sort of projections of embroidered fabric. The man at the rear wore a hat of brightly dyed fur, topped by an enormous feather.

Treating them with respect, Meriwether rose to greet them, pleased to see that Clark joined him. When the visitors spoke, he realized they would not speak English or even the French, which Meriwether only marginally understood. Their words had only faint echoes of the languages he'd learned from the common tribes in the east.

"Flynn!" He called to another young man, Pryor's cousin, whom he judged to be most reliable among the various hirelings.

Flynn had been keeping track of the translators or fur trappers who had joined the expedition. "We need someone to translate."

Soon, a man of mixed race rushed forward to the campfire. Jean Baptiste LePage wore a hunting outfit similar to that worn by many men in the expedition, but he looked flustered, as though not sure of his place in the force. He bowed to Meriwether and Clark, then turned to the four Kickapoo. Meriwether saw his eyes widen, and he bowed hastily. He spoke to the visitors, introduced himself and the expedition leaders. The leader of the natives spoke in measured words, and LePage translated the introductions in turn. "These are Wagohaw, Plecheah, Kechemaqua, and Katewah, chiefs of the vermillion band of the Kickapoo. They bring you greetings, and an offering of meat to demonstrate their peaceful intentions."

Clark formally introduced himself and Meriwether, thanking the visitors for the deer, finishing the pleasantries. The leader of the Kickapoo, Kechemaqua, spoke at some length with gestures.

Every time LePage seemed about to translate, the stranger would continue. Meriwether hoped the translator could hold in his mind everything that the visiting chief had said.

At length the speaker fell silent and looked intently at Meriwether. LePage closed his eyes like a child in Sunday school preparing to recite his lessons. "This is what Kechemaqua says. Listen as if Wisaca himself were speaking, and as though I had ridden the vulture above the sky, to see from there.

"Since the time of my father, we have seen the legends come to life, the stories our ancestors told, about Nenemehkia who lives in the sky and creates thunder and lightning. We always thought these were stories told to children, or stories of things that only shamans could see, but they have come true before our eyes. I, myself, Kechemaqua of the Kickapoo, have seen them. I have sat with such legends around the fire, in their human form, as I sit with you.

"But now there is something new in this land, something that the Kickapoos do not know. Some say the spirit of the land is outraged at the invasion of white men, and it is wounded by the intrusion of white magic. The spirits of our land are wakening and do damage or good according to their nature. The Manetoa, the great serpents of seas and rivers, have drowned many children lately." LePage nodded gravely as he recited what he had heard.

"Worse, some tribes are taken, to serve…someone. We don't know whom, but we know that his reach increases day by day and moment by moment until he reaches the very edge of white settlements. Those of us who do not wish to be ruled by him are fugitives, like rabbits running before the wolf."

LePage squeezed his eyes tightly shut, as if by an effort he could see the words, internally. "But he carries a wrongness inside, a quality that is not in the mind of Kechi Manito. The Great Spirit would not approve of taking the minds of warriors, or the sanity of women. It would not approve of destroying children from within so they are nothing but willing puppets to this creature who grows in evil power. The Great Spirit would not approve of making the dead walk again so they can serve as slaves. And Kechi Manito doesn't want the deer and the birds placed under deadly spells.

"Those of us who wish to stop this force from taking over and enslaving our land have been attacked by all manner of creatures, even squirrels and—" LePage paused, and said, "I have no words, Captain—some creatures that live in burrows in the ground and look like little dogs? He says: And this great evil one has a form that is like the Manetoa, but has wings, a monster that swoops in to burn the encampments of those who won't obey him.

"We've been attacked by all of these, and also by our own dead who have fallen in battle against him. He is making the lands of Kechi Manito a mockery and a reproach.

"And so we ask you, who have the magic of firearms and the knowledge of a magic different from ours—strike at his heart! You must stop the evil one! My band and I, we will pass out of this land and go live among the white men, where we hope we cannot be reached. When we heard you were coming, though, our shaman says one of you is capable of challenging him. And so we beg of you, destroy the evil one so we can return to our hunting grounds."

For a moment, Meriwether absorbed the horrifying story. When he had spoken to other natives back in Virginia, their words had often struck him as more allegorical than real. But what this chief related made his blood run cold. Resurrected "dead servants" and their own dead turning against them? It sounded too fantastic to believe…but Meriwether already knew that other parts of what Kechemaqua said were true. He'd almost lost his life to an attack of ravens.

He bowed to the Kickapoo chief and thanked him for his information, then he spoke with heartfelt fervor. "I will do what I can to remove this blight from the land, this danger from the native tribes."

He offered the four visitors a place to sleep in their camp, but the men said they must go back to protect their women and children. When they left, Meriwether and Clark ate a fine meal of the freshly roasted deer meat. Strangely, the men of the expedition did not ask for an explanation of the native visitors or what they had said, though he supposed there must be great speculation and discussion where Meriwether could not hear it. He and Clark kept their own thoughts to themselves, waiting for a more private conversation. Even the translator LePage didn't ask them anything, but shortly after the Kickapoos left, LePage also vanished from camp, and the expedition never saw him again.

There were squabbles among the men afterwards. The lack of military discipline took its toll, and the men were obviously nervous about something.

But between himself and Clark, Meriwether managed to keep an uneasy peace.

Later, Meriwether went to sleep, wrestling with thoughts in his mind. Was he truly the one destined to defend the unexplored wilderness from this menace? He'd already had two encounters with the dragon thing, and each time the dark creature had touched his mind and mocked him. Surely, it was issuing a challenge—to him. And surely Meriwether had to respond with all the courage at his command.

He feared the dangers he might face, but he was more concerned that he might not prove equal to the challenge. In the dark of night far beyond civilization, it seemed to him that the land at risk was very large, and the forces arrayed against it were great. And he himself was very small indeed.

My Dearest Julia,

This land we traverse is beautiful and untouched. Paradise must have been like this before Adam and Eve ever tasted of the apple. Animals are plentiful, and the soil fertile. If we are being eaten alive by mosquitoes and gnats, it is only a proof of how all creatures thrive upon this wilderness!

Captain Lewis is growing worried that we've found no Natives since our encounter with four Kickapoos shortly after the onset of our journey.

I hesitate to tell this, for fear you might worry, yet I did promise you a faithful account of all that happened to me, and it is not fair to keep you in ignorance of something so significant.

Our Kickapoo visitors said there was some great magical force alive in the land, and it was gathering strength in an attempt to expel white colonists from this continent, although after the Sundering, where would we go? It seems this force, which thrives on the new magic present in America, must mean to kill us all. The native chief also told of tribes enslaved and even of the dead resurrected as servants to this dread power.

Neither Captain Lewis nor I are men to engage in magic, but we cannot turn our backs when such dire misdeeds are being committed. Even if we can't combat this terrible force, we mean to investigate it, which is the charge of our expedition in the name of the wizard Franklin. What this means for our survival, I cannot say, but you know I will exert every endeavor to return to you alive and hale.

Yours faithfully,
William Clark

—Letter from William Clark to Julia Hancock,
June 28, 1804

Wild Spirits

There was a sickness abroad in the land, and the dead would not remain dead. Rather, they were turned into revenants who then attacked and ravaged by the command of the evil creature that had arisen in the world.

—Sacagawea's dictated diaries, Archive of the University
of Virginia, Department of Arcane Studies

MERIWETHER WOKE UP WITH SEAMAN BARKING. IN THE MILD weather they'd bedded down without bothering to erect tents, but rather lay on blankets on the ground. Before he came fully awake, he grumbled at the dog to stop barking, but then a human noise joined the wild yelps, a disjointed screaming.

Clutching his blanket and leaping to his feet, Meriwether faced someone running into camp. The man was disheveled and howling in pain or terror. Men swiftly surrounded him, and Meriwether recognized the tall, lanky form of Floyd, one of the members of the expedition. He lurched forward. "Floyd, for the love of heaven, what's wrong?" He had obviously suffered a great shock.

As Meriwether approached, someone had managed to press a flask to Floyd's lips, but the terrified man pushed the flask away, seeing him. "Sir! Captain Lewis!"

"I am here. Tell me what happened."

"Sir—Hugh Hall, John Collins, and Alexander Willard. They're dead!"

"What happened? Tell me your story, man!"

Floyd took a deep shuddering breath, eyes fixed on Meriwether but seemingly seeing a panorama of horror. "I heard noises in the night. Hugh was supposed to be guarding the provisions, as you know, and—" He shook his head. "I got up stealthily and found Collins and Willard working with Hall. Together they were taking one of the whiskey barrels away from the rest of us." Floyd pointed. "They were dragging it over there, far from camp." They had camped in a rocky promontory, which overlooked the surrounding region and the river. The outcrop and a growth of sparse trees would have hidden them from the main campsite.

Clark strode up, drawn by the commotion. By now only a few faint red lines streaked the eastern sky, the barest hint of dawn. He scowled. "So you followed them?"

"Very carefully." Floyd was trembling. "I thought if I'd challenged them right then, they would turn on me." He made a face. "I didn't want to rouse the whole camp, for I...well, they are still my mates, sir. I thought they'd have an excuse, some story, and eventually they'd find an reason to do me a mischief."

Meriwether contained his anger. Faced with hazards and strangeness, and without the strict discipline of a military force, the expedition had experienced squabbles, and resentments would be held forever. Most of these men were woodsmen, used to silence and their own company, exploring the wilderness according to their own whims. Keeping forty of them assembled with the same goal required all the diplomatic abilities that he and Clark possessed.

"Once I was sure they really meant to steal the whiskey, I couldn't simply confront them. They were three men against me, and they'd have killed me! Instead, I left them to their stolen drink and meant to come back and rouse you, sirs." He still looked utterly terrified.

"But you said they're dead," Meriwether said.

The young man nodded, and tears sprang to his eyes. "Just as I turned away, a group of native warriors rushed out of hiding, savages! Many of them—"

"What tribe?" Clark asked. They had seen no natives since the four Kickapoo who had visited the camp a month ago at the outset of the expedition.

"I don't know. Sir...Captain..." His frantic eyes looked from Meriwether to Clark. "The warriors were *dead*."

"But you said they killed—"

"Sir, they were dead as they emerged from their hiding place. They smelled foul, like a corpse that has bloated in the heat for days. One of them had a big hole in his chest, as though he'd been burned clean through, while another's head lolled on his shoulders, his eyes blank—"

"Are you sure you didn't have any of that whiskey yourself, Floyd?"

"I know what I saw! These dead bodies were animated, walking around...attacking. They carried stone axes and spears, and they fell upon Hall, Willard, and Collins. Those men had moved the whiskey barrel to their hiding place, but they didn't think about arming themselves. They brought no rifles. They tried to defend themselves against the dead warriors. Hall did pick up a log and try to keep the things at bay."

"And did you try to save them, Floyd?" Clark asked. "Why didn't you yell for help?"

"I wasn't close enough, sir! When I smelled that gagging stench, I backed off—and that was just my good fortune the creatures didn't see me or hear me as I crawled away. And when I got to the top of that outcrop—" He pointed again toward the dark silhouette in the increasing dawn light. "I stopped and looked back. Those savage revenants had killed all three of the men, but they hadn't touched the whiskey barrel. Didn't care about it, I don't suppose. Worse, I also saw other native revenants all around. And they're headed this way! That's when I ran, but before I got very far, I felt the blast...nearly knocked me down! Like when a charge of explosives is set off and the warm air and sound carry before it, and when it hit me, it felt like something within me was twisted. But I picked myself up and ran here, yelling. I'm sure those dead things are coming to attack us."

Another man on the perimeter of the camp let out a loud yell. "We're under attack! Indians!"

The men from camp grabbed their weapons and raced to defend themselves. Meriwether saw that there were indeed frightening-looking natives running toward them, but with an odd, jerky gait. At first, he thought the attackers numbered only a dozen or so, but more and more emerged from the shadowy trees...at least fifty or more. If Floyd had not alerted them, the silent, undead attackers would have swarmed in upon them, catching them unawares.

If these had been normal natives, Meriwether would have tried to talk to them, to negotiate a peaceful encounter, offer them some kind of gift to make peace. But they had already killed three of his men, even if they were thieves. This would be no peaceful encounter.

The ominously silent attackers stumbled and lurched toward camp. They did not move like living men, but like people in delirium, or even sleepwalkers. In a flash, he spotted something else. The other natives he had seen, both here in the west as well as those back in Virginia and the other colonies, had a similar type of clothes and ornaments to show the tribe they represented, showing they were a cohesive band. But these were men of all sorts, their clothing so varied as to be a hodgepodge. Some of them were naked, some wore loincloths, some wore skin capes or feather-studded cloaks all dirty and tattered.

And then the smell hit Meriwether: the rank, rotting smell of a corpse had been unburied a good while. It caught in his throat and gagged him. "To arms!" he called. "Man your stations. Get your weapons. Defend the camp."

From the rocky rise where Floyd had led them, Meriwether could see the revenants before they could attack, some even before they came within range of the expedition's rifles. As the first revenant approached, Bill Bratton let loose a shot, which struck the creature in the shoulder, but the native kept advancing, impervious to pain.

Floyd had got hold of a rifle and started shooting as the revenants approached, though like the others his bullets had no noticeable effect. Meriwether remembered the man had said one of the undead had a hole in the center of its chest. Therefore, even shooting them through the heart would only waste ammunition. Taking his own rifle, Meriwether aimed for the head.

His shot was true, and the revenant's head exploded in a shower of gore. The lurching body fell. He immediately yelled to the rest of the men, "Shoot at the head! It's the only way to put them down."

As the men aimed at the heads of revenants who came within range and Clark shouted further encouragement, Meriwether climbed higher up the rock, where he could see the entire undead army. They came out from behind trees and around the rocks, with the front group acting as scouts. As those came under fire and dropped, the latter ranks hesitated and clustered just outside the range of the rifles.

Meriwether realized, though, that if they got closer and rushed the camp, even the guns of the expedition would not be able to put them all down. Just as he thought that, the assembled revenants did precisely that, gathered in a group that suddenly charged toward the defenders in a single mass, their smell and their wordless cry preceding them.

Meriwether's men, to their great credit, stood their ground, shooting and swiftly felling a great many of the undead attackers, but from his clear vantage, he could see that it would not be enough. "Fall back! Captain Clark, get them to higher ground!"

The terrified men obeyed, scrambling up among the rocks and setting shooting stations in the higher promontory near Meriwether, while Clark brought up the rear. The relentless revenants were so close that their miasma was like a physical force, an insult in the mouth.

As Meriwether scrambled up the rock, a hand grabbed his leg—a skeletal hand. His rifle was loaded and slung over his arm but he had no way to take aim. He needed both hands to climb.

A rotting head with bits of skin and hair clinging in irregular patches to the skull grinned up at him, while milky-white, unseeing eyes fixed on him. He let go of the rock with his right hand and reached for his belt knife, remembering the salutary effect it had had back in Tavern Rock.

Before he could yank the knife free, the deathly hand pulled harder, and he had to scrabble for hold with his right hand again. The revenant's teeth clacked together, ready perhaps to rip his flesh off his bones.

A shot echoed close by, and a bullet whistled past him. The revenant's head exploded, splattering brown blood and ooze all over Meriwether's legs. The smell was so overpowering he choked. The revenant tumbled away. Floyd and Clark reached down to grasp him, pulling him to safety.

He had no time to take a deep breath, even with the stench in the air, before he had to turn and take position and start shooting back.

The revenants were hampered by the cliff face, not nimble enough to climb it properly. Many of the undead creatures simply hurled themselves at the base of the rock, as if it would give way to a concerted onslaught. From above, the expedition men picked off many of them, but a few of the revenants—by accident, rather than through cleverness—stumbled upon the less sheer part of the cliff, and they began to scramble up.

Meriwether moved to concentrate on shooting those, as did his companion. He was glad to see that Captain Clark had not lost his marksmanship any more than Meriwether had. Each shot brought down a revenant, and more men joined in to maintain the barrage of fire.

The last undead creature managed to climb high enough to reach for Floyd as he reloaded his rifle, but he reacted immediately, like a man seeing a poisonous snake. With a great cry, he swung the rifle around and smashed the revenant's skull with the stock, using all his might, until its head was battered in. The thing stopped moving, and slid down the rocks. And that was the last of them.

In the camp, strewn with the wreckage of half-rotted corpses, Meriwether surveyed the aftermath. He took a deep breath of the tainted air. "This is—I can't believe what...what obscene magic would kill and then use the corpses in such an awful way."

"One good thing," Floyd said. "None of those revenants wore the clothing that Collins, Hall, and Willard wore. They must have stayed dead."

"That is intriguing," Clark said, coming up behind Meriwether. "And disquieting."

Outside the camp, the men set about digging a mass grave to bury the rotting body parts. Meriwether and Clark helped with the initial digging and collecting of revenant parts, but while the other men finished the unsavory job, the two captains washed in the river to avoid being tracked by their smell, then they hurried in the increasing dawn light along to where Floyd had said the whiskey thieves were attacked. Meriwether felt sick. The three men would have been punished for their crime, but nothing so horrible as being torn apart by undead warriors. He still felt the grasping claws of the bony hand of the undead around his ankle, and he shuddered to think of what would have happened to him if he had slipped...

He and Clark did indeed find a whiskey barrel, which had been tapped. Two tin cups lay strewn on the ground, and they still smelled of whiskey. The ground was trampled and bloodied. "They were killed, that's for sure," Clark said.

But they found no trace of the three whiskey thieves, or their animated bodies. They explored, widening their search, but they found neither their own men nor any more undead warriors.

"Someone sent them against us," Meriwether said, feeling the chill in his veins. "Maybe the same person or force that first sent the ravens to attack me." He could not shake the feeling that like a marksman aiming shots to get the range, the evil force was perfecting a way to attack the expedition. "And I can't help thinking the force wants to harm us because it senses that we have the capacity to destroy it."

Clark gave him a half-surprised look. "I never considered it that way, but I hope you're right—about us having the capacity to destroy it."

They tramped deep into the trees that grew near the river, but they found no sign of the three missing men, nor any more undead natives.

At one point, Meriwether thought he heard someone singing, not distinct words, but an eerie tune. "Clark, do you hear? Is that 'To Anacreon in Heaven'?"

His companion frowned, then answered, "I don't hear anything. Perhaps it's the current against the shore? And what is that song?"

"'Anacreon in Heaven'? It's a tune they used to sing in the tavern near my house when I was growing up," he said, half absently. While it seemed unlikely that the river would echo the melody of an old drinking song, Meriwether had no other explanation.

The two men returned to the camp. Now impressed with the idea that they were under attack by a malevolent force, they knew to set several sentinels, not just around the perimeter, but ranging as far out as possible as they prepared for the day's movement.

The following night in camp, Meriwether had a disturbed dream in which someone sang "To Anacreon in Heaven" with odd lyrics, but he did not understand them.

My Dearest Julia,

Previously, I described the horrific invasion of our camp by a legion of dead-alive natives. Fortunately, in the days since, we have encountered nothing as alarming. Yet this uncharted land remains a cipher, and the mystery builds. We still have not come across more tribes of Indians, although surely the wilderness is not empty. Our expedition has been calm and quiet—too quiet, I fear. Our far-flung sentinels have told us only one odd encounter, that one of them found himself watched, from a safe distance, all night long by a large wolflike creature. The hairy predator neither moved nor took his eyes from our sentinel. It made no threatening approach, but simply stared.

As we proceeded, mile after mile up the Missouri River, we did come across the sites of abandoned villages or towns. We found remnants of old fires, stripped poles from lodges, bits and pieces of equipment, frayed baskets, horse's harnesses, as though the inhabitants had left in a great hurry. Considering the nomadic nature of many of these peoples, however, it's possible they are always in a great hurry. Perhaps there is no menace in what we found.

We expect to run into the Yankton Sioux before long, unless their villages have been abandoned as well.

The only other matter of concern is a report—which many dispute—from two different sentinels claiming they have seen the men we lost at the "Whiskey incident"—Hall, Collins, and Willard. Surely, this is just a matter of overactive imagination and too many chilling stories whispered over the fires in camp, but the men insist they have seen their three former comrades proceeding over valley and dale on a route parallel to ours. Of course, they never come close enough to attack, nor even to be seen clearly.

Normally, I would doubt such tales, but we know there is magic afoot in these arcane territories, and we cannot deny some dark force that seems to have taken an interest in our expedition.

And Captain Lewis insists that he hears eerie snatches of a drinking song, "To Anacreon in Heaven," which I can never distinguish. What could that be about?

If it's true that our reanimated dead are following our route, to what possible purpose? Have they been made to spy on us? If so, for whom?

As a postscript to the Whiskey incident, I regret to report that Charles Floyd has sickened and complains of a bilious malady. Our good Captain Lewis, who is well versed in all medical arts and herbal magic, cannot treat or cure him, even with his strongest tinctures and brews. We are forced to assume the malady is of magical origin, perhaps contracted during his close encounter with the rotting revenants.

I know it is difficult not to worry about me when you hear of such dire doings, but most of our days are quite peaceful, and the untamed scenery adds color to my soul. For instance, in the prairies, we found a small animal that looks like a toy dog, and which lives underground in a network of burrows. We've managed to capture a specimen to be sent back alive to Wizard Franklin for his studies. We have found numerous antelope, and we have dispatched hides and horns for Franklin. The animals also provide very good sustenance for our party.

I will include these letters to you with every set of specimens we dispatch home. Until then, my dear one, I will subscribe myself,

Captain William Clark

—Letter from William Clark to Julia Hancock,
August 15, 1804

Antediluvian

Sgt. Floyd died with a great deal of composure. Before his death, he said to me, "I am going away. I want you to write me a letter." We buried him on the top of the bluff a half mile below a small river to which we gave his name. He was buried with the honors of war, much lamented. A cedar post engraved with "Sgt. C. Floyd died here 20th of August 1804" was fixed at the head of his grave. This man at all times gave us proof of his firmness and determined resolution to do service to his country and to honor himself.

The funeral was conducted by Capt. Lewis. I worry that we could not learn what ailed poor Floyd, nor how to cure it, even with all of Lewis's herbal magic. I fear that our expedition will perish like this from things unknown. I do wish we'd brought with us a competent wizard. It is surely better than a large party of people who know nothing about magic.

—Diary of William Clark, August 20, 1804

THE SIOUX WERE BETTER DRESSED THAN THE KICKAPOOS. THEY wore full coats and pantaloons of buckskin, the whole worked over with quill embroidery. On their heads were cockades made of ranged feathers, all neat and proper.

Now, Meriwether called for Francois LaBiche, the trapper who had joined the group for a time as their boats moved upriver, to act as an interpreter. In appearance, LaBiche was an indecipherable mix of native and white European, and he claimed that this wilderness was his home, much as the woods of Virginia were to Meriwether. While the Sioux waited, LaBiche smiled ingratiatingly both to Meriwether and to the visitors, and plunged into animated discussion with the natives in their language. Captain Clark also came up to listen.

After a while, LaBiche turned back to Meriwether and Clark. "Let me introduce these men." He pointed at one of around thirty years, whose nose made him look like a bird of prey. "This is Chaytan, whose name means *hawk*, Enapay, whose name means *laughs in the face of danger*." The second Sioux was a dour gentleman, whom Meriwether couldn't imagine laughing at all. "And this is Mato, whose name means *fierce bear*." The third native was a scrawny man who looked neither fierce nor bearlike.

The interpreter continued with expansive gestures. "These men heard of our expedition, and they came to see us. Previously, they also witnessed the evil revenants, undead warriors walking through the forests. Although the revenants left their village alone last time, the Sioux warriors have repelled other such attacks, as well as very odd emissaries."

"What sort of emissaries?" Meriwether asked.

LaBiche seemed curious and troubled. "One never knows what to believe, Captain, but with the magic rising... Well, Chaytan and the others say they have driven off talking animals who came to demand that they join with the forces of the land so they can expel the Europeans." He paused while the Sioux continued to speak animatedly, then he continued to translate. "They say they don't trust the magic behind this demand because it is a big and powerful magic, and they are frightened of it. And also because if the force is truly on their side, it would not attack their village or try to intimidate them. Enapay says it reminds him of an enemy tribe trying to compel you to do what it wishes before it will grant you peace.

"And so, the Sioux haven't taken the offer to join the big magic. They remain in their village, though many other settlements are empty. Maybe the people have run away, maybe they were destroyed, maybe they joined the big magic. Now Chaytan and his people may move far away. They say that large beasts roam the land"—the interpreter made a gesture with his hands, to indicate the enormous size of the creatures—"devouring the great herds of buffalo that provide sustenance for the natives. And though the tribes can sometimes scavenge meat and scraps of hides from the torn carcasses after the monsters attack, many young Sioux are also eaten by the big beasts, whose footsteps make the ground shake and the mountains tremble."

Though Meriwether thought this must be an exaggeration, he recalled the illustration of the woolly elephant on the cave wall. Could a creature so large actually roam the arcane territories?

"Why did they come here?" Meriwether asked.

LaBiche listened to the Sioux. "They came to warn us. They say that we will encounter their neighbors in half a day's journey up the river. These people have also been harassed and starved by the Big Magic, but they blame Europeans for wakening that magic, and making their land perilous." He nodded toward the three Sioux warriors. "These men say we should be prepared to defend ourselves against the next tribe."

Clark showed the same concern and curiosity that Meriwether felt. "Thank them for the warning. We will take it under advisement."

"And we want to thank our new friends," Meriwether said. He gestured for one of the men to get the gifts they'd brought along for exactly such situations: medals that Franklin had infused with magic, so that when held in a certain way they displayed a miniature electric storm on their surface. Some other medals had healing properties, curing illnesses and discomforts for those who carried them.

When he and Clark handed the medals to the three Sioux, though, the visitors were clearly not impressed. Enapay spoke in a voice that sounded wrathful, holding his medal as if he were about to fling it in their faces. LaBiche quickly translated. "He says these are no use to them. They need weapons to fight both the Big Magic and the hostile neighbor tribe. He says that you offer them toys to appease children." The trapper looked jittery, uncomfortable.

"These are not toys," Meriwether hastened to explain. "They contain good will, and they have been infused with magic by one of our greatest wizards. The light show is to show their magic. They also possess a healing spell that makes smaller illnesses vanish and minor wounds close." As LaBiche quickly passed along the words, Meriwether continued, "We would give you bigger medicine if we could, but magic is hard to bind, even for a great wizard. His profile is on this medal, and he wants his magic to be useful to you."

The three Sioux listened, then seemed to reconsider the medals. Finally, Enapay slipped his medal in a small buckskin pouch, and the others did the same with obvious reluctance and disappointment. They refused to stay or share a meal with the expedition, which gave Meriwether and Clark the opportunity to discuss plans for defending against the neighboring band of Sioux, the ones hostile to Europeans.

Knowing the location of the hostile village from Chaytan, Enapay, and Mato, the two captains decided to approach along the river rather than sending a party overland. They would keep the keelboat and the majority of their provisions and people on the water, where it should be easier to escape. Captain Clark made sure that the big cannon on the boat was ready to fire and repel any attack.

As the keelboat moved upriver, with lookouts alert, peering intently at the shore, they found the village of hostile Sioux not far from the banks, just as the sun was beginning to set. Meriwether and LaBiche had taken the vanguard along with three other men, moving cautiously along the riverbank after rowing there in a small pirogue, while Clark remained in the main boat, manning the big cannon.

They thought it was important to draw out the hostiles, before they had a chance to set up a proper ambush later on.

A band of young native men, their faces fearsomely painted, emerged from the brush along the shore, glaring at the boat. They held spears in their hands, with rifles slung over their shoulders. They stepped in front of Meriwether, blocking their way. *They must have been following us for some time*, he thought.

One of the painted warriors advanced and barked a series of words at him. LaBiche was at Meriwether's shoulder. "He says he doesn't want you near his village. He says that you and your kind have disturbed the land and caused bad magic. Because of you, monsters are eating all the buffalo, and now his village is starving." The trapper's face twisted as he listened. "He says if you give them your knives and your guns, they'll let you go without harming you."

Meriwether forced himself not to cringe at such a bald and ridiculous demand. He squared his shoulders, looked the Sioux warrior in the eyes. "Tell him no. Tell him there is a big gun in the boat." He pointed at the boat. "And that we will fire upon them if they will not let us pass unharmed."

For a moment nothing happened. The painted warriors held

their position, apparently steeling themselves. Meriwether noted the way they flexed their legs, shifting weight. Now the warriors looked towards the boat, showing telltale fidgets. On the keelboat, Captain Clark stood cheerfully behind the gun. He waved as though greeting a party of friends.

The painted warriors looked at Meriwether again. He understood why they wanted guns and knives, if they were plagued by rotting, murderous revenants as well as other monsters, such as the giant beasts massacring their buffalo herds. These warriors did not appear to be starving, not yet, but it was not yet autumn. And in the native tribes, the warrior men got fed first, because without them, both women and children died.

As the tense face-off continued for several more seconds, the ground suddenly shook. Meriwether thought that his own senses were recoiling, that the uneasy situation made him tremble, but then the riverbank shook again, and he heard a pounding sound.

The painted warriors panicked, crouching to defend themselves. Meriwether prepared to run, perhaps to dive into the river and swim to the keelboat. The trapper interpreter took a step backward, his mouth gaping open.

The largest of the painted warriors seized Meriwether about the chest, pinning his arms at his sides and rendering him incapable of fighting. The Sioux's knife pressed threateningly against his neck, and LaBiche had also been caught and held. But the other three men in the vanguard party darted away, scrambling into the water and aboard the small pirogues they had brought to the bank.

Aboard the big keelboat on the water, Clark looked impotent even behind the large gun. If he fired upon the party of treacherous Sioux, he would also kill the two hostages.

The painted warriors ran toward the river, and Meriwether's big captor dragged him along, not caring if he made him stumble. Meriwether barely managed to keep his feet, then tripped again.

Throughout, the shaking of the ground and the thudding sound grew closer, louder.

Meriwether struggled, helpless, trying to break free. He was completely under the control of the warrior, and alongside him LaBiche squawked and cursed in a mixture of French, English, and Sioux. The terrified trapper translated in a shout, "Captain, he says that if you do not give his men two pirogues, he will cut our throats. And he will! You have to call to Captain Clark, get him to send the little boats!"

Meriwether knew his partner would temporize, seeking a way to send reinforcements. Clark would never call the warriors' bluff, but he also knew that losing the pirogues would fatally cripple the expedition as they would not be able to carry nearly so many men or equipment. Maybe he would trade the small boats for now, then chase the hostile warriors down the river and look for a chance to take the pirogues back.

First though, the shaking of the soil and the thunderous footfalls became deafening.

Once, while hunting in the Virginia woods in winter, he had been jolted about by an earthquake—but he knew this was no earthquake, nor the boom of thunder. It was something else, something that sent his captors into a panic. They would not stand still if Clark wanted to delay hostage negotiations.

The warrior leader screamed at LaBiche, and the translator struggled, unable to do anything. Meriwether's captor held his arms, twisted him around, and he tilted back where he could see the tops of the trees along the river. He was shocked to see the oaks and maples sway, snap, and topple, as though caught in a tornado.

The warriors screamed, LaBiche wailed and prayed in French. Meriwether used the momentary distraction to thrash himself loose, trying to escape. He managed to yank one elbow free, which he brought into his captor's belly with full force.

The Sioux let out a grunt of shock, and the knife against Meriwether's throat slipped aside, enough for him to let himself collapse, dropping to the ground and shifting the balance. Rolling, he slid between the two nearest warriors and dropped down the slope of the bank to the river, where he regained his feet and splashed desperately into the water.

Breathless and scared, afraid of being grabbed again at any minute, he heard the Sioux warriors screaming behind him, and then a great disturbance of some titanic creature barging through the thick trees.

LaBiche had also escaped, as the Sioux had far more immediate concerns than their hostages. He also waded into the water, plunging into the sluggish current with a savage expression on his face. He had a cut on his throat, from which blood oozed.

On the river, the other three men who had rowed off in the pirogues shouted at Meriwether and LaBiche, but they also screamed in terror as they pointed toward the bank. Many other shouts came from the large keelboat. As he and the trapper thrashed and swam with all their might, Clark moved the keelboat closer, and both of them reached the side of their vessel as the pirogues also tied up. A frightened-looking Clark leaned over the side of the big boat, extending his arm to Meriwether. "Thanks be to God!"

After climbing aboard while others helped LaBiche over the side, Meriwether stood on the deck dripping water, gulping for air. The translator was pressing a scrap of cloth to his bleeding neck.

But no one else on board bothered to look at the two rescued men. Rather, they gawked at the shore. They cursed and gasped in a motley of languages. Two Irishmen who still clung to papism even after the Sundering stared as they crossed themselves so vigorously they were like to throw their elbows out of joint.

Meriwether looked at the shore and saw carnage. The painted warriors who had only moments ago held the two men captive were flung about, their bodies smashed as whole trees were uprooted. The soil of the riverbank was a mess of mud and blood, as churned as the site of any great battle.

The monster that dealt such destruction was something Meriwether had never seen before nor even imagined. It seemed even bigger than the woolly elephant pictured in the cave drawings. He imagined this thing might have been able to pick up a giant elephant and snap it in two with a single bite.

The beast's scaly hide was the brown-green of a lizard, and the creature was as tall as the Government House back in St. Louis. Its posture was upright and it stood on a pair of massive legs, balanced on immense clawed feet. Its forearms looked disproportionately small, but as it seized one of the warriors and snapped off his head, the limbs certainly seemed sufficient.

Its head was reptilian, bestial, with a wide-hinged jaw and curved teeth fully the length of Meriwether's arms. On shore, the beast stomped around, devouring the Sioux until only fragments of human bodies remained on the ground.

Then it turned its gaze toward the river and the keelboat.

"Row!" Meriwether shouted. "Row for your lives!"

His words snapped the men out of their trance, and the long

oars went into the water. On shore the reptilian beast let out a bellow louder than thunder. It stomped onto the muddy bank, snorting at the current.

"Row!" Clark added his voice. Before the monster ventured its foot into the murky river, the keelboat was making good speed. The men of the expedition pulled at a frantic clip.

The monster stood on the bank, lifted its bloodstained muzzle, and roared.

"It was a demon from hell!" one of the men wailed.

Clark muttered under his breath. "The Sundering released many forms of magic. And native legends say that giants walked the Earth in ancient days."

Meriwether found words as he continued to stare at the receding thing. "I don't think it is from hell. It is too solid and too real. I think it is an antediluvian beast, a creature that we've never heard of. By rights, it should have been long dead." Then he recalled the rotting revenants that had attacked their camp.

Many things were no longer dead, and no longer legends.

Little People

"I HEARD THEM TALKING, WHILE THEY HELD US," LABICHE SAID. The group of men sat around a fire much farther up the river, as night fell.

Captain Clark had chosen the place to stop after they had gone many miles from the antediluvian monster and the hostile Sioux village. Before bringing others off the keelboat for the night, Meriwether had scouted around the prospective campsite, under the guise of hunting. He'd even shot two antelope, which were now roasting over the fire. He'd seen neither sign of hostile natives, giant reptiles, nor rotting revenants. Even with that reassurance, Meriwether did not allow himself to feel safe.

If that giant beast had decided to track them up the river, bounding along with its immense legs, how long would it take to reach them? It could certainly run faster than the best horse. But they should be able to hear its thundering footfalls announcing its arrival, and so Meriwether listened attentively, ready to decamp and run quickly.

As night gathered around them, the land seemed full of threatening noises.

There could be no defense against a creature that size. It could charge in among them like a full-grown cat into a nest of baby mice. He could only imagine the appetites of such beasts. No wonder the buffalo herds were dying out.

"Those painted warriors wanted us for something," LaBiche said, his voice hoarse.

Clark snorted. "They wanted to trade hostages for pirogues. Now that I've seen that gigantic monster, I don't even hold it against the poor devils. To save our own womenfolk and children, what would we not do?"

"No, that wasn't what they really wanted," LaBiche said, picking something out of his tangled hair as he sniffed the roasting antelope. "That was just a ruse, although they certainly wanted the boats. No, they still intended to abscond with us, so we could be a gift to something they called Canoti, or little people."

"Little people?" Meriwether asked. "And yet the real danger was a giant lizard."

LaBiche sighed. The fat from the roasting meat spat and popped as it dripped onto the coals. "The little people are dangerous in their own way. I've heard of them before. Out here in the arcane territories, a man can't be a trapper for any amount of time without knowing about them. There's a place not far from here, a conical hill that looks shaped by human hands... or unnatural forces. All the tribes hereabouts are terrified of the place. They say the hill is in habited by the Canoti."

"Exactly how little are these little people?" Clark asked. "And why are they dangerous?"

The trapper shrugged. "I've never seen one myself, you understand, but they're said to be about eighteen inches, high, with big heads. Their magic arrows cause sure death if they should strike you, no matter where, even just a scratch. The stories of the Canoti have been around since long before the Sundering, so maybe the magic was here, too." He looked out past the firelight. "The natives say to avoid the surrounding countryside at all costs."

"And did you avoid it?" Meriwether asked. "Or can you lead us there?"

"Lead you?" LaBiche gave a brief, mirthless grin and shrugged. "I never had the opportunity or the interest to go find the little people. I've always felt that staying away from dangerous places is a good way to remain alive."

"Seems like an excellent idea to me," Meriwether said.

The men from the crew working the roast meat used their knives to slice off dripping hunks of the charred antelope, then handed tin plates to Meriwether, Clark, and LaBiche. Meriwether picked at it with his fingers, blowing on the meat to cool it. "But what did these pygmies have to do with us? Why would the Sioux capture us as a gift to the little people?"

"Many tribes blame the Europeans for the comet and the turmoil in the world for the past half century, but that group of natives apparently believed that the Canoti created the present disturbance that is simmering across the whole land. They believe the little people summoned the swell of magic that raised the revenants to walk the land and brought the big lizards that eat the buffalo." LaBiche licked his fingers and held up his tin plate, waving it until one of the men cut him another strip of sizzling meat. "They think the big beasts are also revenants, very long dead. They are raised from bones and dust in the ground and turned into walking menaces that eat the game, which makes the tribes starve."

"From what we saw," Clark said, "the giant beasts are perfectly happy to eat any natives they catch, too."

With a jerky motion, the interpreter quickly crossed himself, revealing his French and Roman Catholic upbringing. "Those warriors meant to kill us, too. Dead is dead." He touched the bandage wrapped around his neck. "What I know is that they believe the little people create and control the dark magic sweeping this land, and that the little people also hate Europeans. It is just a guess, mind, but I expect the warriors meant to kill me and Captain Lewis in front of the Canoti mound, in hopes that the Canoti would forgive the tribes and remove the terrible beasts preying upon the buffalo, and their villages." He scratched his chin, his hand making a grating sound on his half-grown beard. "Not sure as I blame them, to be honest, if they thought it might save their people."

Deep in thought, Meriwether looked across the flickering fire at Clark. "That is exactly the sort of thing the wizard Franklin would insist on knowing. This is our expedition, William. We should find this place of dread ourselves in the morning. Is it far from the river?"

LaBiche cleared his throat. "It is distant. Some hours walking."

"When have we been daunted by walking?" Clark asked with a smile.

The fires blazed bright, and the men ate well with the fresh game. Seaman, the big dog, gobbled whatever scraps they tossed to him. The night closed in, and the expedition huddled together, with sentries posted all around. Meriwether remained on his guard, restless, but he knew he would have a long journey to find the mound of the little people. He stared up at the dark blue sky, against which paler blue clouds were pushed by a wind which also stirred the branches of the trees above and tugged at the flames of the campfire.

Nevertheless, the night was warm enough, and the men had camped without tents, lying on their blankets in the open. The dog lay down next to him, spread out and snoring quietly in his sleep.

Meriwether knew the weather would turn in the coming months. Autumn was setting in, and he already had a feeling that the winter here would be far colder than what he'd experienced back east. He could read that in the way the animals were putting on fur and fat in preparation for the coming snow. He also noted a greater paucity—though unfortunately not a total scarcity—of bugs and vermin, which spoke of a winter cold enough to kill most of them. Eventually, before the autumn grew too late, they would have to build a fort of some sort for shelter during the frozen months.

And was winter the only hardship or danger they had to fear? His sleepless mind was overwhelmed with the thought of what other perils their expedition might yet face. He rolled on his blanket, turning away from the fire. The ground beneath him seemed more rocky and unyielding than ever before, and his mind worried about all the things that he could not change.

He thought of his mother back east, as he often did. Oh, he had a brother and a sister, too, but he did not worry about them. His father had died when Meriwether was too young to know him. His mother, Lucy, had been the only constant in Meriwether's life. She strived valiantly to keep them safe and stable as a family, a daunting task for a frail woman. For a brief time, his stepfather, a man named Marks, had helped, but he'd died as well, leaving Lucy with the burden of three children, no magic of her own, and little source of income.

Young Meriwether managed to administer his father's estate well enough that they would not want for material goods, and when this expedition returned—assuming Franklin held to his promise—the Lewis family would be quite prosperous. Meriwether might even, with perfect propriety and some prospects, seek a wife of his own.

Even if he didn't come back home from this great and terrifying adventure, the great wizard had promised to compensate his family well. But without Meriwether himself there back in Virginia, who would serve as a bulwark for his mother's old age? He wasn't sanguine about John's or Mary's character, in that respect. They were younger than he and were both too set in their own lives and marriages, too impatient and dismissive of their mother's needs. He feared without him, she would have a lonely life indeed....

Morning came too soon, and yet it was a long time coming.

He didn't remember falling asleep, but he woke when Clark touched his shoulder.

The two men did not speak as Meriwether roused himself in the quiet camp, folding his blanket and gathering himself for the day. He'd slept in his clothes, but he knelt at the bank and splashed river water on his face to wake up. While he finished his morning ablutions, Clark went around the camp, waking ten men who would join the expedition to find the little people. As Meriwether returned, refreshed and ready, he received a mug of antelope broth that had been simmering on the fire all night. Then, with far more relish, he drank a mug of the coffee one of the men had prepared over the fire.

Accompanied by the dog, Meriwether, Clark, and a small party took two of the pirogues down the river to a side creek trending inland, where the trapper said they would find the mound. They would still face a long walk overland to reach the mysterious home of the Canoti, but the small boats allowed them to save an hour or two of travel. After they pulled the pirogues out onto the bank and hid them under bushes, the group set off, following the trapper, who himself had only a general idea of where to go, since he had wisely avoided the place previously.

The day grew hot, and the big Newfoundland bounded ahead into the grasses, but soon grew weary, panting, miserable, and overheated. Concerned for his pet, Meriwether left Seaman with John Potts to watch him near a small creek, before the animal collapsed in the heat.

Within another mile, as the terrain flattened and the trees dispersed, leaving a broad prairie that extended before them, they stopped as they got their first glimpse of the mysterious conical mound. The strange hill had squarish sides that looked manmade.

Its shape certainly wasn't due to erosion. Out in the wild emptiness, it reminded Meriwether of pictures he'd seen of an ancient temple, of the kind that had once graced ancient Greece.

The men stared, gathered their courage, and set off again.

With his hunting senses, Meriwether noted as they approached the strange mound that game became scarcer, though the birds more plentiful. They would take wing in great panicked flights as the men pressed forward. Meriwether sensed an uncanny throbbing in the air.

"A simple explanation might not involve magic," Clark suggested, as if trying to calm himself and the others. "Since the mound is the tallest prominence in the vicinity, winds blow all the bugs into it, and therefore they cluster on its sides. Such a feast attracts the birds, which lends the whole place an air of supernatural dread." He looked up as a small flock of red-winged blackbirds flitted up from the brush, flying about in random paths. "That would explain the savages' superstition."

LaBiche gave Captain Clark a sidelong look of impatience. "Maybe." The trapper scratched at his beard, which never seemed to be full grown or fully shaven, but always scraggly. "Or maybe we should accept there's something truly uncanny about the place. Maybe such explanations were once acceptable, back in the civilized world and back before the comet. Newcomers to the wilds would dismiss local knowledge, but I would warn against it, Captain. Right now, such doubts are quite beside the point. We know magic exists in the world now."

Upon setting out on the expedition a few months ago, Meriwether would have been shocked by the brazen disrespect shown toward a man of higher rank and education, but he'd learned that the rules were quite different in these unexplored territories, and an honest, reliable man was far better than one who merely followed authority.

Meriwether added, "Such an explanation would hold for any tall hill. But we can see that one wasn't formed by natural processes."

"If they are little people, they certainly constructed an enormous edifice," Clark said.

"I'm inclined to believe the little people are real, Captains," LaBiche said, sounding nervous. "I've heard the natives in these parts talk about friends or comrades who died from the pygmies' magical darts." The trapper gazed at the mound and spoke toward it, though he was answering the two expedition leaders. "I've heard of logic and I've seen the impossible. It always seemed to me that dismissing such things with so-called natural explanations is a bit simple. We who've lived here, close to the land, maybe know more about the real dangers we might face."

Clark frowned, deep in thought, but said nothing. That prompted Meriwether to say, "From my readings of history, I believe the people in old Europe had similar legends about certain hills and mounds. When they were excavated, the mounds were found to contain the bodies of great chiefs and warriors. This mound might have served a similar purpose for the local tribes, long ago. Many great chiefs or warriors entombed there?"

"Might be," LaBiche said. "But since we've seen the dead walking now that the great magic has been unleashed on the land, even your logical explanation doesn't give me much comfort."

Meriwether nodded, feeling a chill. In a time of dragons, undead revenants, and giant antediluvian lizards, he could not dismiss the existence of magical pygmies.

The party proceeded slowly with even greater caution. As before, when he and Clark had approached Tavern Rock, he again sensed an eerie feeling permeating the area. The others were uneasy, and for Meriwether it was a phenomenon just beyond his normal human senses. But he couldn't deny it. The daylight had a different quality, the air had a different feel as it brushed their faces. The best he could describe it was as if he kept walking into unseen spiderwebs.

And each time he felt such an ethereal web *snapping* in the air, the birds took flight in great flocks—sparrows, blackbirds, crows.

LaBiche muttered, "I've heard that the birds act as alarms for the little people, warning them of the approach of strangers. Sometimes unwary strangers fall under a magical spell and when they return home they discover that centuries have passed, though to them it is mere minutes."

"I believe the wizard Franklin would not want to wait centuries to hear the report of our expedition," Clark said. "And I have a lovely woman waiting for me when I get home."

"No," Meriwether said. "We cannot wait for centuries." He imagined coming out of this to learn that his family was dead and gone. More important, in that time, the magical evil that was gaining strength in these arcane territories might have consumed the entire land. He had a feeling that the brooding evil might be a greater danger than Franklin suspected, perhaps growing powerful enough to push civilization back to the eastern edge of the continent. In a blurred vision, which might have been no more than his nightmarish imagination, Meriwether saw what the populated east could become, a blasted wasteland populated by rotting human revenants and enormous revived lizards, all civilization left in ruins...

Considering the tension he felt in the air, he was glad he had left Seaman behind, for the dog—with his bravado and boundless energy—would have leaped into the danger, barking. But Meriwether also felt glum that he had separated from his friend and protector, leaving him with a stranger in a land where the natives ate dogs.

When he had acquired the dog in St. Louis, he had thought Seaman would serve as sentinel and hunting companion, and in the months of rigorous travel, he had grown much attached to the furry brute. Seaman was now a friend, and a man dealt fairly with his friends.

But at least he had kept the dog safe... or so he hoped. They were all in danger, man and beast.

Another snap, another flock of birds flew up, obscuring the sun, startling them with their raucous chirping. Meriwether pressed on, pushing his worries aside so he could concentrate on the more tangible perils. The Canoti had lethal darts or other spells that humans could not understand, but he and Clark had accepted the task of discovery and understanding of the arcane territories, not just for Franklin's curiosity, but for the future of the Sundered world. They had to go forth.

Perhaps it was the only way to prevent the blasted landscape of his imaginings.

At the front of the group, Clark raised a hand. "Hold up." He stepped carefully, looking down at the tall grasses with an expression of disgust.

Meriwether paused and saw that he had nearly tripped over a bent human leg, a moccasin-clad foot. The rest of the body hidden under a scraggly bush—no, not hidden by some murderer, not dragged there by scavengers. It was clear the dead man had crawled under the bush after being mortally wounded, and he had died there.

While he and Clark watched, grim and serious, their companions tugged to extricate the corpse. The victim, already stiffening in death, had curled one arm around the trunk of the spreading bush, but the men pulled harder, snapping branches and hard tendons to pull the body free.

The corpse was no bronze-skinned native, but a middle-aged white man, with thinning hair. His death had frozen an expression of the utmost surprise on an unprepossessing face.

LaBiche yelped in dismay. "It's Barefoot Johnny!" He shook his head. "I know he's not barefoot now, but that's his nickname. He was a trapper, but not a very good one. One winter, Johnny was so unsuccessful that he boiled and ate his boots to survive." He blinked at Meriwether, then turned back to the corpse. "What is Barefoot Johnny doing in this place? He's not the sort to come here looking for magic... or anything else, really."

Meriwether bent down and quickly spotted three small darts lodged in Johnny's right leg and a singed spot on his left arm. The darts looked too small, barely piercing the skin, to have caused a mortal wound—unless the tips were poisoned, or otherwise impregnated with dark magic. As Clark and LaBiche watched him, he cut away the buckskin breeches with his knife to inspect the man's thigh. But other than the discolored flesh from the onset of putrefaction, he saw no sign of inflamed tissue or bruising by the wound. Instead, there was nothing, not even much blood.

Carefully, Meriwether extracted one of the darts, looked at the leaf-shaped stone blade, and wrapped it carefully in a rag from his pocket to make sure he did not accidentally prick himself. He saved the dart in a pouch at his waist, since their charge on the expedition had been to collect specimens and curiosities for Franklin. Once back in camp, he could test parts of the stone with such reagents as would indicate the presence of poison.

Leaving Barefoot Johnny in the grass, they moved toward the conical mound again, exhibiting even more caution. The air was utterly silent, now without even the presence of chittering birds. As they came closer to the unnatural hill, they saw no movement of inhabitants, heard no shouted alarms, nor did they see any welcoming crew or threatening defenders.

A stray wind whipped against the mound here, stirring showers of dirt and pebbles. They walked to the base of the mound, and Meriwether indicated holes burrowed into the hill, like rabbit warrens. Curious, Clark put the tip of his boot into one, evoking no response. Meriwether did the same, and again felt the curious tension of breaking spiderwebs. "It seems abandoned."

Clark put his hands on his hips and looked up. "You and I should climb the hill, Lewis, and see what's beyond. That would prevent us from being ambushed by whatever killed that poor fellow down there." He glanced at the others. "The men can stay here and give Barefoot Johnny a decent burial, cover him with rocks to keep the scavengers away."

Though Meriwether felt strangely reluctant to touch and ascend the steep mound, he knew the conical top would command a good view of the countryside, maybe even reveal the extent of magical attack the land was suffering. If the great mound was high enough, he mused, maybe they could even see the land clear to the Pacific.

The two men climbed the steep hill, which proved much more difficult than it appeared. The surface was loose with crumbly dirt and pebbles, as if it had been piled up only the day before and had not settled or compacted firmly in place. The bare dirt surface held no plants, no grasses or ground cover, not even any weeds. They had to clamber up by boot-tip and fingernail, and he and Clark were panting and covered in dirt by the time they reached the mound's summit.

Clark stood, drawing a deep breath and letting out an exclamation as he surveyed the view. Meriwether followed him, standing beside his partner. He blinked in surprise, as though by blinking he could force his eyes to see something different.

The panorama was magnificent. Vast plains so flat they seemed to extend forever, as though the hand of God had flattened the terrain all the way to the horizon. From the summit, he felt he could see tomorrow's weather. Under the heat of August, the waist-high grass rippled like a dry sea in the breeze.

The prairie was more than just grass, though—it was an *ocean* of buffalo, large dark forms that moved through the grassland. Meriwether had seen the big beasts before, but not like this. He saw herd after herd, countless thousands of the animals that covered the land all the way to the horizon. These animals provided the native tribes with everything they needed, meat to eat, hides for clothing and shelter, sinew, gut, bone for other uses.

"I never conceived there could be so many in all the world," Meriwether gasped. How could the Sioux claim to be starving?

Clark narrowed his eyes and extended his arm to point. Meriwether saw swift, predatory movement among the massed animals, driving the beasts into a panic. At first he thought it must be native hunters running or riding horseback, because a cloud of dust rose up from the pursuers.

Even from their distance, Meriwether could hear the thunder of hooves, and then another chilling sound, a loud inhuman roar. He had heard that reptilian bellow before—and now the pounding of feet, driven by massively muscled and scaled legs. More roars, and then the bleating of terrified buffalo.

Large ferocious lizard things, silhouettes in the distance, charged into the herd, thrashing their tails, biting and snapping with great jaws to break the buffalo spines directly beneath the large hump. The buffalo males charged, ramming with their sharp black horns, but the reptiles continued to attack.

"They look smaller than the giant that attacked the Sioux village," Clark said.

"But still deadly," Meriwether said. "And hungry."

The great lizards massacred the buffalo, clawing their sides and ripping out entrails, biting their thick necks, running them down and trampling them. The buffalo began to stampede, churning, racing en masse in one direction and then another. The lizards were mottled gray, and they hunted in packs.

"They are coming this way," he said, glancing down the slope of the mound to see their companions finishing the burial of Barefoot Johnny. "And they're running as fast as good carriage horses. It won't be long until they're upon us."

Clark was already moving. "Let's rejoin our party and retreat. We can head back the way we came, retrieve your dog, and find the keelboat. Let's be free of the lizards."

Feeling the urgency, he and Clark half-slid, half climbed down the hill again. He worried about Seaman, though others would surely criticize him for experiencing greater concern over a dog than the men.

After they reached the bottom of the hill and rejoined the rest of the party, they quickly related what they had seen. In the sky, they could see smears of dust from the oncoming stampede, could hear a distant rumbling. "Maybe we better run," LaBiche said, and the men sprinted back the way they had come, though the day's heat was still oppressive and their canteens quite empty.

Not allowing themselves to rest, they finally stumbled to the narrow creek where they had left the dog and the one man to guard him. They could still hear the far-off rumble of the huge buffalo herd, but Meriwether hoped the terrified animals had charged off in a different direction.

Then a crackling fear made his skin crawl. He heard the sound of giant footfalls, thundering steps that only a creature awakened from millennia in the dust could make.

Hearing Seaman bark, Meriwether started running before he had fully realized he was moving, without even paying heed to whether his fellows were following him.

He was already unslinging his air rifle, which had fortunately already been pumped into readiness. He prayed that the oncoming reptile was one of the smaller sort, not the gigantic monster that had attacked the painted warriors. Against such a huge beast, his rifle would be like a feather.

The man left with the dog held out his rifle, too, his face pale and drawn. "Captain Lewis?"

"Untie Seaman from the tree! Keep him at the back," Meriwether said, as his other companions arrived, also taking their rifles in hand. "Let's make this an orderly retreat, but as expedient as may be."

With aching muscles and panting breaths, they trotted away from the noise and toward the river where they'd hidden the two pirogues. Meriwether wished they had left the small boats under guard, because he had no way of knowing if native spies might have been watching them from the underbrush. Too late now.

There was nothing for it but to run and hope they could reach the river before the stampede and the giant reptiles came their way. Of course, the charging buffalo and the antediluvian beasts would not be intentionally pursuing them... unless they were being controlled by the mind of a dark wizard who wanted their doom.

Leaving the wooded banks of the little creek, they ran across flat and treeless land. Meriwether felt exposed, knowing their figures could be seen for miles. Sweat trickled down his back, but then an unnatural chill swept through his veins.

Seaman bounded ahead of them, tugging on the rope held by his guard. He barked now and then, joyously, as though this were a big game. For the dog, perhaps it was.

From the left came the horrifying sound of thunderous steps shaking the ground. Meriwether took a knee and turned, swinging his rifle at the monster, but it was still a formidable predator. He feared that something so tall and full of muscle would not fall to a little rifle ball. Unless, perhaps, that ball were lodged in the eye.

Meriwether had always relied on his excellent marksmanship, but he was not normally required to shoot at an unknown beast as it was charging toward him. Another man took a knee beside him, extending his rifle. It was Clark. "Go!" Meriwether said without turning. "Go on, damn it! I shall hold it."

"Not on your life! The men shall go and Seaman with them, but I am your second in this combat."

Then the beast hove into range, making further conversation moot.

Now he blessed himself that his air gun could fire twenty-two shots in a minute. And twenty-two shots might well be required, although he didn't know that he and Clark had a minute before the thing was on them. He remembered the long sharp teeth tearing the bodies of the painted warriors, the screaming men dismembered before his eyes.

Instead, he focused his mind, his aim on the golden eye of the advancing beast.

He let the rifle fire, and the creature still charged. He shot again and again, experiencing a curious sense of time dilation. Clark was beside him, firing as well with his conventional rifle.

Sweat rolled down his forehead and into his eyes, and he blinked away the sting and blindness to aim at the creature thundering toward them. He fired, always keeping aim on the creature's eye even as it galloped closer and closer.

The creature was so close he thought he could smell its hide, like hot snake skin.

The monster vacillated.

Meriwether prepared his last shot, knowing the creature would be upon him, but Clark grabbed his shoulder and pulled him to the side. Both men fell on the ground, just barely avoiding a mountain of meat that crashed to the dirt.

Clark gathered himself and sprang to his feet. He offered his hand to a grateful Meriwether. "I could tell you didn't realize your shot had struck home. The beast was already falling forward."

"Did I hit it?" Meriwether contemplated the mountainous

beast that lay shuddering on the ground in its last spasms of life. "Or did you?"

"It scarce matters." Clark stood a safe distance from the vicious teeth, walking cautiously around the carcass. "I suppose we can't stay, but what a trophy it would make."

Catching his breath, Meriwether endeavored to laugh, but it came out sounding more like a cough. The fallen beast made a sound like all the flatulent dogs in the world, and then it trembled and squirmed.

Meriwether frowned, uneasy, and this time he yanked his friend out of danger, as the dead monster—had it ever been alive?—shook, groaned as if under great internal pressure. And then it exploded.

The blast was so forceful it hurled both men ten feet backward, and Meriwether cringed, sure they would be doused with a rain of gore and gobbets of shattered reptilian flesh. But he felt nothing.

When he finally dared look up, he saw that where the beast had stood, there were now only . . . bones? The beast had somehow disintegrated.

The two men approached cautiously. As a boy in the woods of Virginia, Meriwether had often come across decayed skeletons of animals. A year or two in the warm and humid climate, most creatures decomposed. But in other places, for whatever reason, the ancient bones turned to stone. That was what these reptilian bones looked like now, glistening with mineral incrustations, with no sign of flesh, scales, or blood.

"They are certainly more easily preserved," Clark said. "I wish we could take them with us."

"Why not?" Meriwether asked, still dazed. "Franklin would certainly want to inspect them. Even such large bones could be accommodated on the pirogues around the men."

Clark smiled and shook his head. "My dear Lewis, I admire your optimistic and unsuspicious nature, but if such bones could be reanimated once, what would stop an evil wizard from doing it again? I would prefer not to have a giant creature come alive aboard our keelboat."

Meriwether shuddered at the thought. "I concur." He didn't give a second glance to the collapsed skeleton as they ran after the rest of their party, heading toward the river. The other men had already uncovered the pirogues. Seaman barked urgently, then yelped with delight to see his master again. He and Clark waded into the green water, grateful for its cool touch, and climbed into the pirogues.

Once they were settled in the small boats and began making their way along the current, Meriwether turned to look back at the bank. His heart leaped. Clark had been right about the bones. The reanimated reptile—undoubtedly the same beast—now stood at the river's edge, emitting its roar-hiss. As they watched in horror, several others of its kind joined it, including one much larger beast, as towering as the one that had killed the painted warriors. Simultaneously, all the monsters let out a blood-curdling bellow.

The men rowed faster.

From the other bank of the river, high up on the ridge, came the tune of "To Anacreon in Heaven," and looking up, Meriwether could swear he saw the silhouettes of Collins, Hall, and Willard stumbling along.

My Dearest Julia,

After our harrowing adventures, we've come to a calmer part of the journey after five months from St. Louis. Life is not too calm, of course, as these travels through the unknown are never fully calm.

We've climbed many a hill, and we've travelled many miles of river. I've charted a good portion of this unknown land, and Captain Lewis has collected countless strange plants and animals to bring back to our benefactor, the wizard Franklin.

We have not, however, found anything quite as exciting as what happened to us near the mound said to belong to the little people. We never did see any tangible sign of the mythical pygmies, other than the small darts we found in the body of the poor trapper called Barefoot Johnny. Captain Lewis has conducted many chemical tests on that arrowhead, but detected no poison that would explain the man's death. Perhaps it was deadly magic. We have seen stranger things in these arcane territories.

Now and then we have seen other glimpses of those terrifying beasts made of long-buried bones, loping along the hilly terrain near the river, but none have approached or attacked. We haven't even heard their distinctive roars. Other than that and the occasional encounter with raggedy, possibly starving Indians, we have been left in peace.

Autumn is nearing its end here in the north, and the air has a distinctive bite, hinting at a hard winter ahead. Our expedition is together now on the keelboat, making our way higher along the uncharted Missouri, but as the weather gets colder we must find a place where we can settle in for winter before we proceed on our way in Spring.

Sitting out the winter adds a frustrating amount of time where the men must sit idle. It takes months from our journey, but all the trappers, guides, and natives assure me and Captain Lewis that the river freezes solid, and so progress will be impossible. Even if the ground is covered with snow, traveling overland while dragging our pirogues and keelboat is not practicable. So winter we must, and we are searching for a favorable spot that offers a minimum of magical disruption.

When you think of me, imagine me snug and safe in a well-defended log home or even a small fort, wintering in the heart of this great uncharted territory, waiting for the warm breath of spring so we can resume our enterprise.

As with my other messages to you, I shall give this letter to some natives who are heading downriver to St. Louis. With the inducement of reward for safe delivery, I believe my words will arrive safe in your hands soon, my dearest.

—Letter from William Clark to Julia Hancock,
October 1804

An Arrival

MERIWETHER HAD NEVER FELT QUITE SO COLD, NEVER IN VIR-
ginia, never in St. Louis...never in his life. Even if their clothes
were adequate to the cold in the east, the warm garments proved
wholly inadequate here.

The expedition had raced the winter along the river, breaking
still-fragile encroachments of ice before it became too thick and
too binding to allow them to proceed.

Despite the discomforts, however, Meriwether had not heard
the dark, taunting voice in his head for more than a month.

He sensed, in the way most magic could be sensed, that the
looming evil force abated somewhat as the Earth went dormant
and the ground froze white under blankets of ice and snow. It
was as though the magic drew its force from the heart of the
land, and once the world went to sleep in the intense cold, the
evil arcane force could not draw enough vitality to threaten the
expedition or the surroundings.

He and Clark had discussed the merits of continuing, despite
the hardships of the cold and snow, so they could take advantage
of the weakening magical adversary, but considering the equipment,
the boats, the supplies, and the increasingly rugged terrain, both
men knew it would not be possible. Snow had started falling, and
they spent more time chipping the pirogues and keelboat out of
the ice than making progress. The expedition would have to find
a place to take shelter under leaden skies and howling winds.

The scouts ranged up the river and out into the countryside,

91

and finally they found a place with plentiful wood, both for construction of a fort and for fuel. The forest would provide game, even in the dead of winter, and they had easy access to water. Several native tribes had settled the vicinity, and the people seemed normal and non-hostile, neither impelled by a magical force nor so starved by arcane disruption as to feel the need to attack the expedition.

Meriwether had made contact with tribe members, offered the usual trinkets, and the natives seemed satisfied. As the expedition members began to cut down trees and build their home for the cold months, the natives and the expedition enjoyed a peaceful coexistence. Meriwether thought this was a fine place to weather the freezing winter.

They had determined to build comfortable winter quarters surrounded by a defensible palisade. With enough men and guns, they hoped to be able to repel any magical or natural attacks that should come. They had begun construction on November 3, and finished within three weeks, before the first truly severe blizzard hit.

So far, in nearly a month of scouting, building, and occupying what they'd come to call Fort Mandan—named after the neighboring tribe—the guards had sounded no alarums of note.

Twice, a whiskey barrel had been drained, and the sentinels on duty swore it had been done by the three revenants of Hall, Collins, and Willard who'd first been killed by the undead natives. Both Meriwether and Clark had been skeptical of the explanation, thinking that more human and less undead influences had stolen the whiskey.

Every week or so during the passage along the river and during the construction of the fort, one of the men would report seeing the lost men, as though their minds couldn't let go of their friends who had been killed, yet remained alive, animated by the evil force. They named Hall, Collins, and Willard the "Whiskey Revenants," and they were becoming a legend of the expedition.

With the fort finished, Meriwether slept in his first real bed in more than half a year. He looked forward to quiet months of rest and planning. He had many notes to compile, reports to write, assessments and opinions to be delivered back to Franklin.

Nevertheless, when he lay back to sleep, safe and sound in the warm fortress, Meriwether dreamed of the dragon again...

the dragon in a rage. The servants of the great dark force had failed to stop the intruders, and the creature was looking for something—a critical piece of its game, without which it could not be successful.

Meriwether stirred, mumbled. Part of him was aware that he lay dreaming on a straw-stuffed mattress in a rough-hewn wooden bed. His miniscule chamber lacked a door or any privacy, a curtain in the doorway providing barely a pretense of some isolation, and nearby he could hear the sounds and movements of the rest of the crowded men sleeping. In the larger common room where most of them spent the day and where they cooked their meals, two men spoke in low voices, probably the inside guards stationed there. Their murmurs were punctuated by the faint slapping sounds of playing cards on the small table.

But as he slept, Meriwether felt cold, very cold, not just under the blankets but inside his heart and soul. In the dream—was it really naught but a dream?—he found himself outside in the falling snow, looking at their boats, so encased in ice that it would be impossible to free them.

He stood amid swirling snow, strangely naked, though he couldn't look down at his own body. Instead, he looked at the river and the gray sky. All at once, the light dimmed and something immense and powerful hovered above the swirling snow.

Son of the Dragon, said the voice that was not quite a voice, but merely an echo in his mind.

Meriwether recognized the voice. It reignited the memory of the wizard Franklin, of the fight against the dragon, of Government House aflame, and of being knocked out for hours. And of that voice inside his head.

In the dream, he tried to see through the white, blowing snow, but found nothing more than an impression of a shape. The blinding flakes stung Meriwether's eyes, burned on his skin. There was something strange about his eyes and his skin, but he didn't understand it.

"I've come for my bird and her egg," the dragon said, the voice clearer and more threatening in Meriwether's mind. "Where are you hiding her?"

He didn't know how to answer, and he clung to the certainty that he was dreaming, that he had entered that disjointed portion of illusion, where only dreams made sense.

"Where is she?" the dragon demanded again, louder.

Meriwether shifted in bed, groaning quietly, but he could not awake himself. In the snow, his dream self also shifted, although he still couldn't see his own body. Cold wind blew, accompanied with gusts of snow. When he spread his arms, the wind caught his wings.

Something very old, an instinctive feeling from past generations, twined in his mind. Meriwether held up his large arms, stretched them wide, and let the wind catch them.

In bed, his dreaming self heard his own voice give a long, low moan, partly in distress, mostly in confusion. His other self outside in the snowstorm wasn't confused at all, though. His body pushed up with one scaled back paw, taking flight, using the wind to soar, banking against the blizzard's sudden gusts.

He smelled the cold of the snow, but also the musky heat of the dragon. He felt an irrational fury toward the creature and what it had done, for burning the St. Louis Government House, the carriage with the horses still in harness, and for the more general attacks on the expedition, how the revenants had killed the three men who had stolen the whiskey. Now the dragon was searching for . . . *my birdie and her egg?*

Meriwether did know that he would defend that poor "bird" against the dragon with all his might.

Due to his anger, a sound like a screamed roar emerged from his mouth, and he found the dragon above him, a huge figure, three times the dream-Meriwether's own size and ten times as threatening.

The dragon didn't expect him flying here in the dream, and Meriwether beat his wings and came at it from behind, half hidden by the dragon's own wing. The dragon tried to turn, to gush flame at Meriwether, but before he could, Meriwether had sunk his teeth in the dragon's neck. Something like liquor flowed down his long throat, powerful, burning, and intoxicating.

Flying and fighting through the winter storm, the dragon let out a cry like the screams of a dozen dying men. And then it vanished.

Meriwether found himself flying alone in the storm, dizzy and drunk on dragon blood, his mind full of thoughts that weren't his.

"Captain, Captain!" a voice called. "Captain Lewis!"

His dragon-self hurtled down through the sky and crashed painfully into his human body.

And Meriwether sat up in bed, soaked with sweat and shivering.

One of the two inside sentries faced him, Captain Clark's man York, who had accompanied their expedition from the beginning. "Are you all right, Captain?"

"I . . . I was just having a nightmare. I will be fine."

Though the large man mostly served Captain Clark, the men had forgotten he'd once been a slave, and none of them asked questions about the turmoil of the territories back east, the wars for and against slavery, the different systems of government that had sprung up since the Sundering. During their perilous journey up the Missouri, York had saved and been saved by them as much as anyone else. He was so good at cards, in fact, that most of the men in Fort Mandan owed him money.

Now, York still clutched his hand of cards, but he didn't look at all happy. "I came to wake you, sir, because we have a visitor. The outside sentries say they have a woman who needs our help. She came through the storm."

"A woman?" Meriwether asked, running his hand through his hair, trying to bring some sort of order to the locks sleep and his wild dream had disarrayed.

"A native woman, sir. She looks in very bad shape, they say. She's pregnant, very much so . . . and, sir, she may be giving birth right now."

As he swung out of bed, Meriwether considered that it might be a trap, some sort of ambush sprung by the evil force, by the voice of the dragon. After walking revenants, giant lizards, and actual dragons, anything was possible. Might not the dark enemy insinuate a weak person, a seeming victim into their midst, and thus take advantage of their compassion?

On the other hand, he had acquired a strange knowledge when his dream self had swallowed the dragon's blood. The dark enemy had truly been running on dregs of strength, trying to find a target, a connection it couldn't otherwise reach. After the fight in the dream, Meriwether knew he had taken the dragon by surprise and nearly killed him. "I'll come. What are the sentinels doing? Where is this woman?"

"Pryor is bringing her in, sir."

Meriwether nodded. "Bring her to my room. Quickly. Is she wounded? I presume she is not a revenant, like the possessed tribesmen?"

"No, sir. She's alive, but she looks like she's been walking for months, and starving most of that time. Her clothes are torn and dirty, and she's not dressed for the cold outside."

He pulled on his buckskin breeches and a heavy shirt, which warmed him from the coldness inside, though the cozy interior of Fort Mandan was not cold, despite the continuous snow and wind outside. The walls were snug, and they kept a fire going in the central fireplace. Without interior doors, the warmth permeated everything.

This close to his disturbing dream encounter with the dragon, he would and could trust nothing. "If she's human, she has survived a land filled with magical depredations. We'll do what we can for her."

He did, however, make sure his rifle was near at hand, should he need it.

The big pot of water that hung near the fire steamed with the heat, and Meriwether mixed hot water with some snow in a basin for the appropriate temperature. He rolled his shirtsleeves and washed his face and his arms up to the elbows, using a hard cake of soap.

If he was greeting a woman, however bedraggled, he wanted to look somewhat presentable, and if she was truly in labor, then he would need to be as clean as possible. In his youth, his mother had taught him much about practical medicine and as the household healer to Thomas Jefferson, it had been part of his duties to deliver the children of all of Jefferson's dependents. Plants and magic often eased the delivery.

By the time he'd dried his hands, some of the men had piled blankets atop his bed. Pryor came in carrying in his arms a girl in native clothing. Her long hair was tangled and windblown, her deerskin clothes caked with dirt, torn, ragged. Pryor laid her carefully in the blankets and one man brought lanterns closer, so Meriwether could see her.

The girl was young, very young. Personally, he'd never found the native women handsome, though he was sometimes shocked at how casually they disrobed in front of men. It seemed to represent a certain lack of modesty. But this one had a striking character, an exotic quality that went beyond her race. He sensed that immediately. Also something akin to a bond, as though they were two of a kind, as though she were a friend, long parted from him. The feeling shocked him, and he forced himself to evaluate her dispassionately.

She had straight black hair, bronze skin, and the wide, flat facial features of the local tribes. In the keelboat, the expedition had passed many such women and girls, hard at work in manual labor, or just standing still in their buffalo hides. She could have been one of the native wives of interpreters who had traveled with the expedition or one of the women who had formed casual liaisons with the men since they'd been at Fort Mandan. This woman was very young, very tired, and very pregnant. The candlelight and the fireplace softened her features and made her prettier.

But when she opened her dark eyes and looked directly at him, Meriwether understood that she was someone unique, special, and again he felt as though they'd known each other a long time. The moment their eyes locked felt like an instant, inarguable connection. It drew an exclamation of startled recognition from Meriwether, and made him say, "Oh."

He asked the men to fetch one of the interpreters, preferably LaBiche, to communicate with the girl, to explain that he meant her no harm and that he would try to help her with the birth of her child, if she was indeed in labor.

He thought she would feel better if a woman were present, but the women still with the expedition were those casual liaisons of the men. Not exactly trustworthy midwives.

He cast his eye at her swollen belly with some misgiving. He'd delivered babies a few times before in his life, but this girl was so young. Her midriff seemed enormous, much too big for her small frame.

From his experience, the native women had little or no modesty. He guessed that what she needed most was gentling, being told that he would help her. When LaBiche did not immediately arrive, Meriwether tried in his rusty and scant French, "I do not hurt you. I see how baby is coming."

The girl looked at him, her eyes wide, and momentarily seemed to reconsider. Meriwether couldn't tell if she understood him or not. He would have to wait for LaBiche after all.

Then the woman shocked him by speaking English. "You are...Son of the Dragon." Her words had a French accent and something else, something deeper that changed the consonants into a faint lilt of the languages of the region. She raised herself up from the blankets, ignoring the fire nearby. "I came to find you—to warn you. But outside, just now in the storm, I saw your battle in the sky. You acquitted yourself well, Son of the Dragon."

He stepped back, reeling, not knowing anything he could do or say. "You...saw the battle? In my dream?" He suddenly lowered his voice, felt a deep chill. "Did the dragon send you?"

"No, no! I escaped. Dragon had us captive, but I got away." Sitting on the blankets, she wrapped her arms around her belly in what appeared to be a protective gesture. "Had to escape before time for the baby. Dragon would have taken him." Then her composure shattered, and she ground her teeth, letting out a cry of anguish. He realized she must have suffered a labor contraction.

"I have delivered babies before. Many. My master back east has many servants, and I have helped many with difficult births. Let me help you," he said. And cursed himself for not having brought those herbs he had used in the past to help with birth: red raspberry leaf, for instance, a tea of which often sped up delivery. He'd thought since none of the recruits were supposed to bring their wives, they would not run into this.

She nodded, her teeth still ground together. Her face had gone pale. She struggled to undo her clothing, but Meriwether calmed her by placing a hand on her shoulder. "Lie down. I'll remove your clothes." He called for York to bring the warm water, cloths that could be used for washing.

Looking into her face, Meriwether could see she had courage, this woman. "Is it your first baby?" He had seen other women so caught in the pains of birth, they twisted and screamed, but this girl showed only a clenching of her jaw.

She lay back down and muttered words in her native language before adding, "First baby. It hurts."

He worked carefully and gently to undo the ties of her filthy garments, having to cut some of the knots free. He freed her of the clothes around her legs and her swollen belly, and made her comfortable in the blankets. A cursory look told Meriwether the delivery would hurt indeed. Before long, the baby was crowned, but the mother was apparently too weak to push it out.

He leaned closer, trying to encourage her. "You say the dragon would have taken your baby?"

"I was his captive. My...husband, his other wife, and I were held. And the dragon was waiting for birth so he could take my baby to..." She winced with the pain, struggled to find the right words. "Take him over? Make him a vessel? I ran. I walk," Another pause for the pain of a contraction. "In winter he is weakest. I walk many days."

Feeling tense and desperate, but forcing himself to sound calm as he struggled to figure if he could ease the child out, Meriwether said, "You speak remarkably good English."

With her eyes squeezed shut, she laughed, as though this were an unexpected compliment. "I am for two years the wife of Toussaint Charbonneau. He speaks English and French and languages of the tribes. I learned." She gasped, caught her breath, let it out in a hiss. "My name is Bird Woman." Another pause. "In my language it is Sacagawea."

Bird. Meriwether remembered the voice of the dragon saying that he was looking for his lost bird and her egg. Did he mean Sacagawea and her child?

He saw Pryor and several of the expedition men standing discreetly and nervously near the door to the chamber. He directed the man to bring some broth, cooled with a little snow, and asked Sacagawea to drink a little. From her drawn, lean face, he suspected she had not eaten for several days. She drank the broth demurely, without gulping. Meriwether hoped it would restore some of her strength, so she could summon the will to push the baby out.

Hours went by. The dawn came, but the morning remained gray with the lingering storm. Sacagawea endured the relentless pain of contractions with a stoic quality that Meriwether couldn't help but admire. He'd seen men in war who suffered with less dignity than this native girl. Certainly, she was much more than a girl.

Among the tribes, Meriwether had seen women no older than twenty years who had half a dozen children, and he realized that back east in civilized America, many white women did as well. He knew that Julia, the woman Captain Clark was courting, was still a child herself. Meriwether wasn't sure he approved of taking a woman who had not yet lived enough life to make a decision for herself. That and the fact that he'd delivered a few babies born to too-young tenant farmers and neighbors, made him leery of the practice of marrying women who were scarcely into puberty.

Women died in childbirth, just as men did on the battle-field, and in both cases it was easier to convince the young and foolhardy to do it, to use them up before they were so old that their bodies refused to do what was necessary.

If he, Meriwether Lewis, had not been young and foolhardy, he would never have been lured to war himself. And if his father hadn't been young and foolhardy, then he would never have gone to war, and therefore would never have died when Meriwether was so young, leaving him and his mother adrift in the world, need-ing to count on each other for comfort and support. The death that had so shaped his life had been that of a man too young to have made a careful and informed decision to sacrifice himself.

He brooded as he watched the young woman labor in vain. Her response to pain seemed to be diminishing, because she had less strength to show it and less strength to suppress it. After a contraction rippled across her distended belly, he heard her gasp. A tear escaped and ran down her cheek.

York stood at the door and spoke so loudly he startled the men in the room. "Excuse me, Captain. In one of the Indian tribes we passed by, the women were talking about the snakes that rattle, the poisonous ones. They said just a bit of the rattle fed to a pregnant mother would ease her delivery. It's a magic that works in these parts."

"I shot that rattler specimen, and we preserved it." He frowned. "I wanted to see if it was the same kind we have out east. I ran some tests on the venom and preserved the rattle in the vials. Do we still have...?"

York nodded. "I'll fetch the specimens from the crates, sir." He left quickly. In his experiments, Meriwether had ascertained that the rattle did not contain the deadly venom, but he did not know what its other properties were, or what sort of magic the natives extracted from it. But he had kept samples for Franklin. He had tested the venom on some rats, determined that it was deadly through the pierced skin, but a small dose administered in food drugged the rats into a daze; larger doses killed them. And how much of the venom, or magic, resided in the rattle itself? He had no idea what the proper dose might be for a woman of Sacagawea's size.

He leaned close to the sweating woman. "Are you willing to try this? I do have a rattle from one of those snakes. We can give it to you." He realized the very idea of the question would seem strange to her.

He had no idea if the magic from the snake's rattle would be effective or dangerous, but he had to make certain Sacagawea had faith in it, and in him as a makeshift doctor. Whether or not the magic was real, its very potency might lie in her confidence and belief.

And he could tell that she might die soon if he didn't do something. Caesar was said to have been cut from the body of his dying mother, but Meriwether was not quite willing to do that. Not yet. That would surely kill Sacagawea, and even if the baby survived, how could the men of Fort Mandan feed it? No, Sacagawea had to survive this delivery. The rattlesnake magic might be their only hope.

Though the faint gray glow of day seeped through the imperfectly fitting shutters in the walls of the main building, they didn't dare open them for better light, due to the raging blizzard outside. When York had retrieved the specimen bottle that held the severed rattle from the snake specimen, Meriwether looked down at his patient.

She was so thin that her bent knees stood out like knobs in her muscular legs, and her fingers seemed delicate, the bones near-visible through her bronze skin. She'd been starving herself, he was sure of it, in her rush to get away from the dragon. Leaving her husband behind.

"Yes," Sacagawea said. "We know of it. The women of my tribe—the tribe I came from, used rattler venom and the tail of the snake. The magic dulls the pain, and I will be able to push hard, hard. I did not think we would find a snake in the winter cold."

Meriwether held up the specimen bottle and removed the severed tail, a sinister-looking lumpy object. "Fortunately, we are a scientific expedition, among other things. And I will give this a try, if you are willing. We will get you and your little one through this perilous situation."

"It's a boy," she said, panting. "I know it's a boy. He's—" Her hand went protectively over her stomach, as though trying to comfort her unborn child. Her face was wracked with pain.

He placed the preserved rattle on a small plate, then used his sharpened knife to chop it into tiny bits, not at all concerned about destroying one of their specimens. He had no doubt that as their journey continued next year in warmer weather, they would find other snakes.

When he was done, the plate held an unappetizing pink mess, the tissues of the snake's rattler. It looked finely granular, as though composed of salt beneath a membrane. Meriwether had chopped it so finely that each morsel was no longer than the tip of his fingernail.

He placed one of the thin slivers between Sacagawea's lips, and she licked, then swallowed. "More," she said.

He was hesitant, but she seemed certain. He pushed another tiny sliver between her lips, and she lay back, waiting for the venom to affect her.

When the next contraction hit Sacagawea, she seemed to have the endurance to push harder. Her expression showed concentration rather than agony. She gasped. "One...more."

Though his own pulse was racing, Meriwether did as she asked, feeding her another morsel.

She groaned, squeezed, and drew a deep breath for a great push. Her entire sweat-slick body trembled. Something tore and gave way inside her, and with a rush of blood and fluids, she expelled an infant onto the blankets. It was a boy, but it was too still, too quiet. His skin was pale and bluish.

Meriwether lifted the baby up by his tiny feet. As Sacagawea saw her son, she made a sound like a long sigh that caught on a sob, perhaps realizing he was too still. Maybe the dragon had got him after all—

"No!" Meriwether said out loud, defying the voice he had heard in his head and in his dreams. The idea of the this child being made into one of the evil force's revenants cut him through the heart. But wait—he saw the baby's chest moving as he struggled to draw breath.

Instinctively, Meriwether pinched the baby hard on his backside. He'd seen doctors slap the bottoms of hapless infants, but his mother had taught him that any sudden pain could work. The baby's eyes flung open wide, and a half-choked cry erupted from his tiny mouth. With a probing finger, Meriwether reached into the baby's mouth and scooped free the clogging mucus. Then the crying started in earnest and echoed through the fort.

He heard men cheering, whooping, and Sacagawea collapsed

in relief on her blankets. Meriwether placed the baby on her chest, then moved to protect the young mother's privacy from the casually staring men crowded around the door.

Remembering what to do, he tied the baby's cord. The little boy was crying and pumping his arms and legs, apparently a healthy specimen, somehow plump and strong despite his mother's emaciated condition. "He is fine and healthy," he told her.

Meriwether reached blindly for a new blanket and wrapped the baby tightly before handing him to the new mother. "Do you have any idea what you'll call this fine young man?"

She was laughing and crying as she opened her shirt to nurse her son. "Jean Baptiste. His name is Jean Baptiste Charbonneau. His father told me he wanted him named after his father's father."

His father. Meriwether did not ask for further explanation. Clearly she considered herself loyal and devoted to her husband. And why should she not be? Who should she be loyal to?

She lay back, exhausted and dozing, no doubt aided by the rattlesnake. Lewis, also exhausted, went to the main room, in search of a corner to sleep.

They built up the fire to keep the main room warm. He had the men bring him more clean blankets for the mother and child, removing the blankets soiled by the birth. They would be stored outside in a sealed shed, so as not to attract animals; with the frozen river and cold weather, the blankets could not be thoroughly washed until spring.

He also knew there were superstitions about a baby's placenta, and his mother had told him many of them from the old, lost world. His own ancestors in the British Isles would carefully dispose of the afterbirth, burying or burning it. Some even held careful traditions of what must be done afterward, from saying special prayers to planting trees over the remains. Others held no such beliefs, and many times the placenta was just discarded, with no great harm that he could tell.

Except here, in the middle of a strange, magical landscape after the comet had unleashed magic on the world and separated the American continent to another place entirely, who knew what might happen? He did not know the traditions here in the arcane territories, and so he was afraid to discard or burn the afterbirth without consulting Sacagawea, once she grew strong again.

Thinking like a scientist, he wrapped the thing in a square

of white linen intended for ligatures and bandages, and ordered it be stored like the soiled blankets, in a secure place where it would freeze.

For hours the men had held a hushed, tense quiet, but now they talked animatedly, relieved. Pryor, the man on outside guard, described Sacagawea's arrival, like a ghost through the gusts of snow. "When she arrived, Captain Lewis, sir, she said she needed to see the smaller dragon. I think now...I think she meant you, sir. Why did she call you the smaller dragon?"

Meriwether hesitated, not wanting to reveal his dream battle, nor to inflame their superstitions. "She was delirious, Pryor. This isn't her language. She must have confused the words for dragon and doctor." He didn't try to explain how a young native woman would have any basis to know what a *dragon* from European legend was at all.

He was dead tired, and curled up in blankets on the floor. As he drifted to sleep, he thought how odd it was that Sacagawea had said she had actually seen him fighting the dragon in the sky, during the blizzard. Could she see his dreams?

Deep in sleep, he dreamed he was fighting the dragon again, but even though his adversary seemed weaker, this time his teeth didn't find their mark on the evil creature's throat, and they both spiraled into darkness.

My Dearest Julia,

Our long winter stay at Fort Mandan has been enlivened by the arrival—isn't it always so?—of a mysterious woman. But you must not be jealous, my dear one, for she is a very young native, married, who arrived in the very process of giving birth. She sought the medical services, and even a little bit of healing magic, from Captain Lewis. Something to do with a snake's rattle. I confess I slept through most of it, and awakened to the cries of a newborn baby.

Since the girl named Bird Woman, Sacagawea in her language, is very young—we think about sixteen—and her baby is a large and lusty boy, she was in dire straits delivering the infant, but our redoubtable Meriwether Lewis used local custom and magic to ease the birth by feeding her bits of a snake's rattle. This did the trick, and ushered her son into the world.

Our confinement continues to be cold and dreary, but more interesting than before. Sacagawea has given a reminder of home to the many men trapped here until the river thaws, and she has even brought some order to the unruly half dozen local women who follow this expedition with their halfbreed trapper and fur trader husbands. They still bicker among themselves, but the women take direction from Sacagawea, perhaps because they are surprised at the spectacle of a strong and determined woman who speaks three languages, as well as numerous native dialects, and who is not afraid of speaking to the white men.

In fact, I doubt Sacagawea is much scared of anything, after her long cold journey after escaping from some sort of evil force to find us in the middle of the worst blizzard we've endured in this forsaken region.

She has already proved her worth. With her son in a snug wrapping tied to her back, she goes out and finds us berries and roots and other edibles to enliven the dreary meals of endless preserved meat we'd been eating. She has shown or directed the other camp women

105

how to create dishes that are palatable to us white men. Perhaps she has fed them to her husband, a man named Charbonneau, before.

Her husband remains captive of whatever force it is that has been directing the sinister magical attacks against us.

Before the thaw is fully set—which Sacagawea claims will restore that unknown enemy to power—we must decide whether we will continue our determined push westward to try to make it to the Pacific Ocean and possible connection to the rest of the world after the Sundering. Or whether we should stay to fight this evil force and neutralize it. Lewis seems to think he has some sort of power that can stand against it.

This will necessitate long conversations with Sacagawea, since she knows more about the magical perils inherent in this region, but she must be fully recovered and clear-headed before she can make a case for what we should do, and before we can weigh it against the danger to our expedition and our duty to the wizard Franklin.

I shall let you know in the next letter what we decided, since I write to comfort myself more than you, an indulgence for which I hope you'll forgive me.

Yours, sincerely,
William Clark

—Letter from William Clark to Julia Hancock,
Fort Mandan, February 20, 1805

Thin Ice

SPRING APPROACHED LIKE A CREEPING THIEF, AND THE MEN WERE certainly impatient to go.

"The ice is getting thin around our embarkations." Meriwether strode into the common room of Fort Mandan. The sun was bright and relatively warm as he made his perimeter inspection. He'd passed the outdoor sentinels stationed at the defensive stockade wall, which today were Gass and Ordway, and entered to find a friendly scene. Sacagawea, with her son strapped to her back, stirred a meal over the fire, some savory potage of meat and herbs. They'd grown used to her potages, which varied their diet and also warmed them through the coldest winter.

In the common room, six men played a game of cards, while Captain Clark inspected his maps and writings in a corner, diligently making clean copies of his surveyor's maps, which would be delivered back east with the next set of trappers whose path they crossed. Sitting on one of the low benches near the fire, Pryor used a cobbler's needle to sew his boots. From the other large room at the back of the main building, Meriwether could hear voices, other men of the expedition mixed with the sharp reply of a woman's voice, one of the wives of the interpreters.

After making his announcement, Meriwether shook snow off his outer garments and hung them to dry on a peg affixed to the wall. Clark looked up from his maps. "Good. It's about time we resumed our way. There's no telling how far we are from the Pacific."

Sacagawea's face bore a worried expression as she looked up from the food. Later, after the meal, she came to speak to the two captains in private. They met her in Clark's little cubicle of a room, which had barely space for a writing desk, strewn with his papers. He preferred to work in the main room and make use of the candlelight while others pursued their own projects.

It said something about how highly Meriwether had come to regard this proud and pensive native woman that he considered it quite proper for the two men to meet with her in a separate room. But Sacagawea's tribe had no concept of female honor, and the fort, which lacked interior doors and had only curtains dividing the rooms, would never be private enough to endanger anyone's honor without the whole expedition knowing.

She entered the room looking grave. Due to her upbringing, she did not smile in the ingratiating way that European women did when they thought to convince men. Instead, Sacagawea looked somber and self-contained, which made Meriwether respect her. Most of the men in the party treated her as a fellow explorer, rather than one of the wenches who fell in with the expedition.

She wore her own clothes again, native pants and tunic in suede, mended now so as to look new. Her slick black hair shone, freshly washed, and she looked ready to face an important social occasion. Even with the baby strapped on her back, she might have been an emissary between tribes.

Which is probably what she considers herself, Meriwether thought.

"You wished to speak to us, Sacagawea?" Clark asked. Disrupting the gravity of the occasion, he extracted little Jean Baptiste from the carrying board on the woman's back, cuddling him, and calling him "Little Pompy" from *Pompy*, a term that meant leader or chief in the local languages.

Meriwether noted Sacagawea's slight tension as the babe was taken from her back, but she relaxed almost immediately, showing that she trusted them now. At first, the young mother had been very protective of her child, refusing to let the others near her. *And why should she not fear?* Meriwether thought. *How strange we must look to her, with our bearded faces, our light eyes and pale skin, our strange clothes.*

For all the time he'd dealt with the natives, starting back in Virginia, he had never considered them normal, but rather strange, exotic. But now he realized, so far from the populated east, it was himself, Clark, and their party who were strangers, not to be trusted until they proved themselves.

Sacagawea looked at Clark with a smile, pleased to see the fondness he lavished on her son, then she returned her grave dark gaze to Meriwether once more. "The keelboat and pirogues will soon be free from ice. I—" she stopped, not quite sure how to proceed. "I wondered what your plans were."

In the silence, Meriwether and Clark traded a look. They both were devoted to fulfilling the commission the wizard had given them, and they were determined to find their way to the Pacific, if such a way existed. There, they would hope that no great wall of nothing blocked the path to the rest of the world, as it did from the Atlantic side.

Meriwether hesitated before delivering a quick answer, though. He held another purpose, just as explicit, that of making sure that this great continent remained safe for the Europeans stranded here after the Sundering.

"We were given a commission," Clark said. Almost apologetically, he handed the baby back to his mother. "We must find a passage through the continent to the . . . to the great water on the other side." He seemed unsure that Sacagawea had a concept of the ocean, or that there was more to the world beyond, but the young woman had lived with her European husband for two years and had picked up an enormous amount of information from Charbonneau, besides language.

"I know there is an ocean in the east, that now ends in nothing since magic came back," she said. "My father and mother knew of the great sea through fur trappers, and they told us of it." She shrugged. "And I understand that your people want to find a way back to the land of your ancestors."

This brought a startled laugh from Clark. "No, our ancestors have been in the new world a long time. I don't know if Meriwether still has relatives in the old country, but I surely don't. Nevertheless, there is a huge world out there, and many people working to solve the problems of magic and natural science, all of them ready to share their knowledge. And there was commerce. We grow coffee in Virginia, but I miss tea from the east that was."

"All your tribes had commerce?" Sacagawea asked with a weird light in her eyes. "Across the great seas? In boats like your pirogues? Or your large keelboat?"

Meriwether suddenly understood. Sacagawea truly couldn't imagine a society that spanned the globe. Born of isolated and often warring tribes, she could not grasp the idea of many people joining, from tribe to nation, and from nation to empire, of free trade among very different people.

"Not quite boats like ours," Clark said. "Much larger vessels that move with the use of sails. The entire world is... much bigger than what you know, and our tribes are very large coalitions of tribes, mostly at peace with other coalitions. They trade with them, using interpreters and travelers—people like your husband."

A shadow passed over Sacagawea's gaze. "And this is your mission? To find the way overland to the ocean that my husband called the Pacific?"

Meriwether nodded. "Yes, and maybe to connect again to the rest of the world, which the magic severed us from."

Quiet, she took Jean Baptiste from Clark's arms, and cooed at the baby as he fussed wanting to go back to Clark. "Would it be possible for you to join efforts with me, first? You might be able to help me free my husband from the den of the magical creature who imprisons him. You could help me liberate this land and all in it from the evil force. But I have no right to ask. You are the ones who helped me in my direst need, not the other way around. You helped save my life and little Pomp's. I have nothing to offer you, in return, except a certain knowledge of paths and languages, as well as edible foods on the way. And that might not be enough."

Meriwether felt a tightening in his chest. She was trying to bargain with them for the rescue of her husband, when simple human decency ought to suffice.

"I believe you have a right to our help, but I'm not sure we can give it," he said. "We have withstood attacks before, from undead revenants to giant lizards, but we barely survived. I don't know that we could fight back against such a thing as the dragon wizard you describe. I saw his fury once before in St. Louis, and he was driven off only by one of our greatest sorcerers. I am certainly no match for him."

She opened her mouth and looked at him. For a moment he thought she was going to ask him about his fight with the dream dragon and what had brought her in search of him. But the look that passed between them cautioned her not to speak. She turned to the door. "I see."

"I'm afraid Captain Lewis is right," Clark interjected. "Any attempts at rescuing your husband would be met with force we couldn't counter. Unless you have some way we could approach the dragon without alerting him to our presence?"

"Please sit, Sacagawea." Meriwether gestured toward the single bed against the wall in the tiny room. "Tell us how you think we could get at this creature. He holds your husband and others in thrall? What other resources does he have? Who fights for him? What is his appeal, besides magic? And why does he oppose our expedition at every turn?"

He felt a chill, not sure he wanted to know the answer. Perhaps he himself was what attracted the dragon to the expedition, a wish to defeat a rival. The dark dragon had called him the son of Wales, an ancient place known for its dragons. But if he was the target of the evil force, he was sure he could never defeat the creature.

Sacagawea hesitated, remained standing as if she wanted to remain on a level with them, perhaps not a physical level but a moral one. She squared her shoulders after she put the baby on his board again, sound asleep. "I think, the creature is the land."

"The land?"

"The sum total of the spirit of these lands that you call the arcane territories. It has become maddened, powerful, resentful." She shook her head. "It is too simple to say the land is outraged by the presence of those who don't belong here, people like you. But it is more complicated than that. From what I heard of Charbonneau, my husband, people are traveling creatures. They always move, explore. No land can belong only to one people. They come in, make themselves at home with the land, where other people were at home before. People merge, they blend their differences, like my husband and I.

"But after the great comet came and exploded in the sky, long before I was born, I think the magic awoke the land, and maybe drove the spirit of the land insane. My parents spoke of magic as something that never happened in their grandparents' day, but now all the creatures are magical. Magical creatures who think and talk like men are common. Some spirit of the land awakened and found he was no longer worshiped or respected. So, that great power naturally blamed the intruders, those who came from elsewhere . . . those who didn't believe in him."

"But why does it appear as a dragon?" Meriwether asked. "The native tribes have no legend—"

"I merely use the English word for dragon, and maybe that is how you think of it. But my people had creatures like him in our legends, seven-headed, flying lizard monsters. Some people said that my tribe was the tribe of the snake people, that we could change into flying serpents." She shrugged. "My husband, Toussaint Charbonneau, says that the dragon looks like a European idea of a dragon because the magic being took over the body of a European. It wanted a body closer to the land, which is why it wanted to possess the body of my son."

She saw the skeptical expression in Clark's eyes. "Feel free not to believe it, but if you believe in magic and revenants and monsters, you should perhaps also credit my heightened senses as well."

Meriwether pressed, "Other than his terrifying form as a dragon, who else works for the creature?"

"Anyone it can capture, across all the land. It can reanimate the dead so that they do his bidding…except for the three drunken revenants of your men, possibly because the liquor protected them. Your Whiskey Revenants are still dead, and still animated, but they're not tools of the dragon. But his other captives live in a waking dream, like my husband. I tried to get Charbonneau to come with me, but he didn't have enough willpower to stay awake and escape. Neither did his other wife." She looked very sad. "Some captives are ill, or otherwise taken over by him. He even possessed the Canoti, the little people from the mound. Now they also do his commands."

Meriwether felt a chill. "We climbed the mound, but did not see the little people."

"They are fearsome fighters even in a dream state." Sacagawea looked at each of them in turn. "I cannot say that the dragon would be easy to overcome, should you try. But I believe you could do it, and that would rid the countryside of this terrible scourge, and free my husband to look after his family. He has never even seen his son."

Meriwether looked at Clark, and he could see that they both agreed. Still, he remained troubled. With magical forces like that, what could their little party do against such a great enemy? How could they storm its lair?

"So far, I judge that our enemy has sent less than its full force against us. If such is the case, we might survive, as we did before. But if we try to beard the thing in its lair, we will surely never finish our expedition."

Clark added, "If we tried to fight all these creatures at once, we will be quite undone, and dead. And then we might be added to its army of revenants."

Meriwether expected that Sacagawea would look impatient or angry at their reluctance. Instead, she inclined her head. "Then we will part ways here at Fort Mandan. You go to the far ocean, while Pompy and I try to rescue his father."

Stark and clear in his mind, Meriwether knew they couldn't let her do that. He had saved this woman and her child at birth, and he could not let her take such a risk without protection.

Sacagawea was competent and accustomed to the arcane territories, but even in good times, without the shadow of evil magic, the land was full of perils. A lone woman with a child couldn't see every danger. That was why tribes formed, and why families traveled together.

He said, gravely, "I understand and honor your wish to rescue your husband, but the truth is, Sacagawea, that we likely cannot do it as we are now. But if you come with us, instead of sacrificing yourself in a fruitless attempt, perhaps we can find some power or discover something—" He took hope from the secret they both shared, from the dream in which he'd defeated the dragon. "Maybe then the dragon will be easier to defeat."

She stood there in the small room, the baby sleeping on her back. She looked from one captain to the other, studying their worthiness and how much they could be trusted. Finally she gave a curt nod. "I shall try. Unless we find a way to strike at the dragon first."

She ducked through the curtain out of the room, and shortly afterward they heard her scolding the wives of the interpreters, directing them to some task.

"I hope I talked her into the right decision," Meriwether said.

"Surely you did," Clark said. "We could not leave her here determined to fight that creature, alone with the babe."

"But what if we can't fight the evil force? What if we get to the coast and find passage? Are we going to leave her alone with this danger?"

Clark looked perturbed. "No. Once we've proved it can be done, we'll come back and save her husband for her. I wonder what manner of man he must be, and what he did to win such an exceptional woman."

Meriwether agreed, but he had no answer.

My Dearest Julia,

The packing is nearly complete. We are sending our keelboat back downriver to St. Louis loaded with our discoveries, journals, charts, specimens, and these letters. Some of our men will pilot the boat back and send a detailed report to wizard Franklin.

The rest of us, though, will venture forth into a land that no European, or at least none that maintained contact with civilization, has ever seen. We passed a remarkably quiet, though cold, winter at Fort Mandan, and now that the river ice has thinned enough to crack, we shall follow the waters again, in hopes of finding the far side of the world. It will be a grand adventure, but perhaps not too terrible, since the local natives assure us we can cross the continental divide in no more than half a day, and then we should have an easy passage to the Pacific—if such exists.

We are all in good spirits. We've convinced our intrepid native woman, Sacagawea Charbonneau, to join our party. She has proved herself quite adept at finding roots and berries to supplement our diet, especially on lean evenings when our hunters brought back no meat. She keeps a strong hand on the few women that straggle along with our party. In exchange, we keep her safe, along with her little boy Pomp. Working together, maybe we all can reach the Pacific.

After a month of frantic planning and arrangements, we have supplies, dry clothes, and even buffalo robes, traded from the nearby tribes. We are now ready to go on.

The locals and even Sacagawea have misgivings about us continuing our journey, but Lewis and I have seen nothing to indicate that the strange magical attacks against us are about to resume, now that Spring has awakened. Perhaps the evil force—Sacagawea tells us it originated from a trapper captured by a local spirit—sleeps still.

We have seen only one recent sign of any supernatural occurrence, when we once again encountered the hideous damned revenants of Willard, Collins, and Hall. We repelled them as they attempted to steal *a barrel of whiskey we intended to pack into the boat. We drove off the undead forms of our former comrades, and they vanished into the forest. We do not know what animates them, nor why they still have such a thirst for the liquor that had gotten them killed.*

Unlike the other undead, our Whiskey Revenants have not decayed visibly. They remain recognizable to us, and Captain Lewis suspects they'd drunk so much of the whiskey that they are now permanently preserved. They keep singing the same drinking song, which is how we were able to detect them and repel their assault on our supplies.

We carry with us a tent built in the Indian manner, with tall poles, covered in tanned buffalo hides sewn together with sinew. As we travel, we have determined that this portable structure will protect Lewis, Sacagawea, little Pompy and myself from the still-brisk air.

We have two large canoes, and five small pirogues. Not quite the grand fleet with which we departed from St. Louis, but we shall be more agile, more mobile, in case we should face something terrible.

Not that anything will happen to us, of course.

I hope to complete this expedition soon and be back home to you without delay.

Yours, faithfully,
William Clark

—Letter from William Clark to Julia Hancock,
April 7, 1805

Dragons and Serpents

MANY MORE MILES, AND ANOTHER CAMP. CAPTAIN CLARK HAD gone out hunting with a party of men, while other members of the expedition erected the tent and built a large fire. Meriwether elected to stay behind, ostensibly to guard their base camp against possible magical assaults, but he hoped to have a private moment with Sacagawea so he could discuss the matter of dragons.

Such a secret conversation had been near impossible in the crowded confines of Fort Mandan, where they would surely have been overheard. Now he hoped to have time alone with her. He knew she had information that he required.

In the midafternoon, Sacagawea went off in search of wild artichokes, and now she stood on the riverbank, running a thin reed into the muddy sand, near scattered driftwood. From the camp, he watched the native woman poke the sharpened stick into the river sand, pull it back, and poke it in again. She withdrew a spiny green ball, made a sound of triumph, and knelt to dig at the hole with both hands, collecting several of the green, spiny balls. The baby asleep on her back bounced without waking.

Meriwether approached her with an innocent question. "Wild artichokes grow like that? Without external foliage?" He was genuinely curious, with his background in various native plants, and he spoke loudly enough that the men starting the fire behind them would hear him and think nothing of it.

Sacagawea looked at him, with the half smile that came to her lips more often, especially when he showed ignorance in what she considered to be everyday knowledge. On anyone else, the smile might have seemed condescending or infuriating, but on her it seemed more amusing, showing neither fear nor undue respect.

"No, they are large thistles and they grow tall," she said. "But the water rats collect them in a hole so they can eat them when food runs low. See, it's a rat's larder."

"Oh," he said, interested. He picked up one of the spiny balls to examine it. "I'll make a note of it in my journals." Now that he had established that their talk was of wild artichokes, he lowered his voice. "You saw the dream dragon. My battle in the sky, on the night you came to the fort."

She looked at him, puzzled. "Dream?"

"That night I dreamed I was a dragon myself, and I fought the great dragon, the creature that holds the land's evil magic in thrall. I battled him in the air, and I bit him on the neck, and I defeated him, at least for a while. But only moments after I thought I vanquished him, I was awakened to tend to you and help you deliver your baby." He furrowed his brows. "But you said you saw me fight."

Confused, she let the prized artichokes drop from her hand down onto the bank. "But it is not a dream." She spoke so loudly that he glanced over his shoulder to reassure himself that the men had not heard.

He put his finger to his lips to caution her. "But I was in my bed, and it felt like a dream. What else can it be? And how did you see it?"

"It is a . . . a spirit. A spirit journey. Part of your essence transforms into your dragon. When I was twelve, I discovered that I could turn my spirit into a bird and go wandering. The things I saw were true, and others could see my bird form. It is not a dream, Captain Lewis."

He didn't understand. "But if it is not a dream, it doesn't matter what—"

"But it does!" She remembered to keep her voice low, but the fierce whisper was full of meaning. "You can fight the evil dragon in your spirit form, and you won this time. I expect he underestimated you, and you surprised him. But he can also kill you. It is not just a dream, and if you fought him without knowing it was dangerous—" She looked appalled.

"And if my spirit dragon gets killed?" Meriwether felt too foolish to finish the question.

"You die. Your dream dragon is a great portion of your spirit."

Though he was quite familiar with the powers and vagaries of magic in the arcane territories, he could not help but think like a natural scientist. "But how can it be both a spirit and a physical entity? And both are part of me?"

Sacagawea shrugged. "Why does the sun rise in the sky? It just does, and it just is."

He considered explaining the sun, but knew it would be futile. Sacagawea meant that not knowing how something worked did not mean it didn't exist. Even though he had promised Franklin he would keep detailed journals and send back a wealth of exotic specimens, he knew that the magic that infused the land was not so easily categorized or interpreted. Nevertheless, the magic must have its own sort of science, its own rules. And his dreams were part of them.

Meriwether had suffered the strange dreams as long as he could remember. He had seen his dream self wandering the Virginia woods around his house, but he'd thought nothing of it, because he had known those places so well. But what if he had been spirit walking?

He thought of the night of the blizzard, when this desperate young woman had fought her way to the fort. "You said you came to me because of the dragon. You sensed me, knew me. Is that why? Because you thought I could fight him?"

"I sensed that you could keep him at bay, at least for a little while," Sacagawea said. "I had no other place to run. The evil had followed me and sent its minions after me."

Meriwether remembered the voice. "He said he wanted his bird and her egg. He meant you and the baby, didn't he?"

Sacagawea's eyes went wide. "I should not have asked you to fight him without knowing how deadly he is," she said. "But you are strong in a very special way, and I think he is afraid of you. That is why he tries so hard to destroy your expedition, before you can discover who you are."

Meriwether found the very idea amazing. How could a creature who manipulated magic so well, and who possessed such resources drawn from the land itself, be afraid of any power Meriwether Lewis could wield? Though he might be good at hunting and exploring, had no notable ability in magic, other than dreaming about dragons.

He remembered the dark force's voice in his head, vowing that they would meet again...and how thoroughly it had knocked him out. Had that adversary rifled through his mind while Meriwether lay unconscious? And what had it found that made it so afraid?

Before she could give him more answers, Captain Clark and his party stumbled back into the camp, carrying a fine buck and a brace of birds they'd shot. The rest of the men gathered with excitement for the feast, and they all spent the afternoon and evening dressing, cutting, and cooking the meat.

That night, as he slept in the large tent of buffalo hides strung over the framework of poles, Meriwether woke to find Sacagawea nursing her son in the half light. Embarrassed, he turned away and tried to go back to sleep.

So much about this woman intrigued him. She knew more about this land than he did, and she had escaped great evil and come on such a perilous journey alone...yet, she had put her faith in Meriwether. When he finally dozed again, he dreamed that she turned into a bird and soared high above the camp, a beautiful eagle, free against the sky....

Hours later, he woke to an empty tent. When he emerged into the chill, damp morning he accepted coffee and a slice of cold corn bread from Pryor. While he ate, the men broke down the tent and stowed what they'd unpacked the night before.

The men remembered how to pack in a hurry, and they did so with little confusion. Guided by occasional comments from Captain Clark, their operation was like a well-practiced military drill, and even the small group of interpreters' wives and mistresses showed a hint of discipline.

Sacagawea returned from the river, gliding through the bustle. She wore one of the new outfits of quill-embroidered leather she'd traded for with the tribe near Fort Mandan, probably using berries or medicinal herbs. Her outfit was butter-colored, and the quills had been dyed many colors. Meriwether thought she looked splendid, but her too-young face bore a worried expression. Tied to her back, Pompy played with her hair.

Stepping up to Meriwether, she reported, "It is still cold for our journey into the mountains. The men had to use the paddles to break the pirogues and canoes out of the ice that formed overnight."

He frowned. The air felt cool, but not bitter on his face.

Granted, they had slept in the shelter of the tent, but he didn't remember the cold being intense enough to justify ice on the river. "Did we really have a hard freeze last night?"

"No," Sacagawea said. "It is the magic, pulling energy from the river. He is not strong enough yet with the spring just awakening, and throughout the winter he could do little more than keep the revenants from rotting and hold his living slaves in thrall. Even so, he can pull power from certain regions, certain places. And the river is now ever-moving and has a great deal of life and power in its movement."

Meriwether pursed his lips, trying to hide his anxiety. "So, what should we do? We need to keep moving."

"I would stay away from the river today, but I doubt you will believe that is possible."

Meriwether knew not to dismiss her concerns, but after so many months of waiting in Fort Mandan, the expedition needed to push west and explore more territory. "Let me ask Captain Clark."

His partner was supervising the packing and the breakdown of camp. When Meriwether explained Sacagawea's concerns about the ice and the draining magical force, Clark considered, then shrugged. "The men say that sometimes the river is colder than the air, and we might find thin ice on it well into the spring. It is no reason to postpone our trip. We can't delay for every inconvenience."

Meriwether was not so quick to dismiss her worries. "But what if the ice signifies another attack on us? The great magic could be testing its powers."

"All the more reason to keep moving," Clark said. "Remember our previous encounters with the dark magic. Only the river and our swift travel allowed us to escape unscathed. If the attack intensifies, what good would it do us to remain here, huddled in camp? Should we all run in different directions along the bank?" Clark surveyed the river's edge, the rocks, thickets of drift wood, impenetrable underbrush. "I would rather be on the river."

Meriwether could not disagree with that, and Sacagawea accepted the decision. Nevertheless, he made sure to have his air rifle close, pumped and ready, and insisted that the four men in his pirogue were similarly armed.

Together, the canoes and pirogues set off into the river, using oars for direction, pulling against the surprisingly rapid current. Before long, the river narrowed and they found themselves passing between quite steep banks of golden stone, dotted with scraggly trees that clung to pockets of soil.

Suddenly, the air seemed to dim, as it had at Tavern Rock nearly a year ago. The sounds of the world grew muffled, as if a thin blanket had been draped over them. Noticing the difference, Meriwether grew tense and wary.

A scream came from one of the canoes ahead, the boat carrying Sacagawea. He saw it tilting perilously, and then the water itself lurched up, raising the canoe. It looked like a green rock...and then the rock moved, curled, slithered. They were coils, semitransparent, glistening, wet coils, like the skin of a great monster.

A roar-hiss erupted from the river, drowning out the alarmed shouts. A sinuous body rose from the current, as tall as both canoes end to end. At the end of the snakelike neck, the creature's head looked part lion, part lizard, with broad golden eyes and glistening fangs. More serpentine coils spread across the river surface, ensnaring every one of their boats, tipping them. In one of the pirogues, the big dog Seaman barked and barked.

As Meriwether's pirogue tilted wildly beneath him, he grabbed his air rifle and aimed, but his shot went wide of the mark. With a yelp, he found himself plunged into the deep, cold water. Sacagawea was in the water, swimming. Baby Pompy was wailing, his head barely above the water. Crates, papers, and parcels floated everywhere, strewn about from the capsized boats. The men frantically struggled to escape the coils and swim for the high-banked shore, although Pryor and York tried to save some of the supplies. Seaman paddled toward the bank, snapping at a coil that came too close to his muzzle.

Struggling in the water, Sacagawea tried to turn a pirogue right-side up again. Meriwether stroked over to her and helped her. Treading water in the swift current, she started throwing packages into the pirogue, saving their supplies. She shouted to him, "*You* have to stop it!"

Meriwether didn't know what she meant. Did she mean he had to become the dragon? How could he do that? He had only dreamed it, and he still only half believed what she had told him. He couldn't just call on some imaginary inner magic.

The water-serpent's coils pulled Peter Weiser up out of the water and dangled him before its maw before popping him in, still screaming. The serpent's tail plunged back into the water, coiled around Meriwether's legs.

As she clung to the side of the pirogue, Sacagawea lifted her hand, palm open. A bird flew from her hand, a magnificent, powerful eagle that appeared out of nowhere. The raptor swooped in, flying directly into the serpent's golden eyes, attacking.

Sacagawea's body grasped the boat, but Meriwether sensed that she was not really there. Her mind and heart were inside that eagle, screaming a challenge at the river monster.

If only he could do the same...

Meriwether used his belt knife to stab at the serpent, but the creature only coiled tighter around him, squeezing, raising him partway out of the water. Sacagawea's eagle continued to harass its face. The serpent snapped its jaws, nearly catching the eagle's wing. Two loose feathers drifted away as the bird swooped in the air.

She had said that if the spirit form died, then the person would die.

Meriwether blocked all thoughts of the constricting slimy coils around him, and he *willed* himself up in the air. He felt something leave him, and suddenly he was the dragon, flying, roaring. He didn't know if he could breathe fire, like that other attacking dragon in St. Louis. He spread his dream wings in the air and evaded the serpent's lunge for him. His dragon form flew closer and interposed himself between the monster and Sacagawea's eagle. Meriwether spread his hooked claws and raked at the eyes of the river serpent. He felt the satisfying snaring of tissue, ripping scales, flesh, and jellied eyes.

The river serpent scream-hissed, and its sinuous glistening neck wavered like a reed in wind, back and forth. Trembling, shuddering...

The monster screamed one more time and then, like the antediluvian lizard, it exploded, tore itself apart, and collapsed inward. One moment the monster thrashed and writhed in its attack, gross and blood-spattered, and then it simply fell apart, spraying in chunks and gobbets.

Meriwether was once again in the cold river water, going down, down, down, into the swift current, striking against submerged rocks, grabbing at fallen, waterlogged trees, rushed along by the current.

Hands grabbed him and pulled him out of the water. He could barely see, but he flailed his arms, trying to help. York dragged him to the shore, while Clark shouted orders to the other terrified men. "The monster is dead! And we'll all be dead unless we retrieve our boats and supplies. Get in the water and collect what you can!"

A gunshot rang out, and Meriwether blinked, saw Clark raising his rifle to shoot at three...creatures, revenants that moved in a halting and strange way. He shook himself, flung river water out of his eyes, and saw that the three revenants appeared to be the tattered remains of Hall, Collins, and Willard, still lurking along with the expedition. The three dead men seized a barrel of whiskey that had washed up along the bank, and they shambled off with their prize. Clark fired again, but his shot missed.

Meriwether lacked the strength to be interested. Becoming the spirit dragon, fighting the river monster, had drained him, as well as nearly drowning in the rushing river. He collapsed on the narrow bank near the high rock walls, but he struggled to sit up, looking around to find Sacagawea. She was dripping wet, and the baby still wailed on her back, but she was alive and intact.

While the rest of the men scavenged what they could and looked about for any appropriate patch of ground that might serve as a camp, Clark came up to him, sloshing through the shallow water. "I saw the dragon." His expression was grim and serious. "I believe that you and I need to talk, Lewis."

Before Meriwether could answer, a cry came from Sacagawea, "Charbonneau!" She scrambled through the shallows, sloshing her way to the rocks and sparse trees toward a rough-looking stranger who sat on a narrow strip of sand, looking dazed. "Charbonneau! Mon ami!"

Secrets and Powers

AFTER THEY GATHERED THEIR BOATS AND AS MANY SUPPLIES AND specimens they could manage, the surviving members of the expedition worked their way down the river to a place where the cliffs rose far enough from the banks to leave space for a camp. In the curved recess and overhang of stone, they also had a defensible position in case they should face another magical attack. As the darkness gathered and they huddled next to several small campfires, trying to dry their sodden clothes before the full cold of night set in, Meriwether kept listening for the sound of wings or big trampling feet.

They had brought Sacagawea's displaced and dazed husband along with them, still trying to learn answers. She squatted by the fire, attempting to tend to Charbonneau. He looked wrung out and pale, like an old threadbare rag. Many other members of the expedition were similarly in shock after the attack of the river monster, and now they gathered their shreds of sanity about them.

Meriwether approached her. "You were right about the dragon, Madame Charbonneau." She nodded, absorbed in trying to get soup into her husband's slack mouth. He was thin, with hanging skin folds, dark and deeply sunk eyes, and had a haunted look as if he'd been dragged through the gates of Hell.

Charbonneau had shown no interest in his son, nor even asked the sex or age of the baby. Pompy, in turn, had refused to go near him, instead crying so shrilly that Sacagawea had handed him to Captain Clark, who had offered to hold the child, while she tended to her husband.

And she clearly did so with great devotion, which elicited a strange twinge of jealousy in Meriwether. Ever since she had come to Fort Mandan, he had done his best to distance himself from Sacagawea and not think of her as a woman. In fact, if he thought of her as a woman, the whole scene of her patiently spooning soup into her husband's mouth hurt. Not only because she was married to a bigamous, no-account trapper, but because she obviously cared for the man, no matter what he had done. And though Meriwether knew that no spark of romance could ever happen between them, no alliance or link be permitted, he could not help the way his mind protested the thought.

"She is so different from us," he told himself. "After all that has happened to her, she seems perfectly happy, so long as she has food and shelter for herself and her child." *Charbonneau's* child.

Leaving her, he went to join Clark, who was feeding Pompy spoons of soup and talking to him, as though the child were an adult. When Meriwether sat next to him and the baby, Clark said, "Sacagawea was right enough in her warnings this morning. I should have listened. She knew that the unexpected ice on the river was an indication of some big magic." He stared at Meriwether a long time. "And while we were being attacked I thought I saw a dragon. I knew it had some connection to you. How do you explain it?"

"I am trying to find explanations of my own, but as yet I have none to give." He gazed into the smoky fire, but felt little warmth from his clammy clothes. "What matters most is that Sacagawea knew. She was correct that the dark force that has lain dormant throughout the winter is beginning to awaken again and gain strength. And she was correct that I would find some unexpected strength inside me that could fight it."

Pompy made complaining noises when Clark forgot to keep feeding him, and the man gave him another spoonful. "What can you tell me about this dragon you summoned? And the eagle that Sacagawea controlled? I certainly know the tale of how you fought beside the wizard Franklin, but I didn't know you were a wizard yourself." He gave his friend a wry smile. "Such great magic could have been useful to our expedition all along the way."

Meriwether let out a deprecating laugh. "I am no wizard. The dragon that appeared to fight the river monster seems to be a part of me, some extension of my spirit or my dreams, which I can't fully identify or control." With a sigh, realizing that this was no time for secrets between him and his close companion, he told the story of his relationship with the dream beast, from earliest childhood.

We will meet again, son of Wales.

Clark looked intrigued, and not the least bit skeptical. "Why did you not tell me before this?"

Meriwether looked down at his hands in the crackling fire-light, then back up at Clark. "Tell you what? That sometimes I dream of a dragon? I had no idea the thing was real in any sense until Sacagawea said she saw it as she was trying to reach Fort Mandan. She explained to me that it is a dragon of the spirit, something connected to me from my European heritage where such legends originated. And if I use my spirit dragon to fight the great magic, I can die—here, in my physical body."

Clark spoon-fed the baby to give him a moment to think. "A dream dragon would have been of great use scouting the countryside. Could you not summon it earlier, if you've known about it all your life?"

Meriwether fidgeted. "I have had the dreams, but I never understood them. They started the night I learned my father died, and I always thought that it was a boy's way to cope with bereavement. I feared that if I spoke about it, people would think I'd gone mad. My neighbors in Virginia already considered me eccentric if not insane because I went hunting in the dead of night, in the dark of winter, sometimes having forgotten to put my shoes on. So I allowed them to think I was just a boy, unhappy at home, rather than a man haunted by a dragon."

Clark got down to business. "Now we do need to talk about it and decide what we're going to do. And how your power could possibly help us. We lost Peter Weiser—that monster devoured him whole. We can't afford to have more of our men eaten by some magical horror, and we can't proceed with the survey if our steps are dogged by infernal creatures doing the bidding of some unknown enemy."

"You're right," Meriwether agreed. "I wish we had indeed brought the wizard Franklin along. Sacagawea insists that we should fight the great magic first, before pressing on to find the Pacific Ocean." He paused. "She had a different priority, though. She wanted to break her husband from the thrall of the evil force.

And now..." He looked across the camp to where Sacagawea was pulling a moist blanket over the seemingly insensible Charbonneau.

Clark frowned. "You think she may no longer have the incentive to battle that great magic, now that she has the man back? If he really *is* back. He seems like little more than an empty shell. My God, the horrors he must have experienced."

Meriwether tried to convince himself that his suspicion was not in any way caused by jealousy. "Though I do wonder at the coincidence of his appearance, here and now. It seems too much like a hunter baiting a trap."

"That fact has not escaped me," Clark said. "Though it is possible that when your spirit dragon killed the river serpent, you weakened the evil force... weakened it sufficiently to make it lose its hold on Charbonneau."

Meriwether nodded, though he wasn't convinced. "That sounds perfectly reasonable. I do not know the rules or the energy required to animate serpents or revenants, or giant reptiles. Even so, I suggest we remain on guard. I don't fancy being the mouse in a game of cat and mouse." He stared over at the huddled, unresponsive man, and Sacagawea sitting close beside him. "And yet, all the reasons we chose not to attack the source of the evil still stand. The great magic is too powerful for us to make any impression at all, even if Sacagawea could guide us to it. We would be sacrificing ourselves in vain."

Clark inclined his head. "And yet we must find a solution."

The two men went to sleep in the makeshift tent of tall saplings and salvaged buffalo hides. Sacagawea collected her baby from Captain Clark and said that she and her husband would sleep by the side of river, under some branches.

In the middle of the night, Meriwether was awakened by the sound of a baby crying, enhanced by a sudden sharp scream from Sacagawea. He was bolting out of the tent, half dressed. He was halfway to the source of the alarm before he realized he had instinctively grabbed his air rifle.

Other men from the camp rushed to the place, crowding at the foot of the little shelter of branches. Sacagawea stood there, pale and shaking, holding her child. "Pompy was crying. My husband turned without noticing, and—"

Even by the scant light of the fires and the distant moon, Meriwether could see the imprint of a palm upon her face. He did not like it. The dazed, miserable Charbonneau had slapped her? Was this no-account bigamist trapper also a wife-beater? He stepped forward, indignant. Why should such a remarkable woman endure such a relationship?

The befuddled, haunted Charbonneau seemed annoyed that he had caused such a fuss, and he crawled back under the meager shelter of branches. After a moment, head down, Sacagawea joined him.

Meriwether watched, but there was nothing he could do. The other men shook their heads, smiling and relieved that the matter was such a minor one. They drifted back to their sleeping places. Those men might all be the same, he thought. More than once, he and Clark had been forced to break up domestic disputes, especially early in the trip, when the interpreters and trappers had brought more wives or lovers along. Such offhand violence might be the common thing of men who lived at the frontier and close to the land.

Back in the big tent, he slept little and badly, worried about the woman and her child as much as he feared the enemy dragon and the great evil magic. He still sensed something deeply wrong about Toussaint Charbonneau. And he was sure that others could see it, too. Even the baby Pompy, who was used to the company of rough men, objected to being too close to his father.

Several times during the night, when Meriwether peered through the tent flap, he saw Sacagawea pacing or sitting by the light of their small fire, rather than beside her husband.

What did she sense? And why did she not do something about it?

My Dearest Julia,

I write with no hope that you will receive this until our expedition is concluded and we are all safely back home, but still these letters make me feel closer to you. Perhaps it is my way of assessing our adventures and ordeals.

I do not wish to engage in melancholy thought, but as our travails grow more and more extreme, it is all too possible that the times ahead may hold death for me. We continue to run across unforeseen and magical perils, and should I die, at least these letters will make their way back to you.

When the natives told us we could cross the continental divide in less than a day, they were either lying or they naively misled us. Great, craggy mountains loom up before us now, and it is clear that it will be at least the work of several days to cross them and reach more hospitable lands beyond. Some of the peaks are so high they retain a blanket of snow, even after the long, warm months of spring.

After the river monster overturned our embarkations, we delayed long enough in our sheltered camp to dry everything and to take inventory of what we had lost. Fortunately, a good portion of our provisions and supplies came through unscathed, though Captain Lewis says we lost much of his stock of medicinal plants. He and the Indian woman Sacagawea hope to find replacement magical herbs as we continue our journey.

Captain Lewis is also very worried about Toussaint Charbonneau, the recovered husband of Sacagawea, and on that account I must agree with his concerns. Having spoken to some of our other interpreters, I know that the man was always considered a lout. He is a mongrel, partly English, partly French, with some measure of native blood too. He has made his living as a trapper and as guide to the occasional party of travelers. Charbonneau seems to have ill-defined morals and few limits to what he will do if he believes it suits him. I gather that he's honest within the bounds of not stealing, *and truthful within the bounds of not getting caught, but he is not a pleasant man. He treats the natives poorly, or any man who has no power over him. He also mistreats his wife, the mother of his child.*

But perhaps there is a reason. Since his escape from the terrible ordeal of the dark evil force, he seems deeply affected, perhaps damaged. If he has his full wits about him, he conceals them remarkably well. Though he reappeared among us some days ago, he has yet to provide an account of his captivity, or explain how he came to be on the riverbank when the monster serpent perished. In fact, he has yet to speak comprehensible words at all. His own dear infant son will not bear his company for any length of time without venting the most pitiful wails.

Sacagawea, who is also not fond of describing her captivity in the lair of the evil force, explains that Charbonneau is still afflicted by the terror of what he's witnessed. I'm am not so certain. Perhaps she is making excuses? But who am I to say? I do not know enough about the magic in these arcane territories to say what could be affecting him, or how it could affect us.

I will watch Charbonneau and keep the little boy safe while we direct this expedition farther westward across the formidable, rocky range of mountains before us. Yes, it will take more than half a day to cross this bulwark that rises before us.

One last point of concern: we have encountered many remnants of native camps where almost everything has been burnt to cinders. We don't understand what might have caused such a disaster, but we fear magic is the culprit.

I will endeavor to remain alert and unscathed so that I return to you, my dearest Julia.

—Letter from William Clark to Julia Hancock,
May 5, 1805

On the Trail

"THESE WERE NOT MY PEOPLE," SACAGAWEA SAID. HER OBVIOUS relief made her voice tremble a little. "Though there is not much left."

They stood in the midst of a burned-out expanse, littered with charred scraps of what had once been fifty or so buffalo-hide tents, much like the one the expedition carried with them. One set of poles still stood, blackened and hollow. Meriwether guessed it would crumble to black dust at a touch. The furious heat had swept through so swiftly, even the burned ghost structures retained their shape. Bits of twisted, charred leather clung to skeletal frameworks, and in other places whole tents had been engulfed in fire, leaving only a black circle of destruction.

"But no skeletons," Meriwether said. "No blackened bones, either of people or horses. For that we can be grateful. They must have survived the conflagration." Then he swallowed hard. "Survived, or been taken."

Clark paced around the camp, crunching ash with his boots. He kicked at the soot-covered rocks laid out in a fire circle, but now the entire village had burned. "Might it not be a natural phenomenon? A blaze sparked by lightning?"

Both Meriwether and his friend knew he spoke nonsense. "We have found more than a dozen villages in the same condition. What kind of lightning deigns to strike only settlements, and burns everything entire?"

Clark kicked another rock.

Sacagawea picked up a moccasin that looked to have been

133

flung down in great haste, then glanced over at Meriwether. Her deep brown eyes met his. "The great dragon can spit fire. The enemy could burn any village it finds."

Meriwether felt his skin crawl. "That explanation would fit what we see." He shook his head, unable to tear his eyes from the destruction. Had the villagers fled the approach of the fiery beast, or had it captured them, placed them in thrall as it had done to Sacagawea? "What would the evil force have to gain by burning native encampments? To inspire terror? Purely for the joy of causing destruction?"

"Some magical creatures draw power from fear," Sacagawea said. She sniffed the ash, moved lightly through the scorched remnants of the village. "It doesn't seem right. I don't think this was a dragon attack, but I don't know what it could have been."

The others in the party cautiously circled the edge of the village, sorting through scattered discarded objects. Since they had seen similar sites of disaster before, their horror had diminished somewhat. But they still had no answers, nor had they found any of the escaping villagers whom they could interrogate.

Thinking of this, Meriwether stepped closer to Sacagawea. "People who ran with very few of their possessions should not be difficult to find. Did they just disappear into the mountains?"

She bent to touch the ash on the ground. "They will have horses, so they can travel fast and far from our route. I hope they are safe."

Clark called the people to order so they could move on, knowing from past experience they would find nothing in the burned village. They had to get back to the river and their boats, so they could press on. As the men prepared to leave, Charbonneau sauntered out of the fringes of the forest. The strange man still had spoken no words.

Meriwether blinked as he caught sight of Sacagawea's husband. For just an instant as the man emerged from the trees, he thought he had seen a giant creature beside him, a dark and furry beast like a huge bear. But then the shape melted into the forest shadows, and Charbonneau kept walking, unaffected.

Meriwether narrowed his eyes, but he could prove nothing. Still, he would keep a close watch on the stranger who had claimed Sacagawea as his wife.

✧   ✧   ✧

"Up, up! *Fire!*" The screams woke Meriwether, and he lunged out of their buffalo-hide tent. Clark scrambled out beside him, rubbing his eyes in the same confused way.

In the camp around them, people ran in a panic, while others just stood and pointed. Meriwether turned to look up at the nearby ridge, and he saw... Fire.

At first he thought a tall tree had caught fire, but then he realized the blaze had a human shape, with a pair of arms and legs. It spread out its limbs, also giving the impression of branches.

And it moved closer, shambling along and trailing bright fire, feathered by intense flames. It picked up speed, loping toward them.

"Faster!" a man cried as he sped past Meriwether. "We can save the tent, and the camp!" He realized he was the last in a bucket brigade line the men had formed. The fiery being still crashed toward them, too far away, but they could throw the water on the hides of the tent, on their own shelters. They drenched their own possessions, and when the flaming being lurched into the perimeter of the camp, Meriwether flung the bucket's contents directly at it.

The water struck the bottom of the creature's legs, sizzled loudly, and sent up a gushing cloud of steam. For a moment, with the fires briefly doused, he saw a tangled mess of human bones before the intense flames came roaring back, like an incandescent skin. The creature roared closer, throwing off heat as if from an open oven.

Meriwether vividly remembered the moment at Tavern Rock when he'd stuck his knife blade into the bluff face, and the pure forged metal, a talisman of civilization, had broken the spell, driven off the attacking crows. As the flaming creature crashed closer, igniting trees and underbrush, Meriwether thought of the dozens of incinerated villages, knew they had no chance.

He had nothing to lose, no matter what his rational mind told him.

He pulled his long knife out of the sheath on his hip. Without pausing to think, he took hold of the hilt, snapped back his hand, and hurled it. Exactly as he had skewered scampering squirrels in the Virginia woods, he flung the blade.

His knife flew true, streaking directly into the fiery being's heart... if such a creature had a heart. He was sure the blade would melt, drip into molten metal to puddle on the ground.

But instead the blazing man shimmered, flickered...then exploded into sparks and whistling flames that spun into the darkness. Burning pieces of trees and human bodies spewed out of its form, as if it had been assembled from the pieces of a thousand funeral pyres. Bones and branches flew in every direction.

On the other side of the camp, Toussaint Charbonneau let out an inhuman scream.

Scattered fires caught in various parts of the camp, and the bucket brigade scrambled around, throwing river water on any small blaze.

Meriwether stared, his eyes dazzled from the brilliant eruption and the sudden darkness as the flame creature was extinguished.

In the aftermath the camp seemed very quiet and very dark. The men were stomping out the last few scattered blazes. He heard someone retching, sick with terror.

"Captain," York said, close by. The big former slave stepped up to him, and his expression looked sick. "Captain Lewis, there are people in there, people twisted in this stuff of roots and branches that made up its body. All broken and burned, but countless pieces, little bodies. Children..."

"I see," Meriwether said in a hoarse voice, but he didn't see. He seemed to be walking in a nightmare. How many more attacks would they suffer before they reached the west coast? Every new landscape they traversed seemed to spawn some new magical horror, like this fiery beast composed of burning trees and bodies. What if they couldn't go on this way?

The sound of loud retching continued, and he saw Toussaint Charbonneau on his knees, with Sacagawea kneeling next to him. She seemed to be whispering something. Now he recalled hearing Charbonneau's scream the instant his knife pierced the shambling creature of fire and horror. Was there some connection?

Shaken men and women went around the camp, putting out the last of the fires and also collecting the shattered and extinguished pieces of the fiery thing, the remnants of the human bodies that comprised its supernatural form. Clark was shouting for the men to get their shovels, to dig a grave where they could deposit the remnants of the humans trapped inside the demon's form. What kind of evil force would kill children and twist them among pieces of trees, then set the whole on fire to create a living golem of destruction?

Even back east, many people considered magic and wizardry to be unnatural, threatening. Despite his fame and his numerous good deeds, Benjamin Franklin was considered a sorcerer and possibly dangerous. Some had even called for him to be burned for witchcraft, as the Bible proscribed. Meriwether had not given it a second thought, for he had revered the great wizard. He remembered how eager he had been just to catch a glimpse of the man in the St. Louis town square. And Franklin's powers were certainly remarkable.

But now Meriwether saw a much darker side of magic, the sort of thing the preachers called black witchcraft, dangerous magic that robbed creatures of their souls. They had seen other instances during their long expedition, but this creature of fire and death that had visited them tonight—no doubt the same being that had torched dozens of native villages—was the epitome of the twisted, evil magic.

In the back of his mind, he felt a stirring, a sinister laughter, and he knew it was the dark dragon, angry, longing for vengeance. He drew in a breath, hard, then held it, used it to control himself, including that spirit part of him that he refused to admit.

Stumbling away in the darkness while the frightened people busied themselves at the camp, he circled around to the main tent where he and Clark slept. Fortunately, because the bucket brigade had doused the buffalo hides, the tent had snuffed out the scattered embers that pelted it when the fiery creature exploded. A pile of debris, smoking remnants from the creature, lay scattered to one side of the tent poles. Even in the dim light, he could see that a grinning, soot-smeared human skull surmounted the pile. The smell of charred remains reminded him both of a fireplace and a charnel house.

"Sir," a soot-smeared Richard Windsor said, hurrying forward to extend Meriwether's knife. "We found it in the main pile of debris."

He accepted the knife, looked at the blackened blade, the cracked hilt. A strange discoloration made the tip shine violet under the scant light of the moon.

Windsor kept blinking at him. "How did you know the knife would kill it, Captain? My granny from old England used to tell me about hobgoblins and boggarts that fear steel, but here in this strange land—"

"Once before, the touch of steel drove back a magical attack." He turned the knife over in his hand. It still seemed warm. "I decided to take a chance."

He helped the men dig their holes and bury the scattered remains, seeing the mixed remnants of human bodies twisted into the roots and branches, all grown together and ignited. He prayed those poor victims had been dead when they were incorporated into the demon's body.

Finally, near dawn, he was utterly exhausted and crawled back into the tent, collapsing into a numb sleep. He vaguely heard Clark stumble in and lie down beside him, muttering, "Good God." Meriwether felt the shuddering dog Seaman come and curl up against him, needing comfort and resting his muzzle beneath Meriwether's chin. With his close companions nearby, Meriwether drifted into a deeper sleep.

And then dreams followed, confused, disjointed. He was the Welsh dragon again, flying free and strong. He woke up startled, wondering why no one but Clark had ever spoken of his dragon form or of Sacagawea's eagle after the encounter with the river monster. He stared at the top of the tent, where the crossed poles poked out. The hole revealed just a bit of gray sky.

Sensing his master stir, Seaman forced his head beneath his hand, and Meriwether patted it, half asleep.

Surely others must have seen his transformation, or had they been too frightened, fighting to get out of the river and away from the serpent? Since then, had the men showed any fear of him? They had so much to accept and absorb.

Meriwether himself had been preoccupied with suspicions over Charbonneau, wondering what danger the strange man posed. No, he admitted, he had simply been jealous of Charbonneau, angry that this thoroughly unexceptional man had captured the attention of a brave and resourceful woman. Even in his altered state, the man commanded Sacagawea's attention and her loyalty. Even though he struck her.

It was so obvious to Meriwether that something was deeply wrong with Charbonneau, but Sacagawea didn't seem to notice.

He chewed on the corner of his lip, trying to tamp down his growing feelings for this native woman.

A tentative voice called from outside the tent, a woman's voice. "Captain?" As if his thoughts had summoned her, Sacagawea pushed back the tent flap, peered inside. She had the child on her back. Though he still found her face beautiful, she looked haggard, and he could see the shadows under her eyes. "Captain?" she asked again, and he realized that Clark also had sat up. She seemed very brave and determined. "I promised to take you to the other ocean, but I cannot go with you further."

Meriwether reeled with the thought, but before he could speak, Clark blurted out, "Why not? You have been extremely valuable to our expedition."

Meriwether said, "Is it your husband? Last night, I saw that he was stricken."

"Not stricken—cursed." She pressed her lips together, clamping away further explanation.

"Cursed?" Meriwether pressed. "Tell us."

She entered the tent and fell, without effort, into that sort of squat that many of the native scouts found so comfortable. Seaman got to his feet, tail wagging, and tried to lick at Pompy's face, while the child squealed and gurgled. He reached out for the dog's ears with his chubby hands.

Sacagawea continued in a grim voice, "You know he has not been himself since he escaped from the great magic." She fell silent a long time. "He's been like a . . . a doll, used by something else." She looked from one man to the other of them and sighed. "I suspected the great magic was reaching through him, but he was fighting it. I wanted to help him, to save him. I did not wish to tell you about his curse, because I feared you would prevent him from coming with us. I have prepared strong potions, tinctures of special magic herbs for him. Sometimes, I almost freed his mind. He told me that the . . . the evil wizard, the servant of the raven, was trying to reach through him and harm us. The great magic needs to be close to cause great destruction, but my Toussaint fought it. He would not allow the evil wizard to reach through him to harm our party. But last night, my Toussaint lost the battle." She fell ominously silent again. "He lost the battle, and the sorcerer reached through him to the . . . to a place where dead lay, and he made roots and trees grow to them and animated them. He used lightning to ignite the creature before he sent it against us."

Meriwether felt a strange relief to hear this. "Those bones, the skulls, the children . . . they were already dead, then?" It was just a small bit of hope. "When they became that thing?"

"And the same sort of thing burned all those other villages?" Clark asked.

Sacagawea nodded. "They were corpses, reanimated and ignited. But not long dead, because there was still life in them, which his sorcery tapped, added to the life in the trees—and then the fire."

"Your husband told you this?" Meriwether asked.

She shook her head. "Toussaint cannot speak. But his mind was sundered when you threw that knife at the creature. He's not . . . himself. No one remains inside his mind to answer me. I think he was being used by the great magic to create the fire monster. It was too strong a spell to make from so little, and so someone had to be present to evoke it. Toussaint. The sorcerer was in his body. But when your knife shattered the spell, Captain Lewis, the shock was like a person being struck in the head. But I also think it is a curse, that some vital part has left him."

"What can we do about it?" Clark asked.

Sacagawea looked at him in surprise. "About Toussaint? Nothing. I have tried everything I can with roots and leaves, but the magic is deep and the damage severe." She shook her head. "This is not why I came to you. Your expedition will continue over the mountains and to the sea, but I will remain here with my husband and Pompy until Toussaint recovers—if he recovers. And if he does not recover, then I will find the great magic and avenge my husband."

"And what if he does recover?" Meriwether asked.

She looked away. "Then I will do whatever he wants, since I'm his wife. But I will try to convince him he must help me fight the evil sorcerer, because none of us will be safe."

Clark was alarmed. "You can't keep Pompy with you!" He had grown very attached to the child. "We will take him with us and keep him safe, feed him, guard him. If you do not rejoin us, then I will educate him and care for him as though he were my own." He seemed embarrassed. "I meant to make such an offer to you, anyway, when the expedition came to an end, but now I must speak. You cannot possibly take this small child into such danger. You cannot!"

Meriwether knew what her answer would be, though. Sacagawea had shown as stubborn a refusal to be parted from her child as from her husband. He interrupted before she could answer, "William, my friend, we can't leave her here, either. We can't go on without her.

Our mission is to cross the continent and reach the Pacific, but we could never survive with attacks every day and every night. We'd lose all the members of our expedition! There won't be anyone to reach the Pacific, let alone come back and report."

Clark pinched the bridge of his nose between thumb and index finger. He knew that his friend missed his young fiancée back home. He'd seen Clark write her letters, which she would never receive, at least not for a very long time. He could imagine that his partner felt a great impetus to finish his mission, to be home and safe and away from these arcane lands.

Meriwether shared the same goal, since Franklin had given them the difficult mission. If he could find a passage across the western ocean to reconnect the rest of the world, he would literally change history. But a part of him felt lost, and he did not want this journey to end.

Clark interrupted, impatient. "I do see the point of your objection to us continuing. I see why you wouldn't want to press on, because of the increasing dangers. The great evil does not have to kill the two of us. He can chip at us, slowly, like an ax against a strong tree. I can see that." He shrugged. "Therefore I agree with what you have not yet been able to say. Our only course of action is to find this evil sorcerer and neutralize him." He gave a determined look first to Sacagawea, then to Meriwether. "But what makes you believe we can do so? This enemy commands terrible creatures, uses revenants of the dead as his puppets, and possesses vast arcane knowledge. What chance to we have? How does it profit us to fight him if there is no possible way we can win?"

Sacagawea spoke first. "If I can bring Toussaint back to himself, he will be able to help us. Because his mind was touched by the enemy, he will have a better idea of what the sorcerer, the dragon, is . . . and how to fight him." She made a face. "I think I understand the state he is in now. I have heard how sometimes a powerful shaman will do this to a man in an enemy tribe, using his body and looking through his eyes as a spy." She shook her head. "I am not sure my herbs will heal him. If we could find the tribe of my birth, the shaman would know."

The tribe of her birth. For the first time, it occurred to Meriwether that she often spoke of it in those terms, seeming to separate herself from them.

"Is your tribe nearby?" Clark asked.

She nodded once. "I think so. I was very young when I was taken away, but I recognize this land as where my tribe roamed. And the moccasins we've found in the burned camps are similar to the things my people wore." She looked intently at them. "We are the Snake People, as the other tribes call us. I'm sure our shaman can help us. He was very wise and full of great power. When I first ran away from the servant of the raven, I hoped to find the shaman. But then I sensed your dragon, Captain Lewis," she said, giving him a smile. "And I realized you would help me."

"Why hasn't your shaman already battled the great evil?"

She made a face. "I didn't say he could fight the sorcerer, only that he can help heal my husband. Maybe then—" Her voice faltered. There were tears in her eyes.

Meriwether had already decided that this is what they should do, but he felt a sudden qualm. "I think perhaps we should put it to a vote among the members of the expedition. We'll be asking them to risk their lives in unequal combat. They agreed to go to the Pacific—"

"And to face any dangers on the way," Clark added.

"And they've faced plenty of them. But even if there is something in Toussaint's mind that helps us understand our enemy, the danger is of a different sort. The overwhelming likelihood is that we'll lose."

"All right," Clark said, conceding. "We'll gather the men and tell them the situation. We'll ask them to vote on it."

"The women too," Meriwether said.

Sacagawea said, "The women left last night, after the fire creature. The interpreters ran away, too."

Clark seemed about to debate, but then shrugged. "Very well. Everyone votes, including Sacagawea." He seemed amused by the idea. "Except Seaman, unless you find a way to interpret his vote."

My Dearest Julia,

Not long ago we held the oddest vote ever taken in the new world or, I daresay, in the old. A month ago, after our camp was attacked by the fire demon, we all decided together that we could not go on as we'd been. The chances of the entire expedition being killed before we reached the Pacific were high. We cannot hope to survive against the continued and increasing attacks of the evil sorcerer who means to destroy us.

Sacagawea hopes that should we find her tribe—called the Snake People, though she calls it Shoshone—the shaman will be able to revive her husband, who is very ill indeed. After the destruction of the fire demon, he lies unresponsive, carried on a litter by two of the men. If he can be revived, he might give us some insight into how to defeat this dark sorcerer, who seems to be part dragon, or at least the Indian manifestation of a similar legend.

I don't know what has gotten into Captain Lewis, though. He seems moody and irrational. If we were back east, I'd say he must be in love, but that cannot be possible here on our expedition. Except for Sacagawea, all of the women have departed, fled with their trapper husbands. Yet he demanded that every member of our party should have a voice on whether we continue to the Pacific or stay and fight this menace that has plagued us mercilessly. He even insisted the former slave York and the native woman get a vote.

Once the perils had been explained, all members voted to find the Snake People and their shaman, hope that he can heal Charbonneau, so that we can all try to fight the great magic that has been attacking us.

Yes, Julia, after great consideration, even I voted to stay and face this menace, though with a heavy heart. I want more than anything to reach the western edge of our world, so that we can consider our mission complete and then I can return to you. How I long to hold you in my arms and to finally celebrate our wedding, which will make you mine forever.

But now that we will fight the evil sorcerer, I do not know if I will survive to reach the western ocean, much less get back to you.

For the past month since the attack of the fiery creature, we have continued to search for Sacagawea's people, without success, though yesterday some chance-met natives warned us about a fierce party of warriors in this region. Charbonneau remains unchanged.

Hopefully we will find her people, and her shaman. They may not even be alive, considering the local wars that often result in entire tribes being taken captive or killed.

With a heavy heart and a fear of not seeing you again, I must sign myself,

Yours, ever,
William Clark

—Letter from William Clark to Julia Hancock,
June 1, 1805

Flying

FOR DAYS NOW, AS THE FRUITLESS SEARCH CONTINUED, MERI-
wether had been aware of mounting despair. Because he knew he
was prone to despondency since an early age, he tried to pay it
no mind, to focus on their goal. Ever since his father's death, his
moods were at best an unreliable instrument. For no particular
reason, a black gloom might descend upon him, so deep and dark
that he could not muddle through it, nor even write in his diary.

Because of his own preoccupation, he did not at first notice
that the same mood had taken hold of everyone else. As they
plodded on, the men had stopped talking among themselves,
except for the most necessary things. Even Clark rarely spoke,
and when he took Pompy from Sacagawea to hold, he no longer
smiled or laughed at the child's cooing and antics.

Other than the brief excitement of a bear chasing Meriwether
through the forest, and another strange dream or vision when
he thought he had seen Charbonneau conversing with the bear,
they had not faced any great peril and no further supernatural
attacks since the fire demon. Meriwether had shot and killed the
bear which, when they inspected its carcass, seemed to be nothing
other than a normal animal, though of unusual size.

One night two bull buffalo had rampaged through the camp,
seemingly disoriented rather than driven to a mad frenzy. They
had both been shot before either of them could trample the men
in camp.

While disruptive, those incidents needn't have been caused

145

by dangerous magic. Though she seemed concerned, Sacagawea was convinced that the evil sorcerer would still be weakened by the wound that Meriwether had inflicted on its fire demon, and the enemy could not attack them. Or so she hoped.

Meriwether, Clark, and Sacagawea had spent some time with a map, sketched from Clark's best charts with additional anecdotal information from local natives. They discussed where the lair of the sorcerer might be, but Meriwether could not believe how far away Sacagawea said it was. It was impossible that young woman, weak, starving, and about to give birth, had managed to cover so many miles on her own to reach Fort Mandan.

Now, they were not searching for the lair of the sorcerer, but following rumors of where Sacagawea's people might have gone. Meriwether also remained concerned about reports of a dangerous party of young warriors with a warlike chief, who were searching for something or someone among nearby villages. At least they weren't revenants.

In fact, the only undead they had seen in more than a month were the three persistent revenants of Hall, Collins, and Willard, who continued to haunt their former comrades in hopes of stealing more whiskey, although the expedition's supplies had dwindled to nothing. Several sentries insisted on having seen the three men, but Meriwether was not absolutely sure he believed that tale.

It didn't seem to matter, anyway, as his black mood deepened. He could not summon the enthusiasm for their search, for fighting the great magic, for finding his own spirit dragon. Not until today, when he walked up a verdant slope under a bright sun. Sacagawea strolled ahead, and birds circled overhead.

The big dog bounded ahead, feeling none of his master's depression, then ran back to Meriwether, then up ahead again. Only Seaman showed any energy. Everyone else seemed dispirited, sweaty, and exasperated. Even the baby, carried alternately by Sacagawea and Captain Clark, seemed listless and uninterested.

The men carrying Charbonneau's litter often changed places, but every one of them seemed to carry an unbearable burden. Sacagawea's husband looked very ill indeed, though they could occasionally rouse him into a sitting position to take some broth, or water, which Sacagawea assiduously gave him. His eyes remained fixed and blank, staring ahead into a land no one else could see.

When he or Clark questioned the man's health, Sacagawea

responded with shrugs or sounds of exasperation, which were often—Meriwether thought—downright rude. He decided that she didn't know what to do either.

They made camp on a small hillock and posted sentinels, but Meriwether saw Sacagawea leave in the dusk, wandering away as if continuing her futile search for the Snake People on her own. At least she had left her son in Clark's care, but Meriwether thought she was taking unwarranted risks. Wanting to protect her, he took his air rifle and followed.

Though the light was dim and fading, he followed her using his woodcraft, the trail of her moccasins, the few broken twigs or disturbed grasses in her path...only to find himself, quickly, utterly lost, such as he'd never been back in Virginia.

He found himself in a clearing of native grass, amid scrubby trees and surrounded by rugged mountains. The pristine clearing showed no sign of Sacagawea's passage, as though her moccasined feet had failed to disturb the grass or break a single twig of surrounding vegetation.

His rifle slick with his own sweat in his hand, he turned in a slow circle, letting out an exasperated sigh.

Meriwether had learned, young enough, that the superior and almost magical forest skills the Europeans attributed to the native tribes was little more than a projection of their own wishes, a way of imagining that the original inhabitants of the new world were both more and less than human. They could supposedly walk without leaving a trace, never disturbing the world around them, like some kind of wood sprite.

But he had become friendly with the natives near his home, and he quickly discovered they were in fact perfectly human. There were swift ones, clumsy ones, garrulous ones, and reserved ones, as well as those remarkably skilled in woodcraft.

Their ability to walk in the forest unnoticed, or to sneak up on people or animals, was simply a manifestation of those skills, although perhaps enhanced with magic in the decades after the Sundering. Such woodcraft, passed down through the generations, was essential for a people who survived by hunting and gathering. Meriwether himself had learned a form of it, and he too could walk through the woods leaving little trace.

But was Sacagawea skilled enough just to vanish, even beyond his ability to track her? Why would she want to lose anyone who might follow her from the encampment? Did she know he was following her?

Annoyed and irritated, both at the young woman and at himself, he concentrated harder. He could hear the river, so he could always return to the encampment. But what about Sacagawea? Despite his own gloom, he worried about her.

True, these were her native lands, and her own tribe came from this region. She was hardy and resourceful, but if that party of young warriors came upon her—

His mind failed him.

What if she had simply abandoned her abusive and now mindless husband, as well as her child? If she couldn't find her people, and the shaman, she might go fight the dragon sorcerer herself.

For a moment he considered trying to manifest his spirit dragon form so he could scout the area from above and maybe he'd find her. He was not sanguine about leaving his body behind, here in an empty clearing. He looked up and saw, against the deepening blue sky an eagle, wings spread against the sky, turning and turning.

It was Sacagawea. He was sure of it.

He ran to the middle of the clearing, swinging his arms and his rifle, trying to get the bird's attention. "Sacagawea!" he shouted. "Sacagawea!"

He careened past saplings and shrubs, ignoring spiny plants that tore at his pants. He made his way until he was beneath where the eagle circled, and he found her standing by a pair of small pines. "Sacagawea," he said, panting. He stopped two feet in front of her and waited. The eagle's immaterial form approached and flew down to melt with her body.

Aware of herself again, she turned to look at him with dark eyes. "I was looking for my people. I need to continue the search."

He had trouble catching his breath. He'd feared...he didn't quite know what. At first he'd feared she was leaving, and would be alone and exposed to the dangers of the wild, both natural and arcane. Upon seeing her spirit eagle, he'd feared she was looking for the evil dragon to challenge him.

"You cannot face the great magic alone," Meriwether said. "I know he hurt the man you love, but..."

She blinked at him, in shock, and repeated the one word. "Love?"

"Your husband."

"My husband," she repeated.

For a moment he was afraid that something had left her incapable of understanding human speech, but then she shook her head. "Toussaint is my husband. I did not intend to search for the evil sorcerer alone, only to find the Shoshone." She sounded terribly weary, and he recalled how tired he felt when he had brought forth his own spirit dragon.

She reached down to pick up a basket, which she'd filled with roots and berries gathered in the dusk. "I was out, and I thought to send the eagle to look, and also see if that raiding band was anywhere near."

"We should return to the camp." Meriwether felt inexplicably embarrassed and guilty for overreacting. In wildly coming out to look for her, he might have attracted the attention of the very creature they wished to avoid.

Sacagawea walked away, but not toward the camp.

Meriwether said very formally, "Madame Charbonneau, you're going in the wrong direction."

She kept walking and led him up a slope until the trees parted, and he saw they had come to a high overlook, a bluff that dropped down to the river. Sacagawea set down her basket of roots and berries and sat near the edge of the precipice, looking down at the glistening ribbon of the river in the twilight.

For a moment, Meriwether had the horrible idea that she would jump, but she just stared out at the river. After a while, she spoke. "Before we return to the camp, I should explain."

Hesitantly, he took a seat next to her. "Explain?"

"How I came to be the wife of Toussaint Charbonneau."

A thousand guesses fled through Meriwether's mind, but he could think of nothing that didn't sound stupid, so he just waited. Presently, she spoke again in a dreamlike tone. "I was stolen from my tribe at twelve."

"By Charbonneau?" Meriwether decided that he should have killed the man while he had the chance.

She shook her head. "No, by the Hidatsa. Enemies of my people. They made me do much work and follow their tribe for years. Three years, I think. I learned some languages then, because they came in contact with French and English fur traders and trappers. But then—" She stopped. "Toussaint Charbonneau came to the Hidatsa, and he won me and another girl in a card game, and we became his wives."

Meriwether thought he heard a loud whistle in his ears. "A card game?"

"He won. It is a fair way to marry someone among my people. I belong to him, until he should release me. I owe him loyalty. And he treated me well enough, far better than the Hidatsa did. He gave me food, clothes, and moccasins."

"And that... that is the extent of your feelings?" Any woman from the more civilized parts of the world would have broken under such treatment, taken away as a child, badly used by hostiles, and then given away in marriage as a gambling prize.

"Life is food, clothing, and shelter. Everything else is just a bonus." She gave him a look over her shoulder, one he could not interpret. "I believe that one should abide by the terms of a bargain, and Toussaint lived up to his. I have a contract with him, and we have a son together. Jean Baptiste will require his father's influence and protection as he grows. I can't simply let Toussaint die."

Meriwether could say nothing to that. "Thank you for telling me," he said, understanding her more fully now. It made it easier to comprehend her behavior as the demands of duty. He himself had served in war, and he understood the need to save or rescue comrades with whom he had no other connection. After what Sacagawea had suffered, she would bury her inner feelings and concentrate only on survival. And Toussaint meant survival.

He extended his hand to her as he rose from the overlook in the thickening twilight. "Let us say no more of this. I understand your sense of duty, if nothing else, as well as the desire to heal the father of your son. I will do what I can to help. We really should get back to camp."

Her expression was filled with deep thought, perhaps calculation. Maybe she had meant to throw herself down to the river, but he didn't think she would give up that way, not from what she considered a solemn duty. She was not acting desperate, but rather showed disappointment, or perhaps exasperation, with him, but Meriwether couldn't understand why.

She took his hand and stood. Her hand had a rough texture, quite different from the ladies he'd grown up with. Her life had consisted of rough work, fetching and carrying, digging for roots.

"My eagle saw no trace of the Snake People, but I will continue to look." She picked up her basket.

Following the path Meriwether had marked, they stepped over broken branches and walked through areas of disturbed dirt. Why had he been so desperate when she left? What sick fancies had taken possession of his brain? And why should it matter to him? Perhaps because she was the only other person he knew who could send forth a spirit animal. Idly, he wondered if he should summon his own dragon from inside his mind, inside his spirit. Maybe his spirit dragon could see what her eagle couldn't.

He felt a quickening of excitement within himself that drove away the syrupy gloom that had so plagued him. What were the powers of his spirit dragon? He remembered his dreams of flying, as well as the power in his great body. It felt like an itch, an uncontrollable desire to send forth the dragon.

"I didn't find my people," Sacagawea said quietly. "But I did see something."

He paused. "Yes?" He held up a branch to let her pass through.

"I saw a raiding party, ten warriors on good horses, headed in our direction."

"Good heavens, Madam! We have to get back to camp as soon as possible. They may be hostile."

"They were too far away to arrive before sundown. They will make their own camp, and we'll be gone by morning. Our paths may not even cross."

Something in the way she dragged her words, and the distance in her voice made it seem as if she was thinking of something quite different. He waited for her to continue.

"Something about them disturbs me," she said. "I sense that I should know them, but I can't quite fully explain it."

"You could not recognize anyone from the eyes of a spirit eagle so high above," he suggested. Or did she mean in a general sense? Maybe they belonged to the tribe that had taken her captive at a young age and grievously mistreated her.

There were howls suddenly, echoing from many places. "Coyote," Sacagawea said.

"Yes, I presume they are," Meriwether said. He'd seen the canids, though not yet shot one for his collection.

"No, no," Sacagawea said. She pulled a knot of colorful string from inside her tunic, and clutched it. "Coyote. The . . . spirit. The god."

Lewis looked at her bundle of string curiously. "That's his symbol?"

"No. It is what banishes him."

"You'd banish a god?"

"He is the god of chaos," Sacagawea said, seriously. "And we've had too much chaos. It can be good or bad. But it's often bad. As . . . as you know."

They hurried back to camp, delivered their news, and Clark dispatched additional sentries while the rest of the men settled down to dinner, using the roots and berries Sacagawea brought back.

They had just finished dinner when a tall native man on a dark horse rode into the firelight, carrying a long, deadly lance and looking quite warlike.

The Man on the Dark Horse

THE MAN ON THE DARK HORSE WAS QUITE HANDSOME, EVEN regal in a way, Meriwether thought. He had an air of being accustomed to command. He wore clean new garments made of soft hides and a sort of fur hat topped with feathers. The horse was in good condition, the spear was new, the point wickedly sharp. He wondered if this meant their owner was skilled at rapine and pillage.

Around the camp, men moved into position, rearranging themselves for defense as they stared silently at the warrior. They did not yet reach for their rifles, but they could reach them easily. Many of the natives they had encountered thus far dealt in trade rather than war, but with a party of young warriors, well-armed and provisioned, Meriwether expected the worst.

The thought struck him, though, that after all the expedition had survived, from revenants to fire demons, river monsters, and giant lizards, a mere raiding party seemed almost quaint. But Meriwether knew that a spear could kill them as easily as a dragon sorcerer.

The dark rider was isolated, but his proud confidence spoke of strength, and Meriwether guessed he must not be alone. With a whistle, he called Seaman to his side, and under the pretext of looking for his dog, he swept his gaze around the perimeter of the firelit camp. He could discern little beyond the circle of light, but he thought he could see darker shadows out there in the trees, the size and bulk of men on horseback.

Finally, the tall warrior spoke. "Good evening, gentlemen," he said in excellent English. "My companions and I would like to know what brings you so far into the territory of the Shoshone... and how you are creating such a magical disruption that terrible beasts are eating the buffalo and fire monsters are consuming the camps of our friends and neighbors."

Clark advanced to stand next to his partner. "We have done nothing." He, too, flashed a quick glance to the shadowy figures just out of view. Neither of them wanted to provoke a confrontation. The rider carried a spear, but the other warriors beyond the camp might well carry firearms. Between trade with trappers and fur traders, even theft, the native tribes had plenty of access to firearms. "We are traveling across the land and over the mountains in search of the great western sea."

The warrior on horseback responded with a skeptical frown. "Prove it." The campfire cast eerie shadows on his face, making his smile look to be a leer. His eyes shone with an intense fervor. "No one else is causing trouble, and yet the great magic throws our land into turmoil. The people suffer—and all since your party moved into these territories."

"We mean no harm," Meriwether said. "Your enemy is the evil sorcerer. He is tearing this land apart."

The warrior did not seem convinced. "Our shamans tell us this is foreign magic, magic from that land across the sea, from invaders who came here before the comet."

"Shamans can say whatever they like," Clark said. "That doesn't mean they know the truth."

"What else could cause this much disruption? Prove to us it is not your fault."

Meriwether felt a trickle of sweat down his back. "And how can we prove that? If we have done nothing, then no proof can possibly exist." He doubted this young warrior would understand the nuances of legal logic.

Sacagawea might be able to explain, though, since she had suffered more at the hands of the dragon sorcerer than any. She knew who he was and what he had done to the land and to the other tribes. She could vouch for them—if the warriors believed her.

He looked over his shoulder and saw her standing by the fire. He immediately realized something was wrong. She clutched her hands at her chest, and her face was vacant, her mouth half open, her eyes huge as if caught in some new magical attack. As she stared at the tall man on horseback, she seemed to see something entirely different.

Immediately on guard, Meriwether dug deep inside himself and prepared to release his spirit dragon, as he had done against the river monster. He didn't know if he could do it, or how he would fight against this raiding party, but the appearance of the supernatural creature connected to him would certainly startle these natives. Then Clark and the rest of the expedition members would have to fight and hope to survive.

"Cameahwait," Sacagawea finally spoke, breaking his concentration. "Brother."

The warrior swung about, staring at her as if poleaxed. Sacagawea spoke in a rush, a language Meriwether couldn't understand. The man responded, shaken, as she stepped closer, so he could see her. His voice had lost its assurance, growing husky with disbelief, like a man fighting back tears. He secured his lance and leaped down from the horse in a single, sudden movement. Ignoring Meriwether and Clark, he strode past them, opened his arms, and Sacagawea ran into them. She was crying and talking, her voice gone higher with excitement, as if she'd become a young girl again. Meriwether heard the same word again and again. "Cameahwait." Her brother's name.

While the men in camp murmured in confusion, the two of them were lost in a world of their own. From the darkness beyond the firelight came the shuffling noises of men and horses. The rest of the raiding party drifted closer, possibly threatening. Meriwether hoped that their leader would call some kind of truce.

Cameahwait had Sacagawea by the waist, hugging her frantically. She grabbed his shoulders, said something, and broke away to where she'd left her sleeping son. She returned holding Pompy, the baby blinking and half asleep in her arms. She proudly held him up to show her brother, the leader of the band. She said the name "Jean-Baptiste Charbonneau."

With an expression of wonder on his face, Cameahwait stroked the baby's head, his wisps of dark hair, and he looked up, as if waking from a dream. He found the two captains and spoke, his voice thick with emotion. "Forgive me. My sister says that you have been kind to her, and that you are trying to secure help for her husband, who has been cursed by the great magic. She also tells me you did not cause the disturbances my people and I have endured, but rather you intend to combat them, so that the land may be at peace." He looked specifically at Meriwether. "She tells me you have great magic of your own."

He didn't know how to respond or explain, but Cameahwait did not seem to want conversation. He shouted something in his native language, directed to the other warriors hidden in the trees. Out in the shadows, he heard the sound of people dismounting, horses moving forward. The other members of the raiding party advanced just enough to reveal themselves, but made no other threatening moves. The men who stepped forward carried spears, but no rifles. Meriwether thought they all looked very young, perhaps even sheepish.

Sacagawea seemed in a daze as she explained to Meriwether and Clark. "This man is my brother, Cameahwait, and these are his men. They do not intend to harm us."

Meriwether could feel a tangible sense of relief as the tension in camp eased. Some of the men slowly sat back down on boulders or blankets. York fed more branches into the waning campfire.

Cameahwait's people came into the firelight, curious and wary. "We are friends now," he explained, then shouted something to his men, presumably the same words in their language.

Sacagawea cradled her baby in one arm and slipped her other arm around her brother's waist. "We need to sit down with Captain Lewis and Captain Clark, so that we can compare what we know and talk of what is happening to the land. Can you help us with what ails my son's father?"

The big Newfoundland joined them, slumping to the ground and wagging his tail by the firelight, as the others sat near the fire. One of the men brought out some of the leftover food from their dinner, as well as coffee. Gesturing to his warriors, Cameahwait had them offer preserved meat and nuts from their packs. As in all human encounters since the dawn of time, Meriwether thought, eating together symbolized peace.

During the meal, Meriwether described the world of the European settlers back east, how they had made their own American civilization after the continent was sundered from the rest of the world. He explained that if they did reach the far ocean, they might have another route to rejoin the old world. But first, they had decided to battle the evil force that was using the awakened magic to tear the land apart. In a halting voice—with Sacagawea's prodding—he also described his dreams, his spirit dragon, and his previous encounters with the dark sorcerer.

Her brother listened with great interest as Sacagawea described her captivity with the Hidatsa tribe. At some parts, the big warrior turned his head aside, as if to hide a shimmer of tears in his eyes. While Meriwether understood that she had been very badly treated by her own people, it seemed that Cameahwait understood more of her ordeal, being familiar with the customs and habits of the region. He seemed to grow calmer as she spoke of her time with Charbonneau, then fraught again as she described being captured and enslaved by the dragon sorcerer. As she sat with her son asleep in her lap, she explained her escape, and why she had been drawn to the men at Fort Mandan.

"It had to do with my baby," she said. "The dragon sorcerer wanted him, meant to steal his soul and take his body."

Meriwether confirmed. "The dragon sorcerer said he was searching for the bird and her egg."

"But Captain Lewis fought him, defeated him," Sacagawea said.

Clark took over the tale, explaining what the expedition had encountered since the spring thaw, especially the attack of the fire demon, and how the evil sorcerer had been wounded, weakened.

"My husband is his anchor," Sacagawea said, her voice growing more urgent. "He remains in a spell, in a trance, but that is how we can fight the dragon sorcerer. I need the help of our tribe's shaman, so we can rescue Toussaint."

Cameahwait nodded. "The Snake People are only half a day from here. We can take you in the morning."

Though he had no reason to be suspicious, Meriwether half-expected them to be attacked in the night, but other than a small disturbance, the sentries claiming to see the three Whiskey Revenants lurking about again, they had an uneventful sleep. Waking early, they packed and prepared to make their way to the camp of Sacagawea's people, the "snake people." Not a very auspicious name, he thought.

The camp of the Shoshone was a small village, the dwellings covered in long grass, rather than the customary buffalo hides. During the long march that morning, Meriwether spoke with Cameahwait, who explained that most of his tribe had been killed or kidnapped in the same raid by the Hidatsa that had taken Sacagawea captive. They'd recovered some of their members, but not all. The Hidatsa's superior strength had forced the Shoshone to move away from the buffalo-rich lands and closer to the mountains.

"The attacks began before my sister or I were born. For a long time, my tribe could only hunt in buffalo country for some months a year, then we would retreat to the mountains, where we could defend ourselves. Now that the buffalo are growing more scarce with the turmoil in the land, we have had more trouble with our enemies straying here, looking to steal what they can." He narrowed his eyes at Meriwether. "The fire demon burned out many of their camps, which turned them loose to prey upon other villages. The Snake People are very poor right now."

Meriwether understood that the raiding party had intended to steal the expedition's supplies, if they could get away with it. Fortunately, Sacagawea had stopped them. But now Cameahwait's band of warriors was returning with no food or weapons to help his people survive.

Looking at the man's face, Meriwether could see wrinkles of worry. Would he have done the same, if his mother, his family, faced starvation? He could defend himself against the raiding party, but perhaps he should not judge them. Cameahwait was the chief of his tribe, and he bore the responsibility for their survival.

Their arrival was greeted by several young women who rushed forward after the tall warrior called out that their sister had returned. They threw themselves into Sacagawea's arms, exclaiming with joy to find her still alive. Pompy awoke, fussed, but Sacagawea displayed her son and passed him around to the eager arms. Then, devoted to her duty, she went back to her senseless husband. He lay on a litter carried between two horses. She directed two younger men from the tribe to carry him into one of the grass huts.

Meriwether felt awkward, knowing he could not follow to ask her what was happening. He hoped that someone from her people could bring Charbonneau's mind back to such an extent he could help them find, and then storm, the dragon sorcerer's lair.

For now, he and Clark had to observe the important customs of their initial meeting with new friends. Natives were as punctilious and exacting as any society in making sure the observances of politeness were met.

Gifts were exchanged, the Snake People offering garments made of buffalo hide, which were much appreciated, since the rigors of the expedition had left many of the men with ragged and threadbare clothes. After a hundred setbacks and travails, the men were starting to look disreputable. In exchange, after much consideration and discussion, the expedition offered a dozen rifles and a considerable amount of ammunition as their valuable gift.

Cameahwait and his village received the weapons with great joy, for that gave them the ability to hunt buffalo more efficiently, and even to defend themselves against their enemies.

Finally, when the reception of visitors had progressed to the point when they sat down and exchanged food, Meriwether noticed the absence of Sacagawea. He was concerned about her, and he stood, leaving the cook fire as if to relieve himself in the trees, and slipped off in the direction of the grass hut he'd seen Sacagawea enter.

Finding the Spirit

HE FOUND SACAGAWEA IN THE SHELTER, SITTING ON HER HEELS beside Charbonneau, who remained unresponsive, his eyes glazed, as he had been for days. She looked up, startled when Meriwether entered.

"I came to see how you were," he said, embarrassed. "Can your people help him?"

She made a face. "The shaman was not here. He is gathering leaves and mushrooms for his work, and two young boys were sent to call him back. Until he arrives, I know nothing more than I did before."

He leaned against one of the poles supporting the structure. "What if your husband cannot be brought back? Can we still find the dragon?"

She nodded. "With difficulty. But I was hoping for more. Toussaint made the focus of the dragon sorcerer's magic, and I suspect he has some insight into what flaws the magic might have. We need to know anything that might make it easier for us to defeat him. As you and Captain Clark said before, our chances of winning are very small indeed." She gave Meriwether a sad smile. "Besides, he is my husband, my son's father. I need to rescue him."

"Yes, I understand that." He felt a strange impatience that was not justified by the woman's quite reasonable explanations. "But what if the shaman can't waken him? Can you lead us to the evil lair? Can we still attempt to defeat the enemy?"

She hesitated. She opened her mouth, closed it, then finally said, "We can at least try, Captain. And I would want instruction from the shaman on how to approach our fight. This will be a magical battle as well as a physical one, and in magical battles, shamans are useful people to know."

Meriwether heard the sound of feet running outside, and a young boy poked his head into the grass shelter and said something in the Shoshone language.

Sacagawea stood up from her husband's side and brushed the wrinkles from her tunic. "The shaman comes," she said, apparently expecting Meriwether to leave. And perhaps it was logical for him to leave, but Meriwether felt a great need to stay, both to learn what was about to happen, and also to see how reliable this shaman might be. He wanted to form his own opinion on whether the man was a charlatan. For centuries, Europeans had assumed all shamans were fakers, creatures pretending to great magical powers.

But after the comet, after the Sundering, anything might be possible.

Like the sorcerers and witches of Europe, shamans in America had come into their own. As a young man, Meriwether had seen shamans perform what seemed like miracles. But it all depended on tribal lore, and the individual in question. As with European magical lore, some of it seemed to work and make sense, while some was merely the remnants of tricks and dissembling.

He thought it more and more possible that at some point in the past there had been another event like the Sundering, and that magic had existed for a while. Some people had found ways to control it and use it, but then magic had vanished from the world again.

The question was, how real was this shaman of the Snake People? And how much did he truly know about fighting the dragon sorcerer?

A tall man bent and entered the grass shelter. He was taller than Cameahwait. Older. His face was tanned and wrinkled, like that of a man who has spent most of his life outdoors. His clothes and hair were rumpled, looking like he'd been on an expedition over some rough terrain. Grass stains marked the back of his tunic, and brambles had pulled at his sleeves.

He carried a sack in his hand, which he dropped to the ground as he came in, offering both hands to Sacagawea. He said in a

hoarse, emotional voice, "We thought you lost! The others managed to escape and come back, but when you didn't, we thought
we'd never see you again."

"I know, Dosabite," she said. "But I survived. Now I am back."

Only then did the shaman notice Meriwether. He paused in
surprise and concern, as if not sure what to say or do.

"This is Captain Lewis," Sacagawea said. "He is one of the
leaders of the expedition from the white men of the east. They
have come to find what was happening in this land, and also
to find the edge of the world, where the sun sets. That way he
hopes to sail away and reunite with his people."

The shaman, Dosabite, scratched at his chin in deep thought,
then spoke, with Sacagawea translating. "I am not sure I would
consider it a good thing for you to find a way to rejoin the men
of your tribe. If the way is open across the sea where the sun
sets, then more and more of your people will come, until there
is not enough land or buffalo for everyone."

Sacagawea insisted that this was not the captain's intention,
and Meriwether explained that even if they found a way back
to Europe it would be an arduous, difficult way, and that large
numbers of people could never come here quickly, but that trade
would make life better for everyone, including the Snake People.
The shaman made acerbic comments about the manners and morals of fur traders, and how plentiful they were all over this land.

Which made it awkward for Sacagawea to show him to her
husband and ask for his help. But the fact that Charbonneau was
married to her made him one of the tribe, or at least someone
related to them, so that the shaman was interested.

He lifted Charbonneau's eyelids while Sacagawea explained
what was wrong with him and how it had happened. The shaman frowned. "Bird Woman, I caution you against challenging
this dragon wizard. He's very powerful, both in our magic and
that of the Europeans." The older man lowered his eyes. "The
dragon wizard did not start as a man. He might be Raven himself, in his trickster aspect, and he has taken over the body of
a European. With the new magic, all the land responds to him.
It will take more than you or your husband, or this man—" He
glared at Meriwether. "—to make the dragon wizard give back
your husband's spirit, or his hold on this land."

Sacagawea made a sound of protest, and after he heard the

translation, Meriwether also spoke indignantly. "No shaman can just tell us to leave things be. I do not know if we can rescue Charbonneau, with your help, but I know it is incumbent upon us to try to fight that evil force. As his magic continues to grow, his depredations in the land will make your people starve." He came closer to the shaman, looking him hard in the eye as Sacagawea translated. "Your greatest danger is not that *my* people will overrun these territories, but that this dragon sorcerer will destroy you and the entire land."

The shaman seemed to deliberate. It impressed Meriwether that even though he clearly wasn't fond of Europeans, the older man could consider the situation. After a long silence, the shaman turned to Sacagawea. "Do you believe what this man says? Do you think he is an honorable man?"

She did not hesitate. "Captain Lewis is an honorable man, and has rendered me great assistance. He saved me and my son on the night of his birth." She hesitated a moment. "Also—"

Meriwether interjected. "I am connected to the dragon wizard, through dreams and through my own dragon spirit. I know the enemy's mind."

The shaman considered further, then slowly nodded. He explained what he knew of the evil force. "It might be Raven, or an aspect of Raven, but if so, Raven has lost his mind. Our legends tell us that Raven can be cruel and visit death upon us all. The mind that inhabits the dragon sorcerer is not a sane mind, and not a benevolent one. Maybe its anger started because it was irate over the strangers in the land, but it now despises everyone in the land. You know how many camps it has destroyed with fire, how many men and women it has killed and then used as his slaves."

The shaman was silent a long time, scratching at his chin and looking now and again at Meriwether and then at the motionless form of Charbonneau. Then he gave instructions to Sacagawea in a rapid-fire barrage and left the grass shelter.

Sacagawea bent over her husband, but she spoke to Meriwether. "The shaman says to light a special fire, and he will do a rare invocation to see if he can divine what happened to Toussaint and how it might be put right. Come with me."

Outside, away from the normal cooking fires of the village, they followed the shaman and helped him build a fire. He scuttled into his tent to change into a different garment, while Meriwether and Sacagawea went to bring her husband's litter, laying him by the ceremonial fire. Charbonneau remained insensible.

When the shaman came out, he wore a mask made of the head of a coyote and a robe made of many pelts of the same animal.

"Coyote and Raven are friends, at least most of the time," Sacagawea explained, though she sounded dubious. "And they are at the same level of power. This will allow Dosabite to use Coyote's power to learn if it's Raven who has possessed the dragon sorcerer. He will also learn what happened to my husband and how we can help him."

With a stick, the shaman had drawn a wide circle in the dirt, and he indicated for Sacagawea to stay inside with him, near her husband, while Meriwether must remain outside.

He obeyed, though he remained tense, ready to rescue Sacagawea should she need him.

Dosabite threw a handful of dry black leaves on the fire, producing acrid smoke that made Meriwether cough and step away. When he recovered his composure, Sacagawea remained standing, very still, inside the circle. The shaman began dancing, a sort of shuffling dance along the circle, singing in a low and hypnotic voice while waving a rattle down near his feet, then at the level of his head.

The pungent smoke swirled into the sunset sky like a dark smudge against the blues and reds. Meriwether thought he saw movement of a different kind against the sky. Alarmed, he waited to see dragon wings, but he saw nothing. He blinked, dizzy.

Then came a sound like a million shrill screams, and a black cloud of ravens appeared from nowhere, cawing and swooping in a tight spiral around the guardian circle Dosabite had drawn. Meriwether lifted his arm to shield his face from the black flurry, felt his breath catch in his throat. But unlike the previous encounter at Tavern Rock, the ravens ignored him.

He watched as the shaman let out a scream, then collapsed to the ground, barely missing the smoky ceremonial fire. The ravens dispersed, flying off in all directions, like shots fired from multiple guns.

The abrupt silence in the absence of ravens and chants was deafening, and gradually the natural sounds of the sunset camp filtered back into his hearing. He heard distant conversations in the village, Cameahwait and the expedition members.

Meriwether noticed that the smoke from the central fire was rising toward him, but stopped inside the circle, as if it hit a glass barrier. The shaman lay on the ground, not stirring.

Within the protective line, Sacagawea stood by her prone husband, waiting. Her posture and expression showed that she was scared.

Meriwether feared that the shaman had died, or been taken over by the dragon sorcerer. Though he had been told to remain outside the circle, he took a step closer, not sure how to break the line. He knew very bad things sometimes happened to people who broke spells—but he had to assist the poor woman trapped in there!

Before he reached the invisible barrier, though, the shaman sat up. The older man was unnaturally white as milk, his dark hair contrasting with his skin. He seemed to have aged years in those moments of unconsciousness. From inside the protective barrier, Dosabite stumbled toward the circle. He took his knife from his side, and slashed at the air at chest height, cut at the circle, all around. Where he stabbed, the smoke channeled through, pouring beyond the invisible barrier and out into the world. The acrid smell of burnt herbs made Meriwether dizzy.

Like a statue, Sacagawea remained standing by her husband, even when the circle was all cut. The shaman came up to her. Meriwether approached the line in the dirt, but stopped, standing near the prone form of Charbonneau.

The shaman's breathing was ragged and wheezing in the thick curls of smoke from the burning herbs. Dosabite spoke to Sacagawea, his voice raspy. "I am sorry."

Meriwether felt a pang of disappointment, but Sacagawea inclined her head, much more accepting. "You can't cure my husband?"

Dosabite's face looked even older, weary and sad, as if he carried the weight of everyone's disappointed dreams and hopes. "There is nothing we can do to cure him." He pointed at the man on the ground. "That is not your husband, but only your husband's body. His spirit is a captive of the creature who is the dragon, but also Raven." He leaned closer, his voice even more hoarse. "Your husband is dead, Bird Woman. Only by magic does he breathe at all. The dragon emptied him, and filled him with his own will and spirit, using him as an anchor for his spells at a great distance. You can't make live that which has no spirit anymore."

Sacagawea sat down heavily by Charbonneau's side. Meriwether remained just outside the circle, desperately wanting to help but not daring to break the connection now. The shaman tottered away with hesitant and painfully slow steps, walked out of the circle in the dirt, and disappeared into his grass shelter.

Meriwether cleared his throat and called to her. "I am sorry, Madame Charbonneau. I am very sorry."

He expected grief or despondent tears, but when she turned her face toward him, her eyes were alight with a desperate determination. "This is not the end, nor is Toussaint beyond hope. I have seen ways of rescuing him, and I hold myself obligated to do so."

Measuring Hope

THOUGH HE WOULD NOT SAY IT ALOUD, MERIWETHER BELIEVED that Sacagawea was fooling herself. The shaman's words only matched what he himself suspected of Toussaint Charbonneau, that his spirit had departed from his body, leaving him hollow. Even baby Pompy sensed it, pulling away from his father's presence.

He didn't know what Sacagawea hoped to do. If the man was dead, but his body still alive by magic, he was himself a revenant, with no more likelihood of being restored than Collins, Willard, and Hall. But he had also seen some people set in stubborn refusal at the loss of a loved one. They would invent some hope, or grasp a measure of insane planning. Such audacious plots didn't work, but the idea allowed them to deal with the immediacy of death, so the pain could pass.

Sacagawea had made it abundantly clear that she had no love for her husband, but she did have feelings. Even though he beat her, Charbonneau had supported her, fed her, kept her safe, and now that he was gone, she was left at the mercy of a cruel and capricious world.

She did not speak, and after a while he helped her carry the living corpse back to the grass tent where they had first lodged him. As she just sat there, glaring, as though Meriwether were responsible for her predicament, he chose to leave and walk back to the main fire. He felt comfortable here, where expedition members and villagers were talking and laughing. Little Pompy was sleeping, cradled in Clark's arms, who sat next to Cameahwait.

Meriwether joined them, and after some prompting, he told them both what the shaman had said. Sacagawea's brother and Clark reacted with suitable sorrow, and Cameahwait withdrew from the fire circle, going off to the shaman's shelter.

For the expedition, and the plan to fight the dragon sorcerer, they had no further answers.

Eventually, late in the night, the Snake People showed them to comfortable grass huts, where they would sleep. Clark still had the baby boy and turned to find Sacagawea's shelter, but her brother returned, shaking his head solemnly. "She is too grieved now." He gave the child to his own wife to care for the night.

Deeply troubled, not knowing what they would do now, Meriwether lay back to sleep with Seaman pressed against his leg. The big dog seemed discomfited by the strange people and lodgings, and he did not leave his master unprotected.

Meriwether woke up with Seaman growling loudly beside him.

In the moment of disorientation after waking, he spotted his dog's ruffled fur, and his tense position, ready to attack. From long association with the animal, he knew that this type of growl signified that Seaman was warning of a threat.

From outside the cool, shaded tent, came the sounds of women working and talking. This was not unusual. Usually women and young hunters rose earliest to make sure there was food for the tribe. The light coming in through the triangular door of the tent was pale with the dawn of a warm and peaceful day.

And yet, Seaman's growls grew louder.

As Meriwether rose, the dog accompanied him out of the tent. His shelter was located on the periphery of the camp, near a path that led into a grove of birches interspersed with large, lichen-covered boulders.

Meriwether felt the dog's hackles stand up. He turned to his left, in the direction of the village, sensing the prickle of someone watching him.

He tensed, half expecting to see the enemy dragon or some other monster summoned by the great magic. Instead, he saw Sacagawea, fully attired for travel, walking across the village. Her face was set in a hard, determined expression. Her eyes did not notice him, not even when he called her name. She did not carry her child, but instead of the child board, she wore a bow and arrows on her back. She gripped a spear, arrayed for war.

When she walked past him, Meriwether followed her, half mesmerized. Again, she didn't respond when he called her name. Had she decided she'd go on her own, on a mission of honor to kill the evil wizard who had taken her husband? She knew the dragon sorcerer would be impossible to destroy even with Meriwether's spirit help. She could not possibly face the evil defenses by herself. He knew Sacagawea was a rational and brave woman, but in the throes of grief, no one was quite rational.

He called after her again and ran to catch up with her. Although she did not seem to walk faster, she stayed just out of his reach, no matter how hard he ran. Puzzled and suspecting magic, he paused to catch his breath at the edge of the water, a stream running into the main river, where they had placed their canoes and pirogues and provisions, ready to continue on their expedition, should they find out where to go.

Carrying her weapons, Sacagawea seemed even more distant than ever, and he called out again as she waded into the shallows and pushed one of their canoes into the current, then climbed in and rowed away.

Then she disappeared.

It was exactly like seeing a soap bubble burst in midair. Sacagawea, canoe and all, rowed into the middle of the water and vanished with only an impression of shimmer.

He stood gasping, staring at the empty space on the water. He turned around, calling the name of one of the night sentinels, who would soon be relieved. "Gass! Patrick Gass!" When he heard no immediate response, he thought the man was asleep. He'd deserted a post of duty! He—

"Captain Lewis?" The youth came out from behind the trees, where he had apparently been keeping watch. He looked awake enough, his rifle in hand, his eyes bright. "Sir? What is wrong?"

"How can you ask what is wrong?" He gestured toward the river. "Can't you see that the Indian woman took one of our canoes? Why did you not stop her? You're supposed to be guarding our boats and provisions!"

The young man's mouth opened, as though in shock. "Sir! When did she do that? I have not seen her at all. Was it in the dark last night, when I might not have seen her?" Agitated, Gass ran to the river, then turned back in confusion. "Sir...all the canoes are here."

"Impossible. I just watched her take one." Meriwether ran to the river and counted the canoes tied to the shore. None were missing. The more he pondered what he had seen, the more he realized that he hadn't seen Sacagawea cut loose one of their vessels, only that she sat in one. "Impossible," he said to himself.

When he'd been very small, Meriwether acquired a habit of sleepwalking, perhaps due to upset by the sudden death of his father. His mother would find him outside, wandering, and in his groggy state he would tell her of his father coming back, and the games they'd played. But that phase had long passed.

Had he sleepwalked now? Had he imagined the dog growling, and how he had run after Sacagawea? He suddenly noticed that Seaman hadn't accompanied him as he followed her.

Confused and troubled, he walked back to his shelter to find the dog at the entrance to the tent. Seaman ran to him and greeted him with every impression of great joy. But that meant nothing. Had he actually dreamed seeing Sacagawea wander off?

He looked at the women working around the fire in the dawn, saw Cameahwait's wife, but not Sacagawea. Meriwether rushed to the grass shelter where they'd put Charbonneau's empty form, expecting to find her lying there alongside her husband. When he saw her there, his first impulse was to think that Sacagawea was asleep, but he noticed several things wrong. She wore the exact outfit he'd seen her wearing in his supposed dream, a new outfit of buffalo skin ornamented with many beads. It was a fine formal garment, the sort a respected person would wear when acting as an embassy to another people. It was both sturdy and practical, though also ostentatious to denote the wealth of the wearer. By her side lay the spear and the bow and arrows he'd seen her carry.

She didn't stir.

The hair rose on the back of his neck. He noted how pale she looked, how shallow her breathing. He called out "Madame Charbonneau?" and then "Sacagawea?" three times, with increasing alarm. She did not move nor awake. In fact, she looked as comatose as her husband.

Her chest rose and fell in the regular motions of breathing. He touched her hand, and she felt cool to the touch. Meriwether tested, lifting her eyelid to reveal an unseeing eye that stared at nothing.

Had she sent out her spirit form with all the trappings, leaving her body behind? That might be what he had seen, or dreamed.

Alarmed, he left the tent and looked for Cameahwait, and then he asked the warrior's wife. Though the woman spoke no English, he repeated Cameahwait's name again and again. She answered in words he couldn't understand. Cameahwait's wife made an exasperated sound and bustled into a tent. He heard her voice raised in an irritated tone, and a man's sleepy voice answering her. Finally, after more debate, Cameahwait emerged, looking worried and groggy. He had pulled on his clothes in haste.

He approached Meriwether. "What has happened?"

"It's Sacagawea," he said, and led Cameahwait to the tent. He knelt down beside his unmoving sister, quickly performed the same tests Meriwether had done.

"I don't understand," Cameahwait said, whirling to look at Meriwether. "Did the dragon sorcerer perform the same magic on her that enslaved her husband?"

Meriwether couldn't take his eyes from her. "I don't think that's what happened. I think she did this herself." He quickly described how he'd awakened and followed her form—exactly as they saw her now, with the same weapons—to take a canoe and vanish in the river.

Her warrior brother listened gravely. "I think I know what happened. There is a story...Come with me. We must see the shaman."

Moments later they entered Dosabite's shelter. As shaman, the man lived alone, and he slept in a corner of the tent, on an elaborate buffalo-hide robe. In the other corner sat knives, three pots, and woven sacks. He slept in the same clothes he'd worn the night before, although the coyote mask lay discarded by his sleeping mat. It looked like a predator watching them.

"Dosabite," Cameahwait shouted, then spoke a string of words in his own language to rouse the man and beg his help. Exhausted from the magic he had invoked the night before, the shaman was slow to awaken. He moved sluggishly, rubbing at his eyes, but when Cameahwait described the state in which they found Sacagawea, the shaman's expression grew more alarmed.

Dosabite pushed his way out of the tent, passing between Meriwether and Cameahwait. As they ran after him, he ducked into the shelter where Charbonneau and Sacagawea lay. After checking her, the shaman spoke a series of liquid syllables to Sacagawea's brother, who protested. He turned to Meriwether. "Dosabite says that she has gone with her husband to the world of the dead."

Meriwether stared down at the woman, who was still breathing. "So she is dead then?" Was dear Sacagawea now another terrible revenant?

"That is not what I said." Cameahwait released air from his lungs, exasperated. Leaving the shaman, he waved at Meriwether to follow him. "Come with me."

The two men took the same route when Meriwether had followed Sacagawea. Her brother stopped when they reached the river. "The Shoshone have a tale," Cameahwait said. "I always thought it was just a story, but you know, since the comet brought the magic back, our people have found many creatures that we thought were only myths. We have a tale about women who get married to dead warriors and follow them to the world of the dead. Sometimes, their relatives would try to rescue them, and often the relatives themselves died. Other times, the grieving women would leave in spirit, abandoning their bodies, barely breathing, until the spark of life slowly faded away."

Meriwether nodded "People back east have found magical creatures they believe in were real, too, after the magic comet." Looking out at the empty river, Meriwether said, "You speak as though people can just choose to go on this journey to the land of the dead."

Cameahwait made a face. "Yes, according to the legends, some people can. There are potions you can drink, magic-infused herbs that will send you there. Dosabite and I think that is what Sacagawea did. Last night, she must have made herself a tisane with herbs that sent her spirit out. Before she separated from her body, she dressed and armed herself for the battle against the great magic. The stories say a person can take the things she is touching when she goes on such a dream journey."

Meriwether didn't need to hear more. "That is exactly the sort of brave and gallant thing she would do."

The other man did not disagree. "When she was a young girl, Sacagawea was always as brave, as daring, and as capable as any of the boys."

Meriwether felt as though a great tragedy had befallen them.

"How is this land of the dead, then? And do people often succeed in returning, in bringing people back?"

Cameahwait frowned. "They are stories, Captain Lewis. Brothers set out to rescue their sisters who married dead warriors, so there must be some possibility of getting them back. If it were always a forlorn endeavor, surely no brother would do it?"

Meriwether nodded, feeling sickened. "So, who will go rescue Sacagawea, since she seems to be married to the dead? You are her brother."

Cameahwait's frown deepened, like lines chiseled onto his face. "She is my sister, but I am the chief of my tribe. Without me, the Snake People would be lost and directionless. If it is possible for Sacagawea to come out of this unscathed, she'll manage it on her own."

Meriwether left, trying to be contented with the answer. But later, when he spoke to Clark about it, he muttered, "It is Sacagawea. I feel like I should go and rescue her myself."

This drew a very odd look from his partner. "You do have more magic than anyone else on the expedition, and you have your spirit dragon. Who better for the task?" He smiled. "But are you sure it is a good idea, Meriwether? She's gone to rescue her husband, and she is loyal to him." His question had added layers of questions beneath the surface.

"He won her in a poker game." Meriwether realized he sounded defensive.

Clark gave him an even odder look, then sighed. "That's not an unusual form of marriage in these parts." He let out a sigh. "In fact, in some ways it sounds better than courting a lovely young girl for a year, and from a great distance. But that makes the marriage no less valid. You see she is willing to risk herself for him. She must have some feelings for him."

Meriwether shook his head. "Or maybe she just understands the stakes for the world. Sacagawea has been a member of our expedition for months. She helped us find food, she blazed paths for us and guided us through unfamiliar territory. It doesn't seem right that we should just leave her alone to a dangerous expedition in an arcane place from which few return." He sat down heavily, touching the blackened handle of his belt knife. "If we must rid ourselves of the dragon sorcerer before we can complete our expedition, we need to have her help. Sacagawea understands more about the magic of this region than either of us. Without her help, we will no doubt die in the battle—for nothing."

"Surely the wizard Franklin would then dispatch another expedition, and another should that one fail," Clark said. "He seemed a persistent sort." He frowned at Meriwether a long time, then admitted, "Yes, I can see where we need Sacagawea, or at least where our mission will be easier with her. But how do you propose to follow her to some mythical land of the dead, where it is more likely that you'll be killed in a trap. What good will it do me or the rest of the expedition, should you die?"

Meriwether did not want to add too many explanations, which he didn't even admit to himself. Instead, he mumbled, "I might have to risk it anyway? If the only way we can complete our mission is to have Sacagawea back, then I must go and find her... wherever her spirit has gone, no matter how difficult the task."

Clark seemed as unhappy with this idea as Meriwether felt. "Give it a couple days. Sacagawea might very well succeed at this without our help. Perhaps by tomorrow she will have returned with Toussaint's spirit. Maybe we'll find them both awake and breakfasting around the fire with the rest of their village."

Meriwether agreed to wait two days, while villagers continued to care for Charbonneau and Sacagawea, and others took turns with the baby. But the next morning brought no such relief, and they could only keep feeding dribbles of broth between the pale lips of the two motionless forms. Meriwether employed water and honey, which he felt should sustain them, until he could go rescue her.

When she didn't stir on the second day, he knew he had to do something.

Sacagawea looked as though she had shrunk, with dark circles around her sleeping eyes. She seemed near death, and Meriwether vowed that he could not let her die without trying to save her.

In the privacy of his own mind, he had always considered her one of the most fascinating, bravest and noblest women he'd ever met. Her manner might be strange, but she was worth a dozen of the beautiful, well-mannered ladies of Virginia. Those ladies would never have survived the simplest of tragedies and rigors that Sacagawea had suffered, nor would they have managed to find the joy she did in little Pomp, or even in exploring the land with the expedition. Even among rough men, she had held her own with such dignity that they had never harassed her. None dared treat her as less than anyone else on the expedition.

Meriwether admired her, perhaps more than he'd ever admired a woman in his life, save his mother. And he could not let Sacagawea die like this.

In the afternoon, he set aside in his tent the items he meant to take with him on the spirit journey, just as Sacagawea had taken the spear and bow. He chose his air rifle, as well as a bag with dried meat and nuts. He set aside his knife, and, after deliberation, his old army uniform, which he'd brought with him—because he'd thought that if he should die on the expedition, he wanted to be buried with dignity.

When he was ready, he went in search of Cameahwait.

He had tried to convince the chief of the Snake People to give him the recipe for the herbal potion that would send him to the world of the dead, but her brother said, "If you were to die, your comrades would hold it against me and my people. They would wreak havoc upon us."

"Captain Clark has been informed of my intention, and I explained to him again that I do this of my own free will. He will know it's not your fault."

The warrior shook his head. "I have led my people through many tragic times. What a person says he will do, whatever reassurances he gives, often turns to rage when grief strikes. Should you not come back, and should your entire expedition perish at the hands of the dragon sorcerer, there will be other white men who come after you. How can you be sure they will understand? They will think the Shoshone killed you, and they will attack us without listening to our story."

Dejected, Meriwether went in search of LaBiche, to use his services as translator for Dosabite. He hoped the shaman would see the more pressing problem, the threat to all the people from the great magic, though he did know the older man had shown hostility toward Europeans and toward the expedition's goal. Maybe he would feel less responsibility toward men who were mere guests of the tribe. Meriwether didn't know what else he could do.

LaBiche answered his summons, coming to him accompanied by an elderly Shoshone woman whose face was inexplicably familiar. The translator bobbed his head.

"Captain Lewis? Sir, this lady is Sacagawea's grandmother, and she would like to speak with you."

Intrigued, feeling his pulse race, he gestured them to the meager privacy of his own shelter. When she entered, the old woman cast a sharp glance at the things he'd prepared for the spirit journey he hoped to make. Her dark eyes showed understanding and approval.

She spoke in a whispery voice, and LaBiche translated, "She says she knows what you want to do. Her grandson told her what happened to Sacagawea, and the old mother has been looking at you, observing you. She knows you are a brave man, with a great power, and that you wish to rescue Sacagawea from the country of the dead." The trapper looked very disturbed by the words he said.

"She is right," Meriwether said, which did not reassure LaBiche at all. The interpreter seemed to be adding color to Meriwether's motives. He insisted, "It is essential to this expedition that we have Sacagawea's spirit eagle, her knowledge, and frankly her courage. If we are to confront the dragon sorcerer so that we are free to continue our journey, then we will need all the brave people we can find."

"Yes, sir. I remember we voted," LaBiche said. "The old grandmother says she can make you the herbs and the magic that will send you on the journey to the dead. She will make it possible for you to find and rescue Sacagawea."

"I see," he said, feeling weak with relief. "Thank her, and tell her that I plan to depart as soon as possible. Her granddaughter's body only grows weaker with each day. I shall go inform Captain Clark, and you have her make the potion. We don't know how long Sacagawea can last."

"It's too dangerous, sir. I don't understand—" LaBiche said.

Meriwether cut him off, not wanting to test his resolve. "I did not ask your opinion. My duty is to do the best I can for this expedition, and that means I must rescue Sacagawea, by any means possible. Even magical means."

After the man translated, the old woman departed to make the herbal tisane, promising to have it ready for his journey at sunset, explaining that a journey to the land of the dead was best undertaken when the world was between one day and the next.

He presented his decision to Captain Clark as information,

not as a matter for discussion. His companion was uneasy about being persuaded, though. Meriwether tried not to plead. "All I ask, William, is that you look after Seaman. Make sure he doesn't become some meal for a tribe."

"I can see how it is," Clark said with a forced hint of humor. "By the end of this expedition, I will be saddled with raising a child and caring for a large dog." His voice took on a sudden deeper edge, growing serious. "Don't get lost on the other side, my friend. I am not sure I could lead this expedition without you." He sighed. "I can't prevent you from going, but I can only assure you with the greatest vehemence that this expedition needs you . . . and that your friendship is very important to me."

Meriwether felt his eyes burn. "I know. And I promise you I'll do everything possible to return. With Sacagawea."

As he waited for sunset, he carefully changed into his old uniform and mentally reviewed his plans. The sky had deepened to the color of blood by the time Sacagawea's grandmother approached his tent, accompanied by a nervous LaBiche. She carried a jug of something that smelled herbal and sweet.

The Journey

"EVERYONE YOU MEET IN THAT DARK PLACE WILL SEEM OLD AND decaying to you," Sacagawea's grandmother said, as LaBiche translated. "Though the land doesn't look that way to anyone who is truly dead." She narrowed her eyes. "While you are in the land of the dead, you will know that you yourself are dead—should you die in this attempt—because that dark land will suddenly seem as new and normal as our own world. Until then, the canoes will appear to be decaying, the food offered you will appear to be mere bones or sticks, and the huts and tents will look to be rotting in place. You must not eat their food, no matter how much they insist, for it will kill you. You must take your own food, so it is good you packed your sack with nuts and dried meat. I hope Sacagawea thought to take something."

As the old grandmother prepared her potion and activated the magic and the herbs, she continued to give Meriwether advice and instructions, as well as warnings about the prospect of meeting old friends and enemies. "You must not be tempted to stay, no matter how much you miss them."

He assured her he would not be tempted. She told him to lie down upon a buffalo robe on the floor of the tent. He kept the air rifle, its ammunition, and his provisions close beside him.

He sat up and willingly sipped the brew she offered him, though he knew what it would do to him. The tisane tasted something like mint, with an underlying flavor like anise. He drained the bowl empty and lay back.

For the longest time, nothing seemed to happen. He was dizzy, impatient, queasy, and he realized that he had stood up. At least, he became aware of standing, but when he looked back he saw his own body, pale, unconscious, and stretched on the floor. Though he remained on the buffalo robe, his soul, his anima, that part of him that went beyond the body, had broken free, ready to go on his journey.

Now his body was likewise an empty vessel, until he could return to merge with it again. He experienced a moment of panic, wondering how his journey would compare with the European stories of death and the underworld. What if the land of the dead was different here in sundered America, and a man of European ancestry could not travel there to find the dead from native peoples? Would he find himself in a heaven with angels and harps, while Sacagawea had gone to the endless happy hunting grounds?

Trembling and incorporeal, he shook his head. No. He would go where he wanted to go—after Sacagawea. He would rescue her, and possibly rescue her husband. He might have to fight.

In his dream form, he took hold of his rifle, or at least the spirit of the weapon, tugged the bag of food over his shoulder, added the ammunition to it, and slipped his steel-bladed knife into his belt. Then he left the tent to begin his journey. The old grandmother did not see him, nor did she react when he departed.

As he walked through the camp, the first thing that struck him was how quiet the world had become. He heard no birds, no voices, no wind. His boots made no noise as he walked across the path of beaten dirt and rock. When he stepped on dry twigs, they remained unbroken. A look back over his shoulder showed him the site of the Shoshone village to be an empty, untouched area, with no sign of human habitation. All sign of the settlement, of Sacagawea's people, had been utterly erased from the world. This vision chilled Meriwether more than seeing himself stretched out and unconscious on the floor of the tent.

Was this what the world would be like if the dragon sorcerer succeeded?

In his spirit form, he hurried to the river, past where he knew the sentinels would be waiting, but they could not see him. Through his own connection with magic, he had been able to see Sacagawea's spectral figure, but now he understood why she had not acknowledged him when he called her name.

He knew he had to hurry. Meriwether stepped into the water of the river, feeling it swirl around his calves, but the sensation felt odd. Just as he couldn't hear the sound of his steps, he felt what seemed like the memory of cold water, rather than actual cold water itself.

In front of him, bobbing gently in the current, was a shoddy canoe, quite the most dilapidated vessel he had ever seen. Its surface was rough, as though it had slowly decayed for years. Holes in its sides had been patched with clay, and moss grew in green clumps. Meriwether knew he must use it, and he saw that the dilapidated canoe had a paddle. He waded to the canoe and climbed inside, barely making a ripple in the water. After settling himself, he took the paddle and guided the canoe expertly to the center of the river, where he had seen Sacagawea vanish.

As he reached the empty current, he realized that the flow had suddenly changed direction. The opposite bank had held some trees and a striated golden-red cliff, but now the shore lay wreathed in thick gray fog.

He had no map, nor even a guess, so he let the current carry him, now and then using the paddle to keep from approaching too close to the bank. He felt quite sure he was not supposed to disembark, not yet. He hoped he would know.

The eerie river had become much broader than the little tributary river near the Shoshone camp. He heard singing, now and then, voices emerging from the fog-wreathed lands, first singing in English, now in French, now in Welsh or Latin, even in languages he could not identify. But he saw no sign of the actual men.

The more he floated on the river, the colder and more tired he grew. It had been sunset when he consumed the old grandmother's potent tisane, but now in this world he experienced only a perpetual gloom, a land of dismal light. He felt so weary, he wanted to rest, could barely lift the paddle.

The mists swirled, and he saw that he was approaching a small isle in the stream. He saw the light of a campfire, heard a forlorn voice singing. He paddled up into the waterlogged underbrush around the island and stepped out of his canoe. He was so tired, he just wanted to rest. Holding his rifle and his provisions, he moved inland.

Meriwether found a young man sitting by a small, smoky fire. His features and shock of hair were so similar to Meriwether's own, he felt sure this must be a relative. The stranger looked up, equally startled. "Hello there. It's been many years since I've seen a man of my own race. Most of these lands are peopled with savages. I'm William Lewis. Pleased to meet you."

Meriwether froze as he extended his hand in greeting. William Lewis was his father, and his mother always said her son resembled him very closely. Now that he looked at the man before him, he recognized features he had seen on a small locket portrait that his mother possessed. Lucy rarely displayed it in public, not since her remarriage and the birth of her younger children, but Meriwether had seen it. It was one of the only things he remembered about his father.

And now the man sat here, on an island in the river to the land of the dead. Seeing the confused look in William's eyes, he broke his hesitation and extended his hand all the way to clasp the hand of his father's ghost. The grip felt warm and solid just like any other hand, but Meriwether reminded himself that his own hand—his real, physical hand—remained behind in a tent in the Shoshone camp.

He gave an apologetic smile. "And I am Captain Meriwether Lewis."

"Oh?" Understanding came into the man's expression, and he looked his son up and down. "I suppose all people come here eventually. You were much smaller when I last saw you. I swam a frozen river to get back to see you and your mother... and then pneumonia carried me off within the month. I'm very sorry to see you here so young, my son. I hoped you would live a long and fulfilled life."

William Lewis shifted his position on the rock he'd been using as a stool and resumed grilling something over the fire. "Here, share my dinner with me." The roasting meat smelled foul, and Meriwether thought it looked like a collection of bones and dry leaves clumped around a stick.

William followed his son's puzzled look, and smiled, "It's just a rabbit I caught on the way. Not much. But enough to share."

Meriwether shook his head and took a small step backward. "I am here, but I am not dead. I've come on a journey through magic to look for someone who has also come here, perhaps lost." He lowered his eyes. "And while I would enjoy nothing more than to have a long dinner with my father, I dare not eat any food in this land of the dead. Else I'll have to stay, and I am not ready for that, Father, not even for you. I have a great mission to fulfill back in the world."

"You need not rush," his father said. "Time passes differently in this land."

Meriwether sat across from his father and told the man the story of his life, what he had done, the places he had seen, the great things he had accomplished. He tried to leave nothing out, because his father deserved to know. William interrupted him many times, desperately curious to know the details, although Meriwether made a courteous lie, choosing not to tell his father that his widow had remarried and had more children. He thought it would be cruel to let the man know he'd been replaced, if not forgotten in the world of the living.

More importantly, he told his father about the dragon that terrorized St. Louis and how he had fought it, and how that had launched this grand expedition across the arcane territories. His father listened, cutting invisible meat off the assemblage of sticks and eating the food with every appearance of enjoyment. When he described Sacagawea and how she had journeyed into this land to rescue her husband, William said, "She seems uncommonly brave and resourceful. And you have come to help her."

Meriwether said, "She is an extraordinary woman, although her husband is quite common. He did not court her hand in marriage, but rather won her in a poker game. But she is very loyal and considers him worth rescuing."

His father grinned. "Then he is a lucky man. I have heard of stranger ways to find one's wife. It does not mean he doesn't love her."

It was the first time that Meriwether considered whether Toussaint might actually care for Sacagawea. It might have been more than a mere poker game, after all. What if the trapper had longed for this young woman and gambled everything to get her—and won? It could have happened like that.

"You love the woman yourself, do you not?" his father asked, quietly.

He laughed too quickly. "No, we are from different worlds. I respect her, but I doubt I could ever understand her. You know how different the native way of life is from ours."

Sounding sage, even though he had died quite young, his

father shrugged. "One tends to prefer those who are like us, but some people are so exceptional that it doesn't really matter where they grew up or how they look. Some can command love even from those who come from far away. Like Virginia..."

Though his mother was a tolerant woman, Meriwether couldn't imagine what she would say if he should come home with a native wife and a child by another man.

"It doesn't matter," he said with more of an edge than he wanted. "She has a husband, who is the whole reason she's here. She has to bring him back with the knowledge he has about the dragon sorcerer. That way she can save herself, her little boy, and the entire land." He couldn't help adding, somewhat resentfully, "And she will help save his other wife, too, I presume."

William Lewis offered his son a rueful grin. "Here, where we have left our bodies behind like discarded clothes, we come to understand many things, for we have nothing else to do but contemplate. One of the things I've come to understand is that love is love, even if my own experience was perhaps brief. The physical body that envelops the emotion of love matters little. Love is eternal. As for Sacagawea's husband...well, we'll see. You have little enough chance to bring any of them away from here, especially if he was sent here by a violent magical attack. Toussaint Charbonneau might be as dead as I am, even if his body clings to life back in the world."

His father sighed and looked sadly at his son. "I think you should go now." He pointed at the sky in the east, in which a pinkish light showed in the murk. "It is dawn here, or what passes for dawn. You should find what you are looking for down the river, that way."

He escorted Meriwether back to the rotting, dilapidated canoe pulled up in the reeds. He looked at the boat approvingly, "A fine vessel you have there, son. It will take you far." Departing, pushing the canoe back out into the current, Meriwether knew that this was the last time he would see his father until the end of his own life. As he began to paddle away, William called back at him, "One more thing to know! If you stab one of them with your civilized steel, they fall apart into a pile of bones. That will give you moments to run away, but they will come back even worse than your revenants. One cannot die here in the land of the dead. They will come back full force, and fully alive. Now go, save the woman who has drawn you here from the living world."

With a thick throat and a heavy heart, Meriwether waved goodbye as he continued down the river.

After a long while, the fog thinned and he approached what looked like a fully built-out dock, as he might have found in a river back east. Sure that this meant something, that he should stop, he tied the rotting canoe with a painter rope left dangling from the dock. He climbed onto the remarkably decrepit and decaying structure and walked to the shore, where he faced a road, a beaten-dirt track amid verdant forested hills.

Time drifted along, confusing, and he had gone some ways down the road, when he heard a song he remembered from his dreams, that nagging tune he'd first heard as "To Anacreon in Heaven." He heard masculine voices singing it, far away to his left, but the lyrics were clear, though strange, something about a banner. Meriwether was sure that if he trudged over the rolling lands, he would find Collins, Hall, and Willard, looking just as he had seen them last before that disastrous night of the revenant attack.

He kept to the main road, though, knowing from countless stories that if one diverged from the path in a magical land, it would invite all kinds of disasters. Meriwether kept walking until he heard the sound of hooves, and saw a party of painted native warriors riding swiftly toward him, and their garments identified them as Hidatsa. They bore down on him, carrying spears.

He pumped his air rifle and took a knee, shooting into the massed confusion. A spectral horse screamed and fell, and Meriwether shot again, blasting a man out of his saddle. But he faced too many of them, a good twenty, and Meriwether knew he would be killed or captured.

From his left he heard a slurred, defiant cry, "Hold up, Captain!"

"We'll get those rascals!"

Out of the blue, a whiskey barrel sailed through the air and crashed into the charging natives, its staves splintering, the iron hoops rolling and ringing loose. Wherever the metal touched one of the party, the warrior or horse fell apart into a pile of bones, and the other horses and warriors tumbled into the debris.

Only three of the attackers remained in their charge, and Meriwether shot one of them through the chest. The other two warriors were dispatched by the three Whiskey Revenants.

"Come on, Captain Lewis," Hall said, urging him down the

road. "No time to lose. They'll be back on their feet in a trice, and we can't let them capture you."

"This way," Willard called. "Don't leave the road. This part is dangerous for those still living."

"You are..." Meriwether stuttered, but couldn't bring himself to say the word, openly and coldly.

"Dead, too?" Collins asked. He grinned. "Oh, we know that, Captain, but we're still men of your expedition. We'll give you every help we can, since we have only been trouble to our party in the living world."

"And we would love to give a black eye to that dragon sorcerer who did this to us," Hall said.

"In the other world, the world of the living," Meriwether said a little sadly, "you are revenants, persistent ones. I'm afraid you've stolen a lot of whiskey."

"Aye," Willard said. "Do you know why? Because whiskey is the only thing that keeps the evil one from taking control of our bodies and making us *his* revenants." He spat on the ground. "He uses empty bodies as his own. It ain't right. And we found a way to counter him, even though we're already dead and all."

The three men helped Meriwether over the pile of bones and gore that had, moments before, been a charging band of native warriors and their horses. When he tried to explain his predicament to them, they waved away his explanation. "We know. Toussaint Charbonneau was pulled here much as we were, and then his body was returned to the expedition as a spy, and to trap his wife."

"She came by here some days ago," Willard said, "but we weren't able to help her. She did not know us."

They revenants explained that Sacagawea's spirit form was now being held captive by one of the tribes the dragon sorcerer had killed wholesale and now used as his minions: their bodies in the other world, their souls here.

"Is Charbonneau there, too?" he asked.

Hall nodded. "Yes, and he helped with taking his wife captive. Her husband pleads with her, trying to force her to eat our food, so she will remain here forever." He shook his head. "I think you need her, Captain. You both need to defeat the enemy and free the land's magic he seized."

Collins sniffed. "He knows that and is afraid of you. That's why he has set about to capture your souls. Be exceedingly careful, sir. Don't step wrong, or give him a chance to control you. Here, we are given glimpses of many futures. Many presents too. But we can see the futures of your situation. It is important that you return, both of you. Without either of you, the expedition will be destroyed, and then the sorcerer will get hold of Sacagawea's baby. After which nothing will stand in his way to dominate all of the land. Do you understand?"

Meriwether nodded. His three dead comrades escorted him down the road to where the track diverged, cutting amid other sparsely forested hills. He heard the sound of a swollen creek. Meriwether perked up at this, but Hall clapped his shoulder, "Do not drink water from that stream. You will forget yourself and all that you used to think and be."

Willard said, "You'll forget that you even wanted to go back."

"At the end of this track past those boulders," Collins said, "you will find the village of the tribe holding Sacagawea's spirit captive. They are Hidatsa, because the sorcerer knew that would trigger her worst memories and fears. The ghost warriors use her own fears to keep her subdued. You will have to distract them or convince them to let her go."

"You might even have to fight them to free her. And we'll help." Hall sounded altogether too cheerful.

Meriwether felt his heart drop down to his feet. "I shall do it somehow." Saying his formal goodbye, he shook the hands of Hall, Willard, and Collins. He paused, looked at the three men curiously. "That song you sing, both here and in the world? You use different words than the lyrics with which I am familiar."

Willard explained, "We are beyond death, and we can see all that could have been in the living world. There is another version of this world, one without the Sundering, where this continent was never cut off from Europe. That land is different, and it has grown into a whole, united land, where all men are considered equal, where every person has the right to liberty and the pursuit of happiness."

Collins continued, "In that world, they used the tune of 'To Anacreon in Heaven' for their anthem. We use those words for strength against the murderous great magic. A world that might have been."

Willard urged him on. "Now, go and rescue the Bird Woman. It is up to you, sir."

But Hugh Hall looked sheepish. He cast his eyes down. "I'm

sorry we stole that first barrel of whiskey, sir. That was wrong. We let our greed get the best of us, but believe me, we've been punished for it enough. Anything we can do to help you and the expedition, we will do."

"Anything in our power," Collins added.

As he left them and trudged down the track, he considered the idea the Whiskey Revenants suggested, some strange parallel world that embraced the idea of all men being equal. Such a utopia sounded nonsensical.

He did, however, keep to the road, more determined than he'd been before because he trusted what the three dead men had told him. Once a man needed to trust in whiskey to keep him from being possessed by an evil force, he didn't have much room to invent lies.

He thought the Hidatsa revenants would have placed sentries on the track to guard against invaders, and he did find them. As he approached a large rock outcropping ahead, beyond which he expected to find the village, a native undead warrior stood in the road, pointing a wicked spear at him. "Turn around, white man, or I'll be the end of you." His skin was gray and patchy with rot.

Meriwether braced himself and fired his air rifle at the creature. The revenant wavered, then collapsed into a pile of loose, yellowed bones, no longer barring the way. He did not let himself grow overconfident, though. Doubtless there would be many more of these spectral warriors guarding their captive Sacagawea. From the settlement ahead, he could hear voices: men, women, children.

His air rifle was powerful, and he'd brought a sack of ammunition with him into the spirit world, but neither his rifle nor the bullets were magical. To shoot every one of these undead Hidatsa before they could stop him would be impossible. He would be taken down by the enemy's sheer numbers.

He needed a plan, and he needed to reconnoiter.

He worried about leaving the track to scout, because he didn't want to find himself lost in the land of the dead, but he realized that if he couldn't find Sacagawea, he was already lost.

Before he could move, the rotted body of his vanquished enemy on the path was reassembling itself, the bones pulling together, shimmering as flesh slathered itself into place. In his bony, shaking hand, he still held the spear.

Instead of rounding the rock outcropping, which would put

him in full view of the village, he decided to slip around it and not worry about following the road. When he took his first step off the trail, he felt a roar of terror, as if the ground itself might collapse under his feet. Then he felt soil and rock beneath his boots again, and he climbed cautiously.

He might have taken the risk for nothing. While the outcropping had looked discrete, easily sidestepped with a little scrambling, he realized the outcropping was actually a steep yellow-brown cliff, shrouded in mists. He kept climbing, sure he would get around it so he could approach the village unseen.

As he climbed toward the high point, the crumbling barrier had ledges and outthrust rocks that he could use for handholds and steps. The path up the rock veered and meandered, some of it hidden by crumbling rock. He was panting with the exertion, even here in the land of the dead, but he had a perfect vantage from the high point.

As he grabbed for a prominent handhold, he heard the spine-chilling ominous vibration of a rattler, buzzing its warning. He froze, not moving his hand, providing no target for the viper to strike. He had encountered rattlesnakes before, and fortunately he had solid footing and good balance. He removed his knife from his belt, and watched the snake rise up and slither back, ready to strike. With a swift arc, he sliced off its head in one smooth, clean movement with the steel blade.

Here in the land of the dead, the decapitated snake trembled, then collapsed into a pile of bones and decaying flesh. Since he knew that even a small serpent would reassemble itself once killed, he used his boot to kick at the remains, flinging the bones far from the cliff, where they tumbled in the air. He had no desire to see the rattlesnake again.

At the summit of the outcropping, he dropped to a crawl so he could peer cautiously at the village. He did not want to be spotted. When he finally crossed the summit and made his way to an opening in the rocks, Meriwether had an excellent view of the Hidatsa village.

The buffalo-hide, triangular tents were close to the pocked wall of the outcropping, which provided protection against attack from the rear. He saw the narrow river swiftly flowing on the other side of the village, likewise blocking it off. Only by the dirt road could one enter the village. Or leave.

If he wanted to get down from this cliff and enter the village directly, he would have to learn to fly.

Suddenly, he spotted Sacagawea. She looked exhausted and somehow diminished, as if she had been sapped of so much courage that her physical dimensions had shrunk. Listlessly, she tended several horses. Two men stood next to her, one of them Toussaint Charbonneau, and the other a Hidatsa warrior, both of whom appeared to be supervising forced labor. As Meriwether watched, tense and desperate, Sacagawea stumbled and barely managed to get herself up again, before a horse stepped on her. Her own husband was one of her abusers. Again.

Meriwether knew he had to rescue her.

He wished he'd brought a roll of sturdy rope on his spirit journey, so he could climb down the rugged bluff, but he had only his belt, his clothes, and the strap of his bag. He wouldn't make it halfway down the cliff, much less all the way to the village.

He looked around for any sign that a gradual descent might be possible. On his hands and knees, he crept along the top of the outcropping, but found the dropoff as steep there as anywhere else.

There was a pine tree, growing just five feet away from the far tip of the crescent of rock. If he could jump and hold on to the pine, he might be able to climb down it to more handholds, more jutting rocks so that he could make his way down.

If he couldn't, then he would be left stranded, high on the rocks.

What would happen if he fell straight down? Would he be killed, and trapped forever in the land of the dead? He remembered what the old shaman had said about intrepid heroes who came to the world of the dead, how they were lured into traps and killed. If he failed here, he would fall straight down and kill himself in both worlds. If the Whiskey Revenants were right, and he would condemn the expedition to failure and the whole world to the enslavement of the dragon sorcerer.

He contemplated a long time, studying the tree, measuring the distance. If only he were younger, more agile.

But when he heard Sacagawea cry out and saw her on the ground, while the big warrior stood over her and beat her, Meriwether cast aside all his doubts. He secured his rifle, his bag of provisions and ammunition, and took a deep breath.

He jumped for the pine.

When he was in midair, he knew he'd misjudged. The distance

was too great. He would never catch the tree, and he would fall. But suddenly his fingers touched pine needles. He clutched at a branch, which tore free, but slowed his fall enough that he could grab another bough with his right hand, yanked himself forward, and then he was embracing the pitch-wadded trunk with both arms, wrapping his legs around it for security, trying to recover his breath.

With all the commotion, he half expected to find the whole village rushing toward the tree. It took him a long time of slow, careful breathing before the noise in his ears subsided, before he blinked sweat from his eyes, until he could look around. And see that he was safe.

The villagers below went about their activities, undisturbed. As he worked his way farther down the tree, to wider boulders and a safer descent, he saw some women on the far side of the outcropping. Had the dragon sorcerer killed them all in the world of the living? Meriwether remembered the corpses twisted in tree roots in the fire demon. He found it obscene that someone could kill people and then use them as his puppets, body and soul.

A determination as hard and dangerous as the steel of his knife blade calmed his breathing. Meriwether made his plan, and he worked his way down from the trees into the rocks as quietly as he could. He saw no one below, just a clearing and a scraggly dog, sniffling at the ground as if trying to find something to eat.

Meriwether reached the base of the tree and the broken rocks, afraid the dog would bark at him, but instead the friendly animal approached, letting Meriwether pat him. He thought of big, faithful Seaman, and had to remind himself the creature was already dead, a pet of revenants.

He loaded and pumped up his rifle, then made his way around the edge of the village, keeping to the rocks and scrub where no one could see him. He could still see Sacagawea, dragging herself up, fiercely fighting tears while the big warrior shouted at her. He grabbed a bunch of twigs and shook them in front of her. Charbonneau stood by, also threatening, then pleading.

Sacagawea shook her head, and Meriwether understood. They were trying to force her to eat their version of food, so she would be trapped there like them.

Without remorse, Meriwether raised his rifle and shot the big warrior, who fell in a heap of bones and sloughing flesh. Charbonneau turned to gape at him, then let out a scream of warning to the rest of the enemy village. There was only one thing Meriwether could do if he meant to save her and get them both away from here. Reminding himself that the man was already dead, he shot Toussaint Charbonneau, who also fell in a pile of bones and scraps of putrid flesh.

Meriwether was running, heading straight for Sacagawea, but she had dropped to clutch at her husband's bones, tying them in a ragged blanket. Meriwether couldn't believe what she was doing. "You can't bother with that," he shouted, reaching for her arm. "We must go now."

Outcries and the sounds of running feet surged through the village. Close by, two warriors had nearly reached them, howling with fury. Meriwether shot them, while Sacagawea screamed, grabbing the satchel of bones and debris. "I have to. Toussaint is who I came back to get."

To his surprise, she shoved Charbonneau's skull at him. "Take this. While it is separated from his body, my husband can't come fully alive. He's being controlled by the dragon sorcerer. Sometimes he can overcome it for a short time, but he can't be trusted." As she spoke, she grabbed a horse, untied the halter rope, and mounted it bareback. She shouted at Meriwether. "What are you waiting for? Mount!"

Meriwether stuffed Charbonneau's skull in his bag, then shot three more of the approaching Hidatsa warriors and mounted a second horse, less gracefully than Sacagawea. She rode hard and jumped the fence that held the horses. Meriwether, slipping and sliding on the bare back, spurred the animal with his heels, so that he also jumped.

Sacagawea headed for the river. Meriwether feared they might fall in and swallow the water, but there was nothing for it. She got the horse into the current, and the animal swam hard, trying to reach the opposite shore. Meriwether followed, plunging into the river, which was cold as ice. In a second, he couldn't feel his submerged legs, and he struggled to keep his mouth closed and well above the water as he held on to the horse's neck.

Behind them, dozens of undead warriors chasing them on foot hesitated before plunging into the water, as if afraid of losing themselves as well. But by the time Sacagawea's horse emerged onto the opposite bank, many of the Hidatsa warriors were in the water, swimming hard and closing in on Meriwether's horse.

Sacagawea shouted something that Meriwether couldn't understand, and he realized she had called to his horse. The animal understood and redoubled its efforts at swimming. Finally, they climbed onto the opposite muddy bank. Already riding away, Sacagawea looked over her shoulder to see that he was safe, then she set off at a gallop, expecting him to follow.

For a while the two horses rode down the clear path between tall pines. The howls of the village behind them subsided, then increased. Looking back, Meriwether saw mounted Hidatsa warriors chasing them on horseback. They were more used to riding bareback—Meriwether felt as though he were perpetually in danger of sliding sideways—and they were closing in.

Ahead, the trees thinned, and he saw that the path led to the same road he had followed, which should bring him back to his canoe.

The angry shouts from behind grew ever louder.

Just as they left the pine forest, three men burst out of the shadows. Meriwether was so sure they were enemies, he yelled and swung his rifle around—but then he heard a familiar voice say, "We'll handle it, Captain. Let dead men handle the dead. We should be able to delay them."

Willard, Hall, and Collins, the three Whiskey Revenants, went into battle, throwing another of their empty barrels at the pursuers.

He and Sacagawea galloped as fast as they could along the road. Meriwether took the lead because he knew where he was going.

The horses ran free along the road, and Meriwether began to feel hope, when they heard more sounds of pursuit behind them again, shouts of rage. He saw men on horseback pursuing them, but they weren't Hidatsa, rather a motley of tribes. He spurred his horse on, but the animal began to stumble. Did dead horses lose their wind? He couldn't even guess why.

While still galloping, he pumped his rifle and swung himself around, wishing he had a saddle to secure himself, and shot at the vanguard of the pursuers. Willard, Hall, and Collins would not likely show up to save him again. Dead men might battle the dead, but surely there was a limit to the numbers they could overcome.

A voice emanated from Meriwether's bag, startling him. "Give me to the rest of my body. I can delay them." He remembered he had stuffed Charbonneau's head there. In the blanket satchel at the back of Sacagawea's horse, he could see that the man's body mostly assembled itself with flesh and clothes, and weapons.

"Leave me your knife," the head added from the bag, "so I can fight."

"No," Sacagawea said, holding onto her husband's writhing, headless body. "No, Toussaint. We can't trust you—and I came to get you."

"I am already dead, but you have to stop the dragon sorcerer." Charbonneau's hands reached towards Meriwether. "Let me have my head. I am myself, and I'll make a stand and delay them."

Meriwether thought it was a foolhardy suggestion, but how much worse could their situation be? Even if her husband turned against them, he would be only one more enemy. Meriwether fumbled to remove the head from the bag. It was mostly restored, the eyes alive.

"Throw my head at the rest of me!" Charbonneau's skull commanded.

Before Sacagawea could object, Meriwether obeyed. The head sailed through the air, to be grabbed unerringly by the should-be-blind hands of Charbonneau, who slammed it on his neck.

Suddenly Toussaint Charbonneau was whole and alive, and as Sacagawea tried to grab the body about the waist, her husband laughed. "Farewell, mon ami."

As the man dropped from the galloping horse, Meriwether saw that he had somehow managed to get hold of a knife— Sacagawea's knife. Relief washed over him as Charbonneau ran at the enemy. He didn't know how much effect one man could have, but Meriwether was willing to let him try.

Sacagawea attempted to wheel her horse around, but he blocked her path. "No, your husband has picked his own path. He is a hero. As for us, we will still be lucky to leave here. Come, ride!"

He didn't expect her to follow him, but she did. As he galloped down the long road, he could see the dock and the canoe. But behind them, he could hear pounding hoofbeats and the snarls of an enraged enemy growing nearer.

From the clear hills by the road, a surprisingly familiar man appeared as though materializing out of thin air. He stepped forward, ready to take his position—a man Meriwether recognized. "Floyd!"

"Just so, Captain." The undead man stepped up. "If I may have your rifle, I will delay them."

Meriwether had no time to hesitate. He flung his rifle and sack of ammunition at the ghost of the first man who had died on the expedition. Floyd caught them perfectly in midair as though the movement were rehearsed. Floyd pumped the air rifle and swung toward the pursuing enemy. As he and Sacagawea thundered onward, Meriwether could hear gunshots and the screams of the would-be pursuers.

At last, the two horses reached the dock and the waiting canoe. The soft greenish wood of the dock boards looked to be in worse shape than before. The decaying canoe looked little more than a barely coherent assemblage of wood and moss. Meriwether knew it would hold them, though. He paid no attention to appearances here in the land of the dead. He dismounted and hurried a trembling Sacagawea down to the canoe after turning the two horses loose. He had to remind himself the animals were already dead.

The canoe's bottom held sloshing, brownish water, but they climbed into it, ready to paddle away. With Sacagawea's weight in addition to his own, the canoe rode low in the current, but he started paddling to get out into the stronger current.

He remembered how long he'd rowed downstream to get here, and the prospect of rowing the same distance against the current dismayed him, but he continued paddling, his arms numb, his whole body tired. He just wanted to sleep.

Though quiet, Sacagawea was weeping. She used her cupped hands to bail out the water that kept seeping into the bottom of the boat.

He tried to reassure her. "Don't cry. We're not yet doomed."

As the canoe moved along, finding its way as he paddled furiously, he saw people gathering on the banks, moving out of the mist. He could discern little about them, whether they were white men or natives, friendly or hostile. Quietly, they sang the hymns he'd heard in church in his youth, but his ears were buzzing loudly. He was covered in sweat, and his arms protested with each stroke of the paddle, pushing the canoe back to the land of the living.

"I don't weep because we are doomed," Sacagawea said, bailing steadily. "I weep because I left my husband behind, and now he is dead for all time."

"I am sorry," Meriwether said, and he meant it. A cold gray mist swallowed the riverbanks, or maybe it was his vision growing dim with tears. They passed the island where he'd met his long-dead father, and he thought he saw William Lewis on the shore, waving, but he couldn't be sure. He was so tired he might have been dreaming with his eyes still open.

"He chose his own path, as you say," Sacagawea spoke up. "It was the hero's path, but he died trying to protect me. I never thought Toussaint would do that."

Meriwether was also surprised, and reassessed his opinion of the man somewhat.

He rowed and rowed, in a trance of pain and labor. From the mist-shrouded banks came a song about Jordan, but this wasn't the river Jordan. Whatever land of the dead this was, it had nothing to do with the heaven he'd learned about in school or from the Bible. This was no pious place of order and angels.

Still crying, Sacagawea continued to bail, but the canoe, beginning to sink, took on more water. The sloshing water at the bottom now reached to Meriwether's ankles, making his feet and calves numb. They could not drift much farther.

Gray mist surrounded them, and he couldn't recognize the scenery around him. He couldn't tell if they were close to where he had departed. He needed to find out how to return to the living.

He considered the dismal future the world would face should he die here, his quest incomplete. He drew strength from the terrible thought of his mother receiving news of his death. But that was unlikely. As the dragon sorcerer surged in power from the untamed land, he would swiftly subsume even the eastern lands beyond the Mississippi. He lamented for the poor boy Pompy, who would never know why he was dying, or why the evil force possessed him.

Meriwether vowed to keep paddling, to get Sacagawea home.

He lifted the paddle, which seemed to weigh as much as the combined sins of humanity. He let his arms fall again, and he rowed, and rowed, and rowed. He wasn't even sure that the canoe was moving. He could feel the current the other way.

The mist was so thick around them he could barely see Sacagawea in the front of the canoe. But he could hear her cry softly.

As he paddled, he heard a sharp crack right at his feet, like thunder.

The canoe broke in half, spilling them into the river.

Funeral Rites

"STOP STRUGGLING!" CAPTAIN CLARK'S VOICE SAID, WHILE SOME-one pushed Meriwether's hands aside, firmly. He coughed sour water out of his mouth, and he found himself quite blind. He fought against the hands now restraining his wrists. "Stop! My friend, it is I. I am on your side."

How could his dearest friend be there, when he was in the land of the dead? How could he trust that even Clark was there to help him? "I can't see," he half shouted, his voice echoing harsh and hoarse in his ears.

He heard relieved laughter, the last thing he expected. Finally, the grip around his wrists let go and peeled a dripping cloth away from his face. Clark tossed it into a nearby basin of water.

Meriwether blinked, trying to focus. "Why were you blinding me? It was a damnable prank."

"Not a prank. You were burning up with fever, and you know I've studied your own notes and medical journals. Is it not accepted practice to endeavor to cool a patient in such a state?"

Meriwether blinked again, and took in his surroundings. He was inside the shelter with walls of carefully bound grasses, and he lay on a buffalo robe. His rifle and ammunition were at his side, as was the bag of provisions, all intact. He remembered giving the rifle to Floyd's ghost in the land of the dead, so they could get to the canoe. "I was rowing," he said, followed by a long silence.

He heard a deep voice at the door, recognized it as Cameahwait.

He blinked at the chief of the Snake People. Cameahwait said, "You brought Sacagawea back. She's very tired, but she's alive."

With a supreme effort of will, since it felt as though his arms were dislocated from the efforts his spirit body had made, he raised himself onto his elbows. "And Charbonneau?"

The Shoshone chief shook his head. "My sister is now a widow. Her husband did not return from the land of the dead."

Meriwether let himself fall back onto the thick furry robes, conscious of his failure.

All he wanted to do was sleep, but Clark managed to make him swallow some water and then thin gruel, before he fell headlong into slumber. While he dozed, he was conscious of Seaman crawling in and lying next to his legs.

He woke a long time afterwards when someone entered the tent. When he opened his eyes, he saw Sacagawea carrying little Pomp.

"I wanted to thank you," she said, very softly. "For the risk and trouble you took on my behalf."

"Ah, but I failed you and your husband," he managed to say, his voice very rough. "And your son."

She shook her head. "No. The shaman says what I did was wrong. Brave but foolish. I could never have rescued Toussaint because he was already dead. Long dead, but the magic wouldn't let his body know it. He says if you try to bring spirit bones from the other world, they simply rot, and the person dies twice." Her shoulders drooped. "I didn't know. I thought we could get him back. I thought he could help us."

Finding his words, Meriwether told her what the Whiskey Revenants had told him, that she and Meriwether, the spirit eagle and the spirit dragon, were all that stood as bulwarks against the horrors of the dragon sorcerer.

Though she looked as confused as he felt, she inclined her head. "I don't know how all this is to be." She looked tired, he realized, but composed. Her eyes had that look people get when they've cried so much that they feel drained of grief.

Feeling as if he were a million years old, as if he had seen civilizations rise and fall, he dragged himself to a sitting position. "We must call everyone together so we can organize an attack on the evil—"

"No." Sacagawea shook her head for emphasis. "First, we must bury my husband. The dragon sorcerer took him from me, but

I will see that he is properly returned to the land." She came to sit on her heels next to him before he could ask about her people's traditional funeral customs. "We have sent LaBiche, who knows where there is a Catholic priest who can come and give Charbonneau a proper burial. I shall have my husband buried in the way he would prefer. Perhaps it will ensure his spirit goes to the right heaven?"

Meriwether refused to be drawn into the discussion. He had seen Sergeant Floyd, as well as Hall, Willard, and Collins, all in the native land of the dead. Were there truly different aspects of the afterlife? Or did each person see something akin to what he expected?

Sacagawea left the grass tent, and eventually Meriwether gathered his strength and stepped outside to look at the Shoshone camp. With Seaman by his side he wandered the camp in a daze, not quite believing that he'd come back from the place where everything was changeable shadows.

He saw Sacagawea with the women of the tribe, roasting large haunches of meat. As he wandered, Meriwether came upon her brother, who grasped both his hands and thanked him effusively for saving her. "Twice I lost my sister, and twice she was restored to me. But this time, if the legends are correct, it is a true miracle she came back. You, Captain Lewis, have achieved something even the ancient warriors never managed. If there is anything you wish from the Shoshone, forever, it is your right to ask."

Still overwhelmed, Meriwether nodded, mumbled his gratitude, and walked away. It occurred to him he could have asked for help in storming the dragon wizard's lair, but he was not ready for that battle yet.

Soon, he found York following him, and he let the big man catch up with him. York looked sheepish. "Is anything wrong?" he asked.

York smiled ruefully. "Captain Clark sent me to follow you. He was afraid you were not quite...not quite back from your adventures."

Meriwether realized that Clark feared he might have been taken over by the mind of the enemy sorcerer. He also decided that he no longer felt ill or bereft, merely tired to the bone. "Such a journey takes a great deal out of you. Sojourning in the land of the dead leaches the life and energy, and you feel that you don't have the strength or the interest to go on. I will recover, but it might take a while."

York nodded grimly. "Well, Captain, you hear stories. I grew up amid slaves in Virginia, and my people brought their own stories from Africa, before the Sundering. Every land has legends of those who venture from the world of the living to the land of the dead, usually to bring back a loved one who died, although sometimes to steal a treasure that is otherwise lost. But often the people who come back from such an ordeal are not quite right in the head. They're not actually themselves, or they are . . . broken. Something has gone wrong in them that cannot be fixed. They feel attracted to death from that point on, desperate to go back to that place. Many just wither away and die."

"I assure you, Mr. York, that is not what ails me," Meriwether said. "I am just very tired. And you can tell Captain Clark so."

The big dark-skinned man inclined his head, but apparently he didn't fully believe Meriwether, as he continued to follow him around the camp, sometimes clumsily pretending to other errands, but his intent was obvious. Even Seaman, deliriously happy to have his master back, followed his every step, pressing his warm, furry body against his legs and nearly toppling him sideways in his enthusiasm.

It took two days for the Catholic priest to arrive, and he was the oddest Catholic priest Meriwether had ever seen. The man looked as wild and of mixed blood as most of their interpreters. Dressed in Indian clothing, with long black hair peppered in gray, he appeared less like a priest than Meriwether did, and he spoke a wild patois of English, French, and native language. He introduced himself as Father Avenir.

Stopping outside the tent where they'd laid Charbonneau's remains, Father Avenir prepared for his work. From a tattered shoulder bag, he extracted an equally tattered long black tunic, which he donned, making him look marginally more like a priest. He requested a bowl of water, which he blessed, and then he removed an aspergillum from the same bag, and proceeded to sprinkle his surroundings with the holy water: the tent, the curious Shoshones standing by, even Sacagawea and Meriwether, before he got around to sprinkling the corpse.

He mumbled in Latin while walking around the pale corpse. The dead man, infused with the dark magic, looked little worse than when Meriwether had left him behind to go find Sacagawea in the land of the dead. Toussaint Charbonneau seemed to have shrunk and dried in place, rather than bloating and putrefying in this warm weather.

With LaBiche helping to translate, the priest ordered the body to be carried out on a litter. With Sacagawea following, carrying Pompy, they took Charbonneau to a grave dug at the edge of the camp. Meriwether and Clark watched solemnly as the body was laid in the grave, and the priest spoke final words. Two of the men began shoveling dirt into the grave, covering the body, when they heard the loud, ominous laughter.

At first, Meriwether thought it was just thunder, a heavy rumbling over the horizon. But then he knew the voice, the angry adversary. Before he could react, he heard the loud beating of wings like giant rugs thumping in the air.

The dragon creature flew toward them from the open sky above the trees, very red and more enormous than during its previous attack in St. Louis. Seeing it, Father Avenir fell to the ground and dropped prostrate beside the open grave. The gravediggers from the expedition yelled and raised the shovels, their only weapons.

Inside Meriwether's head, the laughter of the dragon was deafening, and he could smell his stink, a hot reptile smell, oily and thick. Seaman kept snarling and barking.

As the dragon flew low, the men futilely tried to strike at him with the shovels, but missed. The great dragon flew so close over Meriwether, its claws would have ripped off his head, had he not thrown himself aside.

As if toying with them, the dragon exhaled a stream of fire, and the grass-woven tent that had held Charbonneau's body exploded into flames and belching smoke. As villagers ran screaming for shelter and Shoshone warriors scrambled for weapons to fight it, the dragon swooped in a circle around the camp, then returned, spewing more fire to engulf Sacagawea's shelter.

Meriwether knew he had to stop the monster. If he allowed the dragon to continue, it would incinerate the entire camp, tent by tent, roast the warriors, the wives and children, the expedition members, even his dog Seaman. With targeted hatred, the enemy dragon wished to break Meriwether, to dissuade him from fighting back.

But the terrorization resulted in the opposite effect.

"Continue with the funeral, Father!" Meriwether bellowed.

"Break the sorcerer's hold on the body!" He heard his voice distorted because he'd already started his effort to project his spirit dragon out into the open, into the real world. The way Sacagawea had taught him to fight.

Like a birth, the process of summoning and transforming was natural and painful. But when the difficult block crumbled away in his mind, it seemed a great relief to allow his own dragon out. He pushed his other form out into the light of day.

His Welsh spirit dragon materialized in midflight, soaring free and powerful. He dipped a broad parchment-thin wing to bank and then flew hard to intercept the enemy as it returned to attack the camp.

His arrival took the dragon sorcerer by surprise, and the monster backflapped his wings to avoid colliding with his nemesis. Not even bothering to look down at where his human body had collapsed on the ground, Meriwether put on a burst of speed. He raked his outstretched claws against the enemy's wing, feeling his talons snag and tear the supernatural flesh of his foe.

The enemy dragon screamed and tumbled out of the sky, but quickly recovered his balance. He turned and vomited a volley of flame at Meriwether's spirit dragon. The fire caught the tip of Meriwether's wing, which blazed in pain, but he managed to corkscrew and dodge, stroking his broad wings to fly high and gain altitude...to lure the enemy dragon away from the camp.

But the enemy dragon had encountered Meriwether's abilities before, did not forget how Meriwether had wounded it severely, nearly tearing out its throat, and he flew guardedly. Reaching up and slashing, Meriwether managed to rake his talons along the creature's tail.

His spirit dragon fought for height, for breath, for strength, and he played the aggressor. He attacked the enemy dragon again and again, knowing that if he failed to kill, or at least drive off, this adversary, then all his friends would die.

Far below, on the ground, the eccentric priest was singing, swinging the aspergillum in hand, sprinkling holy water on Charbonneau's grave to complete the ritual. With frequent nervous glances up into the sky, the two expedition men filled the grave. Sacagawea was shouting something in her own language, and her baby wailed. Seaman kept barking. Villagers ran about throwing water on fires.

Meriwether watched through his dragon eyes, saw Sacagawea hand her child to a woman nearby, then drop to her knees, swaying. Suddenly an eagle flew out of her, a large bird of prey, that winged up into the air. Joining Meriwether's spirit dragon, she harried the enemy dragon, pecking at it. The enemy twisted its long sinuous neck and shot flame at her, singeing the beautiful feathers of her eagle's wing.

Meriwether plunged in to attack again, but he feared he wasn't strong enough to win this battle, even with the help of Sacagawea's spirit eagle. The enemy dragon was twice their size, seemingly drew its power from the anger of the land, and could shout in streams of fire. Meriwether attempted to do the same, but no flame came out of his mouth.

He tried to press his attack, but the enemy dragon seemed to dance in air, easily eluding the eagle form and Meriwether's spirit dragon.

The evil voice boomed inside his head. *You are lost dragonling, and the little bird too! You can do nothing to stop me. I shall destroy the expedition and the village, and I will continue to remake the land in its primal, angry form.* With a wicked twist, the voice added, *Envy the dead man Charbonneau, for he's the only one who will not feel my vengeance.*

Meriwether could feel the despair at the words seep into his mind, darkening his thoughts like an inkstain. His dragon wings flapped, but seemed to catch less air, and he found himself falling, spiraling.

Then the talons of Sacagawea's eagle snagged his tail, sending a jab of sharp, insistent pain into him. It was like being rudely awakened. Meriwether responded by flapping his wings frantically to break his fall, and did not give up.

In his spirit dragon form, he wasn't large enough or powerful enough to defeat the enemy sorcerer. The giant flying form was in his own element, drawing upon his own reservoir of power. Then Meriwether realized that if they couldn't take the adversary in his own element, fighting with his own rules of magic, perhaps he could attack the physical manifestation of the creature with the weapons of civilized steel he'd brought with him. He remembered the devastating effect his knife had on the fire demon, on the attacking flock of ravens.

No, he couldn't defeat this monster if he remained a spirit

dragon. But maybe he could do it as Meriwether Lewis. Hastily, he forced himself into his human body.

Like a reverse birth, this was considerably more difficult than merely releasing his spirit form. As he plunged back from the sky and the powerful freedom of his giant reptile form, his human body felt turgid, too small, too heavy. But Meriwether took control of his limbs, breathed deeply in his stale lungs, and got to his feet. As Captain Clark shouted to him and Seaman bounded after him, he stumbled toward his tent.

He seized his air rifle, pumped it, loaded it. Bullets of metal, civilized metal, forged to be used with a civilized firearm. Sacagawea's eagle disappeared from the sky, and he watched her collapsed form stir and then struggle up from her knees.

Above, the enemy dragon was still laughing, seeming to think his opponents had surrendered and fled. Plunging down to the village, the monster opened its wide jaws to breathe again, to exhale a miasma of fire onto Meriwether. With undaunted bravery, Seaman stood in front of his master, growling up at the monster.

Defeating him with just a gun seemed less likely than with his dragon form, but the dragon form had failed. If he sent it forth again, it would be weaker.

Meriwether stood firm, did not let his aim waver. He fired several shots, aiming for the creature's heart and head and eyes. The rifle balls seemed trivial, little biting gnats, even if he had tried to imbue them with his own magic, his civilized counter-defense. He thought that he had missed, as the monster's mouth opened wider, building up the fire boiling within it.

Bowling Seaman over with him, he threw himself sideways, rolling away from the thin stream of carefully targeted fire that hit where the two of them had been.

But the fire guttered out quickly, impotent. And then the dragon disappeared.

He didn't explode, or collapse into rotting component parts as the other deadly apparitions had done. Instead, the adversary simply vanished from the air, leaving behind a suggestion of laughter, and the memory of words, *Bah, dragonling. You can only win against my projection. If you dare come to where I really live, you shall be destroyed.*

Oddly, the last taunt seemed more like an invitation than a threat.

With the enemy dragon gone and the fires still smoldering around the village, people rushed at Meriwether, jabbering questions. The eccentric and unkempt Father Avenir stepped up and solemnly splashed holy water on Meriwether's face and clothes, then for good measure, he sprinkled the dog, too.

While Cameahwait fussed over Sacagawea, little Pompy was wailing in the arms of one of the village women.

Clark and York rushed to help him stand up, brushing him off, checking him for injuries. Clark cried out, "Good God, Lewis—your hands!"

Looking down, he suddenly felt the pain from his wrists down. He flexed his fingers, saw that his hands were red and blistered, and he remembered when the adversary had scorched the tips of his wings when he was in the form of the spirit dragon.

Sacagawea held out one of her hands, looking at it strangely, as if wondering at the burns she found there too. Meriwether coughed, found his voice. "York, go fetch the herbal salve I make for burns. It's in a sealed jar among our supplies. Both Sacagawea and I can use it. And bring linen strips for bandages, too."

The man bounded off and returned swiftly. Though his own hands could barely function, Meriwether insisted on tending Sacagawea first, but finally York and Clark took the salve away and forced him to become a patient, spreading the salve on his hands, followed by strips of bandages.

Sacagawea kept talking as she endured the ministrations. "The dragon sorcerer is too powerful. Even if the revenants gave you hope in the land of the dead, they do not know everything. We do not have the power to kill a creature like that. The enemy has already eaten many lives and it is full of power, as the land swells into summer. We cannot defeat it."

Her words echoed with the remembered taunts of the other dragon, but that only increased his resolve. He might fail, but he couldn't give up. He needed to defeat this evil, for himself, for his people, for civilization, for the whole of sundered America.

If he surrendered, he would just as surely die as if he had fought to the death. No, the only answer lay in trying every method they could find, use any weapon, and hope.

Dearest Julia,

I am sending this letter with some of the Shoshone people and members of our expedition in hopes of keeping them safe from the immediate wrath of the dragon sorcerer. Perhaps they can reach Fort Mandan, and from thence dispatch the letters with a trapper heading east.

This may be my last letter to you.

Alas, knowing the titanic evil force we face, I fear the promises I made to you will be forfeit, and I'll never return to claim your hand. But this is a battle that simply must be fought, for the sake of our world and our civilization. If the dragon sorcerer is not stopped, he will grow powerful enough to cross the Mississippi, to burn our American lands all the way to the Atlantic. I cannot leave you to face such a terrible fate, my dear Julia, without knowing I did everything in my power to stop it.

I cannot explain how I know these details, because you'd think me a lunatic. Realize that out here in the arcane territories, the powers of magic have a different sway and strength, built out of different ingredients from the myths and legends of all the native peoples. Let me just say that Captain Lewis has returned from a remarkable journey into a magical realm, and he brought us back news we cannot doubt.

Now, we are about to try a rather desperate stratagem. If we should fail, we will be destroyed by forces beyond our control. That growing, primal force is part native and part European, and wholly malevolent. In future, if you hear warnings about ravens or dragons, do not doubt them but make yourself safe.

But if you hear of such dangers, that will mean we are quite utterly lost, possibly dead or possibly worse. It may be that no one will survive on this continent isolated by magic. I can only hope you will find a place to hide and survive as long as possible.

Yours always, to the death,
William Clark

A Forlorn Hope

AFTER THE SPIRIT DRAGON BATTLE IN THE SKY AND THE JOURNEY through the land of the dead, Meriwether told them everything he knew, everything he'd learned.

Sadly, it wasn't enough to bring any confidence of victory.

After they recovered from the attack, put out all the fires, and finished the clean grave of Toussaint Charbonneau, Meriwether met with Clark and the members of the expedition, as well as Cameahwait, the tribe's shaman, and other Shoshone warriors. It was a council of war.

The shaman Dosabite pressed many questions, asking for details about Meriwether's encounters in the land of the dead, his conversations with the revenants. He expounded his entire story, all over again. He was still as puzzled by finding the mixed clusters of white men and native tribes in the same purgatory of their souls.

"Maybe the magic is mingled," the shaman suggested.

Meriwether took it further. "Maybe our fates are mingled. And we have to fight together to defeat this force that means to destroy both of our races."

As the large crowd gathered, LaBiche translated his entire story. The scruffy priest, Father Avenir, stood among the Snake People, curious and concerned. He seemed entirely unsurprised by Meriwether's fantastic tale, and merely muttered in his thick accent that he had seen many strange things himself as he spread the Word among the peoples of the wilderness.

The priest also seemed worried to set off alone. He feared

211

that the dragon sorcerer would snatch him from the sky and enslave him as a thrall. No one could dispute that was a real matter for concern.

The discussions, the discarded ideas, the arguments, the fears, droned on for so long and without resolution that Meriwether began to slump in his seat, exhausted from his spirit battle with the dragon, not to mention the lingering effects from his journey into the world of the dead. He found himself dozing off, but woke when he heard Sacagawea speaking. She stood by the council fire and spoke in her own language with the authority of someone much older...a leader. The crowded people listened to her, in utter silence.

Nudging Meriwether, LaBiche whispered, "She says that not everyone should go on this expedition against the dragon sorcerer. The enemy will kill women and children with no second thought, and he will use the bodies of those he kills to attack the rest. She says we must choose only the strongest warriors."

Meriwether knew he would be included in that number, even if he still didn't entirely understand the true capacity of his own magic. He heard Sacagawea's voice and drew strength from it, although he couldn't understand her words.

LaBiche listened, then translated, "She says that only a few should come with you and her, warriors from her tribe and from your expedition. The rest should hide where the dragon sorcerer cannot find them, so that he can't turn them into his slaves to thwart us." He scratched his chin, frowning. "If the dragon sorcerer seizes their spirits, then they will be as dead as the rest of you."

Meriwether was surprised. "She sounds as if she has no confidence in our war party."

The translator snorted. "I added a little of my own opinion, Captain. Even so, she says they should leave this area and head along the trail back toward St. Louis, to find someplace to hide in all that vast land."

"And if we do win, how will we ever find them?" Meriwether asked.

LaBiche merely smiled. "She says she will send her spirit eagle, or you will send your spirit dragon. You can search for them from the air."

"Can't the dragon sorcerer do the same?"

"You will keep him busy by attacking him, Captain!" He punctuated his reply with a snort.

"I don't like this plan," Meriwether muttered as Sacagawea continued to make her case to the people. Captain Clark and the rest of the expedition sat hunched forward, listening intently and trying to understand.

Clark stood up, interjecting. "Yes, as many people as possible should evacuate to safer lands to the east, toward St. Louis. If we should fail in our war here, if they hear nothing from us within a month, they have no choice but to give us up for dead. They can send an emissary to the civilized lands, seek out the great wizard Benjamin Franklin and seek his help." His voice dropped. "Maybe he can succeed where we fail."

"Don't assume we will fail, my friend," Meriwether said, levering himself to his feet and swaying until he gathered his balance. Sacagawea looked at him with a warm, defiant smile, and nodded.

But Cameahwait muttered and shook his head, and the Shoshone people argued among themselves. Meriwether listened to the heated discussions as the expedition members looked on, confused. "Why are they arguing?" he asked the translator. "How can they not agree with Sacagawea's very sensible plan?"

The translator shook his head. "Among the Snake People, the most important quality is bravery. The warriors are all vying to go with us. They don't want to be sent back east with the women and children. She's trying to make them understand the women and children need protection, and therefore strong warriors must accompany them, too. She is trying to convince them this is just as brave."

In the end, the long discussions reached only an uneasy resolution, with Cameahwait grudgingly accepting that he must go back with the remnant of the tribe, while Sacagawea would go forth to attack the dragon sorcerer in his lair. Meriwether was shrewd enough to realize that her brother only agreed to his role because he knew the tribe would fall apart without a leader.

The men of the expedition were equally determined, all of them angry and wanting to join the battle rather than escort the larger band to safety downriver. In the end, twenty expedition men were selected for the war party, chosen on the basis of which ones had no wives or families that depended on their survival.

Clark insisted he would go along with his partner, since he had no real dependents except for his potential fiancée, whom he often wrote. In fact, he pointed out that Meriwether Lewis had far more to lose, a mother and siblings to look after, and a duty to return to the east.

But Sacagawea was adamant. "Captain Lewis must go. Both of us must go, if we are to have any hope of winning against the dragon. We learned that in the land of the dead."

Before Clark could protest, the shaman interrupted. "One is not allowed to question such things." And no one questioned his pronouncement either.

Meriwether saw the worry and skepticism in his partner's eyes. He and Sacagawea had already battled the attacking dragon, and although they drove off the evil force, they had been sorely battered as well.

"I guess it's our best chance," Clark conceded.

"But you, Captain Clark, must serve in a different way," Sacagawea said. "Go with my brother, guide the rest of our people to safety."

He drew himself up. "I will fight with you against our common enemy."

Sacagawea shook her head. "I will entrust you with my son, Jean-Baptiste. You have told me many times that you love him as your own child, that you wished to give him the advantages of wider society. Now I must take you up on that promise."

Clark squirmed, searching for arguments, and Meriwether also interrupted. "And I will entrust you with Seaman. My faithful dog does not deserve to die because humans are battling each other. Please, take my dog and Sacagawea's son and keep them safe."

His resistance wavered, then melted. In the end, Clark agreed.

York also demanded to be included in the war party, and few objected. He had once been a slave, but had found his freedom, and had served the expedition perfectly in these uncanny lands. Now he would fight for the freedom of an entire magic-infused continent. Meriwether recalled the words of the Whiskey Revenants, their strange vision of a land where everyone was considered equal. Perhaps through some amazing magic that future could actually occur.

The preparations were made, and after a good night's sleep, the camp split into two groups. Captain Clark embraced his friend and wished him luck, magic, and success. Meriwether gave a fond hug, wrapping his arms around Seaman's shaggy neck, and then watched the others set off in the opposite direction.

The Shoshone had left behind Sacagawea, the shaman, and

ten young warriors, including Semee, Dosabite's oldest son, and Tamkahanka, whom Cameahwait called his brother, though Meriwether was never quite clear about the blood relationships among the Snake People. All of the tribe members who volunteered had at least some grasp of English, which made communication much simpler as they made their battle plans, although Sacagawea could easily serve as translator, along with LaBiche, who also volunteered to join them.

What he came to think of as their war party remained in the near-deserted village, making plans, preparing weapons, and gathering their courage for three days. Meriwether had thought they would set off immediately, to charge into the dragon sorcerer's lair, but Sacagawea insisted that he had to use the time to rest and gather his strength. He disagreed instinctively, but considering the terrible responsibility he bore, he knew she was right.

Inexplicably, Father Avenir had also remained behind, claiming he wanted to fight the evil as well. He had already baptized little Jean Baptiste before Captain Clark took the baby to safety, and therefore his most important duties as a priest lay with the war party. No one dared ask him what he thought his duty might be when they went up against the dragon sorcerer. Burying the dead?

Meriwether forced himself to sleep and rest, viewing himself as a recalcitrant patient. He put the magical burn salve on his hands at regular intervals, and the intense potency of the herbs healed his flesh much more swiftly than the normal course of nature. The shaman also declared that his odd chants had also helped, while Father Avenir credited the potency of his holy water. No matter the reason, he became much stronger and healthier over the course of the three days. He removed the bandages, found his hands and fingers whole again. Likewise, Sacagawea's wounds were also healed.

With intense preparation, she gathered food and weapons for the party, warning that it would be a journey of some days. He continued to be impressed with her work, her dedication, her lack of complaint despite the looming danger. The other men seemed uneasy, dreading the battle ahead, but she kept a completely impassive countenance. Now that her husband was dead, and with all that Meriwether had seen, he understood that her stoic courage and silence were a warrior virtue, as powerful as that of any man he'd ever met. Instead of grieving, she spoke only of practical matters for the coming battle.

Sacagawea suggested that it might take them a week or more to journey to the lair of the dragon sorcerer, since it took her a long time to walk to Fort Mandan. "Fortunately, our group is smaller than your large expedition, Captain Lewis, and we can use the horses that Cameahwait left for us." She turned slowly, gestured toward the north and the rugged, blue-gray mountains. "We are supposed to go in that direction. On horseback it may take only a few days...if we are not attacked by the creatures he summons and commands."

"We will fight our way to him and we will dispatch whatever revenants or monsters he sends against us. You can't say there's no hope."

She shook her head. "Oh, we have some reason to hope. There's always Coyote." Her lips quirked in an uncertain smile, and rather than explain further, she grew pragmatic again. "Our most difficult task will be to carry enough water for our people and horses. In that direction it is very dry, and summer is upon us. The rivers and rivulets will often run dry. When I escaped, there was snow on the ground, but now..."

Preoccupied, she moved off, leaving him to wonder what she meant by "Coyote." If she meant the god of that name, hadn't she said, before, that he should be warded off? He gathered his own provisions, sorted and confirmed the items in his pack, and doublechecked his trusty air rifle as well as his supply of ammunition. Though he had left the spirit echo of his rifle with Floyd's revenant in the land of the dead, the physical weapon seemed to work fine.

The members of the war party were agitated, anxious to be on their way rather than huddling here in dread. The horses were saddled (Meriwether let out a sigh of gratitude), the provisions tied to pack animals, and the fighters took their weapons, ready to set off at dawn.

For their final evening in the village, the war party gathered and the shaman built a fire at the time of sunset. Dosabite added the same pungent magical weeds and herbs to generate thick smoke, and all of the people sat close to hear him chant, whether or not they could understand. Even Father Avenir seemed curious, though he remained apart from the group, standing by a tree.

The shaman wore the coyote-head over his hair, leaving his face clear; the paws and the rest of the pelt draped over his shoulders, like a fine lady's stole. The smoky fire cast weird highlights on Dosabite's face, as he spoke.

LaBiche hunched on a rock and dutifully translated for the twenty men from the expedition. "A long time ago, Coyote and Raven were friends. Some say they fell out because they both loved the same maiden, but that is just a story. Coyote says that Raven was maddened by all the strangers in his land, strangers that didn't believe in the native legends and gods. Other people say that Raven was outraged because the men from the land of iron, the men from over the sea, killed the woman he loved.

"No one can be sure of the true story, because Coyote and Raven are tricksters, spirits that delight in confusing and twisting the minds of humans. More than that, they are creatures that walk between realities." LaBiche repeated the words, but he seemed embarrassed by the superstition.

Meriwether wanted to ask what that meant, but he remembered the canoe and the fog, his desperate struggle to return to the world of the living. He knew what it meant to walk between the worlds, a space outside reality and shrouded in dream and confusion. From his own education, he understood the concept of trickster gods. He had read of Roman myth, knew about Pan and even Mercury, god of thieves and messengers, of illusion and commerce. The natives of the new world had similar gods and spirits. In storytelling, they cherished their exploits. So Coyote and Raven were part of this arcane America.

But Meriwether felt a chill, knowing full well that Raven was associated with the dragon sorcerer, and now he worried that the Coyote spirit was irate with them as well. He felt very tired, and they hadn't even set out yet.

"Coyote is also not fond of these strange people who don't believe in him," LaBiche continued his calm translation, while the shaman gestured with great vehemence. "Europeans who come into this land and mingle with his people, and do things he can't understand. But he also knows that after the great magical change, all are trapped here in the same land. Coyote is saner than Raven, especially now that Raven has let his anger transform him. He would prefer to win against the strangers by guile and persuasion, not war."

The shaman paused and remained in deep thought, before he continued in a lower voice, "Or maybe he thinks he can convince the strangers to believe in him and make him strong. It has happened before."

Out of the corner of his eye, Meriwether saw Father Avenir, under his tree, cross himself.

"Coyote continued as always, a god of guile, a playful trickster spirit, a creature who walked between the worlds and twisted both worlds to his own advantage.

"But Raven went insane, and the spirit of Raven went looking for a vessel. He found it in the body of a wounded, starving trapper, a man partly Hidatsa, partly French, but also with ancestry from a land beyond the sea...a place called Wales, where dragons live.

"The poor trapper had unwisely taken shelter from a storm by crawling into a cave that was once sacred to Raven, where blood sacrifices were made to him. The trapper was almost dead when he arrived, too weak to resist. So, Raven took over the body, and mingled his soul—" Dosabite paused, reconsidered his words, and LaBiche listened carefully. "No, he ate the soul of the trapper and acquired to himself everything the trapper was, his heritage, his legends, his beliefs."

Father Avenir crossed himself again.

"And since the trapper was also a little crazy, joining with him made Raven even crazier. Raven is not accustomed to being bound to a physical body like ours. As a trickster spirit, he can take many forms and is free as windblown sand. Chaining himself to the trapper's body made him feel like a dog tied out in summer and winter, unable to break the leash...which made him grow even more mad.

"With his powers, Raven discovered that he could become a dragon, like the legends bound deeply in the trapper's Welsh heritage, and from there Raven discovered that after the comet and after the great change, he could take the powers of the land from all other gods. Insane, he grew great in his conceit, and he began expanding his destructive influence over the land. Instead of merely tricking people to do his bidding, he now controls them more easily if he takes over their bodies."

Near the thick smoke, Dosabite swayed lightly on his feet, as in a daze himself. "I know these things because Coyote told me. He spoke to me when Sacagawea and Captain Lewis descended into the land of the dead. He told me in a dream that I would need this knowledge." He stroked the head and fur draped over his shoulders. "Coyote is my spirit animal, and the god I evoke."

With a dramatic flourish, the shaman pulled the coyote head down over his face, so that his eyes shone through the eyeholes in the mask. Like a wild animal, he scampered around the circle, racing behind the seated people, as he scribed another circle in the dirt, one that enclosed them all.

Meriwether felt an odd tingle on his back as the shaman completed his protective circle. Sitting outside the group, Father Avenir looked pale, his eyes very large.

Dosabite had left enough space behind the seated people so he could perform his ritual dance around the perimeter. With growing exuberance, he danced and chanted, and when he passed close to the fire he threw handfuls of herbs into it. The smoke twisted and blew like a living thing, finding no direction, as if lost.

The smoke enveloped Sacagawea, who sat up very straight, as though she heard instructions in her mind, and then the pungent smoke curled over Meriwether, too. Within the smoke, he thought he heard his father's voice, encouraging him from the isle in the land of the dead. "I trust you son. You can do this."

The other members of the war party reacted variously when the smoke washed over them. And then suddenly Dosabite drew himself to his full height and shouted, in English, "I am Coyote. And I shall go with you."

Through the animal mask, the shaman's eyes were golden in the firelight. He opened his arms wide and reached upwards, like a maestro conducting music. A blazing wall of fire erupted from where he had drawn the line in the dirt, stretching high, well up into the dark sky. Then magical fire died out, vanishing as it erased the protective circle as well.

As the people muttered, amazed, Meriwether rose and stepped out of the circle, away from the fire and the pungent, hypnotic smoke. Some were elated to know they had a new supernatural ally, but the shaman had never been a friend of the Europeans, their trappers and explorers. Meriwether didn't know if he could trust everything that Dosabite said.

And how could they trust the aid of Coyote, the trickster spirit?

Like the Knights of Old

THE EXPEDITION SET OFF VERY EARLY THE NEXT MORNING. THE air had a curious chill that felt like sweat drying on the skin. Meriwether knew it presaged a hot day.

They drank coffee and fried the last of the smoked sausages they'd brought with them from Saint Louis. Sacagawea had made corn bread. Altogether, it was a rather princely breakfast, appropriate for the start of a challenging war march.

As he ate, brooding and worried, Meriwether kept his eye on Dosabite. The shaman still wore the coyote mask, and he acted strangely, as though he were an animal wearing a human form. He seemed both feral and canine, and held his legs oddly, perhaps expecting them to bend in a much more pronounced way than they did. Occasionally, he stooped over to touch his hands to the ground, then straightened partway, confused about his body.

"Look how the shaman moves," Meriwether said, as Sacagawea gave him a piece of corn bread. "What's wrong with him?"

She followed his gaze, nodded. "He is Coyote."

Meriwether stopped himself from scoffing outright. He had certainly experienced firsthand how a spirit could take over a man's body. "But how do we know we can trust him?"

"Trust Dosabite?" she asked. "Or trust Coyote?" She watched the shaman's strange movements. "I believe we can. I know that Dosabite is ... difficult, especially when it comes to the Europeans that come to this land. It is his role to be difficult. Like his totem animal, like the spirit he serves, he walks between the worlds.

It is not an easy position, and not an easy way to live, but he is loyal to the tribe and to those who wish to help the tribe. As for Coyote...He owes some duty to our shaman, who is faithful to him. More importantly, Coyote is a god of the Shoshone, so he owes us some duty too."

"Your gods owe a duty to people?" Meriwether asked, not sure if he was appalled or charmed by the notion. He wondered if Father Avenir would say the same of the Holy Covenant.

"How else?" She patted Meriwether on the arm in a motherly and reassuring gesture. "We have a great battle ahead of us, and Coyote has some powers. Not as great as Raven, because Raven feeds off the new magic in the land as well as the European magic in the body possessed. Your spirit dragon is powerful, as is my eagle, but Coyote is stronger than us. He might be our best chance to wrestle some of the land's magic away from Raven." She looked up at the shaman in his Coyote mask and pelt. "I'm glad he is with us."

Though the creature disturbed him, Meriwether tried to see the advantages. But now and then, behind his Coyote mask, Dosabite would glance toward him with a deeply malevolent expression.

As the war party packed the last of the camp and mounted up, Father Avenir came up to Meriwether, bowing. He smiled and said, in his oddly accented English, "I cannot go with you, my son. I have other things to do in this ravaged land, but I will give you my blessing, from *our* God, a blessing such as was given to the knights of old when they went into battle against impossible odds."

They were accepting help from a powerful native spirit, so why not the blessing of a papist? "We can use all the help available."

Head bowed, the priest walked up and down the line of expedition members and Snake People, dipping his aspergillum in a bowl of water he carried, flicking droplets of holy water at them. Most of the men weren't sure how to react. LaBiche crossed himself when the water fell on him, and Meriwether was surprised to see Sacagawea also make the gesture, though he supposed Toussaint must have taught her. Had she actually converted to Catholicism? How did she reconcile her beliefs? For that matter, how did the Church reconcile the traditions of the man taking at least one other wife?

Then he sighed. Considering the dragon sorcerer, an insane Raven spirit, the rising power overrunning the land, and his own desperate journey to the land of the dead, such worries did not seem important. The people and even the priests in these largely unpopulated lands were cut off, and adapted their beliefs and experiences as needed to survive in a place filled with supernatural magic.

Father Avenir continued his prayers and blessings, sprinkling holy water. There was a tense and awkward moment when he reached the end of the line to face the shaman in his Coyote guise. As if remembering his human body, Coyote stood straight, grinning at the priest from beneath the coyote head balanced on the shaman's tangled hair. Dosabite's lips spread, displaying sharp, shiny teeth that had not been there before. Startled, the priest paused, holding his aspergillum, then let it rest back in its bowl. He gave a respectful bow, not in the way a man bowed to a god, but more as one bowed to an acquaintance.

The shaman's body bowed at exactly the same moment.

The discomfited priest stepped back and turned toward the mounted party. He said in a very loud voice, "Bless you my children. May you win a victory against the evil one and free the land of his stranglehold."

Coyote grinned wider, and his golden eyes shone.

The priest then walked off to the southeast, while the war party headed out, led by Coyote. The shaman had chosen not to ride, but instead he ran ahead of the group, faster than any horse could move.

Meriwether rode his horse alongside Sacagawea. "I thought you would guide us to the lair of the dragon sorcerer, taking us to where you remember."

"I will help, but when it comes to Raven and Coyote, we aren't always in the real world. After I escaped, it is possible I didn't walk in the real world for the first few days. Or weeks. I know we have to head north, but just following a physical direction might not get us where we need to go." She nodded toward the shaman loping ahead with unnatural swiftness. "But Coyote moves the same way Raven does. He can take us directly to the place where Raven is hiding."

They rode hard for the day, stopping several times to let the horses drink whenever they found dwindling trickles of water in arroyos. The terrain looked arid, increasingly rugged, but Meriwether noticed nothing out of the ordinary. Suddenly, though, the dirt and sparse grass changed to just plain rock. The sound of the thin creek they'd been following on their left ceased. The party halted, uneasy.

Meriwether looked around, realizing that the light had dimmed and that natural sounds had ceased. All sounds.

Ahead of them, Coyote stopped and sniffed the air. Watching the shaman, Meriwether was certain the head on the pelt actually twitched and snuffled.

The path stretched out before them, and the rocks rose up on either side, swiftly becoming cliffs twenty feet tall, funneling the war party in a particular direction. There could be no retreat on either side. Meriwether found the canyon ominous, a likely spot for an ambush.

Coyote made a gesture for quiet, and whispered instructions that were passed down the line from rider to rider. Moving as quietly as possible, they backed their horses, and Coyote led them to the left side of the path and up the rocks. He scampered to the top of the cliff, with the horses struggling to follow. Meriwether didn't believe they could go very far in this manner, but Coyote was more interested in looking down into the canyon, where the path led.

Only moments after they had gotten into position, a rumbling sound like an avalanche of thunder echoed through the canyon. A herd of buffalo exploded down the dry path, hundreds of them, shoulder to shoulder and confined by the rock walls. They bellowed in a panic, their eyes rolling.

Behind them, driving them forward, a large creature lashed out with a hissing roar. Meriwether knew exactly what it was.

From above, he unslung his rifle, pumped it.

Behind the herd of buffalo, their horrible mouths open to reveal rows of sharp teeth, strode two of the giant reptiles he and Clark had met on the plain near the Canoti mound. The enormous lizards snatched buffalo in their jaws, crunching down with a will, sending blood and bones everywhere, but they didn't stop to feed. The huge reptiles simply slaughtered their prey and charged on, thundering along on powerful back legs.

Meriwether shuddered. If they hadn't moved to the top of the canyon, the stampeding herd would have crushed them. But even from their height and presumed safety, he saw that the largest of the antediluvian beasts might be able to reach them and kill them.

He took his rifle to his shoulder and fired twice, aiming for the tiny eyes, which he hoped was the most vulnerable spot, although these magical reptilian revenants might be destroyed simply by being pierced with bullets of civilized metal. He certainly didn't want to fight them with his knife.

Following Meriwether's lead, the rest of the party brought their rifles out and all together they let loose a sharp, booming volley of shots. The gunfire was loud enough to echo even above the roar of the stampede and the bellow of the giant lizards, and it quickly became obvious that the metal of their bullets did not possess extraordinary properties. The sharp gunshots drew the attention of the scaled beasts, however.

They charged the canyon walls, seeing new prey above. The monster lizards stomped on buffalo they had already killed, lunging upward to the humans just out of their reach. One of the largest beasts reached out, extending its short, clawed forelimbs. Meriwether fired again.

With a primal scream, the creature slipped in its scrambling climb up the rocks, taking its companion with it. The maddened buffalo ran ahead, surging out of the confining canyon to the open space beyond.

The two monster lizards lay entangled, struggling. Meriwether and York stood together and peppered them with shots, while several others from the war party reloaded, then joined in the fire. After numerous shots, the giant reptiles trembled and began to exude an awful smell. Then, with a great shuddering noise, the monsters vanished, leaving only dirty, dried bones in their places.

The civilized metal of their bullets did have the desired effect, he realized, but for powerful revenants such as those, the quantity needed to dispel them was great.

Meriwether looked around for Coyote and found the shaman bent over the edge of the cliff, sniffing the canyon. He shook his head. His voice carried quite clearly in the sudden silence when the gunfire stopped. "That was an easy trap. Raven is just testing us."

He gestured for them to follow along the top of the canyon, picking his way. "We will go this direction until we reach the bridge."

Meriwether could see a bridge spanning the canyon ahead, but he swore there had been no bridge before. They rode closer, approaching quickly. It wasn't a simple bridge of fallen logs, as someone might make for a temporary passage. This was a fully covered wooden bridge, with tall sides and a roof, the sort of covered bridge he'd seen in old settlements in the east.

He stopped his horse as they reached the bridge. But he hesitated before getting on, glancing at Sacagawea, who seemed confident. His horse snorted. Coyote didn't seem at all alarmed, though, as he strode forward through the covered bridge.

Meriwether guessed this was Coyote's magic, a way for them to pass not only from one side of the canyon to the other, but also perhaps from one reality to another. He rode forward, and the others followed. The bridge held, steady and solid until they had crossed.

The path ahead cut through a flat, high landscape, and they set off, making good speed. When Meriwether looked back, though, both bridge and canyon were gone, like dreams that vanish in the morning.

Another Way In

THEY STOPPED AND WATERED THEIR HORSES AT A STREAM THAT meandered through a convenient field of high, sweet grass. The oasis seemed entirely out of place in the high, bleak plateau, and Meriwether caught Coyote's eye. The shaman said, in clear English, "The horses needed fodder and rest." Dosabite could not speak English at all, but now the Coyote spirit within him spoke with the Queen's own accent.

"So you... conjured it?" Meriwether asked.

"I had to. This is my land you cross through. I am your host and I owe you hospitality."

Meriwether expressed his thanks, then shook his head. "I don't understand why you threw in with us at all." He still couldn't be certain of the trickster's loyalties, or the shaman himself. "Shouldn't you prefer to have no Europeans on your land?"

Coyote cackled, a distinctly unpleasant sound, holding more amusement than malice. "Where would you go? This continent has been sundered from the rest of the world. Should I wish for you all to leave regardless?" He grinned, displaying a mouthful of sharp teeth, and his golden eyes sparkled in the holes of the coyote mask. "I know Dosabite feels this way, but he's only human. He does not comprehend the... opportunities of this situation. The ways of your people are very different from ours, and sometimes alarming. You have different hair and different skin, but the part here—" He touched Meriwether's head with a finger that seemed to have claws, then touched the center of his chest. "And here. Those parts are all the same. Humans of all sorts have worshipped me in the past, in my own different forms. In the far long ago all humans were once a tribe. Why would I kill those who can bring me their power and their strength?"

"I doubt my people will want to worship you," Meriwether said. "We have our own God and our own religion. Or religions." He thought of Father Avenir, the papists who survived here in the new world, as well as any number of Protestant variations.

Coyote cackled. "It won't happen all at once, of course. Maybe it can't be done at all. But now that the magic has returned here, and the world has changed forever, who knows what will happen? Someday, in the time of the great-great-grandchildren, they will remember me and worship me. I have lived since before humans came. I can wait." Now the grin acquired a bit of malice. "Even so, here you are helping me solve this small dispute with my friend Raven."

His suspicion rose again. He called the evil dragon sorcerer his friend? "Only because Raven has chosen to set himself against us. He has tried to stop us and kill us repeatedly. We would fight Raven, with or without you."

"Remember, our adversary is not merely Raven. In his anger, he took on more than he should, and it has addled his mind." Coyote nodded slowly. "I consider this a mission of mercy."

On the perfect, lush terrain of the magically created oasis, Meriwether lay down in the meadow grass near the chuckling stream. It was strange to think that although they were in such an odd place, and at the mercy of an ancient creature who called himself a god, still they had to camp and rest, just like any other part of the original expedition. After posting two sentinels, the rest of them took the opportunity to go to sleep. Meriwether woke just after midnight and roused York so that they both took their turn at the watch.

The rest of the camp slept, feeling unusually safe, but while Meriwether and York patrolled the area, following the stream, they heard a loud splash. A snakelike form the length of an oar leaped out of the water, arced its body, then dove back into the current. It had a triangular head surrounded by a crown of frills, coppery red against its olive-colored body.

The two men raised their rifles, stared at the dark surface

of the narrow river, but the creature didn't reappear. "That was a huge snake, Captain!" York whispered, surprised that the rest of the camp hadn't jumped from their blankets and sounded the alarm.

"Or a very small sea serpent," he said. "There's no telling what we will find in these lands."

The rest of the night passed uneventfully. The next morning they again breakfasted well, taking advantage of the plentiful water. When Coyote was ready, he set off again.

At midmorning, a sudden flock of ravens appeared in the sky, so many that they obscured the sun. The war party shaded their eyes, pointing in alarm. Some drew their weapons, though Meriwether could see that even among all the packs they would not have sufficient ammunition to diminish the enormous flock. But the ravens did not swoop down to attack, merely flew high overhead, an ominous cloud that eventually passed.

"They are spying on us," Sacagawea said, simply stating a fact. Her voice held a fatalistic tone.

Growing more nervous every minute, looking at the sky, Meriwether kept his air rifle at the ready. He urged his horse forward, making his way to the front of the cavalcade, where he could speak to Coyote. "Obviously Raven knows we are coming. Why hasn't he sent his dragon-form against us? Surely that is next?"

Coyote looked into the distance and shook his head. "Not here. This is my land, and we are safe. The only thing he can do here is send his ravens to spy on us. We'll sleep in my home tonight, and then we can talk about the dangers." He paused. "We need to find how to get you and the bird woman into Raven's home...the dragon's home."

Meriwether took little comfort in that. He followed the shaman quietly, but kept looking at the sky, clutching his rifle.

They traveled for the day without incident, and Coyote finally led them between two pillars of stone, like a strange gateway. When the horses passed single file between those pillars, the war party suddenly found themselves in a land of soft grass. Songbirds wheeled overhead, unthreatening.

They rode along through the grasslands, and Meriwether was surprised to see a puppy bounding through the high grass, but when he looked closer it became a young boy trotting toward them. Grinning, Coyote picked the boy up, swung him around, and set him on his shoulders. "My oldest son," he explained, and ran ahead without diminishing his speed despite the squirming burden he now carried.

Soon the war party reached a village of tents and lean-to shelters. Coyote's people came out to receive them, all acting very friendly. Young men took care of their horses, while other villagers led the members of the party to the central fire, where they were all told to sit. The tired men relaxed and enjoyed a fine meal brought to them, and then they enjoyed the flirtations of the young women of the village. Meriwether glanced at Coyote, wondering if these women might be among his wives, but the capricious deity showed only delight.

"Let them enjoy themselves, Captain Lewis," Coyote said, "for who knows what lies ahead?" He rose from his seat and gestured for Meriwether to follow him. "But first, you and I have important matters to discuss."

The two men left the large fire and walked among trees over-shadowed by thick, arching branches that formed a deep tunnel. Meriwether wondered where they were going, but he held his questions inside, knowing that Coyote would explain when he chose.

"There is something I wish to show you," Coyote said in his strangely British English. Meriwether found it odd that the creature could speak so clearly and so eruditely with such long teeth. "But first let me tell you a story. Many centuries ago there lived a beautiful young woman, of the same tribe as Sacagawea. She was married and had two children, but one day as she was bathing at a waterfall, Raven saw her. He was struck with a love so great that he pulled her into his own land, taking her into a waterfall that seemed exactly like the one in which she had been bathing. But now she could not get back home.

"This was long ago, when the world was young, but before the comet came and changed the magic. When I went to visit my friend Raven, I also saw the young woman. She was indeed the most beautiful woman ever born, and I fell in love with her at first sight. But despite Raven's clear affection for her, and my own obvious interest, she remained a loyal woman, faithful to her husband. She just wanted to go home. After a long time, I couldn't stand her unhappiness. I loved her, and so I helped her escape from Raven and let her go back to her home.

"I thought she would be reunited with her husband, but I

had forgotten how time can run differently in our lands, and Raven had let his own world slide into different days and years. When she returned to her tribe, they didn't know her. Her family was long gone, and many generations had passed. She could not endure the thought that her children had grown up without her, and that her husband was long dead. She ran back to her favorite waterfall, climbed to the top, and tried to throw herself down to be dashed on the stones at the bottom. But I was called by her anguish, and I arrived just in time. I took her, and put her..." His step faltered. "You'll see."

They emerged from the tunnel of tree branches and found themselves in a bright, starlit clearing, where a silvery waterfall poured over a ledge into a crystalline lake. A woman drifted on the water, her hair floating around her head. She looked completely at peace.

Meriwether started. "It's Sacagawea!" But he realized it couldn't be. This woman was younger, and seemed taller.

"The resemblance is great," Coyote said, sadly. "Sacagawea is her many times great-granddaughter, I think."

The floating woman hadn't moved, hadn't noticed them at all. "Is she dead?"

"No, she is in a deep sleep, frozen in time at this most peaceful place. I could do nothing to cure her anguish...but now I think there might..." He sighed. "We will see. But before the battle ahead, I wanted you to see why my friendship with Raven broke apart forever."

"And you intend to use this young woman? For what purpose?"

"I don't know yet." He seemed unable to take his golden eyes from the motionless woman. "But I wanted you to know why Raven is so interested in the Bird Woman. He, too, knows the connection, the resemblance."

After watching the waterfall and the pool for some minutes, the two men walked back in silence. Before they reached the camp, Coyote said, "Tomorrow we may be attacked in many different ways. I have been...rotating my home so that we emerge near places where I need to take you and the Bird Woman. If we are lucky, Raven hasn't thought of this place yet, or this way into his lair. He is Raven and he thinks of the air, thinks of flying. And since you and Sacagawea, yourselves, manifest as spirit creatures of the air, I doubt he'll expect you to approach the way I intend to send you. But until we can get to that place..." He looked away, turning his coyote face into shadow.

Meriwether grew worried. "Yes?"

"Once we emerge from my safe lands, we will be fully exposed to Raven's attacks. I want you to be ready. Protect Sacagawea. If one of you dies, the other may not be able to win this battle."

"But you are going to fight with us. Raven's dragon almost killed us both already, and that was just a projection of himself. Now we will be faced with the whole manifestation, in the place where he is strongest. And he'll have his monsters, his revenants, his thralls." He felt sweat prickle on the back of his neck.

Coyote gave him a sideways glance. "You cannot hope to kill him in the air or out in the open, and there is no way you can kill him in his place of power. So I propose to divide our war party into three parts. The younger braves and the men of your expedition will attack frontally and distract the dragon. Meanwhile, I will find my way inside the lair and kill the human thrall, the trapper body he has possessed.

"And you and Sacagawea will have to kill the dragon." He paused for a moment. "Since I won't be with you then, you must tell Sacagawea that the only way to bind the dragon's heads is with the hair of a powerful woman."

Meriwether's step faltered. "Heads? The dragon has more than one head? In the previous times I encountered him in my dreams or in my spirit form, he was like a dragon of Welsh legend."

Coyote looked somber. "In his real form, the dragon sorcerer has seven heads, huge, powerful, and terrifying."

Meriwether was not reassured. "And Sacagawea's hair will bind them?" The idea seemed preposterous, as did the entire plan.

"A single hair will be like a powerful rope holding the heads still. Such a binding will put the dragon to sleep. That is how the magic works. I know it. Will you remember what I've told you? After all the battles we are bound to face tomorrow?"

"If it means our survival and the success of this mission, then of course I shall."

They returned to the village, where the war party was enjoying the feast and hospitality. The revelry seemed jarring after what Meriwether had just seen, after the terrible things he had just learned. The young village women danced, while the Shoshone warriors and the expedition men clapped and laughed, and sometimes being bold enough to snatch and kiss one of the dancers.

Meriwether did not see Sacagawea, and he immediately felt concern. Coyote said, "I believe she has gone to bed." He sat himself down near the young men and gestured toward a group of tents beyond the firelight. "If you need to sleep, you can choose any of those you wish."

The men of the war party were celebrating as if they might not live another day—which was indeed possible—but Meriwether felt the weight of responsibility like a heavy blanket on him, and he wanted to be alone, to gather his strength and to ponder. As he passed the first tent, though, he heard soft sounds of crying. He peeked through the imperfectly joined flaps and saw Sacagawea sprawled on a pile of hides that served as a mattress. He could tell by the shaking of her shoulders that she was crying—perhaps for the death of her husband, the separation from her son, or their likely fate on this hopeless mission. He hesitated, reluctant to interrupt her, to intrude on her privacy.

Eventually he decided he could do little to console her and quietly slipped to the next tent, which he found empty. With a long sigh, he let himself fall on the hides piled on soft grass. Rather than being rank or stuffy, the interior of the tent smelled clean, like freshly mown hay. Disturbed by Sacagawea's anguish, he thought he would have difficulty falling asleep, but he and York had been on guard duty the night before, when they'd seen the small sea serpent jumping in the narrow river. He could not stay awake.

After a long, dreamless sleep, he woke up rested but tense for the great challenges they would face today. He found some of the young women tending the fire, and the shaman-Coyote drinking coffee from a wooden mug. Since his transformation, his mouth no longer matching Dosabite's human mouth, Meriwether was surprised he could manage to drink coffee at all through his muzzle. It must be some sort of magic, he supposed.

A young woman brought Meriwether coffee and fried bread. "I didn't know your people drank coffee," he said to Coyote.

"I've existed since the beginning of the world. I take the best that humankind invents and make it my own. I like this potion."

As Meriwether ate the bread, the other man continued. "I made time move slower in my home." He spoke in the casual tone of a man telling his guest that the beds would be aired. "I wanted everyone to get a good and restful night of sleep, with no need to hurry. We will need to be at our greatest strength and alertness." He lowered his voice. "Some of the party will not make it to the end of this journey."

Little by little the others emerged from various tents, some accompanied by women who had kept them warm through the night. Meriwether neither envied the men, nor did he feel any interest in taking one of the willing women for himself. He'd certainly enjoyed female company before, and all these native women were uncommonly beautiful, yet he felt no desire right now. His eyes kept turning anxiously toward the tent where he had heard Sacagawea crying in the night.

He told himself he wasn't in love with her. Of course not. Being in love was, at any rate, a thing for swooning maidens and young fools. Sacagawea, an admirable woman in her own world, would never fit in his own world back east. Society would shun them if they decided to marry—this was not the utopia the three Whiskey Revenants had described in the land of the dead. A dream . . . and a dream of dead men, at that.

But still, they had a common cause and great respect for each other. In this, they were perfect partners, but their association must go no further, even if she was the bravest, most loyal, and most resourceful woman of his acquaintance. While the rest of the war party attacked Raven's lair, while Coyote endeavored to kill the human form the evil spirit inhabited, he and Sacagawea would travel together to find the real form of the seven-headed dragon and kill it.

And after that, once he and Clark reunited and completed their expedition to the western edge of the world, Meriwether and Sacagawea would go their separate ways, he to the east and his ancestral plantation in Virginia, and she—

Imagination failed him. What, exactly, would she do? From Sacagawea anything was possible. Maybe she would rejoin the Snake People and live quietly among her relatives. She might marry yet another trapper and travel with him all over the west, living an adventurous and precarious life. He felt a stab of irritation at the idea.

Interrupting his thoughts, Sacagawea emerged from the tent and came to sit beside him after she gathered her own breakfast.

Knowing what lay ahead of them, he wanted to keep no secrets from her, so he told her of the preserved woman in the waterfall, the tale of the love that had broken the friendship of Coyote and Raven.

She had heard a version of the story before, but now she frowned disapprovingly. "So Coyote holds the woman that Raven loves. It sounds like he's intending to use her as bait. Is that how he means to get close to Raven's human form?"

"That may be his plan. He didn't tell me, but I doubt there is much we can do to prevent him." He took another sip of his coffee. "We will all have enough trouble surviving this day."

Sacagawea shook her head sadly. "Coyote is a rogue and a trickster, and he will bend the rules as it pleases him. He is usually not ill-intentioned, and for the most part he is on the side of humanity. We will have to believe him now." She drew a deep breath. "How sad her story is, though. In versions of the tale I've heard, we call her Raven's bride. In most of the stories her husband kills her, or maybe a roving tribe, but this story is the saddest of all. She escaped from Raven and lives on, but finds she no longer has any place in her tribe, and no longer has any family." A quaver in her voice suggested that she understood the woman's plight all too well.

Meriwether braced himself, getting ready for their battle. "The day ahead will be filled with dangers, but I will do my best to protect you. I ask that you stay close to me. Coyote means for the two of us to enter Raven's lair by some particular path he has in mind."

Sacagawea shivered. "I will stay with you, Captain Lewis, but I don't like being a pawn in games. I became a wife because Toussaint won me in a game, but I am done with that. I am not a piece to be won or gambled away by those more powerful than I."

"You are not," Meriwether said firmly, hating the idea as well. "You are vital to this war. We'll never win if you and I aren't alive."

She inclined her head. "Then, let us stay alive."

Doing so proved harder than it sounded. The attacks from the dragon sorcerer began as soon as they rode out, emerging from Coyote's land.

Lewis, suspecting ravens might attack them, had them hold blankets in readiness to cover the horses' eyes.

As soon as Meriwether rode beyond the boundary, he sensed that he passed through some sort of veil that tore in their wake. The war party suddenly found themselves in rocky terrain once more, and climbing toward mountains in the distance. One prominent peak looked familiar, similar to the many crags they had seen in the latter part of the expedition, but this one seemed more massive, with black and vermillion striated rock that looked raw, as though it had been hewn out of the surrounding stone just moments ago, with titanic chisel marks still prominent.

After emerging, he barely had time to look around himself and grasp his surroundings before the ravens came. A hurricane of the black birds descended on the war party just as they had swept down upon Meriwether on Tavern Rock. The raucous screeching nearly deafened him, but he screamed as loudly as he could, breaking the panic. "Use your knives! The steel blades may break the magic!" The horses reared, and the men struggled to grab their knives from sheaths at their hips. "Guard your eyes and cover the horses!"

As his animal churned and prepared to bolt, he threw his blanket over his horse's eyes before the dark-feathered cloud fell upon them. He yanked out his knife as a flurry of sharp, deadly beaks pecked everywhere. He pressed his forearm across his eyes while with the other he stabbed blindly at the avian cloud. He managed a sidelong glance to see Sacagawea also defending herself.

The shaman raised both hands, chanting, trying to summon his own magic, but he was weaker now, in the land of Raven.

Among the myriad shrieks, Meriwether drew gulps of air, continuing to slash the blade right and left. Though his horse's eyes were covered, the frightened animal still sidestepped and jerked, thrashing about. The ravens were attacking the animal, too, and Meriwether flailed with the blade, trying to drive the birds away, hoping the emanations of the steel would be strong enough.

And it worked. Under the onslaught of forged metal, the cloud of birds swirled, screamed, then fluttered away, avoiding the war party.

Shaken, the members of the group recovered themselves in the aftermath, checking torn clothes and small bleeding wounds. Everyone seemed to be whole. After their previous evening of feasting and relaxed celebration, this horror had jarred the men back to the seriousness of their quest. They rode on grimly, more wary of their unnatural enemy. Coyote ran ahead, leading them.

The next attack came in the form of numerous gray and rotting revenants that rushed at them, emerging from the very rocks and dust.

Using his air rifle, not worried about depleting his remaining ammunition, Meriwether shot as many as he could, but here they seemed to be stronger, infused with a greater magic, than the shambling forms that had attacked elsewhere along the river. Unless he managed to place a bullet in the revenant's head, they would recover from the wound and lurch forward again, relentless. When the undead warriors closed in, walking over their own fallen, he had to use the butt of his rifle to beat them away. He urged his horse closer, bashed the head of one tall, gaunt revenant who reached for Sacagawea.

He heard a bloodcurdling scream, and saw one of the young men from the expedition, Patrick Gass, dragged from his terrified horse and torn to pieces by undead teeth and claws.

But Coyote also ran about among the revenants, snarling like a predatory animal. In his canine aspect, he lunged amid the attackers, ripping with his teeth and claws. He mangled enough of the undead that the war party could ride through the mass, spurring their horses on to great speed, and then return to pick off more of the disorganized revenants.

At last, Meriwether ran out of targets and stopped, shaking with exhaustion and the afterburn of adrenaline. The war party surveyed the pile of bodies, fallen dead as well as two casualties of their own, Gass and one of the Shoshone warriors.

At the end of it, they stood in the middle of a lot of body parts, most of them from revenants. The stink from the piles of festering flesh was unbelievable. One of the horses had a long slash torn in its flank from the claws of a revenant, and Meriwether had to put it down. The men groaned, covered with gore, angry at what they had faced. Meriwether didn't want to let their fear set in, and he urged the party to continue.

Coyote set off, loping along with his oddly swift and inhuman gait.

They covered several more miles before Raven came at them again—this time in the fierce form of the spirit dragon, flying low overhead and roaring. Before the dragon could plunge toward them to unleash a mouthful of fire, Meriwether had all of the warriors open fire, hitting the enormous flying reptile with a barrage of metal bullets, and Coyote also summoned his own magic, hurling it at the sky. The onslaught was surprisingly strong, and drove the sorcerer's form away. With the loud, heavy beat of wings, the dragon turned back. The men cheered, but their triumph did not last.

They had nearly reached their destination, though without much of a sense of triumph, when the resurrected antediluvian beasts attacked—not only the towering lizards with great jaws and stunted forelegs, but also the smaller carnivorous reptiles that hunted in packs, as well as shrieking, flying reptiles that looked more like scaly bats than a fearsome dragon.

Meriwether and the war party knew the attack was coming, though, and they were prepared. After everything they had faced that day, their defense was a matter of habit. Loading and reloading, they shot so swiftly and so many times that the creatures collapsed into mounds that smelled of flatulence, and then collapsed further into rotting old bones.

Likewise, Meriwether expected the fire demons, five of them, their forms woven from burning trees and human remains. This time, the component victims twisted into the demon bodies were screaming, an endless wail of pain and anger. The burning constructions of wood and flesh stumbled forward, each as tall as a barn. The arcane heat rippling from them was palpable.

"Hit them with your knives or metal spearpoints!" Meriwether cried, holding his own knife with its blackened hilt. "Now."

Spears and knives flew through the air, and on contact with the pure forged metal, the creatures exploded, blasting apart in an eruption of splintered brands and charred bones. At last, the screams of the component victims died away with the thick, putrid smoke.

Meriwether led them through the confusion of limbs, roots, and skeletons. Though they did not want to linger among the bodies and debris, he insisted that they try to retrieve blades and spearpoints. The day's battle was far from over.

They rode on toward the lair of the dragon sorcerer, when more furtive movement came from the rock formations on either side of the path—children, native children of all ages, from toddlers to teens.

"Not what I expected," Meriwether said aloud. And, oddly, he found them even more frightening. At first he thought the children were alive, refugees of the horrible events in the blasted land of Raven, perhaps kept alive as thralls, the way Toussaint Charbonneau had been.

Sacagawea let out a worried cry. "We have to help them." She shifted on her horse, ready to dismount to go to the children.

Then the smell hit them, the same rotting stench of revenants, like the breath from a thousand open graves. And as the children came closer, like innocent pleading beggars, Meriwether spotted their blank eyes, the greenish tinge of putrefaction on their skin. Some of them even showed grievous festering wounds, the injuries that had taken their lives.

He yelled at Sacagawea. "They are already dead! They're not children. We must free them."

He winced, sickened at what he had to do, yet when he saw Sacagawea looking longingly at the child revenants, he could not hesitate. He shot with the air rifle, dropping one of the waifish horrors.

His shot was the signal for the rest of the horrified party to open fire or stab with their lances. York led a charge forward, trampling some of the undead children under the hooves. Coyote showed no mercy either, wielding his own magic to devastating effect.

When the attack of the small revenants had ended, Sacagawea was sobbing, and the warriors seemed sick and saddened. But they could not stop now, and Meriwether kept his horse moving, with Coyote running by his side.

Finally, just ahead, their path branched, splitting in two directions...with the prominent, raw mountain peak rising up between the fork in the road. Meriwether saw it with a combination of relief and dread. This was the point where the party would divide and make their separate attacks.

Coyote made a sign to York, who led the main war party on their frontal assault against the lair of the dragon sorcerer. The big man squared his shoulders, bellowed to the expedition men and the Shoshone warriors. The bulk of the war party rode off down the leftward fork.

Coyote gave Meriwether a disturbing grin that made his flesh crawl. "Are you two ready?"

On her own horse, Sacagawea looked pale and stunned, but she summoned strength from within her. "We will do what we must."

"We are ready," Meriwether said.

Then, as if sharing a great secret, Coyote nodded at them. "Come with me."

He led them to the right fork, but only for a few steps before he broke from the path and set off overland into a dry field, so pockmarked with holes that the two horses had a dangerous time walking. The animals shied, picking their steps carefully.

Coyote shook his head and told them to dismount. "Make sure you have your weapons. We will all have to go on foot from now." Meriwether and Sacagawea did so, and the shaman made strange but oddly familiar gestures with his hands as he took the horses' reins. He tied the animals to an invisible post in the field, something he must have conjured. The two mounts snorted, but seemed perfectly content to remain behind.

Meriwether patted his horse, saw its blood-spattered hide, the dust on its head and mane, and the weariness and fear in its eyes. He looked to Sacagawea, who was in a similar condition, but her beautiful face showed a hard defiance. "We are ready," she said.

Coyote marched ahead with his lithe steps, walking across the soft, sandy soil pitted with numerous holes. Countless small, tan creatures ran about, like squirrels or rats, while some poked out of burrows and made a chittering warning noise, Meriwether had seen such colony rodents long ago in the early days of the expedition; he and Clark had called them "little dogs of the prairie."

Coyote snapped his teeth in their direction, and the chittering sounds fell silent. The small animals seemed fascinated by the strangers.

Coyote strode out to the middle of the prairie, until the soft dirt and tangled mounds collapsed under his moccasin-clad feet. He squashed burrows near the surface, the dirt slumping down a foot or two. He looked up at them with a lupine grin, as if he had found what he was looking for. He squatted and dug quickly with his hands, scooping dirt wildly, until he opened a hole about six inches wide, large enough for a small badger.

He nodded to Meriwether and Sacagawea. "In you go. Raven will never expect you."

Sacagawea frowned at the little burrow. "Into that? I could barely fit my arm in there."

Meriwether glanced back at their invisibly secured horses. "I have a small camp spade in my pack."

Coyote looked up again, displaying all his fanged teeth, and clicked them together in amusement. He made another gesture, and suddenly the hole looked very big, the size of a cave. Meriwether felt dizzy, and he reached out to take Sacagawea's arm to steady her as she also swayed. He realized that the hole had not grown suddenly huge, but that they themselves had been reduced in size. The two of them were no larger than a pair of the prairie dogs.

Sacagawea looked up at the now-towering Coyote, placing her hands on her hips in impatience. "How can we fight the dragon, if you make us small?"

He laughed. "I may be a trickster, but this is no trick. You will return to your normal size soon enough, once you have traveled through these secret passages. Raven doesn't watch the routes beneath the ground, and so you can approach. Now go, follow the tunnels, and you will pass under his scrutiny."

Meriwether looked at the sprawling rodent colony that covered the prairie leading up to the prominent peak. "But how will we see? How will we find our way?"

"You will know the passage. Follow it, and keep traveling deeper into Raven's secret land, until you find a tunnel that goes up. Then you will climb." Coyote grinned, showing his many teeth. "And that will take you directly to the chamber with the seven-headed dragon. Then remember a single hair from powerful woman will bind each of the heads." He bobbed his head. "That will be your part."

Meriwether had his weapons, but also his doubts. He wasn't sure the two of them, with their spirit forms, would be enough against the greatest monster. But Sacagawea didn't question the instructions, and with just a quick glance to be sure he would follow, she ducked her head and climbed down into the tunnel. The two of them found themselves in a moist, musty underground tunnel, a comfortably wide passage that plunged for a great distance forward, as straight as an arrow shot.

He and Sacagawea set off, silent and determined. Sacagawea put on a burst of speed, as if anxious to have it over with. Meriwether hurried after her.

Side tunnels branched off from the main passage, and Meriwether was startled when one of the burrowing rodents emerged to confront them, as if protecting its home. Now that the two humans were reduced in size, the prairie rodent seemed as large as a bear, with claws used for burrowing, teeth for tearing roots. It was a monster, but fortunately Meriwether found that his air rifle still worked, even if it was tiny now. He fired a shot at the rodent, and the single stinging bullet was enough to drive the creature back. It ducked into the side tunnel and scurried off. It made panicked squeals, the sound of which must have frightened the other rodents in the colony, which shied away from further encounters.

Although they had been reduced inside to fit comfortably within the tunnels of the underground colony, this also made their strides much smaller. Meriwether knew it would take them a long time to cover the necessary miles, so he and Sacagawea ran, covering as much distance as possible. Since they were underground, surrounded by crumbling dirt walls, they had no way of measuring the passage of time.

Finally, they reached the end of the long burrow, which opened up into an immense cavern, but which Meriwether realized was a chamber barely big enough to contain them, had they been their normal size.

"Over there, Captain Lewis." Sacagawea indicated a different sort of tunnel that led in the direction of the mountain, this one irregular and opening into rock. The air was hotter, stuffier, and a warm glow seeped out of the rock passage. He knew that was where they must go.

The ground itself, the rocks, the looming mountain, held a throbbing power, the same dark and twisted energy that Meriwether had felt across the land when he was in his spirit dragon form. Though he knew the danger, he felt drawn in that direction.

He and Sacagawea made their way to the passage, and she ducked, her long hair streaming down her back. She crawled ahead, working her way forward. He followed her, keeping his rifle and pack protected, though they had barely enough space to move. After several minutes of pushing forward, the rock walls parted and Sacagawea emerged into a larger cavern, where they could stand and catch their breath.

Then they moved onward into a larger tunnel. The underground labyrinth seemed to expand, widening as they went deeper into the mountain lair. Another grotto, another tunnel, and another.

He stood straight, brushed the persistent powdery dirt off his shirt and shoulder. Though the reference points around him were disorienting, he felt they had returned to their normal size.

And they were inside the mountain of the dragon sorcerer... Raven, or the mad thing that Raven had become.

From the echoes they heard, he guessed the pitch-black grotto around them must be immense. Ahead, he heard the loud, chuckling sound of running water, and he smelled moisture in the air.

Hearing the rush of the subterranean river, he reached out a hand to restrain Sacagawea, so she didn't stumble into the fast flow. But she took his arm and helped to lead him forward, cautious and blind.

The cave offered no light, and he could not see in the dark, not even with any magic he could imagine. Unless his spirit dragon form was able to see in the dark? But if he let the dragon loose, then his physical body would remain here, collapsed on the floor, and they would never reach their actual adversary.

But no, he had something else! He remembered the tokens that wizard Franklin had given him and Clark as trinkets to distribute to friendly tribes. They were like coins, showing the profile of the old bespectacled wizard, and they had been charmed to emit something like lightning. He fumbled in his pocket, knowing he still had some of the tokens there, though he had not thought of them for some time. His fingers found the smooth metal disk. It wasn't much, but it was a chance to see something.

He removed one of the charms and pressed on its surface to activate the lightning-magic glow. As the faint, bright sparks shone out into the cavern, he could indeed see. Sacagawea gasped, and he pressed the charm again, sending out another small burst of light. "There, now we can see our way." He found a second charm in his pocket and gave it to her, showed her how to use the glowing lightning magic. "Now we can keep going."

In contrast to the utter darkness of the cave, the two small tokens were like brilliant beacons. As his eyes adjusted, Meriwether could see that they stood on a ledge in a large cavern, with a dark river flowing past. He felt relief, realizing how easily they could have stumbled over the brink as they made their way in the darkness.

But the glowing charms revealed something even more terrifying that moved toward them on the ledge. A long sinuous creature the size of an enormous, blind maggot squirmed its way along. Where its eyes should have been, the head showed only lumps of scar tissue...and yet the pale thing crawled toward them, flicking a thin black tongue to taste the air ahead.

"We know of many blind creatures that live underground," Sacagawea said, tensing herself but not retreating. "I do not know if this one is natural or magical."

The thick, pale worm reacted to the vibration of her voice and thumped and rolled closer, ready to attack. "Either way it will be impossible to avoid and hard to kill," Meriwether said.

The rock ledge was narrow, and the hulking snake thing plunged forward, picking up speed. Meriwether barely had room to hold his rifle and his pack; they couldn't retreat, couldn't move. He and Sacagawea drew their knives.

The thing was on them, a sticky, stinking maggot-worm that meant to crush them. Its thin tongue flickered and slashed at them. Meriwether stabbed with his blade, plunging the forged steel into the soft, slimy skin. Mucous oozed off the skin, dripped down his hand, and the knife stabbed and cut. Sacagawea also pierced it with her knife—and they knew that if this was indeed some magical manifestation summoned by the dragon sorcerer, then it would have decayed and exploded at the touch of the civilized metal.

No, this was a real underground dweller...which meant that perhaps Raven had not seen them. Yet.

But as the creature continued to attack them, lumbering closer, smashing into them, Meriwether knew they couldn't kill it, nor could they get around it. The behemoth reared, and he took the only choice he could see.

Rather than letting them be crushed, he grabbed Sacagawea around the waist, and jumped into the dark waters of the river, just as the maggot creature lunged again for them. They dropped off the ledge and fell into the river together. The waters rushed around him, breathtakingly cold, swept them along, bouncing against the rock walls, carrying them away. He flailed, and lost hold of Sacagawea, but righted himself, kept his head above the water and was pleased to realize that Sacagawea was swimming toward the other bank and the security of rocks there. Not wanting to be separated from her, he put all his strength into swimming across the current.

He could barely see the opposite sandy shore and the woman's shadowy form. As he strained to see by the faint light of the Franklin coin that Sacagawea held up, a large, bulky shape rose from the water. Sharp jagged edges—teeth?—grazed his arm, questing, ready to attack. He kept trying to stroke with one arm, while he used his other hand to swing his slime-encrusted knife.

He stabbed blindly, hitting the scaly creature in the current, and this time when the metal blade hit, he gagged from an overwhelming smell of rot. Sudden, magical light illuminated the river and the shore.

In the flare, he saw a very large creature with flippers instead of claws, and an elongated mouth filled with an impractical number of long teeth. This monster was indeed a magical manifestation from the dragon sorcerer. When the civilized metal penetrated its body, the creature writhed, shuddered, and exploded into gobbets of debris and shattered bones that tumbled into the subterranean current. The creaking sound it made as it died was like very old bones being sucked down to the bottom of the river. Freed from the attack, he swam for dear life to the opposing bank, where he found Sacagawea standing, holding up her glowing talisman.

"Do you think Raven knows we're here?" Sacagawea asked.

His head pounded, and he still tried to catch his breath on the sand next to her. "Either that, or he has such a charming reception committee for all his guests. We should keep moving. We must be close... or entirely lost."

They followed the narrow bar of sand that led them to another wide tunnel leading away from the underground river. Before they could enter, though, they saw a tightly packed crowd of tiny people. At first, he thought they would have to face the awful revenant children again, but these creatures looked too outlandish to be children. They had overlarge heads and feet, and diminutive bodies.

"How many?" Lewis asked, dazed.

Sacagawea gasped. "Too many. They're Canoti!"

One near the front of the group brought up a small bow, nocked an arrow—an arrow that Meriwether knew would be deadly. He remembered the legends, the dead body of Barefoot Joe out near the conical mound, his only obvious injury a tiny pinprick in his leg. The other little people behind their leader also struggled for their weapons, but they were too crowded to move effectively. Meriwether took a step sideways to protect Sacagawea with his own body, but she pushed him aside, making him stumble against a rock. He caught himself just before he tumbled into the river. Sacagawea did not need his help. She moved quickly, grabbed one of the Canoti by the ankles, shaking him until he dropped his bow and poisoned arrow to the floor. As if she were having a fit, Sacagawea swung the Canoti's body, using him like a club to batter the other little people who now tried to retreat in panic.

She shouted, her words echoing in the cavern. "I have had enough! You will no longer stand in our way!"

Meriwether concurred, and as he scrambled back to her, he picked up rocks from the cave floor and hurled them into the churning crowd of Canoti. They were panicked, outraged, but they couldn't escape. He and Sacagawea went on the offensive, charging into the little not-people, smashing them and striking at them before they could use their poisoned arrows. None of them escaped alive.

Panting, but satisfied with their victory, they stopped. He touched Sacagawea's hand, which still held the battered corpse of the Canoti leader she had used as a club. She looked around by the light of her talisman, angry for more little people to slay. "Madame Charbonneau," he said, "I think we are no longer in any danger."

"Not from these," she agreed. She looked at the massacre with such a shine in her eyes, he feared that she would use the Canoti corpse to beat him into submission, too. She dropped the broken doll–like form and shuddered. "We should be almost under the mountain. Let us find our dragon."

Proceeding along the tunnel the little people had attempted to guard, they came upon natural stairs hewn in the rock. They climbed, working their way from ledge to ledge, ascending out of the underground until they were high enough to see faint daylight filtering through from above. At last, they could pocket the Franklin coins and no longer depend on the stored lightning magic. Meriwether suspected that the old wizard's spell might have released some emanations that drew the Raven's enslaved creatures. Now he hoped they could move in secret again.

The steps faded, though, leaving them to face a high, rough-walled cylindrical shaft that led even higher into the heart of the mountain, like a chimney. Meriwether looked upward in dismay. "We have to climb."

"Yes, we do." More agile, Sacagawea proved better at climbing the narrow space, finding footholds and handholds in the walls, and Meriwether did his best to follow her, though he nearly slipped trying to dig the toes of his boots into tiny stone hollows. He looked up to the growing light, watching her form climb higher, farther from him. If she should fall, she would tumble down and take him with her. But she didn't fall.

He kept scrambling, but his hands were aching, his legs shaking. His sweaty fingers slipped again and he barely held on. Catching his breath, he saw that she had vanished! He no longer saw her silhouette overhead. Since he didn't dare call out her name in the underground silence, he tried to climb faster, tearing his nails on the rough rock. Finally, he reached an unexpected side shaft, and knew where she had gone. Relieved to be moving horizontally again, he crawled along, trying to catch up with Sacagawea.

Ahead, he could see her working her way forward, and then stand up as the passage grew larger. She still walked crouched, but then straightened. He came up behind her, sore, dirty, and sensing that they had reached the end of their journey.

Together, without speaking, they walked forward, as quietly as possible. Around them, the caves and the chambers ahead were aglow with a mellow, honey-colored light, until suddenly the light intensified. Meriwether had to blink, shielding his eyes, and Sacagawea put a finger to her lips. They crept forward, feeling the air thrum with power.

In the Virginia woods, he had practiced moving with perfect silence, which helped him hunt, but mostly it was the game of a very lonely child. He had been able to approach any animal without startling it. Now the skill came back to him, and Sacagawea also moved as if she were silent and invisible.

They reached a broken opening in the wall, an uneven doorway through which light poured. Before entering, they approached cautiously, trying to see what lay beyond. In the glare, Meriwether could discern a large chamber with a naturally domed ceiling, in which a hole acted as a skylight for the bright glow to pour down.

The center of the chamber held the dragon.

But this was not the dragon sorcerer, not the manifestation of Raven, as they'd seen before in its attacks from the air or within Meriwether's dreams. Rather than the stately dragons that had adorned the prows of European ships, the dragons that had been carved into the lintels of hundreds of cathedrals, or graced the storybooks of Welsh children, this creature was an amalgam of nightmares, a scaly assemblage of horror. The great beast had seven heads, and it was a chimera-creation, a single being formed from seven great river serpents that had grown together, and fused, their bodies twisted and distorted. The dragon sorcerer looked as wrong, as painful as the fire demons made of wood and dead bodies.

Meriwether could only stare, transfixed. He wondered what had happened. When Raven had melded his mind with the part-Welsh trapper in the wilderness, had he imagined the mythical conception of a great dragon from European legend, but the only bodies he could summon and control were the giant river serpents? However it was, he had seized the poor things and melded them, bound them together, forcing them into this strange contorted being as its new avatar.

He shuddered. Beside him, Sacagawea looked sickened. She didn't need to explain: this dragon sorcerer, this *creature* had held her captive, had wanted to possess her unborn son, had held her husband Charbonneau in thrall.

The heads of the river serpents, monstrous enough in their normal form, seemed even worse now. All around the great beast's body lay strewn half-charred, half eaten bodies of victims—humans, buffalo, other animals. And it still looked hungry. Perhaps that accounted for the sharp teeth in seven jaws, the maddened eyes, the look of rage.

No. Though he recoiled, he could sense the powerful evil here, the presence that had taunted him, fought him in his dreams. Despite its different appearance, this was the same dragon he had battled before in his own spirit dragon form. This was his nemesis.

As the thought sparked in his mind, all seven of the dragon's heads turned toward them, though Meriwether and Sacagawea still remained unseen beyond the broken opening to the grotto. With a quick gesture, she pushed Meriwether backward and flattened both of them against the wall.

From within the sunlit grotto, a voice shuddered out, sounding like a thousand squeaking rats. "I know you are there. Come and be eaten." A jet of fire scorched through of the crack in the rock wall and would have burned them to a crisp, but for the curvature of the passage. Meriwether felt his beard and eyebrows become singed.

"Water serpents aren't supposed to breathe fire!" he muttered, as if the reality would change in response to his protest.

Sacagawea looked shaken. "We need to go in there and fight him, you and I, Captain Lewis." She took a breath. "I am supposed to use my hair to tie each of those seven monster heads?"

It seemed utterly impossible. "That's what Coyote said. He's a trickster...maybe he wants us eaten." He felt a chill. "Maybe he and Raven are still friends after all. And they mean to kill us."

Sacagawea refused to believe it. "No, it is up to us to kill him—and we will have to use the power of our spirit forms. Your body will be safe here in the tunnel." She glanced through the opening crack into the main grotto. "You have to release your spirit dragon."

"I will," he said, his lips so close to her ear that his whisper was barely more than a breath. "I will distract the great dragon, and you slip in, try to do what Coyote said." He knew it was almost certain death, but he would do what he could to protect her. For the sake of all the peoples in the arcane territories, and all of sundered America, they had to stop this evil force.

For a moment, they were face to face. He could read her lips as she said, "Is your spirit dragon strong enough? You'll get burned."

"There is a good chance we'll both get burned. But we can either stay safe, or save the world."

For a moment her face looked blank, and then it crumpled. He thought she was going to cry. "I have not been safe for a very long time." He wanted to reach out and hold her, but her features took on a stoic, impassive look. She nodded once.

Safely away from the door crack, Meriwether called upon the strange power and presence inside him, and he let his body fall to the floor of the passage. With his face pressed against the rough stone, smelling the stench of decay and fire from the dragon chamber, he willed his own dragon out from his body.

The desperation and the danger gave him more finesse, and as his form manifested, it became much too large to fit through the cracked opening. But as he took his secondary form in the air, he *projected* it beyond the rock wall into the cavern beyond, where it solidified in the much larger chamber.

Before his spirit dragon had sharpened into reality, he flapped his great wings and swept himself to the side as a jet of flame from one of the seven conjoined heads cut through where he had been.

"I see you've finally come to me in person, son of Wales," said the voice like a thousand squeaking rats. "I have always wanted to know what dragon tasted like."

The seven horrifically connected heads moved unnaturally, one twining around the other, as they breathed fire, one at a time, tracking Meriwether's spirit dragon.

The grotto seemed even more enormous than he had imagined, or his spirit dragon had shifted its size. He swooped up, along the curved ceiling. He felt like a canary whose cage has been invaded by a cat. He was trapped, and he couldn't fight the much larger predator.

He flew fast, erratically, hoping to distract the seven-headed dragon long enough for Sacagawea to do her part. He hoped she was in the chamber, moving forward—

"And my pretty bird, too," the voice said, like broken glass in his head. "You, my darling, I will not eat. I shall keep you as my queen, to reign over my domain with me. And where is your tender baby?"

Meriwether circled overhead and saw that the dragon had seized Sacagawea in a stunted set of claws. She struggled, grasping a strand of hair, but she could not reach even one of the intertwined necks.

Another one of the heads swiveled and belched fire up toward his spirit dragon, while the other heads laughed.

Three of the reptilian heads thrashed and wove in the air, also adding streams of fire. Even if he swooped and dodged like a frantic canary, he could not avoid the trio of jets. Rather, he let himself plunge straight down, his wings and tail scraping painfully on the rock of the cavern. The tangled evil dragon let out sibilant, echoed laughter and lunged out at his falling body with clawed paws. "You will make a tasty snack, to give me strength to court my queen."

As he fought to keep himself free, Meriwether snapped at a paw with his own strong jaws, then clawed at yet another.

"Stop!" a voice boomed, and Meriwether spun in the air.

On the floor of the cavern stood Coyote, accompanied by two dazed-looking people, as if they were sleepwalking. One was a man of rough appearance and mixed race, clad in the buffalo-hide clothes common to trappers. His eyes were wide and vacant.

On the other side of the trickster stood the beautiful native woman that Meriwether had seen preserved in the waterfall, back at Coyote's home.

With a lilt in his voice, Coyote said, "If you breathe fire at me, old friend, you will kill one of them."

Meriwether's spirit dragon broke free and scuttled along the floor, to loom over the dazed male figure, presumably the trapper Raven's mad spirit had possessed.

The seven-headed dragon roared and dropped Sacagawea, no longer interested in her. Gouts of fire burned the ceiling of the cavern, but none threatened the hostages.

Sacagawea started crawling, all dogged determination, towards the nearest head of the dragon, still clutching her long hair. She clearly intended to scale the heads one by one and somehow tie a hair around each of the necks. But that was impossible.

Meriwether knew his spirit dragon could do better with the speed of his wings. With his large scaled form, he reached out and pulled Sacagawea back to the place of safety. As she protested, he used his claw, as delicately as he could, to pull loose a handful of her hair. She cried out as they came loose, but now he had the magical weapon he needed.

Before Raven's dragon thing could tear his attention from Coyote's hostages and ultimatum, Meriwether flew out. Swooping close, he snagged the long, thin hairs around two of the necks, before the horror's other heads swung toward him. He darted away, like a startled canary, back to where Coyote kept his hostages safe. The seven-headed dragon howled in frustration, two of his heads bowed, unmoving.

Fire scorched Meriwether's right wing and his tail, but he forced the pain away, flapping hard again as he flew back for a second attack. He fluttered swiftly past another writhing neck, draped a strand of Sacagawea's hair in place and immobilized it. Then another. Then another.

Now, the distorted monster had only two of its seven heads left to fight, while the others had been rendered immobile, unconscious. He focused on the remaining two heads, darting back and forth, drawing their fire, eluding most of the pain, but he could not get close enough to tie another strand of hair.

Suddenly, one of the two heads drooped, also rendered unconscious. While Coyote laughed on the floor of the cavern, Sacagawea had sprinted up the monster's twined body and plucked another hair from her head, binding the reptilian neck.

The dragon sorcerer roared, swung its only remaining head toward Sacagawea to roast her alive.

Meriwether moved. While the last head was turned away, he slipped a final strand of hair around its neck. And the twined river serpents, the horrific manifestation of an insane Raven and the anger brooding in the restless arcane territories, collapsed, defeated and unconscious.

Meriwether collapsed as well, letting his spirit dragon slide down the cavern wall and slump into a heap, breathing with great difficulty. His skin and scales burned, his broad armored chest hurt.

Coyote let out peals of laughter. "Marvelous! A game and a battle at once! It is just what my friend Raven deserved." Then he turned his distorted, canine face toward Meriwether's spirit form. "Very well done, little dragon."

Meriwether was too sore and exhausted to move. His eyes burned, and through the pain he watched Coyote draw forth a very large blade. He handed it to Sacagawea, while he drew a dagger for himself. "Go on, Bird Woman. Behead the rascal. Seven times the trouble, but worth it."

Sacagawea glanced at his wounded spirit-dragon form, as if considering how she might aid him, and instead took the long blade from Coyote and strode forward.

He couldn't imagine that she had ever used a blade so large or so sharp, but she wielded it with a will, raising it over her head. With a single stroke, she chopped down and severed the neck of the first head. Without waiting for it to roll aside, while dark blood gushed out of the stump, she swung again and chopped off the next head, and the third. She let out a yell, a wild release, and with a great blow she sliced off two heads at once, then stood panting. With dark blood spattered on her skin, face, and hair, she moved forward more methodically and chopped off the rest of the seven heads.

Finally, she stood, shaking with exhaustion and relief. She clutched the bloodied blade in both hands, and stared at Coyote with an odd, shining expression in her eyes, as if she considered swinging the blade at the other trickster as well.

In the transformed shaman's body, Coyote looked unconcerned. He clicked his unnaturally long teeth together. "We should make a clean sweep of it. And I must do the part I promised." Without malice, barely paying attention, he drew his own dagger across the throat of the defenseless man to his right, the hapless, maddened trapper who had been possessed by Raven. He collapsed to the floor of the cavern, bleeding, without even reaching up to touch the gash in his throat.

As soon as the human avatar died, a sound like an implosion erupted behind Sacagawea. The dead, tangled mass of twined river serpents whipped and unwound, then blasted apart. Pieces of putrid reptilian flesh blasted in all directions. She hunched over to protect herself from the barrage.

To Meriwether's unbelieving eyes, still in his spirit dragon form, the whole mass seemed to explode and implode all at once, filling the chamber with a bloody haze. Light glowed all around, and he breathed the distinct smell of rivers and fish and willow trees.

In the place where the seven-headed creature had been stood another figure entirely.

He was a young and muscular native, wearing buffalo-hide breeches. His hair was long, sleek, black as a raven's wing. His eyes were intent, and power rolled off him as he looked at Coyote. "Brother, what are you doing here?"

"I came to save you." Coyote nudged the bloody corpse of the trapper with his foot.

Just as Meriwether thought they had been betrayed, that Coyote would join with Raven to attack them all, Sacagawea turned and bowed respectfully to the youth, bending nearly to the floor. He gave her an amused took, as if such abasement was his due, and turned back to Coyote. "Save me from what?" He craned his neck and peered around the cavern in peevish annoyance, as though he noticed something just slightly out of place.

"From yourself, Brother," Coyote said, then placed his hand on the back of the beautiful woman from the waterfall. He nudged her forward, and she moved listlessly, still sleepwalking. "And I brought your wife with me."

Raven's brow furrowed as he looked at the woman, puzzled, as if he were trying to remember something. The woman drew a quick breath, and her eyes brightened, her expression animated as if she had come fully awake for the first time in a thousand years. Her eyes went very wide. "My husband?"

Even knowing the story, as related by Coyote, Meriwether couldn't fully understand what was going on. He watched as the woman and Raven stared at each other, their eyes meeting and widening. Was that what falling in love looked like?

She reached out to him, and he pulled her into an embrace. "My wife!"

The air rang with a fluttering of wings, and suddenly the young man shattered into a multitude of ravens that flew together, lifting the woman, raising her up and carrying her through the opening at the top of the dome, and out into the open sky.

"Well, that worked," Coyote said, sounding surprised, which did not reassure Meriwether. Then the trickster focused on him, sounding urbane and civilized, much like a lecturer whom Meriwether had once heard explaining the mysteries of mesmerization. "It is possible to rewrite memory. It merely takes much patience or a great shock. The woman took a long time...and I gave him a great shock. All of Raven's madness was intensified when he merged his mind with that of the trapper. A form of insanity occurs when trying to make one mind out of two very different souls."

Coyote looked in disgust at the pieces of monstrous river serpents strewn across the floor. "All of his pain and destruction came from that. He and I are creatures of dream and myth, and Raven had several, contradictory dreams and myths in his head. He could not reconcile them or cause them to fit together. When you two killed the dragon form and I killed the trapper he had absorbed and possessed—that freed my friend Raven. It caused him to fall back into himself, but his recollection remained hazy." He grinned, showing more of his long, sharp teeth. "That allowed me to rewrite his memories about the last several hundred years and fix the error I made centuries ago. She always should have been with him, except for my interference. Now they both know it."

"Won't Raven find out it was a trick?" Sacagawea asked. "Will he not wish to seek vengeance?"

Coyote laughed. "I hope he is too happy with his wife to worry about that. We have been friends and fought each other, as friends do, since the beginning of time. It will make no difference, but it is better if we don't involve humans in our disputes.

Especially in this changed world, where the magic is far stronger and using it has greater consequences."

He sighed, glancing at the wounded form of the spirit dragon still crouched against the curved chamber wall. "And speaking of humans, little Bird Woman, we need to drag Captain Lewis's body in here. I don't think he has the strength to push his dragon back into a body that isn't close to him."

Moments after the two pulled Meriwether's unconscious human form into the sunlit cavern, he released his hold on the spirit dragon, let himself flow back into his human shape... which then slumped in utter pain and exhaustion. He was done. All he wanted to do was sleep, heal, dream...

When he woke up some time later, maybe days—he had no idea—he found that he was being carried on a litter into a very nice camp with beautiful tents, tall grass, and women and children celebrating all around. He saw men from his expedition, including the grinning face of York, as well as more Shoshone warriors, all happy to be back at peace.

"Welcome to my home again," Coyote said, leaning over the litter so he could stare into Meriwether's eyes. "You will rest here, until you are fully recovered. You've been burned very badly, you know. Bruised, broken, slashed. But don't worry." He placed a pawlike hand on his forehead. "It doesn't matter. Everything will be fine now. The land heals. You heal." Coyote leaned closer. "After all, you still have a very long journey to go."

Meriwether let himself fall back into unconsciousness, thinking of vast wilderness and long journeys. Yes, he would need his strength.

My Dearest Julia,

It seems I must wait a while yet, before I head back east to deliver my letters to you in person. Our great expedition is once again afoot! The terrible evil force that corrupted the land and used its arcane forces against us has now been defeated, thanks to the efforts of our war party, especially Captain Lewis and Sacagawea.

I had led a large party to safety back to Fort Mandan, and we waited, hoping for news of our friends—victory, we hoped. Just as we had given up all hope and were preparing to make our way back to St. Louis in retreat, on the very morning when we'd packed everything and saddled our horses, we heard a cry from our sentinels.

At first, we thought the dragon sorcerer had sent some new horror against us, rotting revenants or monstrous creatures. And then I realized that I was hearing cries of joy. Captain Lewis and the war party had returned.

The group of brave fighters we sent against the dragon was smaller. Six men total, three from each group, had been killed, including, alas, Pryor.

The actual plan for the army to go face the minions of the dragon sorcerer was merely to distract the evil force. He expended his energies by hurling terrible arcane creatures against them. The men, even my former slave York, who is quite level-headed, tell wild tales of giant tornado demons and a rain of scorpions. While the dragon sorcerer was thus occupied, however, Captain Lewis and Sacagawea were able to enter the chamber of the dragon and slay his physical body.

Neither of them wish to tell details of that awful confrontation, though my friend has some new and disturbing scars across half of his chest and down his right arm.

As for Dosabite, the shaman of the Shoshone, he will give no answers at all, not even when his chief Cameahwait demands it. The shaman simply goes sullen and says he remembers nothing because a spirit named Coyote made use of his body.

I know this may sound strange, my dearest, but here in these wild, arcane territories, even such fantastic claims must be taken seriously.

On more mundane matters, you should have heard the cries of joy with which my little Pompy greeted his mother. I have promised Sacagawea to give every possible help in raising him, but I'm glad she is back with him. He belongs with his mother, and we still have a long distance to go. Perhaps in the fullness of time, she will not need my help because she may eventually choose another husband. In fact... but that is speculation I'd rather not commit to a letter.

For now, our expedition heads onward to the Pacific, as we meant to. Now that the magic of the land no longer fights against us, we expect to have a much easier time. If we are lucky, once we find the western ocean we can seek a passage to the rest of the world by that far route. Who knows, maybe some intrepid Russian or Spanish explorers have already found the far coast of America. I cannot wait to learn what the rest of the world has done with nearly half a century of restored magic, thanks to the comet.

Although I'll warrant that no one else will have a wilder tale than the one we've just lived through.

Captain William Clark

The End of the Journey

ONCE THEY HAD RETURNED TO THEIR CANOES AND PIROGUES, with the expedition resupplied with new clothes and new equipment thanks to the help of the Shoshone, Meriwether experienced great relief. To be moving again! To see the unexplored continent and see what the vastness had in store for them!

It was strange to make their way to the Pacific Ocean facing only natural dangers . . . but there were enough of those.

They'd left the Snake People behind, with much sadness from Cameahwait because his sister insisted on accompanying the expedition, and especially Captain Lewis, as far as they might go. Sacagawea said she must do what she had promised and see the explorers to the end of her journey, which warmed Meriwether's heart. He was surprised she made such a decision, though he certainly would have released her from any obligations. She had certainly done enough. But her mind was made up, and she promised her brother and her people that she and little Pomp would be coming back.

Then the much-diminished expedition had continued on its appointed route, with Captain Clark meticulously charting their way as they went, while Meriwether collected specimens and kept careful notes of the natural wonders he found along the way. After they passed, the territories might still be arcane, but they were no longer uncharted.

They defended themselves against strange and wild animals. Occasionally, they faced hostile tribes, though many had been cut down or scattered by the mad manifestation of Raven. Once, when departing from a friendly village to navigate a span of harsh river rapids, the natives were so sure the strangers would die that they all gathered on cliffs above to watch the crazy white men perish.

Compared to the other dangers they'd faced already, the churning river and occasional sharp rocks seemed like child's play. Meriwether had, in fact, maintained some small grasp on his spirit dragon, on the magic of the land, and he found it possible to nudge the boats at the proper instant to protect them from sure disaster.

Meriwether wrote in his journal of the time he had shot a grizzly bear—several times, in fact, with each shot making the huge beast angrier, until a bullet to its brain finally killed it. The gigantic form collapsed in a furry heap moments before it could reach Meriwether with its claws.

A terrifying encounter, certainly, but it could not compare to battling a seven-headed dragon who could breathe fire.

Now that they no longer lived under magical threat, Meriwether decided that now and then in the evenings he could release his spirit dragon and fly over the surrounding countryside, scouting their route.

Sometimes Sacagawea's eagle joined him, which made these explorations all the more sweet. He still did not know what, exactly, he felt for the native woman, or what could come out of it. But without the shadow of a doubt he admired her courage and nobility.

From the air, he and Sacagawea's eagle spirit first glimpsed great green forests, extending like a carpet to the horizon, and along the whole horizon they glimpsed a sliver of endless blue.

He knew with certainty this was the ocean they'd been seeking all along!

But the glimpse only made their destination seem closer. Crossing the dense, trackless forest took many days of toil, often requiring them to carry the canoes and pirogues overland when the river was too rough or narrow to be navigated. But they knew the ocean was there, and they continued with building excitement.

On a foggy morning they finally reached the shores of the Pacific, seeing first the pale, rough sands, and then the ocean, roaring in great waves upon the shore.

The seagulls screamed ahead.

He stood with Clark, filled with disbelief and wonder, triumph but also fear. Sacagawea was at their side, staring. "Is this what you expected to find?"

What captured their eyes was the sky. Past the roaring waters, past the blue, there was a strip of... nothing.

It was hard to describe the lack of existence, but the great ocean which had once extended all the way to China, to India, around Africa and eventually up to England and France just... stopped. The horizon ended abruptly in a curtain of mist, churning veils that rose up from an infinite dropoff. Perhaps the literal edge of the world, now that this continent had been sundered from the rest of Earth.

Meriwether stared with tears in his eyes. The gathered men from the expedition were groaning in dismay and amazement. Others were just stunned silent, not knowing what to say.

Of course, Meriwether had seen it before. You'd think you couldn't see, but you could. He knew for absolute certain that out in the water, perhaps no more than a mile or so from shore, they would find the same type of impenetrable barrier that cut off passage across the Atlantic.

Unless the ocean itself simply tumbled off the brink and fell down into an infinite void, as the legends of frightened mariners told. But now that he knew frightening legends were no longer entirely impossible...

His heart sank, but Sacagawea stood by him, looked up, and cocked an eyebrow. "So this is the ocean."

"Madam, this is the edge of the world. And not the world we wanted to find."

Against the whispering roar of the surf, Meriwether heard a tune accompanied by off-key singing. He turned to see three men ambling down the beach with unsteady steps, the Whiskey Revenants, who had come once again to join the lost expedition.

Despite his shock at finding the edge of the world, the sight of these three men gave him a sense of unbearable relief. He'd thought they'd died, their spirits extinguished back in the land of the dead. They should have perished permanently with the defeat of the dragon sorcerer, but then he remembered that these three had never really belonged to him anyway. Now, as they stumbled closer, they kept singing their tuneless version of "To Anacreon in Heaven."

The Whiskey Revenants sloshed into the edge of the sea and raised their hands up in some kind of celebration.

Baby Pompy wriggled impatiently in his mother's arms. By now he was old enough to manage a tottering walk, and Sacagawea followed the child as he moved in wonder toward the foaming line of water that met the sand. He giggled.

Meriwether turned his gaze again toward the abbreviated horizon, wondering how much of the ocean remained intact. Were they really done with their exploring?

Suddenly, in the deep water off the shore, a large dark shape appeared, and a slithering green reptile body, surmounted by a smiling lionlike head, lifted majestically out of the waves. The men shouted, retreating onto the beach. Meriwether fell back and reached for his air rifle as Sacagawea swept up her child and ran back to the shelter of the forest's edge.

But the sea serpent merely looked at them, snorted jets of steam out of a blowhole, then executed a graceful somersault in midair before diving back down into the depths.

Meriwether felt a shudder, though he had sensed no threat. "They look like the river serpents we saw. Like the twined body of the seven-headed dragon."

"Maybe such creatures come from the sea," Clark suggested. "We have seen salmon from the sea leaping through rivers and streams, fighting their way inland. Perhaps the young serpents do the same." He scratched his chin. "You should write that in your journal, Lewis."

Sacagawea said, "I don't think they're hostile without the spirit of Raven enslaving them. They are just animals."

"That grizzly bear was just an animal, too," Meriwether said. "They can still be dangerous. Sailors must beware." Realizing what he had said, he sat heavily on a large driftwood log on the beach. "What sailors would we find? We are cut off here, too. There is no way to make a passage west, over the Pacific, to join the rest of the world."

Seaman ran, barking and wagging his tail to where Pompy and Sacagawea were playing in the foam. He didn't seem to mind being stranded.

"Perhaps that is all to the good," Clark said. "In this slice of land, separated from ancient hatreds and surrounded by magical marvels, perhaps we can carve out a continent that is better than the one we lost."

"Perhaps we can make the new world everything we dreamed," Meriwether replied, recalling the story of the fantastic utopia he had heard in the land of the dead. "Perhaps we are fine after all, and it is the rest of the world that's lost."